· STEVEN JACKLIN ·

THE ADVENTURES OF THE

DWARFGIANTS

SERPENT OF THE SULPHUR SEA

To Cole,
Enjoy the adventure,
Steven.

The Adventures of the Dwarfgiants | Serpent of the Sulphur Sea

Tellwell Talent
www.tellwell.ca

ISBN
978-1-77302-626-8 (Paperback)
978-1-77302-625-1 (eBook)

Dedication

For my children, Charlie, Adam and Jessica
and the best bedtime stories

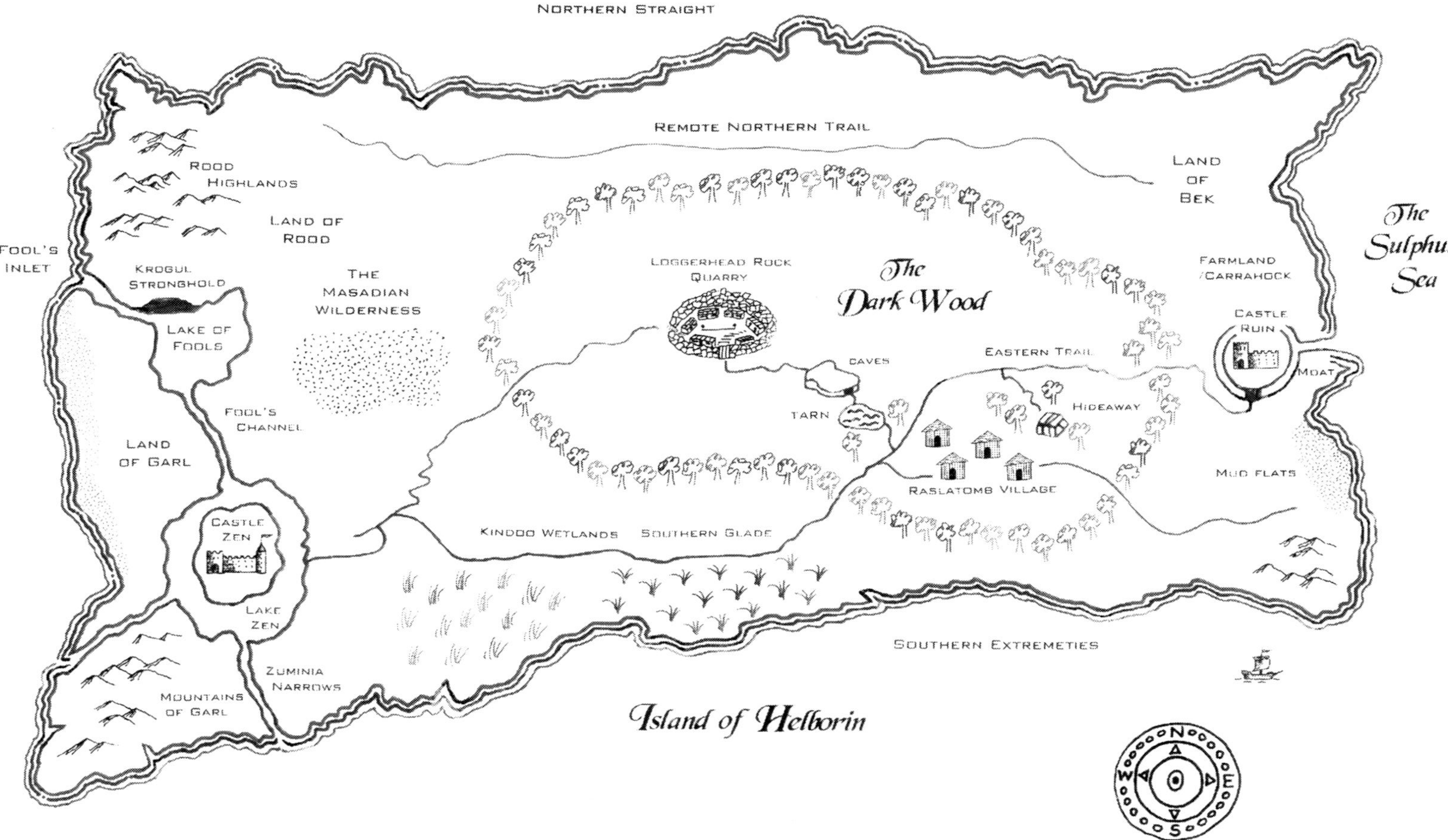

Northern Straight
Remote Northern Trail
Rood Highlands
Land of Rood
Land of Bek
The Sulphur Sea
Fool's Inlet
Krogul Stronghold
The Masadian Wilderness
Loggerhead Rock Quarry
The Dark Wood
Farmland /Carrahock
Castle Ruin
Moat
Lake of Fools
Eastern Trail
Caves
Tarn
Hideaway
Fool's Channel
Land of Garl
Raslatomb Village
Mud Flats
Castle Zen
Kindoo Wetlands
Southern Glade
Lake Zen
Southern Extremeties
Zuminia Narrows
Mountains of Garl
Island of Helborin
N
W
E
S

Chapter 1

It came at midnight. No fanfare, no warning. The room shuddered. The bed shook. Glass jars fell, smashed to the floor. Addi sat bolt upright, his heart racing. In the half-blackness he strained to see. He fumbled for a candle, but before he could light it a white flash filled the window. The room went dark again. What was happening? Was it lightning or just a bad dream? Above, he heard the ceiling crack. Stones and clumps of dirt rained down onto the bed, pummelling his head. Forget the dream, he needed to run, get out of his sleeping quarters before it caved in.

Rolling off the bed he slipped and hit the floor, knocking his elbow, hard. Ignoring the pain, he grasped a chair leg and pulled himself up. About halfway to the door he stopped, and turned to where Tarro slept. Another flash. Tarro's bed was empty. Where was his friend? *Probably on some late-night mission for the Circle,* he reassured himself. In his bare feet he stumbled to the door through a gauntlet of wood splinters and broken glass. He'd almost made it when a piece of glass dug sharply into the soft arch under his foot. He tried to pull it out but the shard was in too deep. It snapped in his hand, a jagged edge smeared with blood.

No time to linger, the walls were shaking. Outside he heard voices, shouts of panic. He peered out the window and saw other Dwarfgiants running by with torches and whatever possessions they could carry. He reached for the door handle but then froze. As suddenly as it had started everything stopped: the shaking bed, the falling ceiling the trembling walls.

All was quiet.

Slowly he turned the handle, pushed the door open and stepped out into the cool air. But before he could take a breath he looked up to see a shadow ripple across the two moons. Then hell erupted. With a *Boom* louder than thunder, the top blew off the Mighty Mountain of Mol. He covered his ears with his hands and stared as a fountain of fire lit up the night. Out of the mountain's red throat, plumes of smoke and ash, swollen with crimson sparks, filled the sky. Rivers of fire ran down the slopes; a torrent headed towards the Dwarfgiant settlements.

"Addi!" said a familiar voice. "Give me a hand!"

Across the way, outside the old apothecary building, a figure was frantically filling a sack. Addi hurried to him, zigzagging between fleeing Dwarfgiants, bumping into some.

"Tarro!" he said, breathlessly. "What are you doing?"

"I was coming for you, but I had to bring this."

The sack was full.

"Tarro, this isn't a drill. We have to leave, now. Get to the boats! Look!"

Up the mountainside, molten lava pushed over the high ridge and into the Dwarfgiants' upper settlement, setting the wooden homes there ablaze.

"It's done," said Tarro, tying the sack.

"What's in it?"

Tarro looked at him, a let's-not-go-there look. "Myvan's counting on it."

Maybe it was the ingredients for the secret power serum, thought Addi.

Tarro threw the sack over his shoulder. "All right, let's go!"

Amid the din of the exploding mountain, the screams of panic and the clanging of the warning bell, they hit the main trail down to the sea. With fireballs of stone and rock hurtling about them, they jostled with fellow Dwarfgiants running for their lives. Chased by the inferno, Addi guessed they'd need to run as fast as they could if they were to get to the boats in time. But the glass in his foot slowed him down.

"You're hurt," Tarro said, running alongside.

"Ah, it's nothing, a piece of glass." But it hurt a lot.

Without looking back they reached the docks where the first wave of Dwarfgiants – about a hundred males, females and youngens – were already scrambling into boats. Watched over by members of the Circle, the evacuation was, as practised, reasonably smooth. Addi was heartened to see, two boats down, his female friends, Reesel and Kulin, helping youngens aboard.

Where there was room, livestock was taken in, including fowl and some milk-bearing creatures – mostly moobeasts and udderlings. One boat was reserved for what looked like items of importance – scrolls, precious stones, pots of Jabunga healing leaves. Although Tarro wasn't saying, the sack he carried likely contained a mysterious concoction of galinsa roots along with potent carrahock grains. It was this special cargo that gave them clearance to go to the front of the line.

"Make way!" said Revel, raising his torch. "Let them through!"

Tarro led the way up the gangplank. He was, after all, Myvan's son, and, being the son of the Dwarfgiants' leader, he was, by right, a member of the Circle, if only a junior. As Myvan's adopted son, Addi, too, had standing.

Revel stood waiting. "You have it?"

Tarro nodded.

"Excellent. Put the sack at the front, under the seats. You go too, Addi, fast as you can."

Revel's encouragement made Addi feel important. Revel was not only Myvan's second-in-command, but his chief adviser. When it came to planning the Dwarfgiants' security, he was the one. Whenever there'd been talk of Kamistra's "silent giant" blowing its top, it was Revel who had made sure there was an emergency plan in place for a quick getaway. After a generation of calm, the volcano had finally erupted, and his escape plan looked to be working.

But there was little time. The burning avalanche surged closer.

"Look!" a voice cried out from one of the boats.

Heads turned towards the mountain, where the bubbling lava was running through the middle and lower settlements, incinerating homes and vegetation, suffocating anything that remained in its path. Addi swallowed hard when the great oak started to burn. It stood in the place where he'd grown up, played games, sung and danced at festivals, learned to fight. The magnificent tree had been at the centre of his world: a titan, indestructible.

It was horrible to watch – Dwarfgiants were still running down the trail.

Distant screams. The smell of death.

Those who were going to make it were now in the boats. All along the dockside the call went out. "Cast off!"

One by one the boats left, urgent paddles splashing west along the rift lines of the Sulphur Sea. Not all the boats were full. Stragglers kept arriving at the dockside, but only one boat remained, until the molten heat forced it away, too.

The cargo boat Addi was in was one of the last to leave. He and Tarro were two of the designated rowers. Of the twenty or so passengers, most were dock guards and members of the Circle, including Myvan. Parchment in hand, the Dwarfgiants' leader looked agitated, concerned.

"All here?" he called out. "Everyone accounted for?" Before anyone could respond, he added, "Someone's missing. Has anyone seen Lucus?"

Addi stopped rowing. He felt queasy. Although he didn't know Lucus well, he knew he was Revel's son.

As junior members of the Circle, Tarro knew Lucus. Tarro locked his oar and jumped to his feet. "Wasn't Lucus at the armoury?"

"I thought I saw him at the food dispensary," said one of the guards.

Looking dazed, Revel stepped forward. "He was supposed to be at the settlement gates, marshalling residents to the boats."

Myvan, his face grave, spoke. "I'm sorry, Revel, I really am, but Lucus isn't accounted for. Wherever he is now, it doesn't look good."

"No. No, it can't be!" said Revel, his voice breaking. "Lucus knew the plan, inside and out. We have to go back!"

Myvan started towards him. "We can't do that. I'm sorry, Revel, we must…"

The blast was so loud – so full of fury – everyone who was standing fell to the boat's deck. Addi fell on his back. Tarro sprawled on top of him. In the dark cacophony, it felt like the end of the world.

For a long time nobody moved. All Addi could do was look up. A monstrous black cloud billowed high in the sky, reeking of sulphur, sparking with flaming fragments. Rolling waves began to buffet the boat. Stinking ash fell like black snow. Addi and Tarro scrambled to their knees to look back. Kamistra, the island they had called their own, was just a smouldering mass of smoke and fire.

No one could have survived. There was nothing left.

CHAPTER 2

Myvan stood on a rocky outcrop overlooking the Sulphur Sea. A fresh breeze blew in. Whitecaps on the morning tide. He leaned on his staff, gulped great breaths of air. It was his spot – this small, quartzite jetty – a serene place in which to think, to conjure ideas, to make a better world for the Dwarfgiants. As their leader, it was his duty.

A gust of wind sent his hair flitting across his face. Sweeping the strands from his eyes, he glanced to his left where a coastal path led to the castle ruin. The old stone fortress – now called home – was surrounded by a moat connected to the sea. Each day when the tide rushed in, the moat filled with sea water. Fortunately, three of the castle walls remained intact: the east wall overlooking the Sulphur Sea, the west wall facing the Dark Wood and the south wall where, still in working order, stood the gatehouse, portcullis and drawbridge. The old keep, the north wall and its castle towers were no more than broken remnants. Fixing the north wall had been put off until homes had been built. Still, in just a season, he was pleased with the progress they'd made. After fleeing the exploding island of Kamistra – the Great Evacuation as it had come to be known – they'd sailed west, five suns and moons across the Sulphur Sea. Then, in the early light of the sixth sun, with food and water running out, they'd sighted land and the sprawling shape of a castle ruin. Set on a low scar jutting out from the land, it gave them temporary refuge. A place to camp.

With plenty of rain to grow crops, and the discovery of sulphur-rich soil north of the moat, the decision to stay was an easy one. Thanks to Tarro bringing seed from Kamistra, a carrahock grove had been cultivated there. Carrahock fuelled the power serum that allowed Dwarfgiants to change up, temporarily giving them the stature of beings more than twice their size. Only Circle members bore this responsibility, linking hands with another Dwarfgiant to effect the transformation. Each change to giant size, though, took its toll; aging the Circle member by about a season. Still, when needed, it could provide an advantage, even be lifesaving. After losses suffered in the cruel cauldron of Kamistra, the life of every Dwarfgiant was precious.

Myvan looked out to sea and marveled at how the Dwarfgiants had survived not only that terrible night, but, as a tribe, had been able to start fresh again. Just how many times in their history had they started again, he wasn't sure. But stories of Dwarfgiant adventures had been passed down: voyages in search of precious stones – diamonds, rubies, sapphires – thought to exist in the igneous rocks on volcanic islands such as Kamistra. Only when the Dwarfgiants settled there did they discover a treasure more valuable – one that grew in the black, sulphur-rich earth at the edge of the sea. Potent nutrients believed to have been washed ashore during the Great Sulphur Gale had spawned germination of the blue-leaf carrahock. It had been Myvan's forefather, Bek, who first tasted the plant, had, by chance, discovered its power for sudden growth. But after realizing a side-affect – that caused the user to age faster than normal – did the leaders limit its use to situations of life and death, and then only to those of the newly formed Circle. In the end, it was this discovery that gave the Dwarfgiants their name.

Again, Myvan cast his eye towards the castle ruin within which the new settlement had sprung up. Surrounding the main square, wooden structures were being built. Rows of houses, an infirmary, granary, food dispensary, stables, armoury, storage sheds for tools and farming equipment. From the beaches to the north of the moat, fishing boats were launched, until a new wharf could be built. Even a name had been given to their coastal realm: the Land of Bek.

Below ground, down the steps of the south tower, an old torture chamber had been transformed into the Chamber of the Inner Circle. The Inner Circle or "Circle" as it was more commonly known consisted of the Dwarfgiants' leaders. Given recent revelations, including one that threatened their very existence on this new island of Helborin, a meeting of the Circle would soon be needed.

He drew a deep breath. Out over the sea, the morning mist had cleared. The orange sun crackled low over the fresh-breaking waves. High up, seabirds caught the wind and soared and drifted. Above the ruin a great seaglut circled the moat. Squawking noisily the strapping king of seabirds seemed off kilter. As if caught in the tidal force of the moons, it swirled, sometimes spinning out of control. Twice it tried to right itself, fighting to keep its balance. For a moment it did so, levelling off in a majestic glide. But then, in a blink, the mighty creature buckled, dropping like a stone into the sea.

Myvan winced, biting his lip. Something caused him to look to his right, an invisible pull. At first he saw nothing, then a shape in the distance: a shadow, moving at speed from the south, skimming the waves. Closer now, the shadow broke up. Then he saw them – six marigores flying in formation. With massive wingspans, the dagger-toothed fisher-birds approached. Black wings flapping, they swept past him towards the moat and took dead aim at the spot where the great seaglut had fallen. The lead bird ascended from the pack. Then, at a steep angle, it plummeted into the sea. The others broke formation. One by one they, too, rose and then angled down, cutting the water with killer precision.

He watched with a mix of curiosity and awe. What were they after? Marigores normally gorged on the bounty of sea life squalling just below the surface. At any moment he expected they would burst from the depths, their beaks filled with flapping fish.

Moments passed. He felt uneasy. There was no sign of the fisher-birds. What fate had they met in the depths of the Sulphur Sea?

Whatever the reason, the voracious sea hunters were gone.

A twinge in his chest took his breath as he suddenly remembered that Tarro and Addi were also gone, late from their mission in the Dark Wood. And while a need for Jabunga healing leaves had become desperate, being lost in the Dark Wood was an even bigger worry, especially at night, where shadows of evil loomed at every turn.

CHAPTER 3

A scream cut deep through the Dark Wood, jolting Addi awake. Like a never-ending nightmare it rang out, echoing through the trees.

"Sweet mercy," he said, sitting up. "What was that?"

"I don't know," replied Tarro, his normally calm voice shaky. "I don't think I want to know."

In their hideaway made of oak branches, thick with leaves, Addi shivered. Rubbing his eyes, he stood and peered out through a gap in the cover.

"Look! There's a light."

In the distance, above a ridge, a yellow glow filtered through the trees.

For some moments they watched in silence. "This is creepy," Tarro said. "I think it's time we…"

"Listen! Did you hear that?"

Low, at first, the hum of voices turned into chants.

"I don't like it," Tarro whispered.

"If someone's in trouble we should help them," Addi said, quickly fastening his belt.

"No, we shouldn't. We should do what we were told to do – gather Jabunga leaves and get back quickly."

"What kind of adventure is that?"

Tarro sighed. "Addi, we've been given an important job. Without medicine many will die. You know yourself if it hadn't been for the Jabunga leaf you wouldn't have survived the infection from the glass in your foot.

The Circle won't be pleased if we deviate from the plan, we're already one sun late."

Addi tapped his foot impatiently, partly because he still could, but mostly because he knew Tarro made sense. This was his friend's most annoying quality – he was prudent and kept his mind on the task at hand. Being Myvan's son wasn't the only reason Tarro was a member of the Circle.

"Wisdom looks ahead" was a well-known saying among Dwarfgiants. But as far as Addi was concerned, wisdom was a pain, and looking ahead was no fun at all. He glanced at Tarro. In some ways, they couldn't have been less alike. Tarro looked more typical of a Dwarfgiant: round, worried eyes, button nose, brown fur, which was thicker than his own yellow, flowing hair. This colour difference, along with his thinner nose and pointed ears was, he guessed, courtesy of a father he never knew.

The scream's echo finally died, but the chanting in the distance grew louder.

"Come on, Tarro. At least let's go and look."

Tarro stayed silent, keeping watch through the gap in the branches. It was going to take more to convince him.

Addi tried. "If the odds are against us, we'll turn back."

Still no answer.

"We're running out of time!"

"All right!" said Tarro. "We'll take a look. But not too close."

Addi could hardly wait to get started. He lit a torch and shone it on a bulging bag of blue-green leaves, which he then hid under a pile of branches. "We'll leave the Jabunga leaves here. We can come back for them later."

"If something happens and we get separated," said Tarro, "we meet back here."

"Agreed," Addi said. After a final check of the hideaway, he turned to his friend. "Ready?"

Tarro straightened his tunic and nodded.

As they headed out, Addi saw him reach down, take a handful of Jabunga leaves and stuff them in his pouch. The master herbalist, it seemed, couldn't help taking some of the precious leaves with him.

Addi led the way towards the yellow glow. As they trudged through the knee-high undergrowth, the light shone brighter, and the chanting sounded more and more ominous.

"It's not too late to turn back," said Tarro. "Nobody would blame us."

"Nobody except the poor soul who screamed," Addi said, keeping up the pace.

The shrubs and bracken thinned out. At the edge of a clearing Addi stopped and pointed. "Over there! There's a trail going up to the top of the ridge." He smothered the flame of his torch with dirt. "Remember, Tarro, as soon as we reach the top, take cover behind a tree or a rock."

Up the slope they scrambled, a steep incline leading to the source of the fiendish chants. But halfway up, they heard a different sound. Something was coming down – an odd marching beat: *dunda dun, dunda dun, dunda dun.*

"What is it?" said Tarro.

"Move to the side."

"What?"

"To the side, and be still."

The beat grew louder: *dunda dun, dunda dun, dunda dun*. And then, around the corner they came – a moonlit column of small, boxy creatures, green-faced with blow-torch eyes, arms and legs like sticks, marching six-wide in perfect unison, two steps forward and one step back. It was as if they'd done it ten thousand times before. Not once did they bump into each other.

"What are they?" asked Tarro as the last row went by.

"Good question. They seem harmless," said Addi, moving back onto the trail. Breathing hard, he clambered to the top of the rise. Sprawled on his stomach, he waved for Tarro to join him. Straight ahead, a cluster of deserted huts could be seen in the flickering light of the campfires. To the right, past a line of trees, a gathering of creatures stood in a circle. Chanting gravely, the rabble held torches and bones.

"We need to get closer," Addi said, pointing to a large forio tree twenty paces away. Before Tarro could protest, Addi ran towards it.

From the shadow of the tree they had a better view. The creatures – at least twenty of them – stood on their back legs, head and shoulders taller than a Dwarfgiant. Their stringy bodies were covered in grey, spiky hair. Curled horns sprouted from goat-shaped heads. When their mouths opened, they spewed their awful chants through the gaps left by missing teeth. It was hard to see, but they were surrounding something.

When the circle split open, Addi felt his jaw drop. What looked like a young female – though not a Dwarfgiant – was lying on her back, tied to a bed of pointed stakes. It was a shocking sight, and yet, in the face of evil, she remained still, looking up at the moons as if entranced. Long black hair ran over her shoulders and down to the ground. Around her waist a thin cord tied a white frock – her only protection from the sharp points.

Addi gazed at the young captive. "I think we've found our scream."

"Who are the ugly ones?" replied Tarro.

"Search me. All I know is that we have to save her."

"And how do we do that? Ask nicely?" Tarro scratched his head. "What are they doing?"

"Looks like some kind of ritual. They keep looking at the moons."

High in the sky shone two silver balls. Ever since the night the Dwarfgiants had left Kamistra – fleeing from the apocalyptic volcano – the moons had been edging closer to each other. Now they were almost touching.

A deep, guttural sound interrupted their gaze.

"What's that?" said Addi.

"Sounds like an ugmul."

"A *what?*"

"A hollow piece of wood you blow into, like a horn."

The creatures stopped chanting. More ugmuls droned. Smoke swirled in from the campfires, an ill wind. Then, in what seemed like a trick of the eyes, a dark, freakish creature appeared to rise out of the ground. Taller than the others, its face, almost without flesh, was painted like a mask: pale circles, red eyes. Great horns jutted from its head, tusks from its mouth. With fingers, half-skinned, it held a sceptre made of bone. Emblazoned over its right breast on a black gown was the image of a serpent.

"Who's that?" said Tarro.

"No idea, but it sure looks mean. And ugly."

"I don't mind ugly. It's the mean bit I don't like."

Framed by the burning torches, the creature approached the bed of pointed stakes. A guard stepped forward brandishing a long, serrated dagger. He drooled then handed the dagger over in exchange for the bone.

Holding the dagger above its head, the creature looked down and sneered at the young captive. It then looked to the sky and spoke to the moons in a hard, dry voice.

"Phul, magic spirit of the moon and mighty protector of our fate, we pay homage to your greatness! The time will soon be at hand when I, Taluhla, Queen of the Raslatombs, will rejoice in your coming, when the two moons join and the serpent returns on the night of nights."

"That thing's a queen?" said Tarro.

"Queen of the Raslatombs, no less," added Addi. "I wonder what she meant by the return of the serpent?"

As if making an offering to the moons, Taluhla raised the dagger higher. The Raslatombs shrieked.

"This isn't good," said Tarro, biting a fingernail.

Addi stared at the young female on the bed of stakes. "She's beautiful," he murmured. With his mind racing he turned to his friend. "Tarro, there's only one thing to do."

Tarro inhaled sharply. "Like what?"

"You've got to change up. It's the only way. Keep them at bay while I rescue her. We have to do it. Now!"

With Raslatomb death chants rising to a crescendo, Taluhla looked to be in another realm – a snarling, blood-lusting ecstasy. Then, as her face caught the full light of the moons, she became calmer, looking up as if to garner one final blessing.

Tarro blew out a long breath, quickly loosened his tunic and pouch. "Addi," he said, solemnly, "if I don't make it, I'll never be friends with you again."

"We'll always be friends, Tarro. No matter what."

Palms up, fingers spread, Addi interlocked his fingers with Tarro's. A surge went through his hands. Tarro's eyes popped, his shoulders spread; his body ballooned to twice Addi's size.

Tarro looked woozy, backed into the forio tree. He steadied himself, holding on to a thick branch. Although Addi had seen the change-up before, he marvelled at the speed of the transformation – at the powerhouse that Tarro had become. If only he'd been a member of the Circle, he'd have been the one going into battle.

"Use the branch as a weapon," Addi said.

Tarro, his arm muscles pumped, snapped the tree branch. The cracking noise, though, alerted the Raslatombs.

Taluhla, about to thrust the knife blade into the young female's chest, looked up. Shrieks of pleasure turned to screams of anger.

This time, Tarro needed no coaxing. Swinging the tree branch like a bludgeon, he charged into the Raslatomb lair.

From the dark shade of the forio tree, Addi watched his friend attack the Raslatombs. Running hard and screaming, Tarro – now almost twice the size of the horned creatures – swung the tree branch at anyone who put up a fight. Some hurled torches, others threw daggers. Four guards with spears encircled him, but when he turned a full circle they were sideswiped. Blood was everywhere.

Others turned to flee. Only Taluhla and six of her guards stood their ground. Eyes flaring, she squawked orders. Fire-arrows were lit. Streaking flames soared past Tarro's head. One struck him in the shoulder. He cried out and staggered but broke off the arrow before the flames took hold. With the tree branch clenched in his right hand, and holding a dead guard as a shield, he resumed the charge. When the next round of arrows missed, Tarro chased the guards into the woods.

Addi clenched a fist. Now it was his turn. In the moonlight he could see the young female shifting under the rope that bound her. He looked for Taluhla. He hadn't seen her leave. And yet there was no sign of her. It seemed the Queen of the Raslatombs had vanished as mysteriously as she'd arrived.

The way was clear. Across open ground he made his run. Leaping over fallen guards he scooped up a dagger. Breathing hard, he reached the bed of sharply pointed stakes. For a moment, he looked down on the young female. Unlike anyone he'd ever seen she was lovely to look at. Dark eyes, dainty nose, her skin was smooth; no hint of fur. She lay still, her pretty face ghost-white, her eyes a confusion of hope and fear.

"Don't be afraid," he said. "They've gone. I've come to rescue you." He reached for the dagger in his belt. She watched anxiously as he showed her the blade. "I'm going to cut you free, all right?"

He wondered if she understood him.

She shivered, nodded slowly. This was good. Even in her state of distress she remained calm, the slender shape of her body tight under the ropes that tied her down. How she'd got into this state he couldn't imagine. Moving quickly, he slid the knife under the rope binding her left wrist. Before cutting it, he looked to reassure her, but her eyes, again trance-like, looked past him. Not so good. Like a last chance to suffer, the moonlight darkened, a shadow crossed her face. He gulped, tightening his grip on the dagger. Something was behind him.

With his heart beating out of his chest, he swung around, blade pointing. No one there. No Taluhla, no lurking Raslatombs. Only a bird – a nighthawk – darted across the sky, taking the moons' shadow with it. The place of sacrifice was now still. Only distant screams in the Dark Wood – Tarro on the rampage.

Addi turned back, cut the rope – a quick slice – and unwound the binding as fast as he could. After returning the dagger to his belt, he held out his hands. She was more alert now and, with a determined look, reached for them. Her fingers were thin and delicate. Holding them firmly, he slowly pulled her up.

"Hold on," he said, slipping his arm under her legs, "I'll lift you."

He helped place her arm around his neck and lifted her easily from what could have been her death bed. She felt limp in his arms, snug. He carried her past the smoky campfires and deserted huts, along the edge of the woodland tract. He hurried towards the forio tree. In a dappled patch of moonlight he placed her on her feet. She wobbled, but his hand steadied her. Then he noticed his fingers stained red, blood from the puncture wounds in her back.

"Can you walk?" he asked, watching her eyes for signs of faintness.

She nodded weakly.

"There's a hideaway," he said. "It's not far. My friend Tarro will be there soon and we have healing leaves for your wounds."

She glanced at the surrounding woods then turned back to him. "What are you?" she said. Her voice was calm, surprisingly clear.

"I'm a Dwarfgiant. My name is Addi."

She smiled. "You have fur. It's soft."

"It's warm at night."

"Your friend, is he a Dwarfgiant too?"

"Tarro? Yes. Right now he's a giant, but soon he'll be back to normal size."

"How magical."

"It comes in handy."

Her smile widened. "My name is Bodessa. I'm a Zenta."

Bodessa. Nice. But who were the Zentas? "Well, Bodessa, we have to get out of this place."

"Which way are you going?"

"To the coast," he said, pointing. "The Sulphur Sea."

"I'm going the other way, to Castle Zen."

"How far is it?"

"Almost one sun."

"I'm supposed to meet Tarro at the hideaway. We can work out directions once we get there."

For a moment she looked distracted. A pink glow emanated from a hole in the base of a tree. "Can you wait here?" she said.

He watched her step gingerly towards the tree, then stop in front of it. She seemed to reach for something, spend some time fussing. When she turned, the glow had gone. She walked back to Addi a little steadier, a hint of a smile.

"What was that?" he asked.

"Nothing. It's all good, now," was all she'd say.

He led the way back down the trail. Halfway, Bodessa lost her footing, slithered into the back of him. For a moment they stood and listened to the woods. But there was nothing. Not a sound. Just a thick emptiness. Where were the Raslatombs and their squalid queen? Where was Tarro? No more battle cries, no more screams. Was Tarro done with the goat-faced savages? Had he finished them off? If so, he'd be back at the hideaway as planned.

Addi peered down the trail, half expecting to hear a *dunda dun, dunda dun* marching beat, but the boxy, bouncing creatures weren't coming back.

Step by step they descended. At times – down some of the steep bits – he'd help her, extend a hand. He liked doing this, liked how her hand felt in his. When they reached the bottom he found his torch and relit it with a friction stick. Surrounded by a wall of black trees, they'd barely entered the clearing when a forlorn cry startled them.

Bodessa gripped his hand.

A second cry moaned through the trees.

"It's a troubled tree howlet," he said, looking up. On this night, the only sounds the Dark Wood could muster were joyless ones.

Out of the clearing, they re-entered the wood. Trudging through dense foliage Addi reluctantly let go of her hand, using the Raslatomb dagger to cut through clumps of stubborn brush. Eventually the congestion thinned out, giving way to a coppice of twilip saplings: small, self-culling trees whose branches twisted and fell to the ground before them, squirming like vipers. A brief dance and they expired like petrified sticks.

Addi reckoned they were close. "Not far now," he said. "The hideaway's through this thicket."

When she didn't answer, he turned. But she wasn't there. In a panic, and with torch aloft, he hurried back. After rounding a bend he saw her motionless on the trail, lying in a pool of moonlight. Slowly he approached her, praying he'd see signs of life. She appeared to have fallen backwards, a leg folded under her.

For a terrible moment he stood over her. Nothing. Then he saw it, the slight rise and fall of her chest. She was still breathing. He needed to get her back to the hideaway. Mindful of her wounds, he lifted her, gently, and carried her the rest of the way.

The hideaway was empty. No Tarro. Not yet. He laid Bodessa down. Near the entrance, he pulled away the pile of branches that hid the bags of Jabunga leaves. He made a bed of them for her to lie on, not caring how many leaves he used as long as she got better. She opened her eyes only once and after he gave her a sip of water she closed them again. He covered her with his outer tunic then extinguished his torch flame.

Outside, under the light of the moons, he sat listless. His mind was on two things: keeping vigil over Bodessa, and worrying where Tarro was.

* * *

Blood-soaked and wracked with pain, Tarro staggered down the woodland path. There were no flames, but his shoulder felt as if it were on fire. His legs too, were burning – a sensation, like melting jelly – but he dared not stop, not with Raslatombs skulking about and night beasts on the prowl.

He'd long since abandoned hope of meeting up with Addi at the hide-away. The Raslatombs had seen to that. He'd chased them far into the wood, through a maze of thickets and halfpaths taking him to who knew where. The arrow that pierced his shoulder hadn't helped either. At first he'd thought nothing of it – a shallow flesh wound – but after snapping off the end, he realized the barbed arrowhead had lodged under his shoulder blade. His gradual change-down from giantsize – the shrinking of his bones and skin – had caused the arrow to nip tight. Had it not been for the healing Jabunga leaf, which he held hard against the flow of blood, he would not have survived. Then by luck he'd stumbled onto the Eastern Trail, lifting his hopes. But how much longer could he last? As the night wore on, he wondered if he'd ever make it home, back to the castle ruin by the sea.

CHAPTER 4

Myvan grimaced as he descended the stone steps to the Chamber of the Inner Circle. Halfway down, a searing pain made him pause. It was his knees, they were not so good. Neither was his neck, or his back. He was beginning to feel creaky. Perhaps his time as leader was coming to an end. He took a breath, remembered who he was – the one who, for over twenty summers, had guided the Dwarfgiants, weaned them from an age of reckless adventure into an era of peace and tranquility. Kamistra had been his one setback.

Gingerly he continued down the steps. By the time he reached the bottom he felt better. His neck may have been stiff but he was satisfied that his mind was sharp, his ability to make good decisions still intact.

The chamber was filled with chatter. Before entering, he smoothed the silver edgings of his black tunic and tightened his belt a notch. When he stepped in, the room fell quiet. He strode towards the stone, pentagonal table and stood behind his chair. Its high back was encrusted with jade and topaz. His favourite gemstones stood for wisdom and peace.

Also dressed in ceremonial tunics, the four senior members of the Circle stood in place. To his right, around the table, were Revel, Havoc, Jeeve and Rimsky. Standing a step behind three of them were their sons, the Circle's junior members. It felt strange to Myvan that Tarro wasn't there behind him. He couldn't imagine how Revel felt without Lucus.

Through a slit in the wall, a beam of light struck the sundial in the centre of the table. "It is high sun," he said. "This meeting of the Circle is now in session." As he sat, so did the senior members. The junior members remained standing.

"The purpose of this meeting is threefold," Myvan continued. "First is the matter of Tarro and Addi. They should have returned from their mission by now. Whether they found Jabunga leaves or not, they had strict instructions to be back by midnight."

"The Dark Wood is a mysterious place," Revel said. "We have only just begun to discover its secrets. When it comes to Addi, who knows where he and Tarro may have ended up. He can get sidetracked."

"Addi can be impulsive," Myvan replied, "but he's brave, has a good heart. And he usually finds a way to get things done. The concern we have is that they're late. We need to find out where they've got to. Get them back safely and quickly, before –"

The beam of sunlight cut out. The chamber darkened to an eerie flicker of torchlight. Then, as if a cloud had passed, the beam returned.

Myvan shivered. "We just need to get them back."

"We also need more Jabunga leaves and Tarro's expertise as an herbalist," Rimsky added, his normally cheerful tone subdued. "The situation down at the infirmary is getting serious."

Jeeve raised his hand. "I propose we send a search party, two or three of our best trackers."

"I agree," said Havoc, glancing over his shoulder at his son. "In that regard, we need look no farther than right here in this room."

Myvan swallowed hard. "I have every confidence in the ability of any of our sons in their capacity as trackers, but –"

He'd found his opening.

"– to help us decide on who they might be," he went on, "I'd like to jump to the second item for discussion – the selection of a new junior member of the Circle." He rose and stood next to Revel. "When Kamistra was destroyed, we were all saddened by the loss of those close to us, but none is more missed than Revel's son, Lucus. Not only was he an upstanding young Dwarfgiant, he was also a valued junior member of the Circle." Myvan put his hand on Revel's shoulder. "Lucus' memory will be commemorated in stone, an inscription right here on the table, next to Revel's seat."

Following a spontaneous moment of silence, Myvan gave Revel a pat on the shoulder, turned and went back to his chair. "That being said, it is now my duty to remind you all that a season after Lucus's passing, we are bound to choose his successor. This means that the Circle's five senior members, including myself, are to nominate and decide on a candidate. As there are presently no male descendants of the Circle to choose from, the successful candidate will, for the first time, be selected from the common ranks. The candidate with the most votes will be sworn in as the new junior member. If necessary, you may consult with the junior members present, although I suspect those discussions have already taken place. Revel, I think it only fitting that we start with you."

Wearily, Revel stood. He too was slowing down – the wear and tear of his long-standing service as the Dwarfgiants' second-in-command, the burden of losing his son.

"I would like to thank Myvan for his kind words," he began. "Lucus was a source of great pride to me." After a pause, he composed himself. "The candidate I choose was not only a friend of my son, but has developed the brave and fearless attributes of a warrior. I speak of Sinjun, the armourer's son."

"Thank you, Revel," said Myvan. "Sinjun's name is duly noted. What say you, Havoc?"

His blood-red tunic glorious in the torchlit chamber, Havoc sprung to his feet. "I too pick Sinjun," said the Master Builder. He flexed his forearms, wrung his hands. "He has a straight forward, no-nonsense approach to completing tasks. He's disciplined, and his physical strength commands respect."

Myvan was taken aback. He'd fully expected Havoc to pick Addi, especially when Addi had been such a willing helper on several of Havoc's building projects. Myvan wanted this honour for his deserving adopted son, but now Addi would need all three remaining votes if he was to become the next Circle member.

"It appears Sinjun has become the favourite," Myvan said, with a hint of surprise. He hoped his tone was not lost on Jeeve, the next to vote. If the head of Livestock and Farming also picked Sinjun, Addi's chances would be finished.

"It's a difficult decision," Jeeve began. "Not only because I find myself with the possible deciding vote, but because, of the two candidates I'm considering, one of them is Sinjun …"

Myvan held his breath.

"… Addi being the other."

At least he's still in the running. Myvan watched Jeeve's brow furrow as he struggled to make up his mind.

"There's no doubt they both have admirable qualities," Jeeve continued, his voice slow and deliberate. "But one of them has more of what I would call gumption – one who's resourceful, shows spirit and initiative. For me, that would be Addi."

Myvan exhaled. "Thank you, Jeeve," he said quickly. "That makes the voting two to one in favour of Sinjun."

To his left, Rimsky, the Keeper of the Castle, sat, head bowed, deep in thought. His vote was critical. "Well, Rimsky, what about you? Who do you choose?"

Rimsky looked up. "I would gladly nominate Sinjun or Addi, for all the good reasons given. However, having consulted my son, I am persuaded to pick the one who gives of himself the most, the one who never hesitates to lend a helping hand, no matter what the need. I speak of Addi."

Yes! Myvan's heart fired up. Struggling to hold back a smile, he took a moment to settle himself. "Very well, then," he said. "Two votes for Addi and two for Sinjun. By rule, the deciding vote falls to me."

All along he'd guessed this outcome – though he'd thought Havoc and Rimsky's votes would be reversed. Still, he was now in the position he'd wanted – the choice of Addi a formality. But was it? He had no doubt that his adopted son would be a splendid addition to the Circle. But so would Sinjun. As leader, the last thing he wanted was to show favouritism. With all eyes on him he opened his mouth. At first nothing came out. Then he said: "I propose we wait until Addi and Tarro return."

There were groans around the table.

"In the meantime," Myvan continued, "we should pick a third candidate."

Now there were gasps.

"A third candidate determined by lottery."

Bigger gasps.

"Myvan," said Revel, "is that necessary? We already have two excellent candidates to choose from."

"It will be a simple matter of drawing a name from our younger male population."

"Then what?" said Havoc.

"Once we know who the third candidate is, he will accompany Sinjun and a junior Circle member into the Dark Wood. They will comprise the search party that tracks down Addi and Tarro. I will cast my vote upon their return."

For a moment the chamber fell silent – a collective mulling of information. Then, before another word was spoken, the rumble of the drawbridge shook the walls. The clang of the warning bell rang out.

A guard burst in. "Myvan," he said, catching his breath, "I bring news of Tarro."

Myvan tried to read the guard's face: good news or bad? "Well … what is it?"

"He's here. Back at the castle."

Thank goodness! "How is he? Where is he?"

"He's at the infirmary. He needs repairs. But he should be all right."

"What about Addi?"

"Tarro was alone."

Not so good.

Myvan stood. With a quick step he headed towards the tower steps. "There's an urgent matter still to discuss," he called out to the members. "But it will have to wait until I've seen Tarro. We'll reconvene post meridian."

Myvan strode across the square to the infirmary. Inside the low-beamed structure the smell of fresh wood mingled with the muffle of screams. He entered the first bay to the right, where Tarro lay strapped to a bed, a rope between his teeth. At his bedside were Mother, a nurse and a healer, who was dipping a surgical knife into a bottle of green liquid. The healer worked the "clean" knife around the entry point of the wound – the arrowhead lodged in Tarro's shoulder. Tarro braced himself, the veins in his neck bulging as the healer inserted the blade farther, twisting it to force the arrowhead free. Blood gushed, but in moments the arrowhead was loosened and the healer pulled it out. Without delay, the nurse placed a fresh Jabunga leaf on the open wound.

The healer turned to leave, saw Myvan in the entranceway. "He'll recover," she said, wiping her hands. "The Jabunga leaf will heal the wound. But we're on emergency rations. Many of the sick are going without."

"I'm aware of that," Myvan said. "I promise you'll have fresh supplies soon."

The healer nodded, and then, along with the nurse, exited the bay.

Myvan approached the bed, and sat next to Mother.

"What do you think, Claris? Did you ever see such a fine specimen?"

Tarro offered a weak smile.

"There, you see, he'll be home for dinner."

Claris reached for Tarro's hand. "Just a little rest, first," she said.

Myvan shuffled closer. "Son," he said, "We need to know what happened."

Tarro's eyes narrowed. He didn't seem to remember.

Myvan spoke more slowly. "Addi's missing."

Tarro's eyes widened. He cleared his throat.

"We'd found Jabunga leaves," he began. "Lots of them. Made a hideaway in the wood. In the night ... a terrible scream ... went to help. A horde of ugly creatures ... horns, missing teeth, chanting. There was a young female tied to a bed of pointed stakes. The leader of the ugly creatures appeared. Said she was a queen ... Taluhla, Queen of the Raslatombs ... spoke to the moons. She stood over the young female, raised a knife. That's when I changed up. When they saw me they fired arrows ... caught one in the shoulder. But they soon scattered. I chased them into the woods."

"Raslatombs," Myvan muttered to himself.

Tarro grimaced. "I wanted to go back to the hideaway where we said we'd meet. I changed down ... but the arrow ... I lost blood ... lost my way. Came across the Eastern Trail ... somehow, got back."

"We're glad you did. But there's concern for Addi. We're sending out a search party of three to look for him. Two of them will be candidates to replace Lucus. The other will be an existing Circle member."

"Me. I'll go."

Myvan had expected this. "Tarro, I can understand why you'd want to find Addi. It's an honourable gesture. But look at you. You're hardly fit."

"I know the way, where the Jabunga leaves are, where the hideaway is ... Who are the candidates?"

"At the moment it's Sinjun and Addi. A third candidate will be selected this afternoon, by lottery. Whoever it is, he will go out and search with Sinjun and –"

"Me!"

CHAPTER 5

Tarro's return was heartening to Myvan, but with Addi still missing, little had changed. And he still had dire business to discuss with the leaders at the reconvened meeting.

In the Chamber of the Inner Circle, Myvan eased his sore back into his topaz and jade chair. He unlocked his stiff knees and slowly stretched his legs under the table. *Remember who you are.* He smiled, surveyed the room and addressed the Circle members.

"I am pleased to report that the arrowhead embedded in Tarro's shoulder has now been removed. In fact, he's feeling so good that he insists on being the Circle member to join the search party to find Addi. He knows where Addi might be and where the Jabunga leaves are. I realize he's not in the best physical condition, but under the circumstances it's hard to deny him his wish."

"Tarro is Addi's best friend," said Rimsky. "If he's able he should be the one to go."

There were no objections.

"Then it's settled," Myvan said. "Rimsky, do you have the names for the selection of the third candidate?"

Rimsky reached down, picked up a small sack and dropped it on the table. Bits of dust danced in the sunbeams shining through the slit in the wall.

"All there?" Myvan asked, reaching over and giving the sack a shake.

Jeeve nodded. "Everyone accounted for: the names of fifty-six young males."

"Excellent. One of these young Dwarfgiants is about to become a candidate for the position of junior member of the Circle."

"Myvan, if I may speak," said Havoc, rising from his chair. "We were wondering – the Circle members, that is – what you had in mind when you proposed a third candidate."

"It's a fair question," said Myvan, nodding. "Let me answer it the best way I can. As we rebuild our lives and make a new world for ourselves here on Helborin we have a chance to look more closely at the things that are important to us – our sense of duty, a stronger feeling of togetherness." He looked around the table – an impatient shuffle, puzzled looks. "Let me get to the point. I must tell you, dark clouds are approaching. We need to bolster our defences, increase our fighting power. We need to have more Circle members who can change up."

"Who are we fighting?" said Havoc.

"When I spoke with Tarro, he told me that while he and Addi were in the Dark Wood, they came across some nasty creatures called Raslatombs. Worst of all is their queen, a moon-worshipper named Taluhla."

There was a buzz in the chamber.

Myvan waited for quiet. "She will signal an attack from a serpent. A sea serpent."

A bigger buzz.

Myvan raised his arms. When the voices settled, Rimsky said, "How do you know this?"

Myvan turned to his right. "Revel, show them what you found."

Revel stood, shuffled to the back of the chamber. On the floor below the window lay a batch of ornamental relics. Leaning against the wall were several scrolls. He picked one of them and brought it back to the table.

Myvan gestured for Revel to speak.

"Along with the items by the window, we discovered this tarnished scroll buried in a box near the crumbling north tower. These are remnants left behind by the Odanus, a tribe who, it appears, were known for their love of art and life, and, like ourselves, a desire to live peacefully here by the sea. But it seems there was one among them, a female known as Taluhla, who, being forsaken in love turned against her sister; against her own people. Using the forces of darkness and the power of the moons, she conjured a monster from the sea – a serpent that ended the hopes of the Odanus forever."

A heavy silence fell on the chamber. Revel, his hands starting to shake, handed the scroll to Myvan who read the last handwritten lines:

On the wind of horn and sacrifice,
Where souls are lost and found,
The blade of fate is risen,
A scream the only sound.
On the night of nights, when the two moons joined
In pleasure for the spoil,
The sea stormed in with tooth and fin
And snapped Odanus' coil.
Taluhla tolled her victory,
The moontide ran its spree.
Beware the mighty devil snake,
Serpent of the Sulphur Sea.

"It is signed Fillan," said Myvan, "Scribe of the Odanus." He rolled up the scroll. "Astral calculations reveal that in two nights the moons will join together for the first time in fifteen summers. The sea will churn and the demon serpent will rise up against us. We are all in danger."

Signalling his intent to speak, Rimsky rose to his feet. "Let me get this straight. We're to believe that in two nights, a so-called devil snake – a giant serpent – will rise from the deep and, in all its grave and terrible aspect, attack us by the light of the two moons?"

"We must believe it," said Myvan. "If we don't, we risk losing everything."

"What about the other sea creatures?" Havoc asked. "We've seen flying jades near the north wall and dragonfrogs in the moat."

"An appetizer for the main course," said Myvan.

"What does an evil serpent want with us?" asked Jeeve.

Myvan shrugged. "I'm not exactly sure. Other writings left by the Odanus suggest that the serpent and Taluhla – its evil collaborator – may have some spiritual connection with the castle ruin. There is a reference to lost souls. But the manuscript is badly damaged, the words difficult to read."

"So what do we do?" said Rimsky. "Run to the Dark Wood – abandon our homes and everything we've worked for? Or stay and fight?"

An image of the Dwarfgiants fleeing Kamistra flashed into Myvan's head. Surely, nothing could be as bad as an exploding volcano. "We stay," he said firmly. "Besides, the Dark Wood harbours its own breed of terror. Revel and I have discussed it and have come up with a plan. First, we have to strengthen the north wall. Use earth, wood, stone, whatever can be found. Build it up as much as possible. Then we dam the sea entrance to the moat. It's crucial we keep all evil at bay. Havoc, your building skills are about to be put to the test. We're counting heavily on you and your workers to make sure the weaknesses in our defences are fixed.

"We'll also need extra power serum. Jeeve, arrange for a fresh batch of carrahock plants to be harvested. Make sure Tarro arranges to process the grains and roots before he leaves with the search party.

"And Rimsky, without causing alarm, make sure that every Dwarfgiant is in a state of readiness – the armouries fully stocked with bamboozies and ammunition, the dispensary with food and water. The infirmary should be ready for those who will need treatment – which brings me to the subject of Jabunga leaves. We must dispatch the search party for Addi right away. Get him and the Jabunga leaves back here before the moons join together – before this serpent strikes. We're going to need his energy – his ability to rally our young Dwarfgiant fighters."

Myvan reached across the table and grabbed the sack. "Right, let's make the draw," he said, loosening the knot at the top. "The person whose name comes out is our third candidate, the one who goes with Tarro and Sinjun into the Dark Wood. Revel, you do the honours."

Myvan gave the sack a shake. Revel took a breath and after a short pause – likely giving a final thought for his son – stuck his hand in, pulled out a name carved in wood and held it out in front of him.

"Well?" said Myvan. "Who is it"?

Revel looked down at the name. "Groff."

There were murmurs around the table.

"Groff?" said Myvan. "Is he one of the carpenter's sons?"

"He is," said Revel, his voice tinged with disappointment, "a pale, thin, studious youth. I'm not convinced he's the best candidate. Maybe we should draw another name."

Myvan's thoughts were mixed. On the one hand, Groff would pose little challenge to Addi being selected to the Circle, or Sinjun, for that matter. On the other hand, someone like Groff, without any adventuring experience, might not be too helpful in the search for Addi, and maybe more of a hindrance.

Still, the process had to be honoured. "If Groff's name was picked," said Myvan, "Groff's the one who'll go. Revel, deliver the news, and have all three prepare for the search."

Chapter 6

Bodessa crossed the stream, danced on the stepping stones to the other side. Addi shook his head and marvelled at her dexterity – at how she'd kept going.

Since sunrise, when they'd set off from the hideaway, she'd kept moving – slowly at first, burdened by the wounds in her back and legs. But by the time the sun was at its highest and the Dark Wood was beginning to swelter, she'd actually got stronger. Except to stop briefly to eat the merriberries they'd picked, she hadn't rested once. The Jabunga leaves, of course, had been a big reason for her quick recovery. Addi had placed five or six fresh ones down the back of her frock, and the young female with the long black hair – the one who called herself a Zenta – now moved with amazing grace.

His decision to accompany her back to Castle Zen instead of returning to the castle ruin hadn't been an easy one. The Dwarfgiants' shortage of Jabunga leaves and the fate of his friend Tarro weighed on his mind. Myvan would not be pleased he'd abandoned the mission, no matter how noble his decision to help a young female in distress. But the truth was that Addi couldn't help himself. Not only had he helped save her life, he was attracted to her. This beautiful Zenta, her dark eyes full of mystery, was hard to give up.

They'd trekked westward and by midday reached the Dark Wood's Southern Glade – a gorgeous, green-lined clearing with a stream running through it. Without saying much, they followed the stream for about an hour, enjoying the sun and the sound of the rippling water. As the sun moved over to the other side of the stream, he and Bodessa did too.

Following her lead, he skipped across the stepping stones – though not nearly as gracefully – slipping on a mossy bit, almost falling in.

She giggled – a sound as lovely as her face.

"Let's cool our feet," he said, sitting on the bank.

She sat next to him, dipped her toes in the pool of water. For a moment their knees touched. It made him tingle. He looked down at their reflection – she, white-skinned, with lush dark hair; he, the furry, fair-haired Dwarfgiant. Through the circling ripples she looked distracted, gazing off into the distance, lost in her own world – a world he knew nothing about. Could her encounter with the Raslatombs – the trauma of facing Taluhla's blade – have finally got to her? What had she been doing anyway, alone in the Dark Wood? Before he could ask, she too looked down into the rippling water. Their eyes met. He looked away.

"I can't believe it," he said quickly. "How much you've overcome in one day."

"It's your Jabunga leaves," she said. "They're like magic. Wait until my father hears about them. He'll want lots."

Her father, that was it – if he asked about her father, he might get to know more about her. Only as he pondered the question did the shadow fall. He looked up. A single cloud blotted out the sun. It was the only cloud in the sky, the darkest he'd ever seen. A breeze picked up. It made him shiver.

"We should go," he said, standing. "You need to get back home."

"It's not far," she said, pointing. "The Kindoo Wetlands are just beyond the curve of pines."

The cloud stuck to the sun like an eclipse.

With Bodessa in front, they pushed on, following the rippling stream. But the rhythm of the water, now running hard, put Addi on edge. He gripped his knife, glanced left and right. Up the sloping banks the pinewood had darkened, grew restless with lurking things. They were not alone. He looked back. High in the muted sky, two pink moons nudged closer.

A roar made him turn. Bodessa ran towards the big rock near the pines. He ran after her.

"What was that?" he said, falling in behind the rock, crouching next to her.

She turned to him, her face anxious. "Addi, I should tell you … here, in the Glade … is where the gorax lives."

He saw her lips tremble. "Gorax?"

"A beast of prey. It has jagged teeth and eyes in the back of its head."

"In the back of its … have you seen one?"

"Yes," she said, "but not alive. Zenta hunters once brought the horrible creature back from the Glade. But not before it had eaten three of them."

"Stay here," he said, brandishing the knife. "I'm going to take a look."

"Be careful," she said. "Don't let it see you."

Be careful. Her concern lifted his heart. He nodded and edged around the rock.

With a deep breath he took in the view. What a sight! It was like entering a new world – where the Dark Wood's Southern Glade ended and the Kindoo Wetlands began – an open vista where, to the right, the pines trees gave way to reedy marshes, and, as far as he could see, the huge skies swirled thick with flocking birds. He ventured a few steps from the rock, his eyes shifting, taking in the rough and tumbling land leading to the marshes. Smaller rocks mingled with patches of scrubby grass and the black holes of bogs, but when his gaze stopped at the edge of a swamp, fear ran through him. Although the dark cloud still half-covered the sun, the light was enough for him to make out the shape of a hulking brown creature – a beast, three, maybe four times bigger than a wild boar. With its head bobbing, it stood over some poor animal, eating it. Addi gulped. Although the beast's back was turned to him, its eyes looked right at him. *It has jagged teeth and eyes in the back of its head.* Addi stiffened, not daring to move.

"Addi," said Bodessa. "What is it?"

He turned. She stood at the corner of the rock.

"Stay back!" he said. "It's the gorax."

The beast still watched him. What could they do? A trail skirted the pines, away from the swamps and around the distant marshes. It would be risky, but if the gorax was busy with its kill, maybe it would leave them alone.

"I saw a trail," said Addi, scrambling back behind the big rock. "If we follow the tree line I think we can get past the beast." He took her hand, gave it a squeeze. "Are you up for it?"

She pressed her lips together and nodded. But he wondered if he was taking too big a chance. The thought of confronting a gorax – a beast he knew almost nothing about – struck him as reckless.

"Stay close," he added.

They set off, side by side, at a fast jog. Knife in hand, Addi kept to Bodessa's left, a buffer between her and the gorax should it attack. He ran harder. He thought she might fall back, but no, she stayed at his shoulder, running strongly. Now and then, through the gaps between rocks, he'd catch a glimpse of the gnawing flesh-eater. But as they passed the point closest to the beast – about fifty paces away – the gorax looked up. Addi couldn't tell if it had seen them, but the bloated pile of squalor stayed put, gorging on flesh and bone.

As they ran on, he breathed easier. Soon they'd be out of danger, his adventuring instincts intact. But instincts can be delicate, and certainly not to be taken for granted. In the moment it took for the sunshadow to pass, his heart flared. It was as if he'd suddenly found himself in a race, with the finish line in sight, but being chased down by something dark. It came from underfoot, a shuddering of the ground. At that moment his instincts changed. He'd miscalculated, knew he wouldn't get to the finish line without a fight. But how much time did he have?

He glanced back. The gorax, blood-faced and snarling, was already bearing down, so close he could smell it. All he could do was shield himself, take the blow, hope to live. Like a sack of stones the beast bowled him over, knocked him flat.

Bodessa screamed.

Face down, Addi could hardly breathe. The gorax, heaving and grappling, was trying to turn him onto his back. The knife! Where was it? Through glazed eyes, he saw his hand stretched out in front of him. His finger was cut – blood, but no knife. What a fool he'd been, stupid. He tried to crawl but gristly hooves spun him over onto his back. The beast's head swiveled. Addi gasped as its mouth hung above him: smelly breath, dripping blood, chunks of flesh. He'd be next. He braced for the gorax's plunging teeth. Instead, a gob of goo fell on his head. The beast's red drool ran down his face. What was this, some sort of sick pre-meal ritual?

He heard a thump – a rock thrown. The gorax squealed, made a creaking sound like something being wound up. Slowly its head swivelled half a turn, and now its eyes – bulging goggles, lids crusted with warts – were fixed on Bodessa. She was about to throw another rock. A creak, another swivel, the beast's mouth opened until it was as big as a Dwarfgiant's head.

"Run, Bodessa, run!"

Before she could even start, the sky darkened. A cloud of green-winged pine-tattles swirled above. In their midst, a huge flapping bird shrieked: "Eeeeah! Eeeeah!"

Without looking up, the gorax clamped its mouth shut. Scrambling to its feet it pushed off, but its back hoof slammed into Addi's chin. For a moment stars danced in his eyes. Then his head cleared enough to see the gorax running towards the open swamps.

He wanted to move – to get up – but couldn't. He felt bludgeoned, couldn't believe he was still breathing.

He felt a hand touch his shoulder. "Addi," Bodessa said, kneeling beside him, helping him sit up. "It's all right, the gorax has nowhere to hide. The mizot will save us."

Together they watched the mizot bank and turn. Then, in a scatter of pine-tattles, the great battle bird swooped down, talons open, beak pointing, hauling the gorax down at the edge of a bog. When the swivel-headed beast screamed, it was because the mizot had plucked out its eyes.

CHAPTER 7

Tarro stood in the main square, burning with fever. Arm in a sling, his wounded shoulder screamed. Even a fresh Jabunga leaf couldn't ease the pain, or the heat in his head, or, for that matter, the dazzling sun. He squinted, gritted his teeth. Although he felt as if his knees might give out, he couldn't show weakness. The mission was too important. After all, he'd volunteered – no, demanded – to lead the search party to find Addi. With his father standing next to him there could be no going back.

"Here they come," said Myvan, his voice full of curiosity.

Using his good hand, Tarro shielded his eyes. Three odd figures approached. Revel, short and stocky, his no-nonsense step led the way. To his right, a tall, raw-muscled youth kept pace, his sledgehammer shoulders leaving no doubt it was Sinjun. To Revel's left, a gangly youth, legs like stilts, struggled to keep up. Groff.

"Sorry for the delay," Revel said. "There were some last-minute details to attend to. Seems our friend Groff here insists on carrying his bag of 'useful' things."

"What kind of things?" Tarro asked.

"F-fire-starters, d-dangerous b-beast repellent," said Groff.

And he stutters.

"That's good!" said Myvan handing him two empty sacks. "Make sure you have room for these. Bring them back full of Jabunga leaves."

"When do we start, sir?" Sinjun asked, his voice sharp, urgent. The armourer's son had cold grey eyes, a fresh scar down his left cheek. A leather fighting tunic hugged his torso, a knife and bamboozie sling were secure on his belt.

"Right away," Myvan said. "We need to find Addi, fast. As Revel will have already told you, Addi, along with yourself and Groff, is a candidate for the Circle's new junior position. On your return, the selection will be made. Tarro will lead the search. He knows the trail. However, the Dark Wood is a sinister place so keep your eyes open, and don't take any unnecessary risks. Remember, you must be back no later than sundown tomorrow. Any questions?"

"C-can we t-trust the moons?" asked Groff, casually. Yet the question was full of possibilities.

"The only thing you should be trusting," said Myvan, "is each other."

"You can count on me, sir," Sinjun said. "I won't let you down."

Below the glare of the afternoon sun, Tarro thought he saw Sinjun smirk.

* * *

Tarro led the search party out of the castle ruin. In single file, he, Groff and Sinjun crossed the drawbridge. His legs were still shaky. And with a walking stick in one hand, his other arm in a sling, he felt ridiculous. The departure was supposed to be an important moment – if not exactly a show of strength, at least strength of purpose. In his aggravated state he couldn't even bring himself to look back, wave farewell.

A yell and a thud made him look back, anyway. Groff was down. Sprawled on all fours, he must have tripped on a drawbridge slat; the contents of his bag scattered all around him. Panicky, the carpenter's son began to gather up the spilt objects: gadgets and tools, toy-like shapes made of wood.

Tarro's humiliation began to rise. He had a Circle candidate who couldn't even make it across the drawbridge. He could only imagine what the onlookers were thinking.

Sinjun grabbed Groff's collar. With one hand, he yanked him back on his feet. This time, muscle-boy's smirk was unmistakable.

"You all right, Groff?" said Tarro.

Groff nodded, straightened his tunic.

"Look, I realize this is a new experience for you, but let's try to keep it together. The mission demands it."

"Tarro, wait!" said a voice behind them.

Mother.

Tripping along the drawbridge, she carried a basket laden with food. "You forgot the dinner I prepared. It's your favourite – roast rosarri on baked bouella bread – and there's a creamy jenjer cake for after. There's plenty for all three."

He didn't need this. "Mother, we won't have time to eat. Besides, we'll be back before you know it."

"Nonsense," she said, "you'll be hungry soon enough. We can put it in Groff's bag."

Together she and Groff fiddled to make space.

Impatient with the delay, Tarro turned away, looked out beyond the moat, up the sandy trail leading to the Dark Wood. Soon the sun would set, shade fall to darkness. He thought of Addi, remembered the last time they were together; the scream in the night, torchlight through the trees, the Raslatombs. Did Addi save the female? Was his friend still alive?

"There!" said Mother. "That should do it. It's packed tight, but it's in."

Tarro braced as she approached.

"Now be safe," she said pinching his cheek. "I want to be able to do this again." He winced as she kissed his forehead.

That was it. They had to leave. "Dwarfgiants!" he bellowed, as if leading an army of thousands. "To the woods!"

As the three headed out, a flying jade jumped clean out of the moat.

CHAPTER 8

Dazed from the gorax attack, Addi stumbled along the wetlands trail. With his tunic torn and gorax drool smeared on his face, his pride may have been mauled, but he was still alive … and holding Bodessa's hand.

Fate was capricious. In less than a day, he'd gone from saving her life, to her saving his. Had she not distracted the gorax by throwing stones at it, the mizot would have been too late.

Addi said, "Where did the eye-plucking bird come from, anyway?"

"It spies its prey from the secluded branches of pines trees. But sightings are rare."

He squeezed her hand.

The boggy scrubland gave way to fresh green marshes. The harsh chatter of birds was everywhere, but it felt safe – a safe place to be. They stopped by a marsh pond: lilies floating, the mingling aroma of reed grass and water mint.

"Your face is dirty and your finger's bleeding," Bodessa said. "You should bathe."

He looked at his right hand; the middle finger was sliced open – the knife – he'd fallen on it when the gorax knocked him to the ground. He touched his face. The sticky goo there was beginning to harden.

While she sat on a flat stone, he wandered down to the water's edge. But he felt awkward. His tunic was loose, torn open at the back. He glanced over his shoulder. She looked away – her lips tight, her eyes amused. He waded into the pond, shivered. When the water reached his belt he let himself fall. A gasp, then underwater he opened his eyes. Blood and brown goo coloured the water, clouded the sunlit reed bed. He tugged at his tunic, retied it. Breathless, he broke the surface.

"You look better already," she said.

"It's refreshing," he said, sweeping the hair from his eyes. "You should come in."

As soon as he'd said it he knew it had come out wrong – too eager. It was hardly time for water play.

Her chin lifted and for a moment her gaze looked through him. Why couldn't he – just for once – think before speaking?

"We should go," she said. "The sun's going down. Need to reach Lake Zen before nightfall."

Although her answer didn't surprise him, he was still disappointed.

CHAPTER 9

Tarro trudged up the trail to the Dark Wood. In silence, Groff and Sinjun followed. The search for Addi had begun, but Tarro knew it wouldn't be easy. The wood crawled with devilish creatures – some with tusks, some with horns; moonworshippers carrying out acts of sacrifice. He'd already confronted the Raslatombs, taken care of a few of them. But he knew the grimy goat-heads wouldn't be blindsided again. Next time, Taluhla would be ready.

As a Circle member, Tarro had the power to change up in size. But with his skewered shoulder aching, he winced at the thought of what that would feel like, prayed it wouldn't be necessary. He knew the path to the hideaway; he hoped Addi would be there waiting.

The smell of salt sea air began to fade. Sandy earth and tufts of coastal grass gave way to forio and pine. Before them, the Dark Wood stood silent, steeped in twilight.

A stumble startled him. Not Groff again! He stopped and looked back. But Groff was steady. It was Sinjun who hobbled. At least he hadn't fallen.

In the distance, down the sweep of the valley, the castle ruin was closing up for the night. The drawbridge was raised, torches were lit. Beyond the ruin, the eastern sun had set. The breaking waves of the Sulphur Sea gave no hint of the giant serpent its waters were said to harbour.

With his walking stick, Tarro pointed to a cluster of rocks. "Let's sit before we enter the wood." In a three-point circle he faced the two candidates:

Groff, his bag lodged between grazed knees; Sinjun, picking at the scar on his face.

"How did you get it?" Tarro asked.

Sinjun paused, looked up. "Battle practice. You?"

Tarro winced. "Raslatomb arrow."

"Will we see them, the Raslatombs?" Sinjun said, flexing his fingers, making a fist.

"Hope not," Tarro said. "With any luck we'll reach the hideaway by midnight. If Addi is there, we should all be back at the castle ruin by sunrise."

Groff was digging in his bag, pulled out a small wooden box. He lifted the lid and scooped a glob of reddish-brown paste, smeared it around his eyes.

Sinjun scrunched his nose. "What a stink! What is it?"

"M-mizot rep-pellent. Do you w-want some?"

"My what?"

"Mizot. A b-bird that plucks out eyes."

"Are you serious?"

"We probably won't s-see one, but j-just in case."

Tarro was intrigued. The Odanus scribe had written about a mizot – a great flying creature with a long pointed beak. But it was known only to those of the Circle. "Groff, how do you know about this bird? Have you seen one?"

"Only f-from stories."

"Then how do you know the repellent works?"

"I d-don't. It's a test sample."

"Do me a favour," Sinjun said sharply. "Put the lid back on."

Groff looked hurt.

"We should go," said Tarro. "It'll be dark soon. Groff, why don't you prepare the torches?"

Groff nodded. But as he pulled out three torches and a flint from his bag, roast rosarri spilled out. "Oops, s-sorry," he said, gathering up the sandwiches.

"No!" said Tarro. "Don't put them back. Mother would never forgive me if we didn't eat them."

Chapter 10

The sun fell in flames behind the distant hills. Across the still waters of the lake, a whispering mist snaked towards the island castle. On reaching shore, the mist rose, engulfing sections of the ancient walls of Castle Zen.

"Wow!" said Addi. "That's where you live? It's … magical."

Bodessa didn't answer. She looked uncertain – apprehensive. "There's a small boat," she said at last, pointing to a bed of reeds.

Addi hurried to retrieve the row boat, untied its rope from a bent willow. Wading along the shoreline he pulled the vessel to Bodessa. He took her hand, helped her in. She settled on a seat facing him. She looked drained. Her pale skin was even paler now, her dark eyes glassy. He pushed out of the shallows and rowed into the purple dusk, across the lake, towards the castle.

A cool cross-breeze rippled the waters. Bodessa shivered, pulled Addi's outer tunic tight around her. As he rowed, he kept a close eye on her. It was as if she'd finally succumbed to the effects of her ordeal: the Raslatombs, the bed of pointed stakes, the run-in with the gorax. She hadn't talked about returning home. Maybe reuniting with her father was something she wasn't looking forward to.

After glancing at her too many times, he put the oars down. Careful not to rock the boat, he unfastened the pouch from his belt and stepped towards her. "Here, drink this." She mustered a smile. As he watched her take a sip of water, he noticed her pendant. It must have been nestled in her chest, but it slipped out now from her tunic.

As she handed the water pouch back to him, she caught him staring. "What are you looking at?"

"It's beautiful," he replied.

Her fingers found the chain and the two stones that dangled from it. "My pendant."

He continued to stare. The stones emitted a faint pink glow. "What are they?"

"Moonstones."

"Where did you get them?"

She shuffled then sighed. "My father gave them to me. They were my mother's."

"Were your mother's?"

"She died."

"I'm sorry," he said, remembering his own mother passing in only his eighth summer.

She tucked the pendant back under her tunic. "Just after I was born. I never knew her."

He waited for more, but that was it. She'd said all she wanted to say. In the maddening dusk he resumed rowing, wondered to what end their fortunes were headed.

Eyes closed, still as a monument, she sat. In her soporific state, her expression showed neither contentment nor concern. Maybe she was shutting out the memory of her recent ordeal – finding her way home. But to what? He wondered what life was like behind the mighty walls of Castle Zen.

"Thanks for the water, Addi." Not until she spoke did her eyes open.

He rowed some more – but not far, it was time to ask the question. "So, Bodessa, can you tell me more about your father?

"He's Zuma, the leader of the Zenta's. Some call him Zuma the Mystic Zenta."

"Mystic Zenta? Really?"

"Don't be overawed. My father is a self-made mystic, more a legend in his own mind. His powers are drawn from the fumes of crushed mizot eggs and viper venom. He claims the concoction gives him the power to know things."

"Like what?"

"Like how and when Castle Zen will be attacked."

"That's scary."

"You needn't worry. You saved my life. I'm the one in trouble. My father, he's very protective. I shouldn't have been in the Dark Wood in the first place."

"Why were you?"

She looked out across the lake. "I was looking ... for something."

"What were you looking for?"

"Something."

She was back in her shell. Except for his oars cutting through the water and the odd splash of jumping fish, Lake Zen was quiet. The last remnants of daylight struggled to fight off the oncoming night. The sky, heavy with blackening clouds, seemed as if it might fall, leaving those below no choice but to take cover underwater. It occurred to him that only Castle Zen, with its massive fortress, could withstand such an impact.

A quarter of the way across Lake Zen the breeze picked up. Banks of mist swirled around them. Suddenly, Bodessa sat up.

"What is it?" Addi said.

She put a finger to her lips. They listened in silence.

"Zentas!" she whispered.

"What?"

"The castle guard."

A rumble of drums, faint at first, grew louder and louder. Like waves of thunder they pulsed to the grunt of rowers, the lash of whips. In a drone of horns, six bloodthirsty war boats broke out of the mist.

Bodessa scrambled to Addi, nearly tipped the rowboat.

"They're coming straight at us!" said Addi.

"But they're not coming for us," Bodessa replied. "Look!"

Over their shoulders, from the northwest, eight opposing war boats burst into view. As the drums and horns climaxed, the sky lit up. Fire-arrows streamed from both sides.

Addi called out, "Who are the Zentas fighting?"

"Kroguls," she said, shaking her head with an air of futility. "Every summer they sail down from the Lake of Fools, try to take Castle Zen and seize my father's treasure."

Addi frowned. "If they always lose, why do they keep coming back?"

"They're pirates, outcasts from bands and tribes from the northern parts of Rood. They try hard but they're not well trained."

As the battle flared, Addi observed the combatants. The Zenta Guard, their heads shaved clean, were swifter, more precise. Clad in black tunics, swords in jewelled belts, they fired twice as many arrows as the Kroguls. Naked from the waist up, the pirates took the brunt of the onslaught. In the lead boat, high on a platform, a mighty Krogul, magnificent with a black plumed helmet and pugilistic nose, stood before the mast, barking orders. "To the death!" he cried waving a great sword. Alas, for him, his words were prophetic; before he could raise another cry, a flaming arrow punctured his chest, pinning him to the mast. Ablaze, he set the mast on fire.

The Kroguls staggered. Confused, and riddled with burning arrows, those who could make it threw themselves overboard, screaming.

Dusk turned into night.

Though outnumbered eight boats to six, the Zenta archers overwhelmed the bigger pirate fleet. Sails blazed, drums boomed amid the fevered cries of battle. Six Krogul boats were in flames – clouds of choking smoke. With only one Zenta boat burning, the fight was over. A bulky vessel – a Zenta holding ship – trolled for prisoners: pirates pulled from the chilly waters.

Fanned by the breeze, more mist rolled in and for a time Addi could see nothing. There were only sounds – harsh commands, the crackle of fire – and the smell of burning wood.

When the mist cleared, a Krogul vessel, its charred hull smoking, veered towards the rowboat. There was no time to get out of the way.

"Jump!" Addi said, grabbing Bodessa's hand. He felt her thin fingers clasp his. They leaped. The cold water made him gasp. They rose to the surface, watched the ghost ship smack the rowboat to splinters. Panic ran through him. But before he could catch his breath, she'd spun away, swimming hard.

"Bodessa, wait!"

She neither stopped nor slowed down. The distance between them grew quickly. Soon she was lost in the mist. He started to swim, clawed through the water towards the Zenta trolling boat. To his regret, swimming wasn't his strength. Twice he stopped: once to take a breath, another time to avoid a floating body – a Krogul, his face black and bubbled, his eyes wide open, an arrow stuck clean through his neck.

Worn out, Addi reached the side of the trolling boat. Treading water he looked up, hoped to see Bodessa, but mist and smoke fogged his view. Before he could call out, something rough slapped his head. Instinctively he slipped under water. The shock of being hit jarred him, and when his eyes popped open he saw it – a thick rope waiting to be grabbed. He pulled himself to the surface and looked up. The mist had lifted, and there, dream-like on the deck, stood Bodessa, dripping in her white frock, her hair streaming down her face. Next to her, a young Zenta warrior – head shaved and striking in black – stood tall, his arm around her shoulders.

Addi gripped the rope.

"Hold on!" Bodessa said, "We'll pull you up."

Surprise. The tone of her voice sounded amiable enough.

With his free hand, the Zenta warrior signalled. Suddenly the rope tightened and yanked Addi up the side of the boat. On deck he scrambled to his feet. All around, Krogul prisoners were being prodded with swords, bound, shoved into the hold.

Soaked and shivering he stood before Bodessa. Next to her the Zenta warrior, smooth-skinned and half again as tall as he was, still had an arm around her.

Addi looked into her eyes, waited for an explanation.

After a few torturous moments she finally spoke. "Addi, this is Andros – my brother."

With a thud, Addi's anxiety fell to the deck.

Chapter 11

Tarro, Sinjun and Groff entered the Dark Wood at twilight. Black trees, shrouds of mist and the smell of damp earth gave Tarro the shivers. He'd been there before, but he and Addi had gone looking for Jabunga leaves in the middle of the day when the birds sang and sunbeams streaked through the breezy trees. Now, the branches, gaunt in silhouette, looked too still – like petrified monsters, all arms and trouble.

Tarro had chosen Sinjun to lead the way. The brash, muscle-bound Circle candidate needed to be tested. Tarro wanted to see how he dealt with whatever the Dark Wood might throw at him. Surprisingly, Sinjun was reluctant to go first, citing a sore ankle. But Tarro wondered if the real reason was something Groff had said about what they might expect. First there'd been the stinky repellent to ward off the eye-plucking mizot. Then, before handing out the lit torches, he'd come up with another creature to watch out for. This one was tiny – with lots of legs and an oversized belly. "It's c-called a chompit," Groff had said in his nonchalant, stuttering way. "Likes to c-crawl in your ear, munch on your b-brain, then, when it's finished, c-crawl out your other ear."

Tarro wasn't sure where Groff had got this little gem, or why he'd even mentioned it. Still, if his knowledge of the Dark Wood was a figment of a fertile imagination, it seemed to have worked, at least strategically. It had put Sinjun on edge, and, it seemed, there wasn't much a set of bulging muscles could do against a brain-eating chompit.

Tarro insisted Sinjun go first. "Keep to the middle trail," he called out from the back. "It goes straight to the hideaway."

They went slowly into the gloom. Sinjun limped, Groff wobbled on his grazed knees and Tarro scuffed along with his walking stick. With a new set of worries to fill his mind, he soon forgot about the pain in his shoulder.

The air was cool and thick, soundless except for the now-and-again grunt of a snodgril, a frisky, burrowing creature with a corkscrew nose. The trail to the hideaway – at times overgrown with gnarly tree roots – was fairly passable. Since arriving on Helborin, several expeditions had been carried out in an attempt to discover the secrets of the Dark Wood. The main trail had been partly cleared and Jabunga leaves found. Some creatures were already known – or known of. The most fearsome was the gorax – which, according to the Odanus scribe, was "a wretched, powerful beast, warty and smelly, with a spinning head and teeth like daggers" – although no Dwarfgiant had ever seen it. And, if Groff was right, the great mizot battle bird might even be waiting around the next corner, looking to pluck out an eye.

Suddenly, Sinjun stopped. He looked slowly to either side, his nose twitching as if he was smelling danger. "Get the feeling we're being watched?" he said, his hand on his knife.

"I d-don't see anything," said Groff.

"It's these trees," Sinjun said, his voice shaky. "They're not real, something cold, like eyes peeping."

Trees that weren't trees! Peeping eyes! What was going on? Just ten minutes in and the backbone of the search party was hallucinating. Not good. In fact, Tarro thought, the way things were going, Addi might as well be made a new Circle member right now, in absentia … assuming he was still alive.

Chapter 12

On the crowded deck of the Zenta trolling boat, Addi and Andros stood facing each other. Up close, Addi could see how Andros could be Bodessa's brother – limber physique, dark eyes, full wide lips which, at that moment, revealed a bemused smile.

He thinks I'm odd, Addi thought.

"Andros," said Bodessa, flicking wet strands of hair from her eyes, "Addi's a Dwarfgiant. He –"

She was interrupted by a Zenta cheer; dry and mocking, it rode the night wind then deadened against a wall of mist. With white flags flying, the last two Krogul war boats had surrendered.

The battle was over.

Andros removed his arm from around Bodessa's shoulders. "I must go," he said, "but I'll be back with dry clothes."

Addi turned to Bodessa. "What was that all about?" he said, puzzled. "Taking off like that, in the water, without saying a word."

"It was like I was being pulled," she said, handing him a blanket from a storage box. "I can't explain."

Addi looked at her, baffled. But she'd lapsed into her solitary state again, content to lean on the guardrail, watching the captured vessels being hitched to the trolling boat.

With the blanket wrapped around him, he watched too as a scuffle broke out near the trap door to the hold. A chained Krogul with an arrow stuck in his leg went berserk. Screaming, arms flailing, he swung his chain and dropped two guards before he too was taken down, knocked silly when his face hit the deck. In the galley, other Krogul prisoners were forced to row. Shackled and lashed, they towed their own boats back to Castle Zen.

Andros returned carrying dry clothes, a smile of victory splashed across his face.

"So the Kroguls tried again," Bodessa said, taking a towel and wrapping it around herself.

"Their annual attack," Andros replied matter-of-factly. "But Father saw them coming. Strange he didn't know you had gone. Where have you been?"

"It's a long story."

"I hope it's a good one."

"Well, I'm here now. Thanks to Addi."

Addi's heart warmed.

He and Andros eyed each other again.

This time Andros looked doubtful. "Thanks to Addi?"

Addi began, "It was –"

"With great timing and bravery," Bodessa interrupted.

Andros looked suspicious.

Addi said, "There were some nasty –"

"Moon worshippers," Bodessa said. "They tied me to a bed of pointed stakes. But Addi cut me free."

Andros frowned.

Addi shrugged.

Chapter 13

In the Great Hall, flickering with torch fires and smelling of incense, Zuma the Mystic Zenta sat on his turquoise throne, the fingers of his right hand drumming on the arm. The drumming usually meant that he was getting impatient, but sometimes he was simply enjoying the changing glow of the Zenstone he wore on his middle finger. Busily he jiggled his finger. The massive stone, clear-cut and blood red, brought him luck and he always wore it for special occasions. He was hoping this was one of those times. But the throne – his for over thirty summers – wasn't helping. Instead of getting softer with age, it seemed to get harder. Sometimes he'd get cramps in his legs, or more often, like now, his backside would go numb.

He shuffled from side to side, working on his circulation. Then he stretched. As he did so, he noticed what fine shape his leg and arm muscles were in: firm and strong. Certainly good enough to be shown off in the thigh-length, sleeveless black tunic he wore. Feeling better, he treated himself to a footrest. Wearing his skin-lined, shin-high boots, he planted his feet on a small treasure chest resting in front of him.

Two more things to check before his patience ran out. First, his ruby-encrusted belt harness. Criss-crossed over his tunic, it held a black-handled knife in a leather sheath. He pulled the blade, eyed it for flatness. Slid it back in. Smooth. Then, feeling a tad self-conscious, he glanced over his shoulder. In the shadowy recesses behind him, four elite Zenta guards stood in place, attentive, silent and still. Satisfied, he turned back and fixed his eyes in front of him. Beyond the treasure chest supporting his feet, a narrow carpet extended some fifty paces along the full length of the hall. It led to two mighty doors, where more Zenta guards were positioned, one on each side.

Zuma had waited long enough. His voice boomed. "Bring in the fool!"

The guards pulled at the handles. Creaking, the doors yawned open. Flanked on either side by two more guards, a slight figure clad in a ragged grey tunic entered. His wrists and ankles were manacled and connected by a chain. He was a familiar sight – the hapless Krogul with his long hair straggling over a thin face dotted with stubble. His pointed ears stuck out from under a dirty red scarf wrapped around his head. Below his eyes – sharp and bitter – his skin was sloppy. Bags hung halfway down his face. But the scars of war were there, too. His nose looked twice its normal size – red and swollen, one part flattened, one part twisted. His main handicap, though, was that he limped terribly. With an arrow lodged in his thigh, he dripped blood all along the carpet. And yet, for all his suffering, he still carried himself forward – a dogged attempt at self-respect. Two paces in front of the treasure chest he was forced to stop.

While the prisoner looked away, Zuma observed the skewered mess.

"Hello, Bardo," he said. "Run into a door?"

Bardo said nothing.

"So, how are you?"

Bardo glared. "Better when I get this arrow out of my leg."

Dry blood caked the area where the arrow had torn through Bardo's leggings and entered the fleshy part of his thigh. Fresh blood trickled down the shaft, falling on the carpet.

"Ooh, nasty!" said Zuma. "Perhaps we can help. Yank it out."

"No thanks."

"It's not barbed, is it?"

"All your arrows are barbed."

"Umm, come to think of it, they are. Still, we really should have it seen to. Twist it out."

Bardo said nothing.

"Tell me, Bardo, you didn't really expect to pull off a surprise attack, did you?"

"It had crossed my mind."

"I mean, it wasn't even dark. Against my archers, not very good odds. Why not try a nighttime attack?"

"We have tried a nighttime attack. Last year, remember?"

"Oh, right! You had bad weather. Half your boats sank and the other half got lost in the dark. Wasn't your finest hour, was it?"

"Bad luck."

"Come on, Bardo, it's got nothing to do with luck! Let's face it, your archers are pathetic. They're no match for mine. They only hit one of our boats. We hit six of yours." Zuma leaned forward, lowered his voice. "Tell me, how many times a week do you practise?"

Bardo was silent.

"How many times?"

Bardo looked down.

Zuma began to drum his fingers, tap his foot on the treasure chest.

"Three," Bardo muttered.

"Three! Is that all? How do you expect to win on three practices a week? Bardo, you really disappoint me. And now, I'm afraid, you're going to have to pay for it."

The blood from Bardo's thigh began to pool on the floor.

Rising from his throne, Zuma strode to the west window and looked out. "I've decided to build a new extension to Castle Zen," he said. "And this should be of particular interest to you, Bardo. Starting tomorrow, you and your Kroguls are going to do all the heavy digging."

Feeling smug, he returned to his throne and snapped his fingers. "Get him out of here!"

The guards went to grab him, but Bardo shook them off, turned and dragged his chains back down the blood-stained carpet.

Zuma, watching his old adversary being escorted from the hall, couldn't resist a parting jab. "Oh, and speaking of digging," he called out, "let's get that arrow out of his leg!"

As Bardo exited the hall, Andros came in. Up the carpet at speed he slipped and skidded and almost fell on Bardo's blood.

Zuma stood. "Andros, my boy! A superlative performance. Another Zenta victory."

"Thank you, Father," he said, straightening himself. "It wasn't much of a fight."

"You're too modest. Bardo's a wily soul. We must always be ready for him."

Andros smiled, then bit his lip. "Father," he said, "I have even greater news."

Zuma prided himself on his ability to predict things happening. Once again he'd warned of the Krogul's surprise attack. Once again it was the Kroguls who'd been surprised. What news could be greater than that?

"It's Bodessa."

"Oh, yes? What's my little Bo Bo up to now?"

"She's back."

"What do you mean, she's back?"

"She's waiting to see you."

"Where's she been?"

"I don't know. I found her in the lake."

"You found her where? Is she all right?"

"Seems to be."

"Right. Well, don't just stand there, bring her to me."

Andros remained. "It's just that there's … there's something else."

Zuma frowned. "There is?"

"She's brought a friend."

Zuma put his hand on his dagger. "What kind of friend?"

Andros's face twisted. "Well he's … he's different. Smallish. Long yellow hair. Maybe fur."

"Fur?"

"Probably hair."

"Well, which?"

"I'm not sure. But he's … different. He calls himself a Dwarfgiant."

Zuma checked the Zenstone on his finger. Its red edges began to ripple. Was it good luck or bad? "A Dwarfgiant, you say? … Well, bring them both in."

* * *

In the waiting area outside the Great Hall, Addi was on edge. A prisoner with an arrow in his leg was being led away – the Krogul from the boat. There was a lot of blood and he had a busted nose.

"What's that you've got?" the Krogul spewed at Bodessa. "A new pet? Just remember who you really belong to."

A guard jammed the length of his spear across the prisoner's back. The Krogul stumbled, cursed and called out again. "You're all weirdos. Weirdos and freaks!" His words echoed down the passageway.

Addi looked at Bodessa. "What did he mean, who you really belong to?"

"It's Bardo," she said in exasperation. "He never changes."

But Addi felt queasy. If this was a taste of life behind the walls of Castle Zen, what could he expect for himself? Here he was, if not a captive then certainly an outsider, an alien figure about to meet Bodessa's father, Zuma the Mystic Zenta.

He'd need to be alert.

He heard the call, and a guard at the door waved them in.

Bodessa turned, put a hand on his shoulder. "It'll be all right, Addi," she said. But her smile, lovely as it was, only stretched halfway.

Keeping close behind, he followed her into the Great Hall.

The smell of old wood and tar smoke hit him first – an ancient essence, pungent yet comforting, hanging in the torchlit air. Not so comforting was the fresh blood that spotted the carpet on which they walked – all the way down to a large blue throne, where the occupant – head-shaved and muscle-heavy – sat, looking puzzled. Although handsome, age was creeping down the lines of his face, accentuating his fading looks. But there was nothing faded about his eyes – deep black.

Zuma jumped to his feet. He sidestepped the treasure chest and, with his arms outstretched, hurried to his daughter.

"Bodessa!" he said, his voice loud. "What's this all about? Andros tells me you left Castle Zen. Said he found you in the lake."

"It's true," she said giving him a quick hug. "But I'm well. Thanks to Addi, here."

Addi felt his face flush.

Bodessa reached back for his hand and drew him to her side. "He saved my life."

Zuma looked at him. A look similar to the one Andros had given him – uncertain, though not so full of suspicion. "Addi, you say? Huh. Well, Addi, it seems I owe you a debt of gratitude."

"I was glad to help," Addi said.

Zuma sat back on his throne. After a moment he said, "So, Bodessa, what happened? A bit chilly for a night swim."

Bodessa shrugged. "It's hard to explain."

Why was it always so hard to explain?

"My dear Bodessa, there's nothing you can't tell your father."

She glanced at Andros. Then back to Zuma.

Zuma took the hint. "Andros," he said, "we'll talk again soon. For now, though, go check on our friend Bardo. See how his leg is coming along."

Addi watched him leave. Then, like Zuma, he awaited Bodessa's answer.

"Father, all my life I've been trapped here. I wanted to do things."

Addi thought her answer reasonable, yet she still seemed to be holding something back.

Zuma sighed. "Bodessa, we're surrounded by unspeakable evil. If ... well ... you know I couldn't bear to lose you."

"I know."

"So tell me, what is it you want to do?"

She shook her head slowly, ran her fingers over her moonstone pendant.

"Very well," said Zuma, "I'll ask Addi. Where did you find her?"

This was awkward – Zuma staring him down, Bodessa holding her breath. What to say? There was only one thing he could say. "I found her in the Dark Wood tied to a bed of pointed stakes. About to be sacrificed."

Zuma went pale. Then, with his eyes on fire, he sprang from his throne. "Who were they!?" he screamed, his words bouncing off the walls. "Who did that to my princess?"

"Raslatombs," said Addi.

"Who?"

"The leader called herself Taluhla, Queen of the Raslatombs."

Zuma gaped. "Did you say Taluhla?"

Addi nodded.

Zuma backed onto his throne. He looked grave, haunted. A moment passed, and then, with a voice that seemed almost lost, he said to Bodessa, "You still have nothing to say?"

"Can we talk about it later? I'm tired."

Zuma studied his daughter. "Very well," he said, softening his tone. "Go rest. Then freshen up. Later tonight I'm holding the victory banquet."

Victory banquet? How odd, the need to celebrate before the dead had been counted. And yet Zuma made it sound as if it was something expected, like a summer habit. As if buoyed by the thought, the Mystic Zenta rose from his throne and said, "Addi, you will be my guest of honour."

Before Addi had time to think, Zuma, stepped towards him and, like an old friend, put an arm around his shoulder. But there might have been another reason; he could feel Zuma's fingers rubbing and stroking as if testing the texture of his fur. Turning his head, Addi could see the huge ring on Zuma's finger. Like a mystic heartbeat it pulsed, light and dark red. For the first time since Bodessa`s scream in the Dark Wood, Addi felt homesick.

Chapter 14

As Tarro suspected, the trees with the peeping eyes turned out to be imaginary. And while the last glimmer of twilight could play tricks – especially in a place as creepy as the Dark Wood – the cold black branches kept their hands to themselves.

It had been hard to convince Sinjun, though. In panic, he'd drawn his bamboozie and let loose a barrage of shots – pinging away, "popping out eyes." Afterwards, in a bizarre moment of celebration, he jumped in the air, claiming to have popped at least a dozen.

One good thing had come out of it: Sinjun agreed to put on Groff's mizot repellent. And now the stinky, reddish-brown paste was plastered around all of their eyes.

Tarro decided to lead. Not only did he have a good idea of where the hideaway was, but he needed to show the two Circle candidates that, when threatened, it was better to be calm than out of control. He pushed trigger-happy Sinjun down to second in line. Groff took a stint at the back, his magnetic wayfinder strung around his neck.

Tarro knew that leading was a challenge – a lonely time up front – especially since he was reluctant to change to giant size, what with his arm being in a sling. With only a torch to defend himself even his fears began to close in; the thought of swivel-headed goraxes, eye-plucking mizots, the revenge of the Raslatombs, all tightened his chest. He thought of Addi. Wondered what his friend would think. He'd probably say there was no point in worrying – trust that fate would be kind. So far, so good. Except for being startled by a brace of smirlies, there'd been no sign of trouble. The ball-like creatures, rubbery and translucent blue, made a bowang sound as they bounced across the path in front of them.

The search party reached a secondary trail. It was narrower, darker. But they were getting close. Tarro remembered the canopy of brambles that led to the hideaway. Down the prickly corridor he pushed on, Sinjun and Groff close behind.

He thought he heard a drone. Far away. Like an ugmul. "We're almost there," he said. "I don't expect trouble, but this is Raslatomb country. So stay alert."

Sinjun and Groff were quiet.

"You two all right?" Tarro asked.

"Yes," said Sinjun, a little too fast. And Groff nodded, even faster.

"Just have your bamboozies ready."

Sinjun tested his, pulled the elastic sling. *Thwack!*

"Good," said Tarro. "Let's find Addi."

The terrain through the corridor was slow going, full of drooping brambles, lined with stinging ferns. The congestion ended with a fork in the trail. Tarro remembered the fork but he couldn't remember which trail to take.

"Groff," he shouted, "we still on track?"

No answer.

He turned to look back. "Groff, we still on … where is he?"

"He was right behind me," Sinjun said, loading his bamboozie.

"H-help! H-help!" Groff's voice was unmistakable.

"Come on!" said Tarro, pushing past Sinjun.

Back down the trail, around a curve, Tarro heard gasping. He stopped, pointed his torch. In a shady nook some ten paces away, Groff was being dragged feet first into the clutches of what looked like a writhing tree stump. A profusion of "arms" – some raw roots, others wiry branches – shot out from its flaking bark and curled around Groff's legs. The creature had an oval mouth – toothless and fully-lipped – with three eyes stacked on top of one another.

Dragasp! What was it doing here? According to the writings of the Odanus scribe, the short, stubby crusher was said to inhabit the Land of

Rood. For a moment he and Sinjun watched the creature tighten its grip around Groff's torso, squeezing the breath out of him.

"We've got to do something fast," said Tarro, "or Groff's a goner."

Sinjun stepped forward. "Drop it!" he bellowed.

But the dragasp, its eyes knotted in a try-and-stop-me look, wrapped more grippers around Groff's chest.

Sinjun aimed his bamboozie.

"No!" yelled Tarro. "You might hit Groff."

Sinjun jammed the bamboozie back into his belt, pulled out his long blade. Holding it low to his side, he edged towards the creature. The dragasp – busy crushing Groff – didn't see him coming. Now only a step and a half away, and with no apparent concern for his sore ankle, Sinjun lunged, swiping and slashing, lopping off tentacles. The dragasp squealed, blood flew, its three eyes bounced crazily. But the creature wasn't finished. Two new grippers sprang out and coiled around Sinjun's arms. His knife spun away.

Tarro's heart raced. He was on the brink of losing both Circle candidates. He watched Sinjun kick and Groff swing his arms. But they were no match. With its three eyes popping, the dragasp's mouth opened wide.

Tarro couldn't see what to do. He'd feared this moment, a chance to save his fellow Dwarfgiants but unable to come through. He had his own bamboozie, but with only one arm to use, the weapon was just for show. He could change up. But dare he? If he did, he'd double in size, but his arm might burst.

"In my b-bag!" Groff called out, his voice frantic. "Use the – aah!" A branch coiled around his neck.

The bag, where was it? Tarro waved his torch over the ground. He saw Sinjun's knife, and then, sitting in a clump of nettles, Groff's bag. But as he reached for the bag he could see there wasn't enough time. The creature had Groff almost breathless. Sinjun, too, was struggling, but in a different way. A root had whipped around his arms. Then a branch snaked between his legs and around his hips. With a jerk, the dragasp raised him above its head, held him up like a prize. Sinjun's legs were free, hanging limp.

"Sinjun!" cried Tarro, waving his torch. "Kick!"

Sinjun winced, stunned, speechless.

Tarro knew fear. He'd taken a Raslatomb arrow, almost bled to death. Alone in the Dark Wood he'd faced it: the shaking, the cold sweat.

"Sinjun, listen to me! You have to –"

"Go!" Sinjun said.

"What?"

"Pee!"

He had to pee. Fear could do that.

"It's squeezing my bladder!"

That could do it too – not so much fear, but physical pressure – a tightening that was about to put an end to Sinjun and Groff, unless he could think of something. Tarro's veins rushed with blood. Then he went dizzy, his head spinning, his thoughts flying this way and that, until, finally, in a sweet moment of clarity, his brain landed on his favourite subject – chemistry. He knew that non-Circle Dwarfgiants lived on a diet of malana grains. He also knew that these grains created a reeky, stinging solution in their urine.

"Sinjun," he cried, "pee on its head!"

"What?"

"Just do it."

"What about my tunic?"

"It'll wash off."

Sinjun hit the spot. The acidic liquid cascaded over the dragasp's head, ran into its three stacked eyes. In a blind fit, the creature screeched – went haywire – its roots and branches unwinding, straightening out, shaking madly. Like oversized fruit at harvest time, Sinjun and Groff dropped to the ground.

One by one, the dragasp's arms sprang back into its stump.

Tarro planted his torch, rushed to help Sinjun back on his feet. Groff was still down. "He's breathing," said Tarro, checking his pulse. "Can you lift him?"

Somehow finding strength, Sinjun threw Groff over his shoulder. Then, one-handed, Tarro grabbed Groff's bag and Sinjun's knife. His walking stick, though, was done for, snapped in two.

"Quick, let's go," Tarro said, "before the thing recovers." But as they hurried away, he couldn't resist a glance back – a last look at the perishing dragasp – its severed arms, its shriveled trunk, its top eye flicking open.

The image of the dragasp giving chase propelled Tarro. He didn't stop until he reached the fork in the trail.

Sinjun, who'd kept pace, pulled up beside him.

"How is he?" Tarro asked.

"He's alive," Sinjun said, lowering Groff's limp body to the ground. "I heard him groan."

"Hold this," said Tarro, giving Sinjun his torch. Then he unhooked the pouch from his belt, splashed water on Groff's face. Groff spluttered, tried to sit up.

"Not so fast," Tarro said, holding him back. "Here, drink this."

Slowly, deliberately, Groff sipped the water. In the flickering torchlight the marks of his ordeal were visible around his neck: a blistering welt, the frayed cord of his magnetic wayfinder.

"What about you, Sinjun? Need anything? A Jabunga leaf, maybe?"

Sinjun sniffed, looked down at his damp tunic. "A change of clothes."

Tarro laughed. "We'll find a stream soon enough. Right now, we have to get to the hideaway – if I could remember which fork to take."

"The right f-fork," said Groff. His voice was clear, his wayfinder still working.

"Good," said Tarro. "You able to go?"

Groff stood shakily. "I'm g-good."

* * *

In a moonlit hollow, the hideaway stood before them, a secret woodland den covered in silvery leaves. In the cool silence, Tarro stood, hardly breathing, hoping to hear something from within. But there was nothing. Not even a shuffle. Maybe Addi was asleep.

"Wait here," Tarro said to Sinjun and Groff. Then, with his torch held high he crunched over bracken and twigs to a low entrance. To his left stood the pile of branches that hid the bag of Jabunga leaves. He pulled the top branches away. But the bag was gone.

"Addi!" he whispered. "You here?"

Silence.

He ducked under a bough and went inside. Except for a bed of leaves littering the ground, the hideaway was empty. No Addi. No rescued female. He stood shaking his head, cursing his luck. And yet, though disappointed, he wasn't surprised. His friend never could stay in one place for long.

Tarro knelt down, picked up a leaf. A Jabunga leaf! Someone had been there. And as he raised his torch, he saw it lying in the corner – the missing bag. It had to have been Addi; he was the only other one who knew where the bag had been hidden. So where was he now? Tarro stared hard at the Jabunga leaf. It was big and bluish and it healed wounds, but it couldn't answer questions, so he slipped it between the strap of his sling and his sore shoulder. As he did so, he felt uneasy, as if being watched. To his right he noticed a shadow, bigger than he was, floating on the wall. He never liked shadows, of any size. They were mysterious and usually didn't come to any good. The one that had crossed the two moons the night before – a shadow of foreboding – had been especially creepy. And then Taluhla, Queen of the Raslatombs, had appeared from out of the earth.

With a quick move, he transferred the torch to his left hand and swung around. The firelight revealed a scarred but familiar face.

"Sinjun!" said Tarro, both angry and relieved. "I thought I told you to stay outside."

"So, he's gone."

"Looks like it."

"That's it, then. There are only two Circle candidates left – me and Groff."

"You believe Addi's no longer alive?"

"I can't imagine he is. Not after two nights in this wood."

Tarro didn't care for Sinjun's tone. Not only had he disobeyed instructions and created a shadow, but he was also quick to give up on a fellow Dwarfgiant – seemingly for his own benefit. This wasn't the stuff Circle members were made of.

"We have no evidence of Addi's demise," Tarro replied, curtly. "If anyone can survive the dangers of the wood, he can."

Sinjun's lips spread slightly, a look of disdain. "Are you saying we go on?"

Although Tarro would never admit it to Sinjun, the question was a valid one. They couldn't wander around the Dark Wood forever. There was only so much time. Before they'd left the ruin, his father had told him that, no matter what, they had to be back at the ruin by the following night, bring home the much needed Jabunga leaves, and be ready to fight a giant sea serpent. Hadn't there been a serpent emblazoned on the gown worn by Taluhla, the Raslatomb queen? There were lots of reasons for turning back, but he'd never live with himself if he didn't do all he could to find his friend.

"We go on," he said firmly. But which way?

As if by magic, the answer came from deep in the wood. Another scream! Dark and distant, lower in register than the young female's had been. Sweet mercy, not Addi!

Tarro brushed past Sinjun and out of the hideaway. In the harsh moonlight he saw Groff rooted to the spot, his face full of worry.

"Groff – the scream – where did it come from?"

Groff pointed. It was neither the way they had come nor the way to the Raslatomb place of sacrifice. But there was a trail.

"Right!" said Tarro. "This is the plan. In the hideaway there's a bed of Jabunga leaves. Groff – put a handful in your own bag to take with us, then put the rest in the two bags Myvan gave you. If you need a third bag, you'll find Addi's inside. Then stash them under the pile of branches by the entrance. We'll pick them up on our way back."

He looked Sinjun directly in the eye.

"We've now had a taste of the lowlife that inhabits this wood. If not for an act of nature, the dragasp would have had its way with us. But here we are, still alive. And that's a good sign. It says we were meant to go on – to find Addi – no matter what."

As Tarro listened to himself he could hardly believe what he was saying. It was as if he was suddenly caught up in the adventuring spirit, the kind that past generations of Dwarfgiants were known for. Addi would have been impressed.

"Sinjun, have all your weapons ready and loaded. You'll go last."

A second cry echoed through the trees.

"Come on, let's go. Groff, you lead."

Chapter 15

Addi found himself in a stone-walled chamber, sparsely furnished, torches flickering on the walls. There was a bed, a wardrobe and, above a small table, a window half open. The night wind whistled softly as it came in. He shivered, went to the window and peered out. He could hear Lake Zen lapping, but all he could see was mist. It was so thick he wondered if he'd ever find his way home. He shivered again then snapped the window shut. He turned and took a deep breath. An hour, the guard had said, an hour and they would come for him.

He was supposed to rest, ready himself for Zuma's victory banquet. And though he was tired – close to exhausted – his mind kept turning, thinking about what he might face next, whether it would include Bodessa.

He missed her already – her lovely face, holding her hand, her annoying secrets. He imagined her alone in her chamber, sunk in a bath; fathoming her mysteries, healing the wounds on her back. But was she missing him?

Tired, agitated, his thoughts at a dead end, he needed a distraction. He spotted a torch by the door and grabbed it. Then he walked up and down the wood-planked floor, making sure that the shadows – especially those crouching in corners – were behaving themselves. Most were, motionless and regular-shaped. Only one was fretful, bobbing and shaking in the firelight. But was it dangerous? He hoped not. It was his.

He paused by the bed. Maybe he should lie down, take a nap. He headed towards the door to put the torch back. But crossing a scarlet carpet, he tripped. Feeling like a fool he fell forward, a breathless freefall, his embarrassment saved at the last instant by quick reflexes. He landed on one knee, the torch secure in his hand. What had he tripped on? He turned to see that the carpet had shifted. Something was protruding from the floor. He stood and pulled the carpet away. What he saw took a moment to sink in: the outline of a rectangle set in the floor planks – at one end, bolted hinges; at the other, a recessed handle. The torch cast a shadow on it, a shadow that bobbed and shook. Forget the nap.

He gripped the iron handle and yanked. The trap door rose easily and 180 degrees later was lying on its back. Angling his torch, the flame lit up a shallow shaft. Fixed to the wall, a wooden ladder stretched down to what looked like the beginning of a passageway at the bottom. His instinct was to set off right away, to see where it would lead. Recent events, though, had made him more cautious, more thoughtful of the dangers he might face. He started to think but didn't get far; the forces of adventure were pulling him forward. And as he stared at the ladder, nothing – except going down it – came into his head.

Torch in hand he descended – slowly at first – testing the ladder's strength. Then, speeding up, he reached the bottom skimming the last two rungs and landed with a thump on his backside. *Ouch! Slow down!*

Back on his feet and keeping his head low he started down the dingy passageway. He'd gone no more than a few paces when a sweet aroma drifted into the air around him: rose petals. Bodessa! He pointed his torch. The light flooded ahead of him all the way to the end, where an arched door stood ready to be opened. As he walked towards it, the scent of rose petals changed to a strong, musky perfume. The sweet aroma made him light-headed. What elixirs could she be conjuring? What mysteries imagined? A strange sound – a cat-like squeal – startled him. He stopped abruptly, then eased forward, put his ear to the door. He could hear a voice, deep and coaxing.

"Come, my little angel, it's time."

The voice sounded like Zuma's. But who was he talking to? Another squeal – this time sharp and angry – made Addi cringe. His newfound caution told him that this was probably not a good time to investigate, and he'd actually made up his mind to go back when the door swung open. He almost fell inside.

"Addi!" hailed the Mystic Zenta. "I've been expecting you."

Zuma looked different. In a jewelled crown and a blue satin gown spattered with suns and stars and crescent moons, he stood bleary-eyed in the doorway, his expression shifting in a swirl of smoking incense. What was more worrying was the black-handled knife he held.

"Come in! Come in!" he said, waving the blade. "Don't mind the mess."

The chamber was a haze. As soon as Addi stepped in he started to cough. Perfumed smoke wisped like spirits around tables and shelves cluttered with bottles and boxes and cages – a veil of fog mingling with candle and torch smoke rising to the rafters.

"I'm testing my new batch of lentilla musk," said Zuma, gliding past sticks of burning incense.

With his hand covering his mouth, Addi followed – past benches strewn with herbs; purple plants sprouting in pots; evergreens with orange flowers; jars filled with resins and balms; bottles of liquid, amber and blue. A cauldron bubbled in a hearth; next to it, a cage on a table. Zuma, his face wrinkling with pride, stopped and knelt before it. "My little musky," he said. "Isn't she beautiful?"

Addi stared. Lying inside the cage, a slender feline creature – long-tailed and weasel-faced – blinked drowsily, its barred and spotted coat patched with blood.

"What happened to it?" asked Addi. "Is it hurt?"

"No, no, nothing like that," said Zuma, wiping the blade on his gown. "On the waxing of the two moons, musk is taken from her scent glands. Just a little scraping." He slipped the knife back into its sheath. "She's one of the lucky ones. Lentillas are hunted for their fur. Dregs like Bardo turn them into caps and gloves. I won't allow it."

Beyond, on a wall of shelves, stood more cages, more lentillas waiting to be scraped.

Zuma inhaled deeply. "It's a potent aroma. But I see you're not used to it. Why don't we go somewhere less ambrosial, a place where we can talk?"

Before Addi could reply, Zuma was off, heading to the far end of the chamber where a ramp led to a gantry. Addi, shuffling behind, followed him across the high walkway and through an open arch. Down a set of steep steps they entered a circular space – a candlelit gallery whose flickering walls were spiked with the heads of wild beasts. In the middle of the floor were two facing chairs. Next to the more ornate chair, a carafe and two goblets stood on a table.

"Drink?" said Zuma, starting to pour.

Addi was thirsty, but could he be sure the carafe's pink liquid wasn't some sort of trickery, even poison? Not wanting to offend, he nodded, but he'd wait for Zuma to drink first.

"Its juice squeezed from suli fruit," Zuma boasted. "The best there is." He handed Addi a goblet then sat with his own in the more ornate chair. But he didn't drink.

Addi sat in the other chair – next to a tall, broad-leafed plant in an earthenware pot.

"So what do you think of my little perfume den?" asked Zuma. "I think you'll agree it heightens the senses. Like the soul, the senses also have their spiritual mysteries to reveal."

Addi was watching Zuma's goblet. The mystic raised it to his lips, was about to drink when a thought seemed to cross his face. He put the goblet back on the table.

"I used to burn frankincense, wondered what was in it that made it so mystical. After a while, though, I realized I was already mystical. So I conjured other types of perfumes distilled from sweet-smelling roots and scented flowers. Along the way, I discovered that wax secretions from the intestines of serpents stir passion, while resins from the fragrant heartwood awaken the memory of dead romances. I now dilute musk. The aroma is enchanting. It clears the mind; calms the miseries of the soul."

Dead romances?

Zuma picked up the goblet, swished the liquid around then put it back on the table. He gave Addi a resigned look. "When you get older, you'll realize the need for a sense of peace – as much as you can get."

Addi's full goblet was still on his lap. As he started to speak he could feel his throat drying up. "Bodessa told me you have the power to know when things are going to happen. She said this power comes from the fumes of crushed mizot eggs and viper venom."

Zuma grimaced. "I did tell her that. But it isn't true. At the time I was in my … my … well, let's just say it was a time I'd rather forget. It was lonely and dark and I made things up, exaggerated a lot. The thing that saved me – the only thing that helped curb my wild imaginings – was to take lavish doses of wintergreen herbal mint three times a day."

"So how did you know I'd find my way to your chamber?"

Zuma shrugged. "It's just a knack I have. I can predict the arrival of almost anybody."

"Like Bardo?"

"Huh! Bardo is easy. You just have to stick your nose out the window and you can smell him coming. What I don't understand is how I missed Bodessa. And this business about the Dark Wood troubles me, deeply." Zuma reached for the goblet. He looked as though he was about to crush it in his hand but then stopped, put it back on the table and stood. A moment passed and then he said, "How did you rescue my daughter?"

Although Addi remembered every detail, he wanted to spare Zuma the nasty bits. "I was with my friend Tarro. While he chased the Raslatombs away, I untied Bodessa."

Zuma frowned. "And how did your … friend manage to do that?"

"He changed up. To giant size. When he charged at them, the Raslatombs ran. But he caught an arrow in his shoulder."

"I'm sorry to hear that. What happened to him?"

"I don't know. We were supposed to meet at our hideaway but he never showed up."

Zuma's eyes narrowed. "And what about the Raslatomb queen, the one called Taluhla. Did she escape?"

"She just disappeared, one minute yelling orders, the next, gone, like she'd sunk into a hole in the ground."

Slowly, Zuma shook his head. He looked as though he wanted to say something important, a confession, maybe, to clarify some dark mystery, but he held back. For a moment he regarded his goblet of suli juice on the table, but then sat back down in his chair.

"So, Addi, tell me something. You're a Dwarfgiant. You can grow in size? How do you do that?"

Addi had expected the question. "Actually, I can't. At this time, the change-up is limited to only those born of Dwarfgiant leaders – members of the Circle. Myvan is the leader of the Dwarfgiants. Tarro's his son. Myvan adopted me when I lost my parents."

There was a pause. Zuma waited. Addi looked down at the juice in his goblet. Zuma broke first.

"You must know how members of your Circle change to giants?"

It was a question Addi couldn't fully answer. Even if he had known, he was still sworn to secrecy – and he'd said too much already. The carrahock plant was definitely the main ingredient. But there were other constituents that made up the secret power serum.

"Only those in the Circle know," Addi said as sincerely as he could.

Zuma's eyebrows rose, but he accepted Addi's answer without further probing.

"You're a discreet young Dwarfgiant," he said. "I like that."

Circle talk reminded Addi of home. "Tomorrow I must get back. I was expected two suns ago."

"Of course you must. Where is it you're from?"

"The Land of Bek. An old castle ruin at the edge of the Sulphur Sea."

Zuma's face darkened. "This castle ruin, does it have a moat leading to the sea?"

"How did you know that?"

Zuma stared grim-faced at the blood-red ring on his finger. Then he leaned close. "Addi, I don't want to frighten you, but whoever lives in the old ruin is in mortal danger. According to legend, tomorrow night when the two moons join, a giant sea serpent will attack those who inhabit the ruin."

Addi laughed nervously. What was this, Zuma having a mystical moment? Or could he actually make predictions based on legend? "I don't know about moons joining or giant serpents, but I do know I must leave at dawn."

Zuma picked up his goblet and circled the table. "If you mean to help your tribe, I'd say that's a good idea. In the meantime, we need to ready ourselves for the victory celebration. But before you go back to your chamber, I'd like to make a toast."

Walking towards Addi he raised his goblet.

There was no getting out of it now. And, as Addi raised his, his hand shook.

"To victories and reunions," said Zuma.

Their goblets touched, but in the pause before taking a sip, Addi gasped. On the wall over Zuma's shoulder, the spiked head of a beast stared back at him. It had no nose or mouth, only diamonds where its eyes had been. For the second time that day he was facing the haunting spectre of a gorax. Zuma turned to see what had caught Addi's eye; it was enough time for Addi to empty his drink into the earthenware pot next to his chair.

"The gorax is a fearsome creature," Zuma said, turning back to Addi.

"It's got a swivelling head – a mouth on one side, its eyes on the other, so it always knows what's going on behind its back. Unlike me, it never takes prisoners. This one was blinded by a mizot."

"I can see that," Addi said.

Zuma gave him a funny look and said, "Come on, drink up!"

Addi put the goblet to his mouth, tilted it and pretended to drink. "You were right," he said when he'd finished. "It is refreshing."

Zuma smiled, tipped his own goblet and took a long swig.

Addi watched closely for signs of distress. But after Zuma wiped his lips and put the goblet back on the table, all he did was burp.

Chapter 16

Through silver bands of moonlight Tarro and Sinjun followed Groff along the trail. As mystic dreams float, so did the way forward – like a river running on a spooky cloud. To the side of the trail, into the darkness of the wood, Tarro pointed his torch: dead trees cowering, fungus feeding on stumps, tendrils squirming, roots crawling to a scene of horror worse, he imagined, than when he and Addi had first found the female. The drone of an ugmul didn't help. The gutter-throated horn blurting through the trees meant the Raslatombs were near, and that Taluhla – calling to the moons – was about to wield her knife. If a poor soul was about to be sacrificed, it couldn't be Addi. It just couldn't.

"What was that?" Sinjun said.

"Shhh," said Tarro. "They'll hear us."

"Who will?"

"Hairy savages you don't want to meet."

Groff, who'd been leading the way, raised his right arm. "Up ahead!" he whispered over his shoulder. "To the left about thirty p-paces, there's s-something at the s-side of the trail."

Tarro and Sinjun joined Groff. Shoulder to shoulder they stood wondering what the "something" was. From that distance it wasn't easy to see – it was just a strange, solitary shape, draped in grey. It stood upright, but as far as Tarro could tell, it wasn't a Raslatomb. No horns.

Sinjun loaded his bamboozie.

Groff swung the skin bag from off his shoulders. He foraged noisily, searching for useful things. At last, he pulled out what looked like a magnifying device. "Spygoggles!" he said, triumphantly.

Tarro was impressed. "Let me try." He took the goggles from Groff and fastened them around his head. There were two small wheels, one to bring the "something" closer, the other to help focus. But the light was too dim, and whatever the "something" was supposed to be doing, it wasn't moving.

"Right," said Tarro. "We go forward together, slowly. Sinjun, make sure that bamboozie's ready."

The "something" stood twenty paces away, silent, dead calm, like a stone-faced sentry guarding the trail. Ten paces away it remained still. At his right shoulder, Tarro could hear Sinjun's breath – short, anxious – and his creaking bamboozie, ready to break.

They were getting close. Within five paces of the "something" the trail suddenly narrowed. Groff, who'd been on Tarro's left, dropped back a step. But his stun-dart peashooter was still pressed to his lips. Tarro raised his torch. The flame lit up a queer figure, almost square-shaped. Short, bulky, smaller than a Dwarfgiant, it stood as wide as it was high. It was clad in sacking and its head – top heavy and also square – was wrapped with a scarf around the lower half of its face up to two pin-eyes that stared blankly out front. Thick arms hung by its sides, but its right hand held a rock.

"Alright," Tarro whispered, "let's find out what we're dealing with. Groff, put your peashooter down and ask it something."

"Who, m-me?"

"Go on, Sinjun's got you covered."

Groff took a breath and stepped forward. "W-who are you?"

Silence.

Sinjun's bamboozie creaked.

More silence.

"N-no answer," said Groff, his eyes still fixed on the "something." "I can't even t-tell if it's breathing."

"Ask again. Ask if it needs anything. A drink, maybe."

"It's got a scarf around its f-face."

"Hmm. Well, in that case, tell it to blink its eyes. One blink for yes, two blinks for no."

Groff hesitated, spoke again. "We were w-wondering if you'd like a –"

A crunching sound stopped him. The hand of the "something" started to quiver. It was squeezing the rock. Crushing it to dust.

Tarro gaped.

"Heck of a trick, eh?"

The voice came from behind, out of the darkness, hard and gruff. As Tarro spun around, his heart crashed. At least ten of them, ten "somethings," stood in a half-circle. Stout and burly, they looked like the stone-faced sentry except none wore scarves. But each had a rock in its hand.

One stepped forward into the torchlight. Its face was full of lumps, its nose zigzagged. Below a red swelling on its forehead, pin eyes darted from one Dwarfgiant to the other.

"Who are you?" said Tarro, feigning a tough voice.

"Uh-uh, you first," said the "something".

Tarro shrugged. Outnumbered, he wasn't going to argue. "We're Dwarfgiants."

A faint smile crossed its lips. "Dwarfgiants? What's that supposed to mean?"

"Means we're betwixt and between."

The "something" banged its head with its fist. "What?"

"Neither here nor there."

Now its smile disappeared. "Are you trying to be funny? Better not be, or we'll throw rocks at you."

The other "somethings" squeezed theirs.

"No, no," replied Tarro. "It's just that ... well ... we're not always what we appear to be."

The "something" bared its teeth. "Oh, yeah, how's that?"

"Well, let's just say that some of us are creatures of change."

The "something" winced as though a needle had been pushed down its fingernail. "Creatures of change?" he screamed. "Look, I don't know what your game is, but we don't like change. We like things just the way they are."

"Don't worry, we don't want to change you, we just want to find our friend."

"You have a friend? Who's that?"

"His name's Addi," said Tarro. He pointed down the trail. "We have reason to believe he might be getting sacrificed."

"Don't think so," said the "something". "It's one of ours they've got."

"One of yours? One of what?"

"Loggerheads," he said, banging himself again on the head with his fist. "I'm Noggin."

"Well, Noggin, I sincerely hope we can be friends. I'm Tarro. These are my companions Groff and Sinjun. I hope they can be your friends too."

"Make him put the weapon down," said Noggin.

For a moment Tarro thought about it. If Sinjun were to lower his bamboozie, the Dwarfgiants would be completely at the mercy of the Loggerheads. But weren't they already? The bamboozie only had a single shot. There were ten of them. Besides, if he was sincere about making friends, there really wasn't much choice. Going on instinct, but mostly hope, he motioned for Sinjun to back down.

"That's better," Noggin went on. "Now, the sling. You hiding something in there?"

Tarro remembered his arm. It didn't hurt so much now, what with the fresh Jabunga leaf. "This? No, it's just a flesh wound. Got it last night when I attacked the Raslatombs with a tree branch. Took an arrow for my trouble."

Noggin squinted. His lips jittered as though they were working out the odds. When he spoke again he didn't declare his friendship but at least he didn't hit himself. "You attacked the Raslatombs with a tree branch?"

"You had to be there," said Tarro, getting impatient. In the short silence that followed he thought he could hear Raslatomb chants, not so far off. Whether the chants were real or imaginary, time was getting short. "So, Noggin, unless there's anything else, we really have to go."

Noggin's eyes looked ready to pop. Instead, he burst out laughing, his breathless guffaws rolling through the woods. Then he stopped, serious again. "You think I'm stupid? Let me tell you something: I'll let you know when you can go –"

A *whoosh*, a murderous, freewheeling *whoosh* swept past Noggin's head; an arrow, followed by another, then another – *bam! bam! bam!* – slammed into the trees behind him, heart-stopping in a flurry of black feathers.

"Raslatombs!" said Tarro.

"Quick!" said Noggin. "This way!"

Into the back wood, along a path of scratchy briars, the Dwarfgiants followed the Loggerheads. It wasn't easy to keep up, as the Loggerheads' short, powerful legs churned fast as whips. The sentry with the scarf, armed with a new rock, ran last. Raslatomb arrows chased after them, whooshing by, skimming heads, until the path curved in a great sweep, rising steeply to the top of a cliff.

As they scrambled up the rocky incline and out of range, Tarro stopped to catch his breath. With his good hand he adjusted his sling – made it more comfortable – then munched on carrahock grains from his pouch. He was thankful for the moment, and as he gulped in air, he realized his life had changed. Scrambling from things was now part of who he was. Not only was it essential for survival, but the more he did it, the better he got, and, if he was honest, the more exciting it became. He wasn't sure that that was a good thing. But as long as his luck held out, he'd be happy to scramble every chance he got – at least until he found Addi.

CHAPTER 17

Light-headed from the wild fragrances he'd inhaled during his visit with Zuma, Addi stumbled down the passageway leading back to his chamber. It didn't help that he had to retrace his steps through the aromatic veil of rose petals dealing with the guilt he felt in thinking the Mystic Zenta might have poisoned him. At least the underground journey was short, and he was happy to see the wooden ladder. Happier still, he climbed up it and squeezed through the open trap door at the top. He wasn't sure how much time he had before the guards would come to take him to the victory banquet. But it couldn't be long. Then he'd see Bodessa again. He must rinse his face. A bowl of water stood next to a wardrobe. The wardrobe, he'd been told, contained a change of clothes. Yet all he wanted to do was to lie down on the bed for a while.

He did neither. Three heavy thuds shook the door. Addi gathered himself. He swung the trap door closed, straightened the carpet and crossed to open the door. Two Zenta guards, shining in black and gold, stood to attention. They weren't heavily armed – jewelled daggers in sheaths – but each held what looked like a ceremonial staff.

"We're to escort you to the banquet," said the shorter one. "I'm Flogg. This is Milo."

"Actually," said Addi, "I'm not quite ready. Why don't you come in and sit down?"

The guards looked him over. "Can't do that," said Flogg. "One of us has to stand guard out here in the hallway."

"What about the other one?"

The silence was awkward. Then Milo began to rotate his shoulders – forwards then backwards – as if trying to release double knots in his shoulder blades. When he stopped he said, "I think I can answer for both Flogg and myself on that one. It just wouldn't be fair."

"What do you mean?"

"It's been a long day. We've been up since daybreak. Fishing. Getting the boats ready for war. Locking up prisoners. It wouldn't be fair for one of us to sit down and not the other."

"Oh, well, in that case," said Addi, "I'll leave you to it. I won't be long."

He closed the door and strode over to the bowl. He washed hard, hoping to rid himself of the lentilla musk that seemed to be stuck in his pores, the sweet scent that followed him everywhere. An array of shirts and pants and tunics hung in the wardrobe. He pulled out a cream, loose-fitting frock-shirt and black leggings. He took off his tattered tunic, folded what was left of it and placed it on a spare shelf. The new linen felt glorious: fresh and soft, fitted perfectly. Finally, he hooked his water and grain pouches to his belt and buckled up. Only his fur felt messy. A quick de-tufting with his hands would have to do.

Anxious to get going, he strode to the door and opened it. Out in the hallway the light was murky: smoky torches. He looked left and then right, but there was no one standing on guard. On the floor, though – with ceremonial staffs still in their hands – the two Zenta guards sat next to each other; Milo, his head resting on Flogg's shoulder; Flogg, his legs stretched across the hall. Both were snoring.

Addi looked past them and down the hallway – distant voices, faint strains of music. The victory banquet had started. He could always find his own way there, leave the guards to doze. After the day they'd had, it would be a shame to wake them. Besides, he couldn't wait to see Bodessa.

Quietly, he closed the door to his chamber. There was plenty of room around Milo, but as he stepped over Flogg's outstretched legs the guard rolled over unexpectedly and his right leg got caught between Addi's – just below the knees. His reflexes couldn't save him this time. He went down like a tree.

The guards awoke with a start.

"Going somewhere?" Milo said, irritably.

Addi disentangled himself from Flogg's legs. "I heard music," he said, trying to smile. "I didn't want to disturb you."

"That's the best you could do?" said Flogg, rubbing his knees.

"I was in a hurry. The victory celebration has begun. Zuma will be waiting."

"He's right," said Milo, scrambling to his feet. "All that food. Lots to drink. We'd better get a move on."

Flogg grunted. Still sitting, he held out both arms. "Give me a hand up."

They pulled Flogg to his feet.

The two guards stretched and dusted themselves off. Then, with Addi between them, they started down the hallway, the music and voices getting louder with each step.

"The last to arrive is always the guest of honour," said Flogg. "Is that what you are, Zuma's guest of honour?"

Addi was surprised by the question. Surprised Flogg didn't know.

"I think so," Addi replied.

"What did you do to earn that?" Milo asked.

"Saved his daughter from being sacrificed. Brought her back home."

"Bodessa?" Milo asked. "You rescued her? No wonder you're in Zuma's favour."

Addi shrugged. "Is she at the banquet?"

Milo smiled.

Flogg sighed. "Princess Bodessa, Jewel of the Zentas."

"Princess?" said Addi.

"Not officially," said Milo. "But she's a princess to us."

Me too, thought Addi.

CHAPTER 18

Tarro was surprised at how organized the Loggerheads were. All ten of them, including Noggin, had avoided the Raslatombs' arrows during the flight through the back woods. Now, at the top of the cliff, they'd found rocks and bushes to hide behind, a silent battery of rock-throwers looking down on the Raslatomb army as it passed below. Tarro wondered where Taluhla had found them all. When he'd helped rescue Bodessa, the Raslatombs had numbered maybe thirty. Now, just one night later, the unbroken line of rabble looked endless.

Tarro found a sunken cleft in the overhanging rock. Even with his wounded arm, he was able to wave Sinjun and Groff over to him. He put his finger to his lips as they hunkered down. They too impressed him, settling into small spaces with little fuss or bother – Sinjun, a calmer presence; Groff, his eyes alert. Survival in the Dark Wood meant learning lessons fast.

For a while they looked down at the torchlit procession: the grungy grey columns of goat-heads strung out along the misty path, armed with spears, daggers, bows and arrows, chanting gibberish, tramping in a daze as if guided by some hell-born force.

Tarro glanced at the sky. Deep black, filled with stars, the two moons almost touching.

"Where are the Raslatombs g-going?" said Groff. "The trail's c-crawling with them."

Tarro looked down. "I'm not sure, but they're going in the direction we were coming from. We'd have run into them head-on if we hadn't been stopped by the Loggerheads.

"L-look!" said Groff.

A new formation came into view. Horned lifters, two at each corner, carried the bed of wooden stakes. Tarro couldn't quite make out who it was, but someone was tied to it. He felt sick. Was it Addi? Did they get him? He was about to find out if he'd ever see his friend again, or whether they'd be returning to the castle ruin with the Circle candidates down to two.

"Groff, pass me your spygoggles."

Groff gave them to him. Tarro fumbled with the fastener at the back "Damn!" he said. "How are these supposed to –?"

"You don't need them," Noggin said, clambering over the rock face, his voice filled with anger.

Tarro put the spygoggles down.

"It's Headlock," Noggin went on. "They have him. Best snoop we had. Always stuck his nose in. Could track a scent from sunup to sundown. Sometimes, though, he'd go too far – too far for his own good."

Tarro thought of Addi. If he was still alive, he hoped his friend hadn't gone too far.

Noggin stamped his foot. "I know one thing. We'll crush the vermin. Crush them all."

The bed of wooden stakes passed by. On it, poor Headlock lay spread-eagled, still as a silent scream.

Noggin, gripping a rock, cocked his arm.

"What are you doing?" Tarro said.

"Letting them have it."

"It's not a good idea."

Noggin turned, aimed the rock at Tarro. "I told you, I do the telling."

"Not any more, you don't," said Sinjun, his bamboozie pulled way back. "Drop it, or I'll split your skull."

Noggin looked befuddled.

Tarro, buoyed by Sinjun's ultimatum, rode the advantage. "He's right, Noggin, the bamboozie stone travels faster than you can blink an eye. And Sinjun never misses."

Noggin stood frozen, not speaking, not daring to blink.

"Look," said Tarro, "we feel for you. We really do. But there's a whole army down there. We wouldn't stand a chance."

Noggin lowered his arm. "You said you clobbered them with a tree branch."

"I did. But there wasn't as many. And look at me now. My arm's in a sling. Together, we can do better."

"How's that?"

"It's the queen we want. Taluhla. She's the one behind all this. If we can –"

A blurt of ugmuls drowned out Tarro's voice. He grabbed the spygoggles. "This might be her now," he said, shouting. Dwarfgiants and Loggerheads peered down.

A row of four two-horned ugmul blowers, their hands full of pipes and tubes, blew at will, their cheeks filling up as they sounded the call of the queen – a braying pandemonium for the she-creature, Taluhla.

Out of the shadows, the Queen of the Raslatombs drifted into the moons' blaze.

"That's her, all right," Tarro said. "She's got tusks."

As though without feet, she seemed to float along the misty path: tall, wretched, her face painted on – on bones without flesh.

"Tell me when," said Sinjun, drawing his bamboozie. "I'll pop her from here."

"No!" Tarro said, raising his hand. "I know it's tempting, but even if you made a perfect strike, there's still too many of them. They'd hunt us down and fry us for breakfast. No, what we need to do is –"

He gasped. What he saw couldn't be happening. The Loggerheads had rolled a massive boulder to the brink of the cliff. Caught in a moment of madness – a moment born of a need to get even – they'd lined up behind it, nine abreast, giddy for revenge. "This is for Headlock!" cried one. And as he put his shoulder to the boulder, the others followed, digging in, knees bent, shoving the rock over the edge.

As if in slow motion the boulder fell, a dead weight taking deadly aim. Only at the bottom of the cliff, where the rock bounced off an outcropping, did the Raslatombs turn to look, and the ones standing in its path took their last breath. Those who could, ran, but the ugmul blowers never heard it coming; four of them were silenced in mid-drone. Some guards were also flattened – legs and arms stuck out. But what of Taluhla, where were her arms and legs?

Tarro focused the spygoggles. Yes! There she was, her black arms flapping like an oily fish, slithering up the trunk of a tree. She turned clinging to the first branch, screeching at her archers: "Fire!"

Waves of arrows soared up the cliff face and over the top. Two Loggerheads went down, struck clean through their chests.

"We're in big trouble now," said Tarro.

Chapter 19

Gay music and the light from a thousand candles greeted Addi as he entered the banquet hall. Smoothing his mane with his hands, he followed Milo and Flogg through the crowd – a merry mix of Zenta guards and nobility. The air, too, was lively: a thin cloud of musk – courtesy of Zuma, no doubt – to mark the sweet smell of victory.

While some guests stood in groups, others sat at long tables. The tables, configured in a "U" shape, were laden with mouth-watering food. Platters of roast roggle, grilled gumplefish – with the barb removed – were delicacies Addi recognized. Along with baskets of freshly baked bouella bread, bowls of soup were brought in on trays – the green mint flavour of polnop, he guessed.

"Make way!" Milo said, using his ceremonial staff to nudge aside a group of revellers. As he passed, Addi noticed the looks of surprise from both males and females. What were they staring at? What he found surprising was that while Zenta males had no hair at all, Zenta females had yellow hair. But Bodessa's hair was black. Addi looked for her, but Zentas were tall; he couldn't see over the standing throng. Not until Milo and Flogg stopped near a balcony, where eight musicians played a sprightly tune, did Zuma's table come into view.

Addi saw Zuma first. At least, that was who he thought it was. No jewelled crown, no blue gown spattered with stars and crescent moons, this version of the Mystic Zenta looked more like a conquering warlord. Studded leather tunic, broadsword, metal-capped club, at least five knives slung into cross-straps. If Addi hadn't known Zuma better, he might have thought of him as someone with the tendencies of a tyrant. As it was, he guessed the flagrant display of weaponry was probably more for show. Still, if there was a demonstration of knife-throwing, Addi hoped he wouldn't be asked to volunteer as a target.

Zuma had been standing, talking to his son, Andros, but now, as the music softened, he sat down – not on his customary turquoise throne, but on a black, hawk-winged chair, raised on a stepped dais, spangled with moonstone and pearl.

"You ready?" Flogg said to Addi. "I'll let Zuma know you're here."

Chin up, staff in hand, Flogg set off. Zuma, who'd been absorbed by the glowing red ring on his finger, looked up at the approaching guard. Flogg bowed and began to speak. As he did so, Zuma glanced over at Addi and nodded. Flogg bowed again, but as he turned, Zuma held him back. This time Zuma did the talking. When Flogg returned, his head was bowed, his face long.

"What's the matter?" said Milo. "You look sick as a Krogul's parrot. What did he say?"

Flogg shook his head, glumly. Then he turned to Addi. "Go on. Zuma's expecting you. Yours is the seat to his right."

"Is there something wrong?" said Addi.

"Oh, just something Zuma has in mind for Milo and me."

"Like what?"

"Never mind. Go on!"

Addi started walking, but before he reached Zuma, he saw her across the room – Bodessa, coming towards him. He knew it was her because she had black hair. It was swept up at the top. A small tiara twinkled at the front. But she looked different. She still moved easily but seemed more certain of herself, startling in a rose-petal dress that made her body look fuller, like a flower in bloom. As she got closer he could see that her face was warmer, her pale skin blushed soft pink. Her eyes, though, were deeper than ever, and when they smiled, he just couldn't stop looking.

"Addi," she said, brightly. "You changed."

He looked at his shirt, down at his leggings, then back into her eyes – eyes that were still smiling, as were her lips, which were redder than he remembered. The moment was so blissful he felt as if he were in a dream: a magical place that would always be. He would make sure of it.

"You look beautiful," he said. And yet, as soon as the words came out, the look on Bodessa's face changed. Her smile dissolved – her look of certainty. What had happened? Whatever it was, the spell had been broken.

Addi looked over his shoulder. But no one was there. Not even Milo or Flogg. He turned back to Bodessa, who was looking down around her feet as though the floor was about to open up. Then Addi felt it, a low rumble, undercutting the din of celebration, quieting every voice in the room. Except Zuma's.

"You two!" he called from his throne. "Come. Sit."

Bodessa's face flashed with wonder. Then she took her place to Zuma's left, Addi to his right.

All eyes were fixed on the entrance, where drums thundered and the blare of trumpets brought a troupe of dancers tumbling into the hall, gyrating with tassels, their sinewy limbs interlocking, forming a rolling carousel. A fleshy female, her skin the colour of amber, cracked a whip, drove the carousel towards a rack of fiery torches. Plucked one by one, the torch flames swirled and streaked; the drums beat on, louder and faster; the girl with the amber skin shook her thighs, rippled like jelly, coaxing the carousel over and over, then slowing down, commanding it to stop, unravelling the dancers from its circle of fire. Round and round they ran, around the floor, free as birds, chasing each other, torchlit, trailing smoke, dizzy, until the whip snapped, the drums stopped and the dancers stood gasping for breath.

Addi held his. He glanced over at Bodessa. She sat rooted to her chair, her lips parted, her chest still. Again the whip cracked and the dancers flung their torches high in the air, watching them spin, then come down; catching the flames in their mouths. The crowd was stunned. Then they cheered. The applause stopped only after the dancers had saluted and left the hall.

The room was abuzz, but became hushed when Zuma rose from his chair and banged his metal-capped club on the table. "Nobles, escorts and guards," he said in a commanding voice. "Tonight we celebrate yet another victory against our irritating neighbours from the Lake of Fools."

This brought more applause.

"Once again, our archers, led by Andros and the captains of the fleet, have won the day."

Andros, who was sitting on the other side of Bodessa, stood to acknowledge the cheers.

Zuma beamed. "I believe," he went on, cheerfully, "this is the fifth attempt by the Kroguls to take Castle Zen. Each time they have failed. This time they failed miserably."

As the cheering continued, Zuma took a sip from his goblet.

"I have told Bardo that, starting tomorrow he and his Kroguls will be digging the foundations for their new home."

A murmur arose from the guests.

"It will be the darkest dungeon ever built."

There was a mixture of gasps and applause. Zuma cleared his throat and continued in a warmer tone. "Now, there's another reason to celebrate tonight." He turned, looked down at Bodessa. "The safe return of my daughter."

This brought the loudest cheers of the night.

"She was rescued by Addi, here, my guest of honour, and rescued before … well, before it was too late. So you see there is much cause to rejoice."

Zuma swigged again from his goblet, then turned to his musicians and waved for them to play. Immediately, the band struck up and, once more, the room was filled with joyful music.

From the kitchens, swarms of servants descended on the tables bringing drinks and more delicious things to eat. As hungry as Addi was, he was more hungry to talk to Bodessa, to let her know of his plans for returning home at the first light of dawn. He could see that she was talking to her brother, Andros, so he decided to start his meal. He was about to try a piece of jenjer cake topped with cream when a servant offered him a drink.

"What is it?" he asked.

"Suli fruit," the servant replied.

Addi sensed Zuma was watching. Not another test! He nodded to the servant, who filled his cup. The suliberry had a curious taste, more like medicine, thick and bitter. He drank it down anyway, trying not to grimace, happy to have survived the real thing.

"It's an acquired taste," said Zuma. "But you know that already."

As their eyes met, all Addi could do was smile.

CHAPTER 20

On Castle Zen's chill south tower Milo straddled the turret wall, his teeth chattering, his backside cold. Next to him, Flogg stared out at the lake. There was nothing to see except a creeping blanket of mist that made lake-watching a futile task.

Across the battlements, the muted sounds of music and laughter could be heard from the banquet hall. Milo jumped down off the wall. "Just our flaming luck," he said. "While they're in there feasting on roast roggle, we're out here freezing our bums. Why didn't you ask Zuma if someone else could stand guard out here?"

Flogg stared out at the lake.

"Did you hear me?"

Still no answer.

Milo shook his head, blew into his hands. Of all nights, guard duty. He was about to feel really sorry for himself when, suddenly, his vision blackened. For some moments he couldn't see. When it cleared he felt anxious, a dire feeling that time was running out – as if his chance to be somebody, to have some greater standing in life, had passed him by. By his own estimation he was now twenty-four summers old – six of them lived as a dedicated Zenta guard. But he'd received only modest recognition. Together, he and Flogg did a variety of jobs. But even Flogg had higher ranking, was the one giving orders.

Their most enjoyable job was to keep an eye on Bodessa – Princess

Bodessa he liked to call her. Nothing too involved. Mainly providing an escort to and from her daily activities, which included tending her garden, practising her reed instrument and playing with the servants' youngens. But even she had slipped out from under his and Flogg's surveillance. She too was breaking away, looking to find her way in life. She'd only been gone for one sun, but now they were being punished for letting her "escape" the castle.

Flogg interrupted his thoughts, a low, pondering voice from the parapet. "You know, Milo, I could've sworn I saw something out there."

Milo looked out at the lake. "Oh, it's misty all right, I'll give you that."

Flogg turned sharply – as if he didn't appreciate the sarcasm. Then he shrugged. "Maybe it was just my imagination. What were you saying?"

"I said we got the short end of the stick – again. They're in there, and we're out here."

"It's our duty."

"If you ask me, our duty's had its fill for one day. Now I need mine."

Flogg was back to peering down at the lake.

"I mean, what more do they want from us?" Milo's breath clouded the air in front of him. "Up before dawn, trolling for gumplefish. Then rigging the war boats, incarcerating Kroguls. What a disgusting lot they are. Stinking filth. And wacko. Slit your throat sooner than give you a smile. Just as well we gave them a drubbing. I've heard stories about how they treat their captives, what they'd do if they ever defeated us. Believe me, it'd be more than tickling feet." He turned to Flogg, who was now leaning over the edge of the parapet. "Don't go falling off that wall."

Flogg shuffled.

Milo went on. "You remember the Krogul with the patch over his eye, the one who ponged. What a stench. I mean, you said it yourself, if ever someone needed cleaning up, it was him. Well, he told me that the Kroguls' favourite torture is to break both shins with a hammer. After that you get a head start before their archers hunt you down. If you ask me, Zuma should keep them all locked up forever."

"They're going to be," said Flogg, turning from the brink. "That's what Zuma told me. Starting tomorrow, a massive dungeon is to be built."

"Oh, no, don't say that!"

"Don't worry. By doing watch tonight, we don't have to lift a shovel."

"Well, that's something," said Milo. "Still, I'd sure like to be at that banquet. All that food and drink, all those lovely females."

"We'll be finished soon. There'll be leftovers."

"Leftovers? That's nice."

Chapter 21

While the hall was loud with joyful voices, Addi was getting frustrated. Why was Bodessa sitting talking to her brother and not to him? He could see her over Zuma's shoulder, turned away, her dress fitting tight down her back; the back he'd recently rescued. Zuma wasn't helping. He'd pulled out one of his knives, using it to punctuate a point as he jabbered on about the glories of old campaigns, favourite battles, most of which he'd commanded from a distance.

"It was life and death," he was saying. "If I hadn't sounded the charge –"

"I'm going to need a boat," Addi interrupted, "to cross Lake Zen in the morning."

Zuma looked startled, then nodded slowly, slipped the knife back in its sheath. "Yes, of course you are. We keep a handful of small vessels moored in a cove below the southern bluffs. I'll arrange an escort for you, first thing."

"Thank you," Addi said, glancing again at Bodessa. "It seems there's not much more I can do here. I need to get back."

Zuma gripped his hand. "I want to thank you again for saving my daughter. She's a spirited one, full of surprises."

"You're right there. She seems to be on a mission, like she's searching for something."

"From now on, I intend to keep a closer eye on her," said Zuma. Then, as if on cue, he turned to speak to her. "Bodessa, you'll have all the time in the world to talk with your brother. But right now, you're neglecting our guest of honour. Addi's leaving at sunrise."

As she turned, the blush on her face deepened. "So soon?"

Addi nodded. "There's going to be trouble at home. The old ruin is in danger. A collision of moons, a giant serpent from the sea."

Bodessa's eyes widened. "How do you know that?"

He glanced at Zuma. "Let's just say it comes from someone whose predictions shouldn't be ignored."

"So you see," Zuma said, jumping in, "you must make the most of the time you've got left together." He turned and signalled to his musicians. They began to play a jaunty tune. Guests and their escorts took to the floor. "Bodessa," he said, "why don't you show Addi our dance of celebration?"

Addi looked at her, uncertain, waiting for her excuse. He was about to save her the trouble when, without a word, she took his hand and led him to join the dance. The touch of her fingers thrilled him. Breathing fast, he followed her as if clinging to the scent of a flower. In the candlelit hall where perfume, colour and music merged, flames quickened. And as they stepped into pools of candlelight, his heart sang.

Caught up in the reel of the jig, he soon learned the steps. And with each merry note, he and Bodessa became one, lost in a whirl of dancers.

Before he knew it, the music had stopped. Bodessa, her chest rising and falling, urgent for breath, held out her hand. "Tradition," she said, "requires you to kiss it."

Was she serious? Her coaxing eyes told him she was. He could do that. In one move he took her hand, pressed his lips to the bony part of her knuckles. He would have kept them there, too, if the main doors hadn't burst open.

Addi turned. Krogul archers swarmed in, faces painted – black war stripes – screeching like maniacs. Still holding Bodessa's hand, he started back towards Zuma. By the time they'd reached the table, the Kroguls were pointing arrows at every guest. Guards, musicians and servants stood frozen; nobles and their escorts were afraid to move. Addi took a chance, pulled Bodessa under the table between Zuma and Andros. From where they crouched, he could see through a gap in the table covering, hear the plod of uneven footsteps.

Bardo!

As the Krogul leader hobbled in, the dancers on the floor backed away. With the arrow no longer in his thigh, Bardo looked different. He was cleaned up. A fresh purple tunic and leggings covered the manacle marks around his ankles and wrists and the wound in his leg. Not as successful was his nose. It was still bent, red and mushy. Still, as he approached Zuma, he attempted a smile. It didn't get far. Probably hurt too much. Instead, he said in a smug voice, "Hello, Zuma. You look surprised."

Addi couldn't see Zuma but could hear him. "Bardo, how did you get here?"

With a sneer, the Krogul unsheathed his dagger and limped towards the table. Bodessa squeezed Addi's hand. Above him he could hear the knife scraping a plate. Then Bardo came back into view, a slice of cream cake stuck on the end of the blade.

"While you were scoffing roggle and jenja," Bardo said, "my second wave of war boats arrived. Your so-called elite Zenta Guard put up little resistance." He bit into the dessert. "A piece of cake, really."

"What have you done with them?" said Zuma.

"Don't fret," Bardo said, licking a blob of cream off his chin. "They're safe, locked up in your festering dungeons. The question is … what am I going to do here? I could destroy every last one of you. Might be fun. First, break some fingers, pull a few teeth, the odd torch burn. Screams, they'd echo all the way to the Lake of Fools. Except that we, the Kroguls, wouldn't be the fools any more. You would. Until, of course the last axe fell, and the only memory of the great Zuma would be of a vain, pompous, blowhard, his shiny bald head sitting on a platter."

Bardo's words hung heavy in the scented air. There were over three hundred bodies in the room, but there wasn't a sound. He milked the moment.

"Then again, if you became extinct, who would we invade next year? Now we have our first victory, I've got a feeling there'll be lots more. I don't even think we need to practise that much. So, what do we do?"

Bardo looked around, turned the knife over in his hands. As if in a game of take your pick he decided on a noble's escort standing nearby. He walked up to her, put his hand around her neck and pulled her close to his face. The noble, pulling a knife, stepped in, but was halted by a whistling arrow that missed his head by a breath. Bardo waved his dagger. "Be warned, Zenta. At times like this, gallantry and stupidity, are much the same thing." He turned to the noble's escort and cut off her jewelled neckband. Holding it aloft, he turned to Zuma. "Now this, this is worth keeping. Makes me feel good, makes me think I might show some leniency. Let you all off with a warning. It'll come at a price, mind you. But what's a victory without the spoils?"

"What is it you want?" demanded Zuma.

"What I want is what I'm going to take. Your treasure. Riches beyond belief."

"Take it."

"My, my, aren't we generous? But there is one more thing."

"What's that?"

"Bodessa," said Bardo, his voice dripping with desire.

It was Addi's turn to squeeze Bodessa's hand. But he'd need to do more than that. Trouble was, he couldn't think of anything.

Zuma spoke sternly. "Bardo, we've talked about this before. My daughter is not involved. She's not bound by any of this. In any case, she's not here."

"Oh yes, she is, I've seen her with that furry creature."

Addi felt a kick in the back. He turned. It was Andros's foot. Then his hand appeared, his fingers twitching, making signs, a language that Bodessa watched intently. She whispered the translation. "When I distract them, crawl out behind me … back passage … tunnel to the cove. Take a boat. Don't stop."

"That's news to me, Bardo," said Zuma. "I always make arrangements to protect my daughter when – "

"Bodessa, run!" said Andros, his voice booming across the hall. "Hurry!"

The distraction. And while heads turned and Krogul archers swung their bows towards the main doors, Addi and Bodessa crawled out from under the table and headed towards the darkened archway at the back.

"Keep her safe," Zuma said, as they slipped past his chair.

Crawling fast, Addi followed Bodessa, keeping low to the floor. A Zenta guard stood blocking the archway. As they approached, he moved aside so they could pass. In the darkened entrance they turned to look back.

Andros was still playing decoy, calling out in the direction of the main doors. "Don't stop, Bodessa. Keep going!"

But Bardo looked suspicious, realized he was being duped. He turned and pointed to Andros. "Take him!"

"Come on, Bodessa," Addi whispered. "We must go."

Down the gloomy passage she ran past him – fast, long strides. Addi followed, thought about snatching a torch from off the wall but decided against it. If they had any chance of reaching the cove undetected, they'd have to find their way in the dark.

They reached an offshoot of passages, left and right. She went left, then down a flight of steps through a cool, dank cellar, stopping in front of a door set flush in the wall. At first glance, the door, heavy with age, looked sealed. But then he saw it, a small keyhole. Bodessa gave him a knowing look and turned her back. She seemed to pull something out from the top of her dress. Turning back to him she held a key.

"Shortcut through my father's treasure vault," she said, pushing the key in the hole.

But it didn't turn. She fiddled, but it seemed stuck. Now there were voices above them, at the top of the steps.

"Here," said Addi, "let me try."

It wouldn't move for him either. He turned harder. But the key started to bend.

The voices were louder now: Kroguls, descending the steps.

"Hurry!" said Bodessa.

Forcing the key in the opposite direction, he straightened it somewhat, then jiggled it some more. He began to sweat.

"We have to go!" Bodessa said. "Take the long way."

The Kroguls had reached the bottom of the steps, their voices wild and urgent. Addi pulled out the key. He was about to give it back to Bodessa when a thought occurred to him, something instinctive, like the obvious thing to do. He shoved the key back in again, this time angled downwards, and turned. The door popped open. They hurried in and locked the door behind them. They could hear the Kroguls outside, shouting and arguing. But then, quiet. The smelly ragtags must have moved on.

Like her father gliding through his perfumed chamber, Bodessa flitted through the treasure vault. Addi straggled behind, spellbound amidst the torchlit chests and cases of jewels – the sparkle of silver, the glitter of gold. He'd seen some of the gems before; the smaller cache of treasure the Dwarfgiants had brought with them from Kamistra he knew by name: the purple amethyst; yellow topaz; the shiny green emerald. He also liked the milky opal and the moonstone's pearly whiteness. He remembered Bodessa's pendant and chain, two stones set like connecting moons. It had been her mother's, but she hadn't said any more.

Near the far end of the vault, Bodessa waved for him to hurry. But he was looking at crowns. He recognized the one Zuma had worn when they'd met – a silver crown inlaid with sapphire moons and stars of pearl. But the one that looked the most magical sat highest on the table: a gold crown set with a double row of rubies, peaked with diamond clusters.

Loud thuds startled him. The Kroguls were back, hammering at the door. He ran to Bodessa, who was busy pulling out the turquoise eye of a snake. A low rumble set the floor moving. A hole opened up and stone stairs appeared.

Addi shook.

Bodessa started down.

He hesitated. A pink gemstone – a rare sapphire, he thought – lay in an open box, exquisite, tantalizing. He couldn't bear to think that a Krogul might pilfer it, that it could be lost to a dirty pair of hands. So he took it, felt its rare smoothness between his fingers, slipped it into his pouch.

At the bottom of the stairs, Bodessa stood next to a marble cat that was as tall as she was. When Addi joined her, she pulled the cat's emerald collar. The floor above them closed.

It was pitchblack in the tunnel. Now he wished he'd taken a torch. He couldn't see Bodessa but could hear her in front of him, her quickening breath, her soft feet pattering. Except for the draft she made as she ran, it was hard to guess how close she was, until he clipped her heel with his foot.

"Ahh!" she gasped, stumbling to the floor.

He cursed himself, then reached down hoping to find her hands, wanting to help her up. Instead he found other parts – the soft line of her leg; the lay of her dress, a bulge or two, smooth and firm. It lasted only a moment, aim misplaced in the dark. Then he found her hand.

"Are you all right?" he said.

She didn't say anything.

Now holding both hands he helped her up.

"Why don't you go first," she said, breathlessly. "It's not far now."

The tunnel curved and sloped, until there, in the distance, a light, soft and silvered.

They stood beneath it, looking up – a cross-barred cover with the moons shining through. Bodessa looked around. "There was always a step to stand on," she said, "to push the cover off."

"Here," Addi said, cupping his hands. "I'll lift you." She placed her foot in his hands and put her arm around his neck. "One, two, three!"

She was easy to lift. Only a slight wobble as her dress brushed his face.

She pushed the cover off and wriggled through the opening. Before he could think about being stranded, a rope tumbled down. He tugged on it to test his weight. Then he pulled himself up, squeezed himself out. For a moment he lay on the ground breathing hard. Bodessa rewound the rope and hid it behind a rock. Then she put the barred cover back on.

Addi got to his feet and looked around. A chill breeze from the lake made him shiver. They were on a shadowy hillside, at one moment lit up by the moons, at another cast in darkness from dense patches of mist. There were some cries and shouts in the distance, the odd scream on the other side of the hill.

He started down the steps leading to the cove.

"Wait!" said Bodessa, pointing to a parallel pathway lined with bushes and shrubs. "The trail's safer."

Chapter 22

Under the fierce light of the moons, Tarro, Sinjun and Groff scrambled for their lives. With Raslatomb arrows zipping past them, they ran with the eight Loggerheads along the cliff top to a tarn whose waters shimmered like silver glass.

They seemed to be at a dead end until Noggin pointed to a way around, a scrubby halftrail leading to a low ridge of rocks on the far side. Not until they'd circumvented the tarn and reached the rocks did they stop to look back. Across the water they could see Raslatomb torches chasing along the cliff top. Tarro guessed that by the time he'd recovered his breath, the arrows would start flying again.

"Where to now?" he asked Noggin.

For the first time, Tarro thought he saw Noggin smile. Not much – it was more a square-lipped smirk.

"Headstrong!" he yelled out. "Open it up!"

The Loggerhead with the scarf over his face jogged over to the base of the ridge. He started to climb the rock face, finding a crevice or two to secure a foothold. A quarter of the way up he reached for the branch of a tree sticking out from a ledge. He grabbed the branch with one hand, removed his scarf with his other. For a moment he looked down. His face was regrettable. He was a Loggerhead, all right – poky pin eyes and a big square head – but he was toothless, had no lips, and his nose was flattened on his face. And yet, whatever had happened to him hadn't affected his agility. He lobbed one end of the scarf over the branch then knotted the two loose ends.

Tarro wasn't sure what the Loggerhead was up to, but, in a weird way, the one they called Headstrong inspired him, made him think about taking off his sling. The Jabunga leaf had eased the pain in his shoulder. Whether he could pull a bamboozie or change up to giant size, he wasn't sure. But he had to take a chance, had to be ready. He unfastened the sling and lowered his arm. There was some soreness but it didn't compare to the freedom he felt.

A hollow thump made him look up.

"That's it!" cried Noggin.

Headstrong was holding onto his scarf, his legs dangling. The other Loggerheads rushed forward. An opening had appeared in the lower rock face, narrow, inviting.

"Let's go!" said Noggin.

"Where does it lead?" said Tarro.

Fire-arrows seared the water behind them. The Raslatombs were almost in range.

"Come quick, or you're dead," Noggin bellowed.

Tarro knew they had no choice. He nodded to Sinjun and Groff and they followed the Loggerheads in through the thin dark gap. They entered a cave – a high, empty place with seep holes that dripped water and let beams of moonlight through. Last in was Headstrong, his face again scarf-covered. He set to work handling the ropes and pulleys that put the tall rock back in place, rolling it on wooden logs, sealing the gap behind them. These Loggerheads were fixated on rocks, knew how to handle them. They were also quick to light torches. Friction sticks, muscled in no time, flared to brighten the gloom. The cavern, now lit up, revealed two passages, one to the left, the other leaning right.

"We'll split up," said Noggin, tossing a rock in his hand. The other Loggerheads began to toss rocks in theirs. "I'll take three of ours and er … what's your name again?"

"Tarro."

"Right. Headstrong, you take the other three of ours, and the other two of theirs – "

"Sinjun," said Sinjun.

"G-Groff," said Groff.

"Right," said Noggin. "Right."

"Wait!" said Tarro. "Why are we splitting up?" He was concerned that without Sinjun or Groff he would have to use a Loggerhead to help him change up. No guarantee there.

"The passages have pitfalls. If we separate, there's a better chance one group will make it through to the end."

"Pitfalls?"

"You ask too many questions," said Noggin. "Stay close. Keep your ears open and your mouth shut."

Noggin and Headstrong lined up their groups.

Slowly, Headstrong's group with Sinjun and Groff set off down the left passage. "Stay alert," Tarro called after them. "See you on the other side."

More briskly, Tarro followed Noggin down the passage to the right.

It was sopping along the way, a smell of mould. Drips of water splashed his face. In the torch light, the lime walls glistened. The heat from the flames helped, but Tarro wondered how soon they would have to face what Noggin had called a pitfall. Maybe it would be a tunnel too small to get through, or some growling creature with hunger pangs. Whatever, he needed to be ready, to attempt a change-up if need be. To give himself a boost, he scooped a handful of carrahock grains, mixed with galinsa roots from his pouch, munched quietly.

Soon the passage opened up into a larger space leading to a stretch of caves full of stalactites and stalagmites and puddles. Above them, still and ominous, clusters of black-winged creatures hung upside down.

"Keep your flames low," said Noggin.

Tarro remembered the blood-sucking bats he'd seen in the crater caves of Kamistra before the Mighty Mountain of Mol blew up, the explosion that had sent the Dwarfgiants fleeing across the Sulphur Sea. Had it been only a season ago? And yet this adventure had seemed even longer – a sun and two moons without sleep. Thinking about it brought a yawn. Soon he'd need to put his head down, close his eyes. Until then, he needed to keep alert, hope that in the other passageway Sinjun and Groff were doing the same.

* * *

Walking single file through a labyrinth of wet caves, Sinjun was weighing the odds – whether he could dispose of the four Loggerheads without bringing harm to himself. But he was fourth of six, and boxed in. Headstrong led, then another Loggerhead, then Groff – his bag of useful things bouncing on his back, his peashooter sticking out the top. That wouldn't help. Not at close quarters.

Sinjun glanced back. The two Loggerheads behind him were breathing down his neck. Maybe a sharp elbow, a hand chop or a jab with his foot would take care of them. But the two in front could be trouble. The best he could hope for would be if Groff got in the way, a lucky stumble.

Yet nothing could be predicted. Best to wait, or, being ankle deep in water, see which way the tide turned. Sploshing along, pondering possibilities, he wasn't ready for Groff's sudden stop. He bumped into his rival's bag, the end of the peashooter grazing his eye. What was going on? In front, Headstrong held up his hand, pointed ahead.

Shoving Groff's bag aside, Sinjun strained to see. The unbroken string of caves had closed in to form a single chamber. At the far end, the only way forward narrowed towards a dark hole in the wall. In the torchlight, there seemed no reason for the hole to be so black. But when the Loggerheads broke into a huddle, it was clear that what lay ahead was a pitfall.

Headstrong, muffled without lips, said. "We have to wait. Be quiet."

"W-what's wrong?" whispered Groff, unhitching his bag. As he did so, his elbow dug into Sinjun's chest.

"Ow!"

"Shhh!" said Headstrong.

"S-sorry," whispered Groff.

Clumsy fool.

"It's a great gorm," Headstrong replied. "Blocking the way."

Sinjun wasn't sure he'd heard him right. "A what?"

"Shhh! Great gorm. Big, furry creature. Sleeps in openings. Can't disturb."

Sinjun whispered, "Will it wake up?"

"Depends on when it fell asleep."

"So, what do we do? Turn back. Catch up with the others?"

Headstrong shrugged.

"I h-have an idea," said Groff, digging into his bag. He pulled out what looked like a projectile, inserted it into the end of his peashooter. "It's a s-stunner. It will knock it out."

This was getting ridiculous. Groff and that bag of his had an answer for everything. "Yeah, but for how long?"

Before Groff could answer, the Loggerheads motioned for him to shoot. Sinjun raised his torch and he and Groff went forward. The great gorm was sitting on the other side of the hole; the opening was filled with its lower back – a mass of black fur – its tail sticking through. Sinjun nudged Groff. Groff sucked in a breath, put the peashooter between his lips, and blew. The dart point sank just above its tailbone. The creature grunted and slumped forward, leaving a slight opening, upper right! Sinjun had a mind to do a runner, get through the tight space before the Loggerheads. Who knew, he might find Addi or, better yet, be the only candidate left. Still, the threat of going down in a hail of Loggerhead rocks made him pause, long enough for them to catch up.

"So, who goes first?" Sinjun said to Headstrong.

"Not us," replied the Loggerhead. "Opening's too small."

Sinjun almost laughed. You mean you're all too square and chunky. Maybe he could do a runner after all.

"Not you, either," Headstrong said to Sinjun. "Your shoulders are too wide."

Maybe, maybe not. But his muscles rippled everywhere. Flexing his biceps was as natural as breathing.

Headstrong pointed to Groff. "You! You're thin as a stick. You go. When you get through, see how the creature's sitting. See if it can be moved."

Groff stepped towards the great gorm. He looked nervous. With his hand shaking, he pulled out the projectile and dropped it in his bag. Then he crawled up the creature's back. Or tried to. He couldn't get a good hold and he kept slipping. Sinjun cringed: The weakling's getting nowhere. It should have been me.

"Grip its fur!" said Headstrong.

Mercifully the creature didn't move and the Loggerhead's suggestion worked. With more confidence Groff reached the gap. But as he put his head through, his bag snagged on a jutting rock.

Here we go again. At this rate the creature would be waking up. He'd better go help. But before he could, Groff tugged at the bag and snapped it free. The sharp sideways motion jolted the great gorm. It began to stir. Then it grunted.

"It's waking up!" Sinjun called out.

Groff froze. But the creature swayed. Groff lost his grip and fell through the hole, out of sight. Then his head bobbed up.

Sinjun waved. "Come back!"

Groff could have, too, could have crawled back. But he didn't. Instead, the creature – now growling – shifted to the right, closed the hole, trapped Groff on the other side.

"What was he thinking?" said Sinjun.

Headstrong shook his head. "Let's hope the creature's not hungry."

Sinjun saw the great gorm's tail wag. Creatures were happiest when their tails wagged – when they were eating. An image flashed in his head – Groff being eaten – teeth gnawing up one arm, chewing down the other; the squirt of blood, the crack of bone, gristle spat out. Not a fun way to end up, even if it did reduce the Circle candidates to two.

Still, Groff had only himself to blame. His stunner hadn't stunned; not really. Even then, he'd had his chance, his moment to escape. Sinjun listened to the muffled cries from the other side, watched the creature wag its tail faster and faster. He glanced at the Loggerheads. They could have thrown their rocks, but seemed reluctant to help. Well, he wasn't about to stand by and do nothing. He'd made his reputation from his strength as a fighter. Now it was time for action – to rescue a Dwarfgiant, after all. As for saving a rival, he really didn't have much to fear from Groff.

He had kept his bamboozie in his belt, out of sight. Now, lifting his tunic, he pulled the weapon out, placed a stone in the sling and took aim. As if sensing danger, the great gorm stood, its back legs exposed. Sinjun pulled and fired. In a blur, the stone struck the crease behind its knee. The creature squealed and wobbled, disappeared from view.

So had Groff.

Surrounded by Loggerhead torch lights, Sinjun reloaded, approached the hole in the wall. He stuck his head through, wondered if there'd be a scene like the night before when he'd tried to rescue Groff from the bone-crushing dragasp. Only a force of nature had saved them then, made him pee his pants. He sniffed himself. Still hadn't taken that dip.

The smell through the hole was worse, a mixture of dead things. To the left and right the cave widened. Straight ahead, a rough-hewn passageway looked as though it might be a way out. But where was the great gorm? Where was Groff? Sinjun heard a squeal, then a whimper – the sound of a creature whose tail was no longer wagging. He stepped through the hole into the dank, stinking place – water dripping, bones on the floor, the smell of rotting food. Then, to the right, another whimper. The Loggerheads, now on each side of him, swung their torches and there, lying in the foul, choking air, was the great gorm – a massive cave bear.

"It fell," said Groff, appearing from the shadows. He looked unscathed, gazing at the creature as if feeling sorry for it. "Fell, when the stone hit it."

"Don't get too close," said Headstrong.

"It fell on stalagmite daggers," Groff said. "It's b-bleeding."

Face down – its tail limp – the great gorm looked finished. Sinjun aimed his bamboozie at the creature's head. "I'll put it out of its misery."

"No!" said Groff. He reached into his pouch, found a Jabunga leaf. "This will heal it. Help me get it onto its back."

"Are you mad?" Sinjun said.

But Groff persisted, slid a hand under the creature's waist. "We can save it. Please!"

The Loggerheads hesitated, but with no sign of a fight from the creature, they stole forward, grasping back legs, front legs and paws. On a count of three, they rolled the creature over. The great gorm groaned; its wet button nose scrunched with pain. Three stalagmites were sunk in the creature's chest; blood was running freely. It wouldn't last long. But now, here was Groff pulling them out one by one, pressing a Jabunga leaf on the wounds until the blood dried and the leaf stuck.

"It's working!" said Headstrong.

After collecting water from the dripping stalactites, Groff gave the creature a drink, leaving the remainder – along with a bowl of malana grains – close by.

"We could have used them!" said Sinjun.

"The great gorm needs it m-more," Groff replied.

"Whatever," Sinjun said, shaking his head. Why should it surprise him that Groff had a weakness for big furry creatures? "Let's just get out of this filthy place."

CHAPTER 23

Addi had travelled some trails; dangerous trails, mostly unknown, mostly on the run. Through the Dark Wood he'd fled from Taluhla and the Raslatombs. In the scrubby bogland between the Southern Glade and the Kindoo Wetlands he'd survived a gorax attack. And now, here he was, still on the run – this time from Bardo's Kroguls. But this trail, the one down to the cove, was easy – the soft, leafy terrain, its quiet twists and turns. Bodessa knew this place. First a gentle slope, then a gradual steepening until, near the bottom, a sharp dip sent them both running full tilt.

Down on the wharf he faced her, panting.

"I can't see the boats for the mist," he said.

She was fixing her hair. Re-clipping some loose strands that blocked her vision, some tangled in her tiara. It seemed odd that she would still wear it. But it did look pretty, full of small diamonds. As he watched her, he was reminded of another oddity, one whose explanation might open a crack in her box of secrets.

"Why do all the other Zenta females have flaxen hair?" he asked.

Her eyes flashed. Then a half-smile. "My mother wasn't a Zenta."

"Really?"

"Hmm."

He waited for more.

Nothing.

"So, what was she?"

Her mouth opened slightly then stopped. She took a breath and said, "I will tell you, Addi. But not now."

Not much of a crack, more, a tease. Still, it was something.

She straightened her dress, flattened the silky trim around her chest. He gasped when her finger caught the pendant chain and her moonstones flipped out. Bodessa held the stones in her hand, gazed at them. She seemed captivated. There was a sound – not quite music, more a lilting note coming from the mist. Then the mist began to lift, sucked into a shape a dream might conjure – a spiralling female shape, all curves and tousled hair. Then, it was gone. The note, too, dragged away.

What was that all about? The moonstones, had they caused some sort of celestial magic? Bodessa stood transfixed, seemingly oblivious to what had happened. Impulsively Addi stuck his hand into his pouch. The pink sapphire he'd taken from Zuma's treasure vault somehow felt alive. Then it didn't.

Bodessa snapped out of her trance. With a vague smile she slipped the pendant back into the top of her dress. Then she looked around. The sky was clear. The moons glared down, and the boats were tied to the jetty.

"You all right?" he said.

She shivered.

Not good, with a night crossing ahead of them, she could easily freeze. He could offer her his tunic, but the thin linen wouldn't be much warmer. But he had fur. Maybe, later, by huddling together he might keep her warm. His thoughts on this possibility were interrupted by the echo of voices back up the trail.

"Let's go," he said. "Before the Kroguls find us."

She didn't move.

"Bodessa, come on!"

She shook her head. "I can't. I can't leave my father. Not in the hands of the Kroguls. It's me Bardo wants. I have to go back."

"You're not serious."

"He'll be tortured."

"And what do you suppose they'll do to you?"

"I have to save him."

He took her hand. "Bodessa, your father and Andros are counting on me to keep you safe. You can't go back."

She gave him that look. Her eyes; they could beat back any resistance. Even break a heart.

"He's right!" said a voice from down the jetty.

Addi turned. A figure stepped out of a boat. And then another. Strange, though, Addi didn't feel threatened. There was something reassuring about them, something familiar. And as they approached there was no mistaking Milo and Flogg.

"What are you doing here?" Addi asked.

"Making sure the boats are ready," Flogg replied.

"We were on guard duty," Milo added, "saw the Kroguls coming – well, Flogg saw them coming – a second batch of boats sneaking through the mist."

Flogg said. "Actually, at the time, I wasn't sure what I'd seen, otherwise I'd have rung the warning bell. Most Zenta guards were at the banquet and the Kroguls overran the garrison. So we came down here, to help Zentas get away, if needed. Then we heard the two of you –"

"They've taken the castle," said Addi, "captured Zuma, everybody. They want Bodessa. She wants to go back."

Flogg threw up his hands. "With respect, Princess, that's not a good idea. You of all people should know what Bardo can do."

As if perishing the thought she shivered again. "He's a brute, I know."

Flogg took off his outer coat and wrapped it around her shoulders. "Princess, being a brute is one thing. Being betrothed to him would be a life of torture."

She gave Flogg a sharp look.

Whoa, what was this? Her box of secrets being pried open?

"My father needs me."

Addi jumped in. "I'm sure your father can take care of himself. 'Don't stop running,' your brother said." He paused. "Did you say you were betrothed to Bardo?"

Bodessa looked at him, her eyes, for once, vulnerable. Then she turned to Milo and Flogg. "Go prepare the boat. I need to talk to Addi."

Obediently, the two guards shuffled down the wharf, the boards creaking underfoot.

Bodessa took a breath, looked at Addi directly. "Believe it, or not," she began, "my father and Bardo were once friends."

The lid was off.

"Bardo was a trader – mostly jewels, precious stones – small amounts, really. Every seventh sun, he'd arrive in his wreck of a boat and my father would be there, standing on the dock, waiting to see the handful of gems he'd brought. When Bardo's boat fell apart, my father had a new one built for him. In return, Bardo gave Father the Zenstone he wears on his finger. But then things changed. Mother's moonstone pendant went missing. It was a family treasure – so important that her distress at losing it almost led to a breakdown. But then it was found – by Bardo, of all people. Said he spotted it in a rock pool wrapped around a coral shell. My father asked him to name his reward.

'Your daughter,' he said, 'when she's old enough,' which, according to Bardo, was when I turned twelve. I was two at the time. Although my father agreed, he said he never intended to keep his promise."

There was a thudding of footsteps on the wharf. Milo and Flogg were running back. "The Kroguls are coming!" said Flogg. "You must leave now."

"Bodessa, I have to get back to the ruin," Addi said. "But I'm not leaving without you."

Bodessa seemed to be of two minds. "What about you?" she said to Flogg.

"Don't worry about me and Milo. We know places to hide."

Her nod was enough. Flogg led the way. At the jetty he helped her into the boat. Then Addi jumped in. Milo unfastened the line.

"Take care," Addi said, locking the oars. "Zuma's depending on you both. Be his eyes and ears. Let him know Bodessa's safe."

The two guards smiled like heroes. Then they pushed the boat out into Lake Zen.

CHAPTER 24

"Halt!" Noggin said, raising his arm. "We've got moonlight."

Tarro stopped, squinted at the light at the end of the tunnel. He knew moonlight was good, but he was too tired and cold and dripping wet to think it was great. Behind him, three Loggerheads squawked with delight.

Noggin signalled them to move forward. His pace quickened as they neared the exit, where the tunnel opened into a cavern whose walls rose like cliffs on either side. Tarro looked up, half expecting trouble – a falling boulder, or the wrath of some back-stabbing cave bird made miserable from being woken up. But all was still. Not even a creeping shadow. Outside could be different – Raslatombs waiting, a moonlit mob, the bed of pointed stakes. And what of the Loggerheads, were they friends or foe?

When he'd asked Noggin where they were going, the Loggerhead had said, "To a place made of rock. Built on rock." It sounded solid. Safe enough. But unless it was a place where they could take a quick nap, the Dwarfgiants didn't have time for side trips. They had to be back at the castle ruin, with or without Addi. The thought sickened him.

At the mouth of the cave, Noggin signalled for the torches to be doused and for everyone to gather behind a block of jutting limestone. Outside, all was quiet – too quiet. Noggin grabbed the Loggerhead next to him and pushed him forward. "You go first. Check things out."

The Loggerhead looked startled, stood his ground. "Me?"

"Go on!" said Noggin. "We'll back you up."

The Loggerhead pointed at Tarro. "What about the Dwarfgiant? Make him go. Let him take an arrow."

Tarro's breath stopped.

"He's already taken one," Noggin said. "Now, get going!"

Tarro breathed again. Even if he were able to change up to giant size, the Raslatombs would be ready for him. They'd make him pay.

"Go on!"

The Loggerhead stood motionless, his tiny eyes glazing over, a forlorn hope lost in a big square head.

Noggin spat, raised his rock and aimed. "I'll count to three. One … two …"

The reluctant Loggerhead gripped his own rock, took a breath and, with his knees shaking, stepped out into the blinding moonlight.

Tarro watched the Loggerhead look left and right – then left again. Moments passed. No Raslatombs, no ambush, no nothing. It was as if the night was waiting for the hammer to fall, waiting for the moons to give it a shove. Then a sound – a slow, scuffing sound, like some dead-of-night creature heavy with scales and multiple feet. The Loggerhead stiffened. His lips began to move, but no words came out, only muttering and gibberish, probably to save himself from screaming. But it didn't last long. Now he was smiling, a manic jumbling of lips. Had to be, because whatever was coming couldn't have been funny. And it wasn't. But neither was it evil.

"Headstrong!" the Loggerhead cried out with no regard for the loudness of his voice or the echo of jubilation. "You're alive!"

One by one they appeared – the Loggerhead with the scarf, three other Loggerheads, Sinjun and Groff.

Tarro felt a sudden kick of destiny. There was no demon to fight, and the Circle candidates had survived their journey through the caves.

"Light the torches!" Noggin ordered, running out to greet them. "We're going home."

Friction sticks sparked flames.

"Where's home?" Tarro asked.

"Down through the ravine," Noggin said, pointing. "Leads to the rock quarry."

"You live in a quarry?"

"Born and raised."

Chapter 25

Heaving on the oars, Addi stroked the boat across the cold black waters of Lake Zen. Bodessa sat facing him, holding Flogg's coat tight under her chin. With her back to Castle Zen she couldn't see what he could – Krogul torchlights dotting the trail down to the cove. He thought of Milo and Flogg, but it was Bodessa the Kroguls were after. For Bardo. If he was to keep her out of Bardo's filthy clutches, he needed to know the truth.

He rowed faster, as fast as he could. With the paddles chopping at the water, he took a wide path, skirting the moons' reflection, hoped to make it to the far shore without being seen. If the Kroguls did give chase, at least he had a big lead.

Halfway across, Bodessa began to shiver, her shoulders and head shaking, moonlit diamonds glittering in her tiara. She still hadn't looked back. He guessed that her decision not to return to Castle Zen was hard enough.

He thought he saw a boat leaving the wharf, lights bobbing on the water. Kroguls? He tried to keep up the pace but his arms ached and he was out of breath. He stopped, and for some moments gasped for air. When he could speak, he said to her, "We'll soon be across."

Through chattering teeth she nodded. He was getting cold himself so he started rowing again. But with increasing shots of pain, he pulled on the oars at only half speed. If the Kroguls were giving chase, he wasn't sure he could out-row them.

Chapter 26

The ravine leading to the Loggerhead rock quarry was a slow-winding, tree-filled gully, a muddy track next to a gurgling stream. He wasn't sure why, but Tarro thought the ravine a mysterious place. Cast in moonlight it seemed old and alone, yet noble and content, with its knotty gnarled tree roots and green carpet of moss. It was also rife with shadows, ready to protect itself – its secrets and ancient habits. But the mist hanging under boughs, the shadows lengthened by moonbeams, made him feel like a trespasser, who, if caught, might never find his way out.

Careful not to dally, he, Sinjun and Groff, along with Noggin and the Loggerheads, pushed on. The track eventually led them up a long slope. When they reached the top they beheld a view that took Tarro's breath: a gorge with a deep drop and waterfall to the side, a night cascade, moonlit and softly flowing. Below, through veils of mist, the stream became a river, and farther along, beyond a breakup of trees, the banks rose again, up to what looked like a fortress of rocks. The Loggerhead rock quarry.

"One false step and you're fodder for the fishes," said Noggin, starting down a steep path.

Sinjun leaned in behind Tarro. "Give me the word," he whispered, "and I'll push them over the edge."

Tarro shook his head. "Don't do that."

The promise of sleep, as well as safety in numbers, had convinced Tarro to go along with the Loggerheads – at least for the time being. Though drawn together by a common enemy – Taluhla and the Raslatombs – he still wasn't sure whether Noggin could be trusted, or if some kind of friendship was even possible. He also worried about Sinjun – all those muscles, all that energy – doing something rash. Groff was doing his part, chatting to Headstrong about something or other. Something about a great gorm.

They reached the bottom of the gorge without Sinjun pushing a Loggerhead over the edge. It wouldn't have been easy, anyway. They'd kept their distance from him.

"Sinjun, you s-stink," said Groff. "Why don't you b-bathe? And your tunic …"

Sinjun glared, puffed out his chest. "When I want your advice, I'll ask for it."

"Groff's right," said Tarro. "In the name of the dragasp, you need to freshen up."

Sinjun looked down into the moonlit pool, made swirly by the waterfall.

"I have a s-spare tunic in my bag," Groff added. "It's a b-bit small, but it's clean and dry."

"As I said, if I need your help –"

But Sinjun had no choice. He was surrounded. If he didn't go willingly, he'd be pushed in. Following the ritual of unhooking his belt, his pouches, his knife and his bamboozie, he stopped short of taking off his tunic. But he did jump in, his splash spraying everyone. The dip did its work, it cleaned him up and cooled him off. Behind a large elm, he discarded his tunic and squeezed into Groff's spare one. It looked so tight, he seemed about to burst. Even the Loggerheads laughed.

The path along the river led to a hillside sprinkled with rocks. The rocks were of ample size and, at first glance, appeared to lie in random groupings. But as Noggin led the way up, it began to look as though they'd been deliberately placed in a staggered pattern, a defensive system retreating all the way to the top. Behind each rock, smaller, hand-sized rocks were piled high: ammunition to repel attackers. But there were no guards, not until they reached the main gate set in a rock wall that stretched across the top of the hill.

The three guards looked surprised, sprang to their feet. They didn't salute but, acting as some sort of ceremonial welcoming party, began to juggle rocks.

"Open the gate!" barked Noggin.

They dropped their rocks. And while two guards rushed off to lift the bar, the third guard said, "Where's Headlock?"

"Dead," said Noggin.

"Dead?"

"That's all you need to know. Make way, we have Dwarfgiants to attend to."

"Can we use them for target practice?"

"Not tonight."

Tarro shuddered, saw Sinjun reach for his knife. Sinjun looked for a signal. Tarro shook him off.

"First we rest," said Noggin, leading the way inside. He strode through the gateway, paused at the top of a long flight of steps.

Tarro looked down at a dug-out basin surrounded by walls of rock and filled with scatterings of low, flat buildings and target ranges. It was as much a compound as it was a quarry. What made him uneasy were the target ranges. Even in the middle of the night, Loggerheads were taking turns throwing rocks at what looked like cabbages stuck on wooden stakes. Others, including females, gathered to watch, shouting and cheering as if it were some sort of tournament. How could they rest with such a racket going on?

Descending the steps, Tarro felt more like a prisoner than a guest. With Sinjun back to being agitated and Groff looking extra-worried, he knew he'd have to be ready at any moment to change up. He grabbed a handful of carrahock grains from his pouch and, careful not to be seen, slipped them in his mouth. Probably more than he needed.

Off the centre square they entered a crumbling building with no windows. Halfway down a dim corridor, Noggin unlocked a door and pushed it open. "This is where you rest." It was an empty room smelling of sweat and straw on the floor.

Groff and Sinjun entered, followed by Tarro, who turned to Noggin and said, "We need to be up early."

"Don't worry about that," said the Loggerhead. "You won't be sleeping in." And with no further explanation he closed the door, shutting out the noise from outside, and locked it.

"I should have shoved them into the gorge when I had the chance," said Sinjun, pounding his fist on the wall.

"What do you th-think they have in m-mind?" said Groff, sitting in a corner, hugging his bag.

"I'm not sure," said Tarro, rolling his shoulder, testing it. "They're hard to fathom. One moment they seem tolerant, the next, they're full of threats. My guess is that with Noggin, it's more bravado – that a life with rocks and living in a rock quarry is one to be glorified. As outsiders, the best thing we can do is to show respect and be as accommodating as we can. I can't believe they want us for target practice – and yet, I don't think all the spiked targets were cabbages. Whatever they're planning, we need to rest – be fresh to face them at sunrise."

CHAPTER 27

Not taking his eyes off the Krogul boat, Addi found the strength to keep rowing. The pain in his arms had eased, replaced by a numbness he hoped would see him through until he'd crossed the lake.

Rolling down the moon-splashed lane, the Kroguls had made up ground and their grunts and screams and yelps were not so distant. About halfway, though, they suddenly slowed down, veered to port. It was hard to make out, but Addi thought he saw another boat in the water, a smaller one.

"They're going back," said Addi, taking a deep breath.

Bodessa looked over her shoulder. He watched her as she took in the scene: the Krogul boat turning back to Castle Zen, torch lights flickering all the way up to the captured fortress. Inside, Bardo would be furious. With Bodessa stolen from under his nose, he'd likely be taking it out on her father. And yet she stayed calm, no sign of any readiness to jump in and swim back.

The boat ploughed through high reeds. Trees loomed in silhouette. "We're here," Addi said, paddling into a shallow inlet.

Bodessa smiled, more respectful than joyous. Still, he'd take it, anything to keep her from despair. Stepping from the boat onto the dry bank, he tied the rope around the trunk of a leaning willow. Sheltered beneath branches, it was a safe spot, quiet except for the occasional gulping of glugs.

He stood on the bank, exhausted. "I can't go any farther tonight. I need to rest."

For a moment she looked at him, her head raised, her eyes thinking. And then, as if feeling guilty for having Flogg's overcoat to herself, she began to undo the buttons. "Are you cold?" she asked, extending her arm. "Come."

He wasn't too cold, but wasn't going to pass on the invitation. When she unfastened the last button, he stepped into the boat, almost tipping it over.

"Body heat," she said taking off the overcoat and re-wrapping it around both of them. "It should keep us warm until sunup."

He knew that his body fur would keep them both warm. With the coat hanging down to their feet, they lay on the floor of the boat, arranged so that her back was to him. He stretched out behind her, not sure how close he should get. She nudged back so their bodies made contact, their legs nestling; the glorious feel of her bottom fitting snug to his stomach. For a moment he held his breath – could have held it all night – except for a distraction, one he hoped could be removed.

"Bodessa," he said, exhaling a cold mist.

Her shoulders stiffened.

"Your tiara, it's twinkling in the moonlight."

Her shoulders released like shifting sand.

He said, "I could put it under the seat."

"I forgot I still had it on."

He withdrew his arm from under the coat and removed the tiara from her crown of thick black hair. Even with so many diamonds it was lighter than he'd thought, more delicate in his hand, made it easy to reach back and slide it below the seat.

Now he was in a quandary: his arm was free. What would she think, he wondered if he put it around her waist – like a hug, to keep warm? He slipped it back under the coat, but just as it was in the darkness of the castle tunnel, his aim was off. Instead of finding her waist he was a bit too high. And just as before, she was quick to move his hand. Then, through the soft tuck of her dress, he found the groove of her waist, narrow and firm, his hand content to settle there. In the short time he'd known her, their knees had touched, they'd held hands; he'd even lifted her, carried her to safety. But this was closer than he could have imagined – the two of them, laying together, the feel of her glorious shape against him, blissfully snug on a clear and shimmering night.

For some time under Flogg's overcoat they lay huddled, not moving, not speaking. The night was still. No breeze, quiet waters. Even the glugs had stopped gulping. This unexpected gush of tranquility gave Addi a chance to rest his head, clear his thoughts. It worked for a while – staring mindlessly at the fall of her hair, soft and lush, right in front of his nose. Eventually, though, it was hard to think of nothing, and thoughts of her and Bardo began to creep into his mind. He wanted to hear the rest of the story about her being his reward, about them being betrothed.

He was about to ask her when her voice startled him.

"You smell like perfume."

Zuma's musk! "It must be from the victory banquet," he said, innocently. "The air was thick with it."

"Was it really that thick?"

Not as thick as the lentilla musk in your father's perfume den. "Does it bother you?" he said, not wanting to move.

Her head shook slightly. "What bothers me is my father's safety."

He withdrew his arm from her waist, found her hand and gave it a squeeze. "Bodessa, I know how you must feel, but your father – and you said it yourself – no one gets the better of him. He'll be all right, you'll see."

Of course, he wasn't the least bit sure of this. But with a shuffle and a sigh she seemed to relax, be more content.

She lay still, her breathing slow and steady. Must be asleep. He was surprised in a way, because the night air bit like ice. In fact, the whole warming process was slow, and his arm – the one he happened to be lying on – had just about lost all feeling. But he didn't care. He'd be pinching himself for the rest of the night.

Eventually, though, his eyelids felt heavy and he gave in to sleep.

When he awoke, his nose was so cold it tingled. Careful not to wake her, he withdrew his arm, rolled onto his back. With both hands cupping his nose, he blew warm breaths into them.

Pleased he could feel his nose again, he remained on his back looking up at the sky. The blackness was filled with stars glittering around the two moons, the moons that were getting closer and closer together. Ever since the second moon had appeared – at the end of the solar meridian – the tides of the Sulphur Sea had not been so friendly; the nightly rush of water flooded the moat, its waves swollen with nightmarish creatures. He didn't know how the moons did it, but knowing that they were the cause, he now looked at them with contempt. One more cycle and they'd be touching …

or, even worse: "Legend says that when the two moons join, a giant sea serpent will attack those who inhabit the old ruin," Zuma had warned. If the Mystic Zenta was right – and Addi had to believe he was – the journey would begin at dawn. He and Bodessa travelling at speed, back through the Kindoo Wetlands, the Southern Glade and the Dark Wood, reaching the castle ruin no later than sunset. If the Dwarfgiants had to battle a sea serpent, what he wanted most was for Tarro to be there. He and his friend – his brother – fighting side-by-side.

In the meantime, he needed more sleep. Slowly, he turned towards Bodessa, slipped his arm under the overcoat and found her just where he'd left her.

Chapter 28

Myvan lay in bed staring up at the shadows dancing in the rafters. He'd kept his bedroom candles lit, partly because he couldn't sleep, but mainly to get some relief from the dark images spinning in his head. An approaching Raslatomb army, wild creatures attacking from the sea, the joining of the moons, the coming of the serpent – all left his stomach jittery, his position as leader of the Dwarfgiants shaky. There was only the following day to fortify the north wall and reinforce the entrance to the moat. Havoc and his gang were already at it, working through the night, piecing together the wooden structures, the framework needed to shore up the moat. Havoc was good – a good builder – but it was asking a lot to put a defence system in place in such a short time, one strong enough to repel forces of such malevolence.

Then there was Tarro and his search party. And Addi. Would they make it back in time with fresh Jabunga leaves and still be strong enough to help fight the terror from the sea? Would he, himself, survive? Probably not. The castle ruin's previous occupants, the Odanus, hadn't. The parchment records had been clear. After the two moons had joined, the Odanus had been annihilated. As leader it was up to him to find a way out – anything to avoid suffering the same fate. And yet, it seemed, fate was all he could hold on to. If the moons were on the side of Taluhla and the Raslatombs, maybe the stars could align themselves in favour of the Dwarfgiants.

Still, the shadows in the rafters flitted.

He got out of bed. At least he tried. A jab of pain. He stumbled and cursed. He held on to the side table, tried to reach his stick.

"Let me get it for you," said the voice practised in the art of knowing when to help, had been helping for twenty summers. Claris arose from her own bed. "Couldn't sleep either," she said, picking up the stick, handing it to him. "Back or knees?"

"Knees," he said, shaking his head. "How can I be expected to fight Raslatombs with knees like these?"

"I've got some emberlea," she said. "Smells like an old root but I'll rub some on."

"Just do what you can."

She backtracked, knelt and pulled a small blue bottle out from under her bed. "There's just enough left," she said, holding the bottle up to the candlelight. She poured the last of the potion onto his knees, rubbed gently.

"That's Tarro's best potion," said Myvan, sitting down on his bed. "Let's hope he's back tomorrow."

She looked him in the eye and smiled. "I'm sure he will be. They all will."

Myvan nodded. But his throat tightened.

Chapter 29

In the darkness of the room, Tarro lay on the floor, waiting – waiting for them to come, the rock-throwers, Noggin and his Loggerheads. The way he saw it, there were only two things they could want: to keep them as slaves, or to use them for target practice. Or both. Of course, he'd hoped there might be a better outcome. After all, they had met by chance, spent most of their time together fighting off the Raslatombs, a shared enemy. Yet there'd been no sign from Noggin that he had any intention of becoming friends, or even being friendly. The Loggerheads didn't seem to have it in them.

As time passed, all that kept Tarro from thinking dark thoughts were the sounds of Groff wheezing in the corner and Sinjun muttering in his sleep – oh, and the tickle of a creeper crawling up his leg. There wasn't much he could do about the two Circle candidates, but the creeper was going too far. Under his tunic it legged its way to his belly, where he felt the sting of a bite. He slapped at it – twice. But it was still there, detouring to the unreachable part of his back, creeping all the way up his neck, stopping just below the lobe of his ear. He shuddered, remembering Groff's story about the chompit, the scrubby little creature that crawled into ears, burrowing – no, eating its way through the brain, then waddling out the other side. Again, Tarro lined up his hand. This time, he couldn't afford to miss.

At exactly the same moment he took care of the creeper – a decisive splat between his neck and hand – he heard pounding on the door. A key jangled in the lock. The door swung open.

"All right, you three," Noggin boomed, his blemished face looking sinister in the yellow torchlight. "On your feet!"

There were at least four of them – square-headed guards, torches blinding, acting tough.

"Where are we going?" Tarro said, rising to his feet.

"You'll see," said Noggin, waving his torch at Sinjun and Groff. "You two, wake up! Let's go!"

Sinjun reached for his bamboozie. But before he could muster a shot a guard stuck a foot on his hand.

"Take the sling," said Noggin to the guard. "Let's find out just how good it is."

In what was becoming a familiar procession, the three Dwarfgiants – with two Loggerheads in front and three behind – were led single file down the passageway.

This could be it. Used for bamboozie target practice. Tarro leaned in and whispered instructions to Sinjun. "Be ready when I change up."

Out through the front door, the air was cool. The moons, screened by a drifting cloud were giving way to the light of dawn, a faint sun streaking the sky purple and pink. Tarro was surprised at this. He didn't feel rested, but he must have slept.

"Over there," said Noggin. "Line them up."

They were escorted to one end of a target range. The crowds of Loggerheads they'd seen when they had arrived were gone. Now, dotting the outside perimeter of the range were shadowy forms, square and still, probably guards. As they walked, Sinjun kept close, but Groff looked as if he was shaking.

Tarro was tempted to change up right then. It usually took a moment or two for his body to react. By the time he started to grow, it was possible for an enemy to get in a first shot. But changing up as they walked would cause surprise.

The surprise, though, came from the sky: a loud, rippling crackle, a forked flash and then another. The cloud had gone and the moons were back, each flaring, not quite touching, but close enough to sound a warning of the bleak night to come.

"That's far enough!" Noggin said. "Turn around."

The Dwarfgiants lined up to face him.

Noggin held out his hand. "Give it to me," he said to Headstrong. The Loggerhead with the scarf around his face handed him the bamboozie.

"Do it now!" Sinjun whispered to Tarro.

More moon-sparks crackled in the sky.

"Wait," Tarro said.

Noggin waved the bamboozie at the Dwarfgiants. "Who wants to be first?"

Nobody moved.

"No volunteers?"

Silence.

"Are Dwarfgiants always so stupid?" Noggin went on. "I want one of you to show me how this works … I'll tell you one thing, if I have to do it, you'll be targets."

"I'll sh-show you," blurted Groff.

"No, I'll do it!" said Sinjun.

Noggin sent the bamboozie skimming. Sinjun caught it with one hand.

"The head on the pole," said Noggin, pointing. "Hit it."

Sinjun squinted. In the dawning light, the target – at least fifty paces away – was a murky orange, like the head of a small pumpkin. But as he dug into his pouch for a stone, sunrays shot up from behind the quarry walls. With a brighter target, he aimed the bamboozie.

"And no tricks," Noggin warned. "Our best throwers are in range."

With his arms bulging, Sinjun pulled on the sling, stretched the elastic back as far as it could go.

Two words came into Tarro's head. Don't miss.

With a tight snap, Sinjun released the stone – a blazing shot, flying so fast it splattered the pumpkin head before Tarro could even blink.

Noggin stood gaping. The first thing he moved was his hand, punishing the rock he held, squeezing it to dust. "Where did you get it from," he said, "the bam … ?"

"boozie," said Sinjun. "We make them. Try it."

Noggin looked at the bamboozie as though it was something sinister.

"If you like it, it's yours," said Tarro.

Noggin turned to Headstrong. The Loggerhead with the scarf around his face blinked once.

"Give me it!" Noggin said. "Put up another target."

While Headstrong spiked another pumpkin – or whatever it was – Sinjun handed Noggin the weapon. Its wooden handle and rubber-like sling were made from the wood and sap of the guttalong tree. Strong and flexible. The Loggerhead looked at it, picked up a stone, put it in the sling and pulled it back.

"You might find it works better the other way up," Tarro said, politely.

Noggin stopped and glared. He turned it the right way and fired. The stone flew hard in the direction of the target, but high. It kept on going and struck the side of the quarry, embedding itself in the sandy rock face.

"That was excellent," said Tarro, "a really good first try."

Noggin looked pleased, quickly reloaded. About to release a second stone, he suddenly stopped. Beyond the target – in the area where his stone had hit – there was a rumble, a crackle, sand spilling, stones and rocks falling.

An alarm went off; a clanging sound, like a hollow pan being beaten by a stick.

With the bamboozie still in his hand, Noggin ran towards the crumbling quarry. Tarro, Sinjun and Groff fell in step, along with other Loggerheads startled by the ruckus. For a time they were lost in a bellow of dust that filled the air around them. When it cleared, they gawped at the caved-in wall, the great mound of rubble piled on the pathway, a huge boulder on top.

"I must have hit a weak spot," Noggin said, shielding his eyes from the sun. "That boulder's blocking the way out. Take us all day to clear it."

"I can move it," said Tarro, his voice urgent.

Noggin smacked himself twice on the side of the head. "I don't think so."

"Try me."

Noggin cocked his head and tapped it lightly on the top as if he were trying to loosen a decision. "Go on, then," he smirked. "It's all yours."

"On one condition," said Tarro.

"Condition?"

"When I clear the boulder, you'll let us leave."

Noggin squirted a laugh, glanced at the massive rock. "If you can move that, we'll escort you out."

"Do I have your word?"

"What do you want, blood?"

Tarro quickly loosened his pouch. Then he turned to Sinjun, hands raised, palms open, fingers spread. Sinjun did the same, both sets of hands flat against each other. He looked into Sinjun's eyes – dark-green and determined. It would be Sinjun's first time being part of a change up, to witness the power that comes from being a member of the Circle.

Tarro had changed-up many times before. The first stage was fairly predictable. A tingle in his feet, a lightness in his head. But there was also the pain of growing so fast, not knowing if his muscles and organs and bones could even stand the shock of such a spurt, a phenomenon born in the essences of galinsa roots and the grains of the carrahock plant, a potion which he'd personally helped to improve, but whose origins and strange effect remained mysterious.

Yet, somehow, he'd always come through.

Their fingers interlocked, and when Tarro closed his eyes, he was overcome with a sense of mellowness, a feeling of floating to another place. Somewhere heavenly.

If only it were that easy!

A jolt wracked his spine. Blood raced through his veins like high tide filling up a moat. His eyes opened, watery and blurred. His skin tightened around his feet, legs, arms; torso elongated, neck pulled, chest bloated, one after another the buttons popped off his tunic.

Sinjun sprang back.

Taller and taller Tarro surged, his shins splintering, his wounded shoulder stretching. But the stitches held. There were noises, some shouts, a scream, maybe, but they were muted; his ears were blocked. He looked down. Sinjun and Groff, side by side, appeared anxious. The Loggerheads were all over the place, some running away, others buffeting around their leader, Noggin, whose jaw, limp as the bamboozie in his hand, looked stunned, as if he'd hit himself too hard.

Tarro guessed he'd grown twice as tall as any of them, and the way his body had swelled, he had to be at least ten times as strong. He felt dizzy, wooziness extending down to his knees which, at one point, almost gave out. But his body began to settle. Now giant-sized, he could demonstrate the immense strength he possessed – after he'd wiped his nose. With the back of his arm he took care of it. Well, most of it. This time his nosebleed was quite runny.

Loping towards the boulder, he waved at Sinjun and Groff to join him. He wanted to make sure they were close by in case Noggin had some treachery in mind. They hurried after him – glad, it seemed, to be on the side of a Circle Dwarfgiant fully changed up. He glanced back at Noggin. The Loggerhead still hadn't moved except to skew his jaw across his face as if he were talking out of the side of his mouth but without the words.

The boulder was a monster, higher than Tarro, bigger than the one the Loggerheads had pushed over the cliff. He stood before it wondering if he could actually move it. Luckily, it was roundish in shape and rested on a curved part of its circumference. Should be roll-able.

By now Loggerheads were streaming out of their rocky abodes, huddling in groups, murmuring excitedly.

Tarro found himself preoccupied with a blob of dried blood caked on the end of his nose. He picked it off with his finger and thumb, stopping only when he realized that all eyes were on him.

Back to the task, he wrapped his arms around the mass of rock as if he was giving it a hug, heard some in the crowd gasp. He'd let them think he was going to lift it. Instead, he leaned on it, testing for movement. It rocked slightly, a good sign.

He stepped back. Taking a long, slow breath, and with both shoulders and arms ready to heave, he moved forward again, more a sideways approach. He shoved the boulder hard. It rolled forward – about a quarter of a turn – then it hit a flat spot and stopped. Pulling it back in a series of rocking motions, back and forth, back and forth, he finally unleashed all he had, adding power from his legs and back. The boulder took off, rolling past the flat spot, crunching over piles of quarry rubble, down a gradient to the side of the path and stopping on a patch of grass and sand. He'd done it. The way out was clear.

More gasps, then silence. The Loggerheads turned to Noggin, as if looking for a response.

The Loggerhead leader straightened his jaw and cleared his throat. Then, appearing to have regained some of his senses, he moved forward, slow and steady. Like a peace offering, Noggin held out the bamboozie. "Here," he said. "You can have it back."

Tarro, now in full command, looked down at Noggin. "Keep it," he said, the deep power of his voice echoing through the quarry. "Call it a gift."

Noggin shook his head. "I don't think so," he said, handing the bamboozie to Sinjun. "Like I said, we like to keep things the way they are."

"Suit your self," Tarro said. "And like I said, we now have to go. Find our friend."

"What's he look like – this friend?"

Tarro pictured Addi. "Like us, he's a Dwarfgiant, except his hair is long and golden." He was tempted to add, He's also brazen and foolhardy – too impulsive for his own good. Instead, he said, "He might be with a female – somewhere in the Dark Wood."

Without hitting himself Noggin placed two fingers on his right temple, looked to be thinking. "This female, what does she look like?"

Another picture formed in Tarro's head. He remembered her, vaguely, lying on the Raslatomb bed of pointed stakes. "She had pale white skin, long dark hair."

Noggin's eyes widened. He looked impressed. "Sounds like Zuma's daughter."

"Who?"

"Zuma, the Mystic Zenta."

Now Tarro was befuddled. "Her father's a mystic?"

"They say he is."

"So, where would we find this Zuma?"

"Castle Zen. On an island about half a sun's journey from here."

"Which way?" Tarro asked.

"Just follow the way out."

Chapter 30

Morning broke to the sound of glugs. Floating on marablooms, gulping and splashing around the boat, they rejoiced as though the world belonged to them. The inlet – full of reeds and marsh marigolds – was their world, along with gauzy damsel flies and a blizzard of butterflies that came and went, except for one that settled in Bodessa's hair. Addi watched its sun-yellow wings, opening and closing, as if trying to wake her.

Still, she slept.

His hand was still in the groove of her waist, his favourite place in the world. The last thing he wanted was to move it. But the day was in a hurry, held possibilities that spun his mind. To get back to the castle ruin before nightfall he would need all his adventuring skills: a keen ear, a sharp eye, a clear sense of direction. Not able to change up, like Tarro, he'd need to be alert, ready to take a chance, but not to the extent of being surprised by a gorax.

Being with Bodessa added to his feeling of excitement. For someone so new to the outside world she'd learned quickly, shown surprising toughness and a nose for survival – a lovely one, at that. And, if he were honest, he could no longer deny she'd taken over his heart. Still, he'd need to watch out for her, keep her safe from the evil they'd no doubt face: creatures of the Dark Wood, crossfire from Raslatombs, the serpent of the Sulphur Sea. If it was to be a full-blooded adventure in the old Dwarfgiant tradition, luck would have to favour them. One good thing: at least the first stage would be in daylight.

He slid his arm out from under the coat and sat up. Covering a yawn with his hand, he looked back at the lake. Castle Zen was out of view but the sunlight shone from that direction, burning off remnants of mist, chasing the moons to the east, to the far coast and the ruin.

He heard a splash behind him. Not the sound of a glug but something bigger, something less playful. Had it been a jumping fish – a flying jade, maybe? He turned to see. All he could make out were the ripples from something like a thick rope gliding across the water towards the boat. Then a gurgle from the tree above made him look up. He cringed. Curled around a drooping willow branch, the black and green bands of a snake – its head hanging down, its mouth wide open – flashed hollow fangs.

Vipersniper!

The one in the water glided closer. Addi didn't expect it to slither up into the boat, but he drew his knife anyway. As he did, the vessel tilted and bobbed. The butterfly fluttered away, Bodessa awoke with a start and the sniper in the tree fell into the boat. Bodessa's scream rang out like the first time he'd heard it – thankfully, the never-ending nightmare part wasn't quite so long. And while everyone had their pet fears – even he had a loathing for vipersnipers – her distress was upsetting, especially with the other circling the boat. As the one onboard uncurled itself, he wondered if the two snipers were working together – one to get them into the water, the other to finish them off.

He turned to Bodessa. She was wrapped in the overcoat, shaking. "Try not to scream," he said. "I don't think it helps."

The paddle was in reach. He stepped in front of her and picked it up. The sniper slid forward, its head disappearing under the seat where the tiara lay.

"Bodessa!" he called over his shoulder. "Jump ashore. Run!"

"What about you?"

"I'll catch up."

With the paddle in one hand, his knife in the other, he waited for the sniper to reappear. Only when Bodessa jumped and the boat rocked did the creature show its scaly head, hissing and flicking its tongue. It could posture all it liked but Addi wasn't about to wait for it to strike first. He threw the paddle like a spear. As the sniper recoiled under the seat, he shoved his knife back in his belt and jumped. But his push-off was awkward, his angle slanted, and though he cleared the water, he landed clumsily, his back foot stubbing the lip of the bank. Off balance, his knees folded and he slid down into the shallows below. When he glanced back, his legs went even weaker. The sniper in the water was coming … no, wait … both were coming; the one in the boat had slipped over the side, its queer up-and-down eyes fixed on revenge. He knew his chances against two snipers weren't good, but he pulled his knife anyway, waving it about, chopping at the water. For a moment the snipers stopped, circled around. Then they disappeared.

They were coming underwater. At this rate the adventure would be over before it had begun. He looked up. There was no sign of Bodessa. But there was the rope tied to the willow tree. He jammed the knife back in his belt, flung himself at the line. His fingers burned as he grabbed it, and hung on with all his strength. But he was dangling; his legs still in the water, the snipers a fang bite away. Pull yourself up! said the voice in his head. Pull! He moved his hands and started to tug on the rope. But the pain in his arms returned – his punishment for rowing across Lake Zen – a deep soreness right up to the sockets of his shoulders. Pull!

As much as he tried, he was getting nowhere; just a mind filled with fateful flashes – stings, venom, blood, being dragged feet first into the depths, or, at the very least, watching his arms drop off.

"Addi!" said the voice. "Here!"

He looked up. Bodessa, still in Flogg's overcoat, lay overhanging the bank, her hands reaching down. She gripped his sleeve and collar. He was closer to the top of the bank than he'd thought, and now, as his feet cleared the water, the pain in his arm sockets dulled; his head was dizzy with hope that he might elude the snipers after all. With remarkable strength she helped pull him up.

For some moments after, he lay on the bank, panting – more from relief than breathlessness. And though happy to have escaped, he felt disheartened that in his role of keeping her safe he had, so soon, fallen short.

"I thought I told you to run for it," he said, guiltily.

"I'm not fond of vipersnipers. But I couldn't leave you alone with them."

He nodded his thanks and, sitting up, looked down at the water. "Where did they go?"

There was a splash and a croak near the boat.

"Looks like they're more interested in glugs," she said. "At least one of them is."

"So … where's the other?"

The rope sagged. Already over halfway up, the second vipersniper – fork-tongued and slippery – was weaving a pattern of green and gold.

"Come on!" Addi said, starting to run.

Bodessa chased after him, throwing off her coat on the fly.

Chapter 31

They'd barely left the Loggerhead quarry when Tarro began to feel his pulse slow down, the muscles in his legs go weak. He needed to sit. Find somewhere soft, a patch of grass that would cushion his head should he faint, which he often did when he changed down from giant size.

"What about over th-there?" said Groff, pointing to an open, grassy space beyond a ragged wall of rocks.

They headed towards the wall, and while Sinjun and Groff scrambled over, Tarro, in one giant step, cleared it with ease. He found a flat spot and, with his knees bent and his arms held out for balance, lowered himself to the ground. For some moments he sat, braced in a kind of stupor, letting his body change in its own time – bones shrinking, joints cracking, skin slackening and tightening, a stilling of his heart as if his life were being drained out of him. Then it came, a wave of wooziness that made his eyes blur. He was determined to fight it off, show that he was strong enough to resist the spectacle of collapse, what with Sinjun and Groff looking on. He shook his head and concentrated, thought about the day that lay ahead.

Not an easy trail. With or without Addi, Myvan's orders had been for them to return to the castle ruin before sunfall. Even if they set off right away, they couldn't be sure of getting back in time. The plan didn't allow for unexpected trouble. And Addi might have even found his way back home by now, even with the daughter of Zuma the mystic Zenta.

As his dizziness began to clear, his body easing back to normal, he wasn't sure what to do: keep looking for his best friend, or follow his father's orders and return home. One thing was clear. He'd need to decide quickly. He observed Sinjun and Groff. The two sat facing him – one strapped with weapons, the other gripping his bag, both a little grubby, showing signs of adventure. But as Circle candidates they needed to do more, show how they could handle sticky situations, make choices that gave them the best chance of survival.

"So that's it," Tarro said, rubbing his knees, getting the circulation back, "the physical part of being a member of the Circle. Changing up – it's the advantage we have over those who might threaten us, or, those we can escape from – like the Loggerheads – simply by moving a rock."

Sinjun and Groff sat open-mouthed, waiting for more.

Tarro checked his nose for blood, picked at a crust. "Still, there's more to being a Circle member than swelling to the size of a giant."

"Well, I can't wait," said Sinjun, finding his voice, "to become giant-sized. I can't wait to do that."

"D-does it hurt?" Groff asked, pointing.

Tarro checked his wounded arm, rotated his shoulder. The pain was bearable but blood trickled again. "It can be painful. It affects Circle members in different ways. For me, my head suffers, takes a pounding, sometimes taking a full sun to settle down. The one thing it does for anyone who changes up, is that it ages them. You may not know it, or believe it, but my real age is seventeen summers. I've been told I look more like twenty-five. So you see, there is a price to pay; changing up is not something to be taken lightly."

Groff reached into his bag and pulled out a Jabunga leaf and a greyish cloth. Without fuss, he fastened it under Tarro's arm, around his shoulder.

"Thanks," Tarro said, rising to his feet, testing the bandage for tightness. "Now I'm ready to go." But where? He had a good idea what Sinjun and Groff would say but he wanted to hear them say it. "So, Sinjun, we have a decision to make: whether to keep going and hope to find Addi, or go back home and help Myvan defend the castle ruin."

"What would we be defending against?"

He needed to tell them. How could they make a decision if they didn't know? "A sea serpent," he said, with intended heaviness.

Sinjun squeezed his eyes. "Sea serpent? How big?"

"As big as they come."

After a pause, Sinjun said, "We should keep going."

Tarro was taken aback. Not the answer he'd expected. "Are you saying you would defy Myvan's order to return?"

"Are you?"

"You're a Circle candidate, I'm asking you."

"Like I said, we should keep going."

"And why is that?"

"We might get to meet the daughter of a Mystic Zenta."

It was Tarro's turn to tighten his eyes. Was Sinjun mocking him? Ever since they'd had words at the hideaway, Sinjun had shown little desire to find Addi. Now he seemed more interested in meeting this female.

Tarro turned to Groff, who was gripping something in his hand. Some sort of gadget. "Groff, what is that?"

"A w-wayfinder. It's magnetic."

"Timely. Which way is it pointing?"

Groff hung on to it. "It's not p-pointing. It's p-pulling."

"Pulling? Where?"

"This way."

Chapter 32

Addi had always been a runner, had the physique for it, the legs, the lungs. He loved running trails, hard and fast, hilly or flat, the blinder the better. Growing up he'd run the trails of Kamistra, through the wooded mountains, the high passes, past streams and volcanic lakes. On hotter days he'd run by the sea, sunlit and breezy, just as now – a golden gazelle running free, until his breath ran out.

The trail from Lake Zen was narrow and full of curves – a dry, sandy track splashed with pebbles, ferns spilling out waist-high from both sides. But it didn't matter. He blazed along, oblivious to obstacles, or anyone following. He'd been so anxious to get off to a fast start, he hadn't even looked back to see where Bodessa was. He swept along a section that wove like a viper, rounding corners, ready for anything. What he got surprised him. A flap of gauzy-winged follyflies, white as lies, filled the air above him, zigzagging busybodies whispering in the wind. He wondered what they were saying. Maybe they were trying to tell him something: tales from the gossip mill. It may have been his imagination, but, amid the buzz, he thought he heard Bodessa's name, as though he was being reminded of his promise to watch out for her. As if to emphasize the point, several of the thumb-sized bugs clipped his head as they flew by. And yet, not until the trail straightened and his breath began to run out did he glance back. The blue waters of Lake Zen were now long out of sight. But not Bodessa. No more than ten paces behind, she ran easily, long, graceful strides, her usually pale complexion blushing in the sun.

They ran together taking turns to lead and by mid-sun they'd reached the edges of the Kindoo Wetlands. In the distance, across the marshes and scrubby bogs, loomed the Southern Glade, the green-lined clearing with a stream running through it. Had it only been yesterday he'd been set upon by the drooling, swivel-headed gorax? Had it not been for Bodessa throwing stones at it and the mizot battle-bird plucking out its eyes, he would have been eaten alive. But he was in no mood to dwell on it. He forced the thought from his mind. Nothing was going to spoil the thrill of their run, which had taken them a third of the way back to the castle ruin in only a quarter of the time. They could even afford a short rest. In a grove of fruit trees they stopped to pick bulloo plums. Sitting in the shade, the tangy juice quenched like bliss.

"You are quite a runner," Addi said, polishing a plum on the sleeve of his shirt.

Bodessa, about to take a bite from hers, paused. "Zentas are natural runners. We were born to it."

"What, living on an island?"

"We're natural swimmers, too."

"Yes, well, I know that."

"We have big lungs."

He glanced in the area of her chest. Her breathing was light, her skin glistened with perspiration. Within this scene of delicate recovery, he noticed that the thin chain carrying her moonstones lay askew. As if by coincidence, she straightened it. The moonstones, though, remained hidden away, bottled up down the front of her dress, a dark secret that drove his curiosity.

"Big lungs have their advantages … but your moonstones … they're really something. They seem to have a hold on you, a strange power. You said they were your mother's. Then after she died your father gave them to you?"

Bodessa took a bite from her plum. Then another. "He did," she said at last, running her tongue over her lips. "Last summer he came to me, told me to keep them safe, protect them with my life."

"What, from Bardo?"

"Bardo is happy with anything that sparkles."

"Like you."

Bodessa smiled. "That's where it gets complicated."

Addi waited for her explanation, but she just took bites from her plum. "Complicated?"

She took a breath. "My father has told me snippets. This is what I know. My mother wasn't always a Zenta. She was born Odanus, a tribe that lived, like you, by the sea. There had been a spring festival in the Southern Glade, not far from here, where my mother and father met. She liked his merry voice, the way he danced. He liked everything about her – her grace, her dark, sultry looks, even her name, Falice. Isn't that a pretty name?"

Addi nodded.

"But she had a younger sister, Tally, who was ambitious, liked my father more for his fame – the splendour of his jewels, his reputation as a mystic. She and my mother became rivals. When my father chose my mother, Tally turned sour, delved into dark magic. She became an outcast."

Bodessa was finally confiding in him. He wanted her to keep going. "What happened then?" he asked.

"My mother left her life by the sea. Moved to Castle Zen. Just before she and my father got married, Tally came to visit, intent on changing his mind. But he loved my mother. Rejected again, Tally was distraught. To try to ease her pain, my father arranged for her to meet Bardo."

"Bardo?"

"Father thought the two of them might become friends."

"And did they?"

"It was love, but on one side only. It was Tally who rejected Bardo. But not before she'd beguiled him, convinced him to steal Mother's moonstones."

"Why?"

"The Odanus moonstones are thought to hold great power; protect anyone who wears them. They also possess the gift of eternal love, whether in this life or the next – or even during the time in between. Tally thought that if she wore them, Zuma's affection would change and there would still be a chance for her."

The snippets were spilling like beans. Addi could hardly keep up. "So, under Tally's spell, Bardo took the moonstones. I thought you said he gave them back?"

"He did. When he found out Tally had been using him to punish Mother for stealing Father."

"So, was Bardo really to blame?"

"Yes and no. Under Tally's spell, he did steal the moonstones. But he was also expecting a reward for returning them. As I said before, that reward was to be me. Later, though, over too many drinks, Bardo told a Zenta noble what had happened. Zuma soon found out."

"So, what happened to Bardo?"

"For a time my father wouldn't confront him. You see, Bardo was not only my father's jeweller, he was also an expert tooth-puller, could take one out without the sufferer feeling any pain. It was a powder he used. My father isn't as brave as he likes people to think. He'd rather suffer toothache than have it pulled, unless the one pulling was Bardo. In the end, though, Bardo, who drank more and more after Tally left him, lost his touch, became clumsy. He spilled too much blood pulling the wrong tooth. It was all Father needed. He told Bardo to leave the island and never return."

"But he still comes back," Addi said. "He brings his Kroguls and his war boats."

"He is persistent."

"So, is it you he wants?"

"All I know is that on this day, fifteen summers ago, my mother died. She was visiting her family in their castle by the sea – helping them deal with problems they were having with Tally. When darkness fell, a serpent rose from the waves, killed the Odanus people and destroyed everything. There have been stories of dark magic driving the serpent on that awful night. I am more and more convinced that Tally was behind it, changing her name to Taluhla."

Addi gasped. "The Queen of the Raslatombs!"

Bodessa put her hand on her chest. "Unfortunately, the moonstones were no help to my mother. Travelling the safe way, by boat, she'd didn't think she'd need them, left them behind at Castle Zen. But I have them now. I believe they will help me find the truth, whether Tally … Taluhla, was responsible for my mother's death."

Talk of sea serpents forced Addi to his feet. It was time to go. He offered Bodessa his hand. She took it and stood. For a moment he looked into her eyes – a little tired, a sentimental tear. "Bodessa," he said softly. "Thank you for telling me this. Whatever happens today, be it serpents or Kroguls or Raslatombs … whatever the truth, we'll face it together."

Chapter 33

The manacles on Zuma's wrists nipped tight, rubbed his skin raw. After a night without sleep – holed up in a stinking dungeon cell with six of his own Zenta guards – the Kroguls had come for him. Deprived of water, he dragged his feet down the passageway, prodded in the back by a Krogul sword.

He was mad at himself, disgusted even. His ability to predict events – to warn his people of impending threats – had been the crux of his mystical powers. Admittedly, he'd not always been perfect. Only last summer, a burst of eyeball-plucking mizots had crossed the lake, blackened the skies over Castle Zen. With plated wings, they'd swooped down like squealing cats, leaving a swath of Zenta guards blind.

Still, when it came to Bardo, Zuma had always found a way – an extra sense that allowed him to anticipate the Krogul's intentions. Until now. Now, with the spell broken, not only would there be doubt about his leadership, but he couldn't escape his feelings of humiliation, reminding him of the dark days after he'd lost Falice. It was a time, fifteen summers ago, when the two moons – and the shadows they brought – had first appeared in the western sky. He'd no idea what they meant, told his people they were an aberration; that they would soon pass. They'd passed all right, but not before a great tempest had been wrought upon the sea, and his lovely wife had succumbed to the terror of the serpent. Oh, Falice, why didn't you take your moonstones like I said? No, she said, she'd gone many times before and could take care of herself. Why hadn't he insisted? Why couldn't he have saved her from all that evil?

After that, his guilt had taken him to a dark place, a self-imposed exile of loneliness and self-pity, locked away in his chamber. A hermit in his own castle. Eventually, his obligation to Andros and Bodessa had brought him out of the gloom. Since then he'd tried to erase them from his memory, but those times of bitterness and sorrow would still creep back – haunting him, just like now. And yet, being summoned to the Great Hall – his own Great Hall – having to answer to the likes of Bardo, seemed somehow worse. He'd underestimated his old enemy. It was a mistake that had left him with little bargaining power and even less hope.

Even the Zenstone on his finger was dead.

The great doors opened. As he passed through, all he could do was lift his head. If he was about to face the worst – an end to the Zenta way of life – he would do it with as much dignity as he could muster.

The walk along the blood-spattered carpet was excruciating. The jangling of his chains echoed through the hall, his eyes stung from a drift of burning incense. Barely halfway down he heard Bardo's thin, snaky voice calling out.

"Step right up, Zuma. Don't be shy." The sneering Krogul was sitting sidesaddle on the turquoise throne; his legs flopped over one of the arms. While Krogul guards loitered behind him, a handsome Zenta female attended him. It was the escort whose neckband Bardo had cut off at the banquet. She appeared uninterested, begrudging, as she squeezed the rubber bellows of a small bottle, squirting what looked like fruit juice into his mouth. The sight of the liquid heightened Zuma's thirst, but his throat was so dry he couldn't even swallow.

"That's close enough, Zuma," Bardo said, spitting out a pip. He waved the female away. Careful not to aggravate his wounded thigh, he slowly swung his legs back over the arm of the throne, stretched them out in front of him. "So, you've had time to sleep on it. What's your answer?"

"Sleep? In that black hole?"

Bardo shrugged. "It's your black hole."

"Where's my son, Andros?"

"I'm asking the questions."

"You'll get no answers until I know he's safe."

Bardo laughed, high-pitched and shrill. "You really are something, aren't you? Remind me, who's the one in charge here? And who's the one in chains?"

Silence.

Bardo sniffed sharply. "All right, forget the formalities. Where is she?"

"Andros, first."

Out from the shadows a Krogul guard aimed an arrow.

Bardo stuck a finger in his ear. "You know, Zuma, you really have become annoying." With one eye closed he drilled with his finger then pulled it out.

Zuma braced himself, felt an ultimatum coming.

"All right Zuma, you want to make a deal? We'll make a deal. Let's see, now, what could it be? Or, more to the point, what could you offer? Oh, I know. How about an exchange? I get all your treasure and Bodessa and her moonstones. In return, you get your teeth fixed. Maybe I could yank a couple."

Zuma finally swallowed. Two of his teeth were achy, but he wasn't going to let Bardo touch them, not after the last bloodbath. "I'll take Andros instead."

"Uh, keeping up the oral hygiene, are we? Good for you. At least I won't have to put up with all that screaming and whimpering." Bardo put a finger in his other ear, poking and twisting, seriously cleaning. "Anyway," he continued, taking his finger out, wiping it on the sleeve of his tunic, "the decision's made. I don't want your castle. Now, don't get me wrong, it's a mighty fortress, but it's a lot of work. Kroguls aren't big on keeping house. We prefer … well, let's just say you can keep your turrets and dungeons. You can even keep this hall. Oh, and bonus, you can keep your people, too. As I said last night, I'm not that interested in slaughter. For the time being. No, your life can continue as it was. Well, sort of … you know, once you've explained to your citizens that the coffers have been cleaned out. That all your Zenta treasure has been taken. Thinking about it, I suppose we are good at cleaning some things."

"But what about –?"

"Boats! Yes, I almost forgot. We'll need … oh, at least six of your war boats to make up for the ones you sank, plus your cargo boat to transport all that sparkling treasure. It's only fair. Besides, it'll give your boat builders something to do, you know, replace your fleet. Anyway, I think that just about does it. I'm happy."

Zuma felt shellacked. It seemed there was little else he could say that would sway Bardo into giving up Andros. Still, he had to try.

"What about my son?"

"Your son? He comes with me."

"No! I told you –"

"Stop worrying. He'll be safe … safe-ish." With his hand, Bardo appeared to brush the ear debris from his sleeve. "As soon as you honour our old deal and bring your lovely daughter to me – along with her moonstones – you'll get Andros back. Any funny business and slaughter's back on the table. You've got three suns."

Zuma glared. "Three suns? What about two moons and a serpent? In case you haven't noticed, the moons are back. And by tonight the serpent will be too."

"Not here it won't."

"Don't be so sure. Anything's possible if Tally's behind it."

Bardo's face softened. A splash of regret crossed his eyes. Then his expression stiffened. "There's nothing for her here. She made her choice a long time ago. Now she's a prisoner of her own ambition – to a sea lashed with waves of blood."

"Perhaps," said Zuma, sensing an opening. "And yet, if Tally … or should I say Taluhla, Queen of the Raslatombs, has her way, then Bodessa, like her mother, will be the next prize victim. My daughter and the moonstones will be gone forever."

"That's why I'm letting you live. If you want your son back, you'd better get to your daughter before tonight's bloodletting."

"She's long gone. But if we had boats there's a chance we might get there in time."

Bardo folded his arms, sighed deeply. "All right, Zuma, I'll tell you what. I'll give you one boat. You and no more than five of your guards take the sea channel. Go and find Bodessa, bring her to me and I'll give you Andros.

In a confusion of manacles and chains Zuma held up his wrists. "I must leave now."

Bardo nodded to the guard with the key.

Chapter 34

"Groff, we seem to be going round in circles," Tarro said, flicking a solarbug off his nose.

"The w-wayfinder says we're going s-southwest," Groff said. "According to Noggin, it's the w-way to Castle Zen."

"There's no way of knowing," Sinjun added. "The terrain's all the same."

They were caught in a drift of sun-baked gullies – clumps of trees, juts of rock – a twist, a turn, one after the other.

"So what do we do?" said Tarro, forgetting for a moment it was his decision to make.

"You're asking me?" Sinjun replied. "We could be in the Masadian Wilderness for all I know."

"That may not be so mythological," Tarro said, smacking another solarbug. The yellow pyro-critter with its flat back magnifyer had scorched a patch of fur from his arm.

"There's no other t-trail," said Groff. "It has to lead s-somewhere."

"As long as it doesn't bring us back to the same spot," Tarro said. "We're running out of time." He guessed they'd already gone too far to get back to the castle ruin before sunfall. If they found Addi, at least that would be something. But if they didn't and did not make it back in time to fight the serpent, the mission would be a disaster.

"What!" Tarro exclaimed as they reached the brink of the gully and looked down into another. The groups of rocks and trees were almost identical. "We're getting nowhere."

While Sinjun swigged from his water pouch, Groff fiddled with his wayfinder. He seemed agitated, turning the gadget this way and that.

"You sure it works?" Tarro asked.

Groff tightened a sliding bar, then angled the wayfinder a few degrees to his left. "There could be another t-trail, crossing the m-main one."

"And I could be standing on water," Sinjun said, sarcastically. "What are you, anyway, some sort of conjurer of secret paths?"

Groff didn't answer. He put the wayfinder on the ground, reached into his bag and pulled out his spygoggles. "There is a t-trail," he said, adjusting the focus with a small wheel.

"Here, give me that!" said Sinjun, extending his hand. "Let me see."

Groff shrugged him off, continued to peer through the goggles.

"What kind of trail is it?" asked Tarro. "Is it clear? Accessible?"

"L-looks like it," Groff said. "Wait … there's s-something m-moving."

Tarro's heart stopped. So far they'd avoided really vicious creatures. "How do you mean, something?"

"It's r-running."

"Here, let me see that."

Groff handed him the goggles.

Holding them steady, Tarro scanned the gully down to the left of the main trail. The view through the lens wasn't clear. But he could see another trail, overgrown. Something was moving.

"What is it?" asked Sinjun.

Tarro waited for whatever it was to run into the open. "I'm not sure, but it's not …" His voice trailed off. "It's more like …" Suddenly he felt woozy. His hands started to shake. Through the gaps in the trees, he could see not one, but two figures running – a female, with dark hair, and a male with flowing yellow hair. He lowered the goggles, rubbed his eyes. He'd always believed he'd find his friend. Even after they'd been separated in the Dark Wood, swarming with Raslatombs, he'd never lost faith. And yet, the odds … maybe he'd only seen what he wanted to see – the strain of adventure leaving its mark, his imagination a bit too lively. He raised the goggles again. No. They were still there, like two birds, free and easy, running together as if they'd never taken a breath.

"You're s-smiling," said Groff.

Unable to speak, Tarro nodded.

"Is it Addi?" asked Sinjun, stiffly.

Tarro nodded again. "And he's got the young female."

* * *

The rough trail they'd been travelling on decended into a gully with a main trail running across it. As they neared the junction, Addi slowed to a walk. He was hot and could smell the sweat that dampened his shirt. With Bodessa next to him, this was not a good thing.

He looked up. The sun was high. No clouds. So far, though, the moons hadn't shown themselves. As soon as they did, the real race would be on.

"We're making good time," he said. "We can walk up the other side."

"To the Kindoo Wetlands," said Bodessa. "There'll be a pool there to bathe in."

She could smell him.

They reached the point where the trails crossed. Given that they'd seen no living thing since escaping the vipersnipers, it seemed silly to stop to see if anything was coming. But Addi's madcap ways had changed. He was more cautious. He looked left – a rocky treed gully likely leading back to Castle Zen – and then right – a rocky treed gully with … what on earth? Three figures charging towards them!

"Bodessa!" he cried. "Go back! Hide!" He pulled his knife, ready to make a stand. But as the trio drew close, the one leading waved. More unlikely, he wore a blue tunic with the crest of a Circle Dwarfgiant. Tarro's tunic was blue. Was it possible? The chances were as remote as the gully they'd entered, and yet, as the Dwarfgiant approached, it was clearly him.

Addi dropped his knife. "Tarro!" he cried, joy rising in his chest. He sprang forward, ran towards his friend. He hadn't far to go – about twenty paces – just a few strides before they'd be together again, sharing stories, catching up. But sometimes, euphoria can turn dark, even at the height of day. And in the time it takes to play a trick, the air turned putrid. Not the smell of his own sweat, or the boggy marshland that lay just over the hill, but a choking stench coming out of the ground, the soft, peaty soil in front of him. Five paces from Tarro, he stopped. Tarro stopped too, and the other two Dwarfgiants. A cloud rose up between them, thick, swirly and black, pushing his friend farther away.

"Addi," Tarro called out. "Nice way to greet a friend. What's happening?"

Before he could answer – a cry from the sky. A bird with red eyes mourned a broken whistle. Above the bird, the two moons, separated only by shadows, had vanquished the sun.

Where had they come from? It didn't matter. It had begun, the unstoppable lunar convergence, a cycle that had started fifteen summers earlier, only to end later that night with the serpent of the Sulphur Sea. Would they live to see it? Survive to help Myvan defend the ruin?

Through the billowing stink he could hear Tarro, spluttering. "Groff, in your bag. Anything we can use?" There was clatter, pieces of wood spilled, but nothing else. For his part, Addi couldn't think of anything that might bring the foul wall down, except …

He swung around. Bodessa was at it again, back in her otherworld, eyes transfixed, moonstones exposed. More celestial magic? Yes! He looked up. The liquid whistle broke. The red-eyed bird fell from the sky. In the consoling heavens, the shadows hugged the moons. Then the wall collapsed, the black mist folding in on itself, sucked back into the earth – gone except for the popping of putrid bubbles.

Addi glanced at Bodessa. Now more normal, her eyes clear, she tucked the moonstones back down the front of her dress. Back to their secret place.

"Addi!" said Tarro, jumping across the churned earth, extending his arms. "We've been searching all over for you."

"We got sidetracked," Addi replied, receiving the strong, one-handed hug.

"I can see that," said Tarro, releasing his grip, moving back a step. "Still, it's good to see you. We'd almost given up."

"Glad you didn't. You've hurt your shoulder? Was that from the Raslatombs?"

Tarro put his hand on his wound, gave a token wince. "I'll live."

"You'd better," said Addi. "Seems we have a serpent to fight."

"How do you know that?"

"A mystic Zenta told me."

"Zuma, right?"

Addi frowned. "How did you know?"

"A little Loggerhead told me," said Tarro. He cast his eyes on Bodessa. "Said there was a mystic Zenta who had a daughter who looked just like …"

Bodessa stepped forward, stood at Addi's side. "Well, Tarro," said Addi, "your little Loggerhead – whatever that is – was right. Allow me to introduce Bodessa, daughter of Zuma the Mystic Zenta. You may remember her as the one tied to the Raslatombs' bed of wooden stakes."

"I remember," Tarro replied, his eyes stuck on Bodessa. It was the first time he'd seen a furless creature up close. "I'm heartened to see you safe."

She walked towards him. "Tarro, I'm glad we've finally met so I can thank you for being so brave." Careful to avoid his wounded shoulder, she put her arms around him and hugged.

Addi couldn't remember being hugged by her.

Tarro's face turned red. "We would never have left you at the mercy of Taluhla, or those goat-headed Raslatombs."

Addi was amused. He remembered how much coaxing it had taken to get his friend just to investigate the scream. "Bodessa's coming back with us to the castle ruin," he said. "Castle Zen has been overrun."

"Who by?" said Tarro, his face returning to its normal colour.

"Kroguls."

"Who are they?"

"It's a long story," Addi said. "I'll tell you about it on our way back." He was eyeing the two Dwarfgiants standing on either side of Tarro. The strapping one, fully armed with sword, knife and bamboozie, he knew of, had seen before. The other, the bony one down on his knees stuffing wooden gadgets into a bag, wasn't so familiar.

Tarro turned to introduce them. "You may know Sinjun, the amourer's son? As you can see, he's strong and fit, got the fighting skills to match. Groff, here … well … he was picked by lottery."

"Picked?"

"Both are candidates to fill Lucus's Circle position."

"Really?" said Addi. It was odd, the two couldn't have looked more different. He wondered why he hadn't been considered. Had he missed his opportunity?

"Along with yourself," said Tarro, smiling.

A surge of pride shot through him. "A candidate? Me? How?"

"The decision will be made on our return to the ruin. I'll explain as we go."

"Well, then," said Addi, "we'd best get going."

Groff smiled wryly, slung his bag over his shoulder. Sinjun, who'd been busy watching Bodessa, turned and gave a cold stare.

"Right," said Tarro, "let's be off." He looked this way and that, but didn't seem to know which way to go.

Addi put his arm around his friend. Spoke confidentially. "If we continue along this rough trail, it will take us out of the gully and to the Kindoo Wetlands. By then, we'll be halfway back. But we need to watch the moons. Keep pace. Or we'll be too late. Bodessa will lead the way. Come on!"

Bodessa started out. But the others, their faces filled with doubt, followed slowly. Addi guessed it was because they weren't used to being led by a female. He knew better.

Chapter 35

Myvan grimaced. The emberlea on his knees had worn off. The painkiller had got him through the night and most of the morning, but now, in need of more, his supply had run out. Still, he had to keep going, make sure Dwarfgiants didn't see their leader hobbling about like some worn-out cripple. Pushing on his stick, he stepped onto a wet ledge overlooking the entrance to the moat.

"You all right?" said Revel, his face glistening with sea spray.

"I have to be," Myvan replied, "at least until after tonight."

"The night of nights," said Revel, remembering the words of the Odanus scribe.

Myvan remembered too. Especially the last part: *Taluhla tolled her victory, the moontide ran its spree. Beware the mighty devil snake, serpent of the Sulphur Sea.*

"Can we dam the moat in time?" Myvan asked.

After thinking for a moment, Revel replied, "Well, the tide is about to turn. But it won't be easy."

"How deep is the water?"

"Right now, high tide … six body lengths."

"Hmm. Deep enough for a serpent. What about low tide?"

"One."

"Where's Havoc?"

"Still fixing the north wall."

"Is he nearly finished?"

Revel shook his head. "To do it right will take the rest of the day."

Myvan winced, gazed out to sea. Should he pull Havoc's work gang from the north wall and continue with the moat? Could they dam it before the night tide returned? As he tried to decide, he felt the urge to look over his shoulder. He turned. In the distance, even in sunlight, the Dark Wood lay heavy like a brooding monster. Where were Tarro and the search party? He could have really used their help: his son's ability to change up, Sinjun's strength. Even Groff – there had to be something he could do. Obviously, finding Addi would be an extra joy, but right now he needed bodies, as many as he could get.

Suddenly, his breath tightened. Beyond the Dark Wood, to the far west – something faint, something spectral hung in the sky. The moons – dual spheres soon to be one – appeared, bringing with them grave helpings of shadows and death. As he leaned on his stick, his thoughts were as painful as his knees.

"Myvan … what do you intend to do?"

All he could think was that if the serpent breached the moat, the north wall wouldn't matter. So, that was it, his best stab, and with as much conviction as he could muster, he said, "Dam the moat."

CHAPTER 36

Milo yawned until his eyes watered. After a late night decoying and dodging Kroguls, he and Flogg had slept long into the morning. Outside their sand-bunkered hideout the day was well underway – a keen breeze off Lake Zen, the sun already high above them. Odd, though, the circle of gold looked strangely wishy-washy, as if it had melted itself.

"All clear?" said Flogg, sticking his head out.

"Not a dicky bird," Milo replied, looking both ways down the rolling dunes.

"The Kroguls must be somewhere," Flogg said.

"Probably doing torture up at the castle. It's a fine day for it."

"You and nail-pulling. You're fixated."

"I don't like Kroguls."

"Yeah, well, they could smell better. Look, Milo, we've got to find Zuma. Let him know Bodessa's safe."

"How do we do that, storm the battlements?"

"Funny! No, I was thinking more … wait, what was that?"

On the other side of the sandhill, a flurry of voices echoed down the cove.

Milo crouched down. "Kroguls?"

"Sounds like it," said Flogg. "Go take a look."

"Me?"

"Hurry!"

Flat on his stomach, Milo crawled up the slope, stopped just short of the top. On the other side he could hear hoots all the way to the docks.

"Must be them," he said, turning to Flogg.

Flogg slithered up beside him. "Wonder what they're up to."

Milo flipped onto his back, brushed sand from his shirt.

"Well, go on then!" said Flogg.

"What?"

"Take a look. Then report back."

"Report back? I only have to lift my head."

"Exactly. Don't let them see you."

"What if they do?"

"Don't let them."

"How do I do that?"

"Use your instincts."

Milo thought about it. But he wasn't sure. There were so many voices, so close, jabbering like barbarians.

"Look, Milo, I'll tell you what. Take a peek over the top. Slowly. If you get spotted, and you won't, but, if you do, just remember we're in this together."

"What, we both run?"

"We'll think of something."

Milo shook his head. Story of his life: always the one testing for poison. "All right, I'll do it. But I'm telling you right now, if we get caught … if we get tortured, they'd better not hammer my shins. Because if they do …"

Flogg crept to the top of the hill.

"Hey!" said Milo. "What are you doing? I'm supposed to do that."

"Shhh! Come take a look."

Back on his stomach, Milo clawed up the sand to join him. He lifted his head and peeked over. He gasped. There were Kroguls, all right, floods of them, hauling boxes and caskets and chests down the trail to a squat cargo boat, the largest vessel in the Zenta fleet.

"Zuma's treasure," said Flogg. "They're cleaning house."

Not all of it was concealed. Some boxes had been pried open: mountains of jewels, pieces of silver sprinkled onto the trail. Some Kroguls – the screeching ones – wore crowns. Others donned studded belts and rubied chains. A flash pierced Milo's eyes – the glint from a golden nugget.

"It's Zuma's treasure, all right. But where is Zuma?"

Flogg shook his head. "Depends on what kind of mood Bardo's in. By the look of all that loot, the Krogul may have let him off lightly – a yanked fingernail or a tooth. Then again …"

A scuffle broke out – four Kroguls tugging at a plate emblazoned with emeralds. A whip cracked. The melee stopped. Down the trail came the beat of drums, an armed guard. Milo eased up onto his knees.

"Get down!" said Flogg.

"Nobody's looking at us. They've got their eyes on … well, well, well. I'll give you one guess."

"Zuma?"

Flogg was on his knees too.

Even in the middle of an armed escort, Zuma stood out; his studded belt harness, his shaved head held high – a look more of victory than defeat. He even walked freely, wasn't chained. So where was he going? Five other Zentas were with him, familiar faces, armed with sword and bow. But there was no Andros. Zuma's son must have been kept prisoner.

As the Krogul guard led them past the cargo boat, Zuma didn't even glance at his treasure being loaded on. They marched on to the main docks, halted at the gangway of a familiar vessel.

"Well, look at that," said Milo. "Zuma's about to board our boat."

"We need to join him, get on board too," Flogg said. "Come on!"

Milo knew the sandhills around the cove like he knew Krogul tortures – every cut, every spike. First, he boarded up the hideout – a hole under a ridge – and covered it with sand. Then he was off, tramping through a channel of dunes, the sand whistling underfoot.

"We're close," said Flogg. "Stop at the gap. See where we stand."

They reached the gap, peered around a lopsided boulder. The Zentas had boarded the boat. Only Zuma lingered on the gangplank, telling the Krogul-in-command something that sounded like a threat, something about Andros. The Krogul ignored him.

"We'd better get moving," said Flogg.

"How do we get aboard?" Milo said.

"We swim."

Zuma was still yapping at the Krogul.

"Now!" said Flogg, starting to run.

Head down, Milo followed. They crossed the gap, past Zuma's Rock and the storage racks at the far end of the dock. From behind the repair shed they watched Zuma finally go aboard, followed by two Zentas who pulled in the gangplank. Ashore, a Krogul unfastened the tie rope and pushed the boat off with the end of his spear.

"Ready?" said Flogg. "Come on, get those shoes off!"

Milo unbuckled them, threw off his coat. "So how do we get on board without the Kroguls spotting us?"

Flogg was testing the water with his feet. "The fishing net. The one we always leave hanging over the side. But we have to time it perfectly."

"How's the water?" said Milo.

"Swimmable."

It was freezing! So cold Milo thought his heart would stop. Underwater, he swam as far as he could. He bobbed up, then Flogg. The boat veered towards them – the mainsail in a flutter – but he could still see Kroguls back on the docks, which meant they could see him. He took a breath and went under again. In a froth of bubbles he and Flogg watched the shadow of the hull approach. *We have to time it perfectly,* Flogg had said, referring to the moment they had to break the water and grab hold of the net. But Milo's breath ran out. Kicking frantically he reached the surface, luckily, just as the boat was passing. He lunged, and, with his left hand, caught a piece of net and hung on. But Flogg missed. Fell back in the water.

Milo, stuck out his right hand. "Take it!"

This time Flogg didn't miss. He was able to grab Milo's hand and leg.

Milo wasn't sure how long he could hold on to the net. Flogg's feet were dragging in the water and, with its mainsail full, the boat was speeding up. Time to take a risk.

"Help!" he shouted, hoping the Zentas on board would hear and not the Kroguls on shore. Moments passed and nothing, except for Flogg's grunts and the rush of water.

Then from above, a voice called out, "Well, I'll be a duck in thunder!"

Milo tilted his head upwards. Zuma was leaning over the side, looking down.

"Looks like we've got ourselves a catch," bellowed the Mystic Zenta. "Hold on! We'll haul you in."

Chapter 37

"So you see," Addi said, his voice rising triumphantly at the end of his story, "already it's been an adventure for the chronicles: the gorax, the battle of Lake Zen, Zuma, Bardo and his Kroguls."

For some moments Tarro didn't answer. Instead he looked ahead, content, it seemed, to watch Bodessa scramble up a slant of rocks. "She seems sure of herself," he said at last. "You could say *liberated*."

Addi didn't say anything.

"She's also very shapely."

"Ah!" said Addi.

Tarro turned quickly. "What?"

"It's just that Bodessa, well … she's … she's starlight … vapours of musk. We've been together for two suns, looking out for each other, staying alive. We've held hands, we've danced. And yet, throughout that time, she's kept her feelings to herself, remained more or less a mystery."

Of course he wasn't going to tell his friend what he *did* know about her, that her secrets had started to unravel. Not yet, anyway.

"Mystery?" said Tarro. "I was talking about her … wait, you've fallen for her!"

"Well, yes. But there's a lot more to her than meets the eye. She's very determined and has a strong spirit of adventure. Except for vipersnipers, she's quite fearless."

"Huh."

It was time to change the subject. "So, Tarro, tell me your story. Looks like you've had quite the adventure, too – blood on your tunic, on your arm. And what is a Loggerhead?"

"The blood on my pants is from a nosebleed – when I changed up a second time. The blood on my arm … well, my arrow wound has been slow to heal. As for the Loggerheads …" He glanced over his shoulder. "It'll take too long to tell. Sinjun and Groff are behind us. I can't look to be playing favourites."

"You changed up a second time?"

Tarro winced. "How I didn't blow out my arm I don't know," he said. "Had to move a giant boulder. I will tell you about it, but right now I'm going to drop back, have Sinjun and Groff come up front. That way I can keep an eye on all three candidates. I'm so glad we found you."

Addi smiled. "And we can keep an eye on Bodessa."

A shriek cut the air.

Up ahead, Bodessa was sliding backwards down the rock face. She bounced off a lip at the bottom, hitting the ground heavily.

Addi ran.

He reached her first. Face down, she lay still. Her dress was lifted, torn up the side. Her leg scraped with blood.

"How is she?" asked Tarro, arriving with Sinjun and Groff.

"I don't know," Addi said, straightening her dress. "Help me turn her over." He took her shoulders, Tarro, her legs. "Gently."

She lay on her back. Except for a covering of dust and a graze on her chin, her face was unmarked. Her eyes, though – those onyx gems – remained closed.

"What are th-those?" said Groff, pointing.

Bodessa's moonstones had slipped out of her dress.

"They're … they were her mother's." Addi dampened a cloth with water and smoothed her brow. "Bodessa, can you hear me?"

Nothing.

"She's knocked herself out," Tarro said.

Addi looked for a bump. Found it under the strands of hair above her temple. *Bodessa, what have you done? I promised to look out for you, and you do this.*

"What now?" said Tarro.

"You keep going," Addi said. "We're running out of time. I'll stay with her. When she comes around we'll catch up."

"What if she doesn't?"

A pang filled Addi's heart. He looked down at her. "She will. I know she will."

Silence.

"T-take her with us," said Groff.

"There's no time to build a stretcher," said Addi. "You go. I'll stay."

"S-Sinjun can carry her. He's s-strong enough."

Sinjun stood bulging like a tree.

"What do you say, Sinjun?" said Tarro. "Are you up for it?"

"It would be like carrying a baby."

Addi didn't like the sound of that, didn't like the idea of Bodessa being carried by someone else – especially a rival with muscles to spare. But was there a choice? He could carry her, had done it before, but only for a short distance. Tarro couldn't do it, not with his wounded arm, and Groff, he could barely carry himself.

"Very well," Tarro said. "Sinjun it is."

Re-slinging his weapons behind his back, the strongman lifted Bodessa into his arms. As he did, her jet-black hair, loosened from its clip, fell halfway to the ground. She looked delicate, vulnerable. And the scrape on her leg shone bright with blood.

"I have to patch her leg," Addi said.

"Let m-me do that," Groff said, fishing two Jabunga leaves out of his bag.

"Hold them in place, Groff," Tarro said, jumping in. "I'll fasten them."

As Addi watched her being fussed over – secure in the hands of everyone but himself – he felt strangely unfit. It was as if he was losing part of what he and Bodessa had become: a couple – united by stars, driven by adventure, sometimes running for their lives, other times leaning on the edge of romance; at all times, caring for each other. Already, he missed her. Prayed she would open her dark, beautiful eyes. But she lay in Sinjun's arms, fixed in a cold swoon, absent from the world. Addi swallowed hard. If only he could have changed up, become twice his normal size, he'd have had the strength to carry her. As his frustration grew, he vowed to himself that by the time they got back to the ruin, he'd be the one selected to join the Circle.

"Lead the way, Addi," said Tarro. "Find a way around those rocks."

With a heavier step, Addi set off. He kept to the trail. It was a longer way around, but soon they were skirting the Kindoo Wetlands. The vast, water-pooled landscape was alive. In the tasselled reed jungles, glugs gulped, snakes rattled, birds squawked – flew in sequence, in clusters, in couples, alone. Bands of follyflies darted overhead, whispering as they went by. But Addi ignored them. He tramped past the marsh pond where he'd gone for a dip after being attacked by the gorax. It was still full of lilies and reed grass, smelled of mud and watermint. He looked back to see if the aroma might have aroused Bodessa. But no, her head was still lolling sideways, bobbing slightly with each step Sinjun took.

Under the pale sun they pushed on, all the while keeping an eye skyward. Up ahead, the moons had already reached the Southern Glade. If the Dwarfgiants were to make it back to the ruin in time, they'd need to catch up.

Addi wondered how.

CHAPTER 38

Evil raked the walls of Bodessa's nightmare. Heads with horns, cankered faces, Raslatombs – toothless and hunched – spewed chants ... low ... discordant ... choking.

She exhaled – more a gasp, loud as a siren.

The chanting stopped. She'd been seen.

Heart screaming, she ran through the trees. But the wood was thick and tangled and her legs were heavy, like logs. She glanced behind – a gang of goatheads, shrieking, chasing her down. Hide the moonstones ... in a hole, in a tree. On a trail going nowhere she was cornered; grey spiked hands pawed and grappled, snapped her up.

* * *

Myvan looked down from the crumbling ramparts. He felt anxious, ground his teeth. The tide had finally gone out, leaving a quagmire of mudflats. Only a few hours and the waves would return with the serpent. Down at the moat's entrance he could see Havoc standing on a platform, bellowing instructions, his exhausted work party blocking the opening – mallets hammering, setting posts and boards and beams.

Revel stood to Myvan's right. "The dam should hold the force of the sea," he said, sounding hopeful.

"Perhaps," Myvan said. "Will it be enough to stop the serpent?"

"Do you think it will come?"

Myvan looked over his shoulder. The moons were closing in. Already, above the Dark Wood, they looked unstoppable. "Count on it," he said. "As soon as the moons join, we'll need everyone in position. How many bamboozies do we have?"

"Over a hundred. Hopefully it's enough."

The sky darkened, smothered the fainting sun. A scream rang out. Myvan turned back to the moat. A construction ladder was toppling, crashing down. Two workers flew off. Both lay in puddles, still as night.

Myvan looked on in disbelief.

"Overworked, overtired," Revel said. "It was bound to happen."

"A bad omen," Myvan said, gravely. "Very bad."

* * *

Bodessa breathed hard, terror rising in her chest. It was getting close to the end … the last gasp. She tried to stop it – forcing her breath, in, out, in, out – but it had taken hold … *they* had taken hold: the rough, hard boned hands that gripped her arms and legs, the chants that drowned her fading hope.

She wished it to end – a flash of light, a return to darkness – anything but this. But it wouldn't stop. She was strapped to a bed of wooden stakes; the points were punching through her dress, digging into her back.

Out of the mist came a dark shape – a tall, horned thing, half flesh, half bone, waving a long blade. The knife edge, bright by moonlight, made its sacrificial way to the altar of spikes, made the nightmare real. Bodessa wanted to scream again, but couldn't.

Mother! Mother! I'm still searching!

Her lips moved but no sound came out. All she could do in her last moments was to pray that her moonstones woundn't be found.

CHAPTER 39

Chasing the moons, the old boat lunged into the freshening waves. In the shade of the billowing sail, Milo stood shivering, dripping wet. Next to him, Flogg dripped too.

Zuma, accompanied by five Zentas, stood facing them. "That was daring," he said, his voice oozing approval. "Swimming out, catching the net, didn't know you two had it in you."

"Your trusted servant," Flogg said, with a bow of his head. "When it comes to the well-being of your daughter, there's no risk too great."

Milo cringed. There was Flogg again. Anybody would think he acted alone; he certainly liked to take the credit.

Zuma's eyes widened. "You know something about Bodessa?"

"We helped her escape," Milo blurted.

Flogg nudged him with an elbow as if to say I'm doing the talking. "She and the Dwarfgiant took a boat and crossed the lake. The Kroguls gave chase but we distracted them, acted as a decoy."

"So she's safe?" said Zuma.

"Unless she fell off a cliff," Milo joked, but then realized it probably wasn't funny.

Zuma frowned, asked Flogg, "Was she all right?"

"She was upset that you and Andros had been captured. But happy enough being with that Dwarfgiant."

"Good."

There was a pause. And while Zuma appeared to be thinking things over, Milo wondered why the Mystic Zenta asked so many questions. With his visionary powers, wasn't he supposed to know about such things, especially when it came to Bardo? Why hadn't Zuma known more about the well-being of his daughter? Just as important, in the teeth-chattering cold, why wasn't he offering a dry towel and a warm drink? Flogg wasn't helping; he kept asking questions.

"My lord, Zuma, we were surprised you'd been given our boat. Did Bardo set you free? Where's Andros?"

Zuma sprung a bitter smile. "We've been released conditionally. Bardo's holding Andros for ransom. He wants Bodessa and those confounded moonstones. If we don't deliver within three suns, I cringe to think what might happen to my son."

"Three suns?" said Flogg. "What do you intend to do?"

"Find her, of course. She and Addi are likely travelling overland to the coast, to the old castle ruin. We must get there by nightfall."

"Is it possible?" asked Flogg.

"Depends. We're taking the Southern Extremities to the Sulphur Sea. If we get a prevailing wind, we have a chance."

"And if we don't?"

Zuma sighed. "We'd better. The serpent takes no prisoners."

Milo's teeth began to chatter, his knees were shaking out of control.

"Well, don't just stand there," Zuma said. "Get below and dry off. Then, after you've had some dogfish soup, you can both row."

Chapter 40

The moons were blinding but Bodessa squinted into the glare. She preferred not to see the skin-torn creature raise the knife. Only the chants – Death! Death! Death! – made her eyes fill with tears, red tears, running down her face onto her frock. If that wasn't enough, a new pain throbbed above her temple … and another … a raw scratch, down her leg, burning like an open wound.

* * *

Addi picked up the pace. Past the Kindoo Wetlands they approached the scrubby fields leading to the Southern Glade. Gorax country. He felt queasy. The last thing he needed was to run into another swivel-head at snack time. He scanned the barren terrain: flat and soggy, clumps of grass, brown as mud. But nothing moved – a good sign. Then his breath stopped.

Eeeeaah!

The squeal echoed in the distance, high in the pines of the Southern Glade. Was it the mizot, the great battle-bird that plucked out eyes?

"What was th-that?" asked Groff, tramping behind.

"Whatever it is," Addi replied, "we need to be ready."

"Might b-be a m-mizot."

Addi stopped and turned. "You know about mizots?"

"From stories my f-father told me."

"What does your father do?"

"He's a c-carpenter. But he knows folklore and m-myth."

"There's nothing mythological about a mizot."

Groff smiled, pointed to the reddish-brown circles around his eyes. "That's w-why I have repellent."

"Mizot repellent?" Addi said. "I wondered what reeked."

Groff dropped his bag to the ground. He pulled out the small wooden box and lifted the lid.

"Ugh!" Addi recoiled, covered his face with his hand.

"Would you l-like some?" Groff said, cheerily.

Eeeeaah!

The sound from the high pines filled the boggy air. Was it a warning or a battlecry?

Keeping his distance from Groff and his repellent, Addi waited for Sinjun and Tarro to catch up. While Sinjun carried Bodessa, Tarro carried an air of concern. For Addi, there was no bigger concern than Bodessa. It was hard for him to look at her, so helpless, in someone else's arms. She was clearly breathing, and though there was colour in her cheeks, her face was creased with torment: crazed mutterings, jibberish in a bad, bad dream.

"Something wrong, Addi?" asked Tarro.

"I think we have a mizot."

"What, the bird that's supposed to pluck out eyes?"

"Believe me, Tarro, that's exactly what it does. And it doesn't care who its victim is. Somewhere out there, there's a blind gorax running around."

Tarro's face turned pale. "See anything, Groff?"

Groff aimed his spygoggles in the direction of the Southern Glade. Slowly, he turned the focusing wheel. "There is something. In a tree. Something large, something d-dark. And the branches are filled with small b-birds, a thousand black dots."

"Right," said Tarro. "We all put on Groff's repellent."

"I don't think so," said Sinjun. "The stuff stinks. Anyway, I've got my hands full with the female."

"Then put her down."

Sinjun didn't move.

"I'm not keen either," said Addi. "We don't even know if it works."

"We don't know that it doesn't."

"Tarro," said Addi, "there's got to be another way."

"Like what? We have no cover. If we're caught in the open, we're done for."

"Not necessarily. I thought we might –"

"Repellent! My decision is final."

Addi grimaced. It was one thing to have to put the stuff on; it was another to have to deal with a bossy Tarro. He wasn't used to it.

"Put Bodessa down," Tarro said to Sinjun.

As Groff offered the box, Sinjun glowered.

* * *

Dazzling moons and death chants were all very well as distractions, but Bodessa's imagination could only hold out so long. Soon, the knife's blade would arch over her, cut her defences, have its way. Her heart pounded as a dark figure filled the moonlight. Her mother's sister, now Taluhla, Queen of the Raslatombs, snarled like some carnival monster: painted circles, face peeling, lips foaming. In no mood for mercy. The blade was lifted high, and when the ghoul's quivering jaw opened, its teeth shook – all three of them.

* * *

"I'll take her," Addi said, holding out his arms.

"Don't worry yourself," Sinjun replied. "She's in good hands."

Addi wasn't convinced. He could see that Sinjun was holding her as if she belonged to him. "Look, Sinjun, I appreciate you carrying Bodessa this far, but she is ... well ... she and I are what you might call ... close friends. She knows my voice. I can talk to her. She might come around."

"Talk to her from there."

"No," Addi said. "You don't understand. She needs to feel a familiar presence."

Eeeeaah! Eeeeaah!

In the far-off trees the mizot was getting jumpy. The haunting squeal of the battle-bird seemed to unsettle Sinjun. He lowered Bodessa onto a nearby patch of grass.

* * *

The release from misery came with screams. But not Bodessa's screams, she had no more to give. It was the horned creatures, chased by a furry giant wielding a tree branch – one whose friendly face had surely come to save her. At that moment, darkness changed to light, her nightmare left behind – the knife's edge, the bed of stakes – to lie on soft grass, to awaken to the warmth of the sun. Only a few irritants lingered – a sore leg, a thick head, a pungent smell. As she opened her eyes, the first thing she saw was Addi. Like the first time he'd rescued her, his eyes shone down with happiness. But his face was covered in goo. Smelly goo.

Chapter 41

Addi was amazed by Bodessa. In keeping with her knack of making quick recoveries, she was soon on her feet, even if a little groggy.

"Addi, where am I?" she said, making sure her moonstones were safe around her neck. "How did I get here?"

"You had a fall, it knocked you out. Had some bad dreams, but here you are, awake with just a scraped leg and –"

"I carried you," said Sinjun.

Addi felt Bodessa's look, one that said, So it wasn't you?

"Well, thank you, Sinjun," she said. "I promise it will be the last time I'll be a burden."

While Addi took some satisfaction from this, Sinjun looked disappointed. He was eager, it seemed, to further prove himself: to carry Bodessa across the mire of the wetlands to the Southern Glade – even as she daubed herself with mizot repellent.

"If you weaken," Sinjun added, "let me know. I'll be happy to carry you."

"Phew!" she said, her lovely eyes crinkling. "This repellent's strong."

"We'll need all the help we can muster," Tarro said, scanning the landscape. "Grave swamps, sucking sands. But we have to make up time, so keep moving. Groff, you go first. Use your spygoggles. Sinjun, you're second, have your bamboozie ready. Bodessa, if you're fit to walk, you're third. Addi next. I'll go last. When we reach the Southern Glade we'll see about getting this repellent off."

Addi liked Tarro's confidence – this new trait in his friend – but he also knew their odds of reaching the Glade were even at best. He could only hope that whatever evil they might face would be part of an adventure he'd live to tell about.

For a while they meandered along a soft peat trail, the one that he and Bodessa had taken a sun earlier after the gorax attack. He stayed close behind her, promised himself he'd do a better job looking out for her. She had a slight limp, but the Jabunga leaves held fast to the nasty scrape on her leg.

She hadn't said much since she'd awoken from her fall. Still, there'd been joy all around with new admirers Sinjun, Groff and even Tarro fussing over her with offers of food, water and a helping hand. As for himself, he was relieved she'd come back from what seemed, at times, like a dark place. Twice, as Sinjun carried her, she'd cried out as if in some tortured state. But if she had anything more to tell – any more secrets to reveal – she was again keeping them to herself. She seemed happy to see him, had given him an amiable smile, but not much more. As far as her affections for him went, maybe he'd have to start all over again.

Suddenly she dropped back. "Can you explain something to me?"

Addi glanced back. Walking some paces behind, Tarro was out of earshot. "What is it?" he replied.

"Zentas have fair hair," she began. "I have black hair because my mother was born Odanus. As for Dwarfgiants, it looks to be the opposite; Tarro, Groff, Sinjun, all have short, brown, curly hair. You have long, straight, fair hair. I wondered why."

"I wondered when you'd ask. Most Dwarfgiants do have brown hair. But in my case my father's hair was fair."

"Was he a Dwarfgiant?"

This wasn't Addi's favourite story, but for the sake of being open about things he decided to tell Bodessa. "He was a nomadic fisherman, an occasional visitor to the shores of Kamistra, the island we used to live on. My mother met him at, of all places, the fish market. He had a stall there. Sold gumplefish."

"A delicacy."

"So they say. Anyway, my mother visited him often and soon she was expecting me."

"I see. Where is he now?"

"The idea of becoming a father didn't appeal to him. Soon after my mother told him, he set sail. She never saw him again. I never saw him at all."

"I'm sorry. What about your mother?"

"She died a few summers later. She was in the sea, wading, stood on a venomous prickler."

"Oh, no!"

"My mother was Myvan's sister. He tried everything to save her, to find a cure. One was found, but too late to help her. Today, the Jabunga leaf saves many lives. In her memory, the leaf was named after her."

"A bittersweet story."

"It's the reason I have fair hair, and why I was adopted by Myvan and Claris, Tarro's parents."

"Still, you're not a member of the Circle."

"Traditionally, the Circle is all male. You can only become a member if your father was one."

"You might be the first one with fair hair."

"We'll see," said Addi.

Halfway across the mire they reached an area pitted with swamps, bog-holes skimmed with green slime. "Watch your step," Addi called out. "One slip and you'll be chasing your last breath."

Ready for anything they kept to a trail that lacked any real definition yet somehow went forward. So far it had been quiet. No more creepy calls from the mizot. Now, though, black wings flapped in a swamp – common croobs, yellow beaks dripping blood, feasting on chunks of flesh. Nearing the fray, the carnage was plain to see. The gorax, blind and done for, was being picked clean.

It was then that Bodessa slowed down. Not to gawp, but to turn to Addi. She didn't say anything; she simply held out her hand. Addi took it. He felt reassured, reminded of how close they had both come to being finished off by the saw-toothed beast. He held her hand only long enough for the others to see. Sinjun looked peeved. In a huff, he loaded his bamboozie and fired a shot at a croob. The bird fell with a splat.

"Might be the gorax we encountered yesterday," said Addi, "or what's left of it. The mizot saved us. But the great bird might not be so kind today."

It was as if the mizot had heard him, and its followers – a swarm of green-winged pine-tattles, shifting on branches, swapping places, chirping with excitement. In a cloud they rose from the pines, darkened the sky.

"We need to find cover," Addi called out. "Anywhere!" He took Bodessa's hand and ran.

With the Glade in sight, the terrain began to change. The ground was turning green, and rocks and trees dotted the landscape. With an eye on the pine-tattles, they hurried towards a line of boulders to gain shelter. Addi took the lead. Familiar with the terrain, he would get them to the boulders faster than anyone else.

The land began to rise and fall. Addi let go of Bodessa's hand and scrambled up a bank to firmer ground. He'd almost reached the first line of boulders when the cry rang out.

Eeeeaah! Eeeeaah!

It wasn't a warning.

The mizot sprang from the tall pine – a black hulk, almost too big for itself, its massive wings pumping to keep airborne. In the swirl of pine-tattles – so many chirping fanatics – the great battle bird banked over the open terrain then turned towards where Addi stood – where Bodessa and the others were racing to get to.

"Come on!" Addi said, waving to them. He could see Bodessa limping. *If anything happens to her ...*

But the mizot took its time. Flanked by the pine-tattles it swept across the far bogs then looped above the stream of the Glade. Only then did it circle towards Addi, cruising overhead, squealing with joy. Or was it hunger? As it passed he got a clear look at the creature. Its body was as big as Sinjun's, its wings dense like armoured feathers. It had a fixed grey eye and its beak was orange, very long and very pointed. In a rush of flaps and glides it headed towards the Wetlands. Maybe it would find an eyeball or two there. But it didn't come close to landing. Instead, in a wide arc it turned and headed back. Was this it? Were they about to face the battle-bird head-on? What about Groff's smelly repellent, would it work?

"Here!" Addi said, reaching out, giving Groff, Bodessa and Tarro a hand up the last rise. Sinjun refused help. He was messing with his bamboozie.

"Groff," said Tarro, "what have we got?"

Groff aimed his spygoggles. "It's c-coming straight for us, blinding speed."

Nice one, Groff.

They huddled behind the boulder leaving Sinjun to take his shot.

Eeeeaah! Eeeeaah! The black-suited eyeball-plucker squealed like a cat.

But Sinjun held his fire. Surely the thing was in range.

"Sinjun," said Tarro, "what are you waiting for? Shoot!"

Sinjun sounded hesitant. "It's … it's over us."

Addi looked up. The mizot, like a dark cloud, hovered above them, its eyes fixed on them as if sizing up the juiciest eyeball. Even though the bird was all but stationary, Sinjun seemed unable to release the sling.

"What's the matter with you?" Addi said.

"I've only got one bamboozie ball left," said Sinjun, his hand jittery. "Got to make it count."

"Just fire it!" said Tarro. "While you still can."

Sinjun pulled and released. Thwack! The bamboozie ball jetted upwards, strong, powerful … and wide.

"You missed!" said Addi. "Our only chance and you missed."

Sinjun slumped to the ground.

Amidst the squawking pine-tattles, the mizot squealed, and, as the great bird flapped its wings, Addi wondered how it could possibly be stopped.

"Groff, check your bag," said Tarro. "We need ammunition, more stones."

Groff was already rummaging, pulling out stuff, mostly torches. Bodessa opened the box of repellent, began to dip the torches in it.

"Addi," she said, "light them."

Addi looked at Tarro, who nodded.

In his haste, Addi pulled the wrong item from his pouch. The pink sapphire, his keepsake from Zuma's treasure vault, lay in his hand. It was a gem he'd planned one day to give Bodessa in remembrance of all they'd been through together. Given the dark threat looming above, he wondered if he should give it to her now.

"Addi, quick," she cried.

He stuffed the sapphire back in his pouch and pulled out a friction stick. Sparks flew, and one by one the torches flared.

"Hold them high," said Tarro.

Sinjun, scrambling to his feet, joined the line. With their backs against the boulder, torches were raised. Addi stood between Tarro and Bodessa. If this was to be their last stand, he couldn't think of a place he'd rather be. No matter what happened, he would make sure he'd defend to the finish his best friend and the girl who owned his heart.

Hovering above them, the mizot seemed caught in the cloud of pine-tattles, the chattering birds criss-crossing giddily. The battle bird screamed again. The pine-tattles scattered, then, like obedient servants, gathered above it, waiting for the eyeball-plucker to strike.

Addi watched nervously as the yellow plume of combusted repellent drifted upward, its acrid smell filling the air. A batch of low-flying pine-tattles were the first to whiff it – flitting like cry-babies to a place where they could breathe.

The mizot blinked, its talons clenched, its beak agape. With a great whooshing, its wings flapped harder, and it banked clumsily away from the rising fumes.

"It's working!" said Tarro. "Groff's repellent is working."

It was the first time Addi had seen Groff smile. It didn't last long. The mizot had flown out of range but now turned back towards them.

"Hold steady!" Tarro said, pointing his torch at the approaching malevolence. "Hold the line!"

Addi braced himself, then glanced at Bodessa. She, too, pointed her torch, stood brave and unflinching, as any true adventurer would.

For an instant the mizot was lost in the cloud of repellent. Then, like a black ghost, it emerged, tilting and swaying, trying to keep its balance. Still, it came towards them, descending rapidly – its beak an orange spike.

Addi had a mind to stand in front of Bodessa – to shield her – when a Dwarfgiant moment took place. Or was it a moment of madness? Sinjun broke from the line, ran into the open, waving his torch, screaming. Addi had no idea what language he was using. It sounded made up. But it could have said: Come on. Come and get me!

"Sinjun, don't be a fool!" shouted Tarro. "Get back!"

But it was too late. The mizot shifted direction and veered towards Sinjun, who pointed his torch, braced for the hit.

What happened next was a blur. Addi heard the slap – likely from the bird's wing – that sent Sinjun sprawling, his torch spinning away, setting fire to a patch of tall grass. In disarray, the mizot, its wing bent back, squealed as it tried to rise up – sharp, pathetic squeals, unbecoming of a battle bird.

"Its wing's b-broken," said Groff, aligning his spygoggles.

Still, the mizot lurched and flapped.

"We have to get Sinjun," Tarro said. "Before his eyeballs are plucked out."

At the foot of the boulder the bamboozie lay abandoned, just where Sinjun had left it. "Here, Bodessa, take this," Addi said, giving her his torch. He ran to grab the weapon. "Groff, do you have anything in your bag I can use to –?"

For a second time Groff smiled, held out his hand. A perfectly round stone lay in his palm.

"Where did you find this?" said Addi, snatching it up, loading it into the sling. "Doesn't matter," he added. "Hope is just a shot away."

Some thirty paces distant, the mizot, seemingly unable to fly, edged along the ground towards Sinjun, its busted wing dragging. Sinjun lay still.

Was he dead?

Down on one knee, Addi lined up the shot. Thirty paces – not too far. He'd used a bamboozie before, but not lately. It would take all his concentration. And his strength. The guttalong sling was tough to pull back. His hand shook from the effort. He was aware of the others watching him, counting on him to make a strike. What he didn't expect was a hand – delicate, yet firm – gripping the back of his, steadying the bamboozie. He didn't look up, but knowing it was Bodessa made his confidence rise.

The mizot was almost on Sinjun; the battle-bird's beak was flipping up and down. Addi aimed at its head. Who knew, he might give the mizot a taste of its own medicine – an eye for an eye.

He released the sling. The stone whooshed towards the bird. It looked good – hard and straight – but then the mizot scuttled forward. The stone hit its other wing, going right through it and plugging into the soft part of its side. The mizot squealed, collapsed and rolled to within a breath of Sinjun.

Euphoric, Addi stayed on his knee, hardly hearing the praise from the other Dwarfgiants. He felt Bodessa though, her hand gripping his hand even tighter.

"You did it," she said. "The mizot's dead."

The mizot lay still. Sinjun lay still.

"We need to be sure," said Addi, letting go of Bodessa's hand. "I'll go look."

"I'm coming with you," Tarro said. "Groff, you stay here with Bodessa."

Groff nodded, then, like a cheap conjurer, revealed another bamboozie stone, this time from under his foot.

"You're full of tricks, aren't you?" said Addi. "If you've got more stones, Groff, let's be having them."

"It's all I've got at the m-moment."

Addi looked into Groff's eyes: mizot grey, like a magician's, all-knowing, giving nothing away. There was something about him that belied his fragile, spindly look, his fumbling ways, his stuttering. It was something hard to reckon, but not to be taken for granted, especially when it came to being favoured by the Circle. What with "finding" ammunition for the bamboozie, his effective mizot repellent and the power of his spygoggles, he must already have impressed Tarro. What was intriguing about Groff was that he had been picked for the search party by way of lottery. What had that been all about? And what of Sinjun? If he was dead, then the choice for a new Circle member would be down to two. If alive, his chances of being selected had also increased, what with the strength he'd shown carrying Bodessa and his brave, if crazy, dash to distract the mizot.

"Let's go, Addi," said Tarro, impatiently.

Addi smiled. He still couldn't get over Tarro's new lust for facing danger head on. Addi took Groff's stone and loaded the bamboozie, then he and Tarro set off, tramping through high grass towards the crumpled battle-bird.

"Don't take your eye off it," said Tarro.

Addi pulled lightly on the sling.

They closed in, straining to see through drifting smoke. The torchlit flames had almost died out, but a stretch of scorched grass still smouldered.

With bamboozie aimed, he and Tarro stood over the mizot. Its damaged wing – the one that had clipped Sinjun – was trapped under the hulk of its body, the hole in its side leaking blood. Its eye was wide open, frozen, without hope. Addi breathed easier, lowered his bamboozie. The cold truth was that the battle bird was dead.

Then they came, waves of green-winged pine-tattles silent in the grieving wasteland, a fluttering fly-by, respectful of the creature they had worshipped. Once they had past, they kept on going, out of repellent range, never looking back.

"I'm over here!" the voice gasped. Nearby, almost hidden, Sinjun lay groaning in the tall grass.

Addi and Tarro hurried to his side.

Sinjun lay on his back, his face contorted in pain. Addi could see the muscles pulsating in his shoulder.

"It's popped out," Sinjun said. "My shoulder's out of its socket."

"Do you know how to fix it?" Addi asked Tarro.

"You have to turn the shoulder blade. But I can't do it one-handed."

Addi looked back. Bodessa and Groff were on their way.

"Sinjun, y-you're alive," Groff said, arriving. "What's the m-matter?"

Sinjun winced.

"His shoulder's out of its socket," Addi said. "It needs putting back in."

"Let me do it," said Bodessa, confident. "We need to sit him up."

Addi and Groff hooked their arms around Sinjun's back and lifted him into a sitting position.

"Aaagh!" Sinjun cried.

From out of his bag, Groff pulled a short coil of rope and straightened it. He said to Sinjun, "B-bite on this."

While Sinjun chewed on the rope, Bodessa flexed his elbow, rotating his injured shoulder outwards. Then, with a click, she snapped it back in.

Sinjun's muscle spasms stopped and he released the rope from between his teeth.

"How's your arm?" Bodessa said to Tarro.

"Getting better, why?"

"Sinjun needs a sling."

With only a slight grimace, Tarro slipped his arm out of the blood-stained sling. He reached into his pouch and pulled out a fresh Jabunga leaf.

Bodessa took them and tended to Sinjun.

As Addi watched, he took stock, weighed their chances of getting back to the castle ruin in time. Not good. Bodessa was still hindered by a badly scraped leg. Tarro and now Sinjun were nursing shoulder wounds.

At least they were all still alive.

CHAPTER 42

Strung out in single file, the Dwarfgiants and Bodessa trudged towards the Southern Glade. Addi, who was leading, pushed the pace as fast as he could, but the injuries to Tarro, Sinjun and Bodessa slowed their progress. Their goal of catching the two moons seemed all but hopeless.

Still, there were no signs of trouble, and by the time they reached the Glade the sun had regained its strength, radiating warmth, making the waters of the stream glint. They passed the deep pool – the same spot where, a sun earlier, he'd sat with Bodessa, toes in the water, her reflection rippling like a beautiful mystery. And now here she was, again at his side, looking not so mysterious, her hair loosened, her dress torn, a bloody scrape down the side of her leg.

"We're losing ground," Addi said. "The moons are already over the Dark Wood."

"Sinjun's struggling," Bodessa replied. "His arm keeps popping out."

"At this rate we won't get back in time. And if we don't, the serpent could finish them all – Myvan, the Circle, our friends …"

"Female friends?"

Bodessa's question – more interested than casual – surprised him.

"I don't have much time for females," Addi said, a little too quickly. "Too busy adventuring." But the truth was that there were two – Reesel and Kulin – whose company he enjoyed.

Bodessa remained silent.

"Tarro and I sometimes play Chizzy," he continued. "Some of the females play, too."

"Chizzy?"

"It's a game where you throw large round stones at a small one. See who gets closest."

"Sounds like fun. Who usually wins?"

Addi laughed. "The females. They've got the knack."

"It could be that their eyes are keener."

"Oh, definitely," Addi replied. "Especially Reesel –" He stopped, felt caught in a trap. "But she doesn't have eyes like yours. I've never seen eyes like yours. There's no one like you."

Bodessa laughed. "I should think not. I'd need to grow fur."

"Female Dwarfgiants have fine, smooth fur," Addi said. "And they sing well."

"Oh, they sing, do they?"

"Usually. After they've won at Chizzy."

"I must try this game."

"We will. Once we get through today."

Tarro caught up to them. "Addi," he said, "we're dragging. The two moons are so far ahead they're laughing at us."

"You don't have to tell me. How's Sinjun?"

"Busy keeping his arm in its socket. He should be all right, but at this rate we don't have a hope of getting back in time."

Addi winced. "Maybe I should go on ahead, take Bodessa with me."

"I don't think so," said Tarro. "We went through life and death finding you. Whatever happens now, we stick together."

"That's noble of you, Tarro. But if we can't get back to help Myvan, we might end up being the only ones left."

"There is a way," Bodessa said.

Addi looked sharply at her.

Without explanation, she pulled the moonstones out and held them in front of her. Gazing at them, she spoke words he had never heard before, a sort of lilting mumbo-jumbo. The moonstones seemed to respond, to brighten, change colour, at one point to an amber glow. "Corasma lunus," she said, finally. Then, as if nothing had happened, she calmly slid the moonstones back into her dress. "There," she said, sounding satisfied, "it's done. The moons have been held up, hopefully long enough for us to overtake them."

Addi could only stare.

Chapter 43

Down the breezy Zuminia Narrows, Milo rowed for all he was worth. In time with Flogg and the Zenta guards, he pulled on the oars, his arm and leg muscles feeling the pinch. Their efforts to reach the Sulphur Sea, to find a prevailing wind that would carry them to the Dwarfgiants' settlement in time, were going well. Even the moons – above them and to the left – seemed to be in a stupor, as if held by some invisible grip.

Flogg, rowing in front of him, glanced up at the sky. "What happened to the moons? We've almost caught them."

"Don't know," Milo answered. "Maybe they're resting, like I should be."

At the prow of the boat, Zuma the Mystic Zenta stood fearless, posing like a carved figurehead. "Not far now!" he boomed over the splash and the rattle of the oars. "The gap to the sea approaches."

"Keep rowing, Milo," said Flogg over his shoulder. "This is not the time to rest. Bodessa's counting on us."

Milo wondered about that. Their young "princess" had changed lately. He felt he didn't know her well any more. Indeed, Zuma's daughter had become rebellious and unpredictable. Growing pains were one thing, but lately Bodessa's behaviour had become erratic. Inflamed by the moonstones she wore around her neck, she seemed determined to find out what had happened to her mother. No matter what advice she'd been given by those closest to her, she was driven to find the truth. Even at the risk of death. And what of her new friend, the Dwarfgiant? Addi seemed safe enough;

a bit high-spirited, maybe, but at least the caring sort. It might not help, though, that his interest in Bodessa seemed more than just friendly. Who could guess the repercussions if a budding romance turned sour, especially with someone of a different tribe; one whose body was covered with fur?

Still, Bodessa's well-being had always been Milo's first responsibility. He wasn't about to give up on her now. But he did wonder whether a mission to help save her – more from herself than from a killer serpent – would prove fruitful.

Killer serpent. The very thought of it made his stomach churn. He looked up and swallowed hard. The moons were moving again.

Chapter 44

Myvan stole into the sanctuary of the Circle chamber, slumped into his jade-and-topaz chair. In the dim quiet of the room, he yawned. For over two suns he hadn't slept. Not good. Lack of sleep always made him grumpy; left his head fuzzy, his thoughts slow. If he was going to be any use in leading the Dwarfgiants against the serpent, he'd need a nap, at least a short one. But his knees wouldn't let him. He tried stretching his legs, but the joints screamed from a lack of healing potions: emberlea or Jabunga leaves. Finally he found a more comfortable position – tucking his knees to his chest. Staring blankly across the table in front of him, his eyes felt heavy. He let them close but, as soon as he did, realized the danger. If he nodded off he could fall into a sleep so deep that he might not wake until after the battle – or maybe not at all. Not ever. He forced his eyes open. Suddenly more alert, he wondered if today might be his last. If it came to pass that fate struck him down, was he satisfied with his life? Had he any regrets? As leader, had he done all he could to encourage the Dwarfgiants to work at what they did best, at what they enjoyed? Had he made their lives safe? Did they live without fear? These questions bounced about in his head. After a bump or two they settled down and he began to think more clearly.

One thing he knew was that Dwarfgiants were adventurers. It ran deep in their blood, especially with the younger ones. In generations past, however, too many adventures had gone bad; too many Dwarfgiants had been lost to shadows and fates. In his own youth, he remembered the time when he, too, had been struck with a passion for adventure: the excursions through the mountains and forests of Kamistra, the thrill of meeting Claris – a first kiss as fresh as a mountain stream. But bliss had lasted less than a season. His closing adventure – a males-only expedition to the Mighty Mountain of Mol – had deadened his nomadic appetite forever. The memory of the trip had left him empty, reeling from the loss of his closest friends – Circle members, all. Even now he wondered if he could have prevented it: a dare to traverse the high ledge of Kamistra's volcanic chasm, to stir the giant Mol from its lair.

In heavy mist the way had been uncertain, the narrow path slick with moss. It happened between heartbeats, so quickly that before anyone could help, the leading five – tethered together for safety – had slid over the edge. In a trice they'd gone flailing, screaming down into the blackness.

After he'd returned – along with Revel and two others – he'd been plagued by nightmares: the helplessness, the last cries of those young, vibrant beings – their familiar faces, never to be seen again.

Although he'd struggled to recover, the irony was that those who died had been the ones ahead of him in succession as leader of the Dwarfgiants. And by the time the golden leaves had been painted over with snow, the current leader was also dead. Most said that losing a son on the Mighty Mountain of Mol had been too much to bear.

As the eldest Circle survivor, Myvan had been chosen leader. Since that day his life had been what he would call content; his steady hand brought, if not a lot of excitement, peace and harmony, at least, to the lives of three generations of Dwarfgiants. Essential to this was making sure adventures were kept to a minimum, allowed only when decreed by the Circle.

Luckily, his own son, Tarro, didn't have an adventuring bone in his body. But then, just three suns ago, with a desperate need for Jabunga leaves, he'd made an exception; he'd allowed Tarro to accompany his stepson, Addi, into the Dark Wood. When Tarro returned alone with an arrow wound, he'd felt sick. And yet, when Tarro insisted on going back to find Addi, he was so proud of his son's loyalty and courage that he gave his blessing. But what good was pride if Tarro never came back? If his son had been lost to the fates, his own achievements in life wouldn't matter.

A strange light shook him from his thoughts. Harsh and silvery, it beamed in through the slit in the wall, striking the sundial in the centre of the table.

But it wasn't the warm light of the sun – too late in the day – more the cold light of the moon. The moons! They were moving again. They were here.

He jumped up from his chair, grimaced as his knees buckled. But he was in no mood for pain. Gripping the hilt of his sword, he hobbled to the steps. The time had come. If the battle was to be won, the Dwarfgiants needed him.

Chapter 45

The race was on, and all the Dwarfgiants had to do was find a way back to the castle ruin before the moons did. Hopes of achieving this had been boosted when Bodessa's moonstones had stopped the silver circles cold. That had bought the Dwarfgiants some time – almost enough for them to catch up. But somewhere over the deepest part of the Dark Wood, in a spark of lunar brilliance, the spell had broken and the moons, separated by only the thinnest of shadows, had resumed their journey to the coast.

Sitting under a canopy of pines, Addi waited for the others to catch up. In the dimming light he could make out the approaching shapes of Tarro, Groff, Bodessa and the ailing Sinjun, who trudged along, his right shoulder useless. Bodessa – herself hampered by a slight limp – held his good arm, making sure he didn't fall. Alongside them, Tarro fussed with Groff's wayfinder, turning knobs, adjusting settings, aiming it as if seeking direction.

Addi knew exactly where they were going. It was the pace that dragged. They were falling behind. Fidgety, he could feel his pulse, his frustration rising. He couldn't accept that they'd come all this way only to fall short at the end. He felt like calling out to them, Hurry up! But what was the use? Thanks to Sinjun, they couldn't go any faster.

Tarro was the first to reach him. "It's getting gloomy."

"We're in the Dark Wood," Addi replied. "It's supposed to be gloomy."

Tarro pointed. "Those rocks, ahead, where the trail widens, let's rest up and light the torches."

"We don't have time to rest," Addi said. "We have to keep going."

"No, Addi. We're stopping. We need to gather ourselves, collect our thoughts."

Thoughts! What thoughts? We need to act!

"We won't stay long."

Addi ended his protest as Groff and Bodessa arrived, along with Sinjun, whose arm – at least for the moment – remained in its socket.

"We'll rest over by those rocks," Tarro said. "Get ready for the final push. We're in the eye of the Dark Wood, the deepest part, so Groff, I want the torches lit."

Addi caught Bodessa looking at him. Concern etched her face, matched his own exasperation.

She looked drained, worn out; not surprising after all she'd gone through – tortured by the Raslatombs, worried about her father, her brother, looking for the truth about what happened to her mother. And the spill down the rock face had almost killed her. Yet, for all of that, the dark-eyed Zenta, leg-scraped and chin-grazed, bedraggled in her torn floral dress, was still able to carry herself with a sure and graceful ease. Even as the gloom of the Dark Wood preyed heavy on her, there was nobody in the world he would rather be with. He wanted to go to her, hold her, let her know he'd find a way to sort everything out. Instead, Sinjun squealed. His arm had come out of its socket again, and she went to help him put it back in.

They tramped to a clump of rocks and sat among them in a rough circle. Legs were stretched, water drunk, wounds looked at.

"Sinjun," said Tarro, "your shoulder, what's the verdict?"

"Verdict? If it wasn't for Bodessa … she's kept me going."

Addi squirmed. So it was all about returning the favour. Sinjun had carried Bodessa after she was knocked out, now she was expected to take care of him. Normally there was nothing wrong with that – Dwarfgiants, after all, were never left behind, even if it put others at risk. The thing that bothered Addi was the number of times Sinjun's arm had popped out and how much time Bodessa had spent coddling him – keeping him going. Sinjun, he thought, might actually be enjoying it.

"It's just that we're lagging behind," said Tarro, his voice urgent. "We need to go faster."

"We have to keep his arm in place," said Bodessa, "with a strong cloth, long enough to wrap around his body."

Groff opened his bag and rummaged. It took no time for him to do his rabbit-out-of-a-hat trick. A familiar scarf spilled out.

"Where have I seen that?" asked Tarro.

Groff held it up. "It was a g-gift," he said, "from Headstrong, the Loggerhead. For s-saving them from the great gorm."

Great gorm! Addi couldn't wait to hear about that adventure.

Groff handed Bodessa the scarf. While she helped bind Sinjun's shoulder, Groff dished out torches. Using a friction stick to spark a fire, he lit them.

"Use them as weapons if you have to," Tarro said, standing, waving his torch. Then after sticking it in the ground he said, "I think we all realize we've reached a moment in our lives – maybe in our history – when we have to show who we are … what we're made of. To put it bluntly, if we don't speed up, we won't make it back in time to fight the evil that wants to take away everything we have. To finish us. Sinjun, what do you think? Can you pick up the pace?"

Bodessa completed her wrap-around securing job, finishing with a crossover knot.

Sinjun grimaced. "I'll try." And he gave Bodessa an appreciative nod.

"Good," Tarro said. "We're in the heart of the Dark Wood so stick together, keep alert and, above all, keep going. Once we get through this stretch we'll be in sight of the sea."

"What about the Jabunga leaves?" Addi asked. "We'll have to make a detour."

"No. You will."

"Huh?"

"I'm making an exception," Tarro said, "about us all sticking together. Right now, Addi, you're fitter than any of us. When we get to the fork in the Eastern Trail, take the south path to the hideaway. Collect as many leaves as you can carry – two bags if possible – then loop back. With any luck we'll meet up as we come out of the wood."

Addi was of two minds. In one way, he thought Tarro's plan was the best one they had – as long as Sinjun could hold himself together. What bothered Addi was his promise, to himself and to Zuma, that he'd watch out for Bodessa at all times. Could he think of leaving her, if only for a short while? She sat opposite. He looked for some kind of sign – a nod, a shake of her head – a clue that would help him decide whether to go along with the plan. But she seemed aloof, distracted. Her face, normally pale, looked ghostly in the torchlight. Her eyes, pools of worry, looked straight past him.

"Bodessa, what's wrong?"

When she didn't answer, Addi followed her line of view, turned to look back over his shoulder. The trail, rising slightly, opened into an oval-shaped clearing tufted with grass. Lined on both sides by high, dark pines, it resembled an arena where blood might flow, where screams would never be heard. He felt a chill. There was always a chill in the Dark Wood, but this was different. It was ice cold. And quiet. It was as if all the woodland creatures had gone into hiding. Then he caught his breath. About fifty paces away, he could see something – greyish, brownish – fiendish. A piggy-shaped hulk on stubby legs stood motionless. For a moment Addi just stared, not wanting to believe it. Then its head swivelled.

He thought about running, urging the others to find somewhere to hide. And yet, even though he'd been at the mercy of a gorax before, he was overcome by a calmness he couldn't explain.

"What is that thing?" said Sinjun, holding up his torch.

"It looks d-diabolical," Groff said.

"The main thing," said Addi, "is not to panic. If you let a gorax know you're scared, he'll come for you."

"What will it do if you don't let it know?" said Tarro.

Addi hesitated. What he did know was that – unlike the last time when the gorax had jumped on him from behind – they had a few precious moments to prepare for what would be a fight for their lives.

Groff's mouth dropped open. "That's a g-gorax?"

"The worst kind," Addi said. "A blood-and-bones butcher, eyes in the back of its head, dagger teeth in front." As he spoke he felt oddly detached, as though describing something from another place, somewhere safe. He looked at Bodessa. She didn't look safe at all. One hand gripped her torch, the other her pendant chain.

"What do you have in mind?" asked Sinjun.

Addi looked skyward. The mizot had saved him last time, but having just slain one he could hardly expect a favour from another. So, what did they have? Each had a knife and a torch. Sinjun was down to one arm. Tarro's shoulder still leaked blood. Bodessa limped and Groff looked scared.

Don't look scared.

Addi turned to Tarro. "Is there any chance you could –?"

Tarro shook his head. "I can't risk another change-up. My arrow wound … it would explode."

Addi exhaled a long breath. "Right," he said, loading the bamboozie with his last stone, "looks like it's up to me."

"Has it s-seen us?" asked Groff.

Addi saw it drool. "Use these rocks as cover. Whatever happens, don't get caught in the open. It will pick you off like a plum from a tree."

Huddled around the top of the largest rock, they watched the gorax staring at them.

"What's it w-waiting for?" said Groff.

"Probably for one of us to make a move," said Addi.

"Maybe it's not alone," Tarro said. "Maybe it's got an accomplice, hiding in the bushes."

"I smell a trap," Sinjun said.

"There is no trap, and there's no accomplice," said Bodessa. "They're loners. They don't share."

"But they love to eat," Addi said, testing the pull of his bamboozie.

"Take your best shot," said Tarro. "It's about to attack."

The gorax hunched its shoulders. With a wrenching creak, its head swivelled half a turn, now just a mouth – bloodstained daggers, black tongue shooting out. Addi remembered the slobbering stink of the creature's breath, its rotting teeth. Its head swivelled again and its eyes were back, leering and hungry. As if to find a secure footing, its feet churned the dirt. And then, with a jolt, it sprang forward.

"Here it comes!" said Tarro. "Torches! Knives!"

Addi steadied his elbow on the crown of the rock, aimed his bamboozie. One shot.

"Wait for it! Waaaait!"

With all his strength he pulled the sling. The gorax thundered towards them, swaying from side to side, snorting, fat rolling. He aimed at its eyes, released the stone. A good shot – strong and straight – but the beast dipped in a rut and the stone skimmed high. Missed! He tossed his bamboozie, pulled his knife and stood with the others bracing for the onslaught.

Tarro, in the centre of the line, stepped forward, pointing his torch in defiance. Was he being brave or stupid? Like a bloated slingshot the gorax leapt straight at him.

"Scatter!" Tarro screamed, throwing his torch at the beast then flinging himself off the rock. The others spiralled in all directions. Addi grabbed Bodessa's hand and jumped. They fell to the ground, Addi landing on top of her. He thought about staying there, protecting her, but the idea backfired.

"Addi, get off!" she pleaded. "You're on my leg."

A tortured squeal made him turn. The gorax had crashed on the rock, mouth first, blood and teeth everywhere. Its head must have swivelled too early – a blind leap. Now flattened, it lay with its mouth open, gasping and groaning. It still had teeth left, some jambed askew, others dangling from threads of flesh. The beast was hurting, but it wasn't finished. Like a giant slug it slid off the rock, leaving a red smear.

With eyes like glass the gorax staggered to its feet and swivelled its head. Up close, the beast was as nasty as Addi remembered: caked in blood, reeking with filth. It was a hulking mass, twice the height of Tarro who, only five paces away, waved his knife. The gorax snarled, signalled Tarro as its first victim.

Addi felt Bodessa grip his arm, urging him to do something. His torch was out of reach but his knife was close. He scrambled for it, had it in his hand, but before he could even think about how he might use it, he froze.

In a moment of unbridled fury, Groff struck. Charging at the beast from behind he jammed his torch into its mouth. The gorax shrieked, whipped its head around. The torch flew out, and more teeth, a canine lodging in Groff's arm. Before Groff could pull it out, the beast rushed at him, knocked him on his back. The gorax stuck out its tongue. Not only was it black, but now it was charred and blistered. Surely it couldn't eat! But the creature, baring the teeth it had left, lowered its head over Groff as though he were a trough. About to feed, its eyes watched its back.

Tarro closed in, pointing his knife. "Off!" he cried.

"Stop!" shouted Addi.

"Go!" yelled Sinjun.

"No!" screamed Bodessa.

Surrounded, the beast rose up in panic, its head swiveling – left then right – from one voice to the other.

"Off!" "Stop!" "Go!" "No!" – the words repeated as its head spun and spun, this way and that, turning almost full circle, its neck stretching to the limit.

"Circle around," Addi said. "Keep it confused!"

"Come on!" cried Sinjun. "Over here!"

"Take *me*!" said Tarro.

"No *me*!" Bodessa cried.

The gorax tried to keep up; its head was creaking, its neck twisting all the way around, going farther and farther past the point where the muscles tear and the spine snaps. A hard, cracking sound stopped the beast dead.

Addi stood and gaped. For a moment nothing moved. In the strange stillness, and with its black tongue hanging limp, only the beast's smell hinted of life. Then, in a crumple of knees, its legs folded and, like a pile of bile, the gorax slumped to the ground.

"W-what happened?" Groff asked, sitting up.

"Its neck's broke," said Sinjun.

"What were the chances?" said Tarro.

"We had its head going," said Addi, "like a spinning top." He saw Bodessa looking at the beast as if she didn't believe it. "I'll make sure," he added, wanting, in some small way, to make up for missing his bamboozie shot.

Picking up a torch, he stepped towards the fallen beast. Holding his breath from the stink, he looked down, prodded and poked the thing with his torch. The mouth side of its head was splattered with blood, its neck purple. Still, there was a queasy moment when he thought the creature's leg moved. But he knew it couldn't have. It wasn't breathing. He turned to the others. "It's dead!" he said. "We can move on."

Addi joined the others who gathered around the surprising hero.

"Hold steady," Bodessa said, getting set to extract the Gorax's tooth.

Groff braced himself – the dagger-shaped canine had plugged in deep, just above the elbow. Like an expert, Bodessa massaged the skin, wiggled the tooth and, with a quick tug, pulled it out. Addi wondered if she'd watched Bardo at the height of his teeth-pulling days.

Bodessa handed the tooth to Groff. He held it up.

"That's quite a prize, Groff," said Tarro. "And well deserved."

"Let's hope it's a good omen for fighting serpents," Addi said.

Groff smiled and dropped the tooth into his bag.

Chapter 46

Through the late afternoon, the boat plowed through the Zuminia Narrows, its rickety hull creaking like old bones. Although lacking the timbers of its youth, the vessel made up for it with toughness and grit, and apart from a brief entanglement with a shoal of basking gumplefish, it made good time.

The waters widened leaving the shoreline adrift. Ahead, in the near distance, the Sulphur Sea beckoned, its green-tinged waves roughened by wind gusts whose direction was hard to read.

Milo, drenched in spray, rested on his oar. This had better be worth it, he thought, panting from a stretch of rowing that had brought them to the verge of finding out which way the sea wind blew – with them, or against. If favourable, they could expect a fast twilight run to the old castle ruin: to find Bodessa, to save her from the serpent.

Zuma filled a jug of water from the scutterbutt. The Zenta guards drank first, then Flogg. Milo was last. The pecking order was in tact.

"Hurry, drink up!" Zuma said. "We need to find out if fortune is with us."

Milo took a long swig and belched.

"Do you mind?" said Flogg sitting directly in front of him.

"I don't have a good feeling about this, Flogg," said Milo, holding back another belch. "We're about to hit the sea, with a serpent in it. A giant serpent that can do things to you … things that would make a Krogul torture seem like a sunny day at the beach. I mean, who wants to be sucked up and swallowed like suli fruit in a goblet?"

Flogg looked back over his shoulder. "Milo, you know what you need? You need a more positive outlook. You can start with that jug of water. Think of it as being half full – not half empty. Oh, and while you're at it, scratch my back, will you."

"Scratch your … where, exactly?"

"Under my left shoulder blade."

Milo ditched the water jug and began to scratch.

"Ooo … yes, that's it," said Flogg. "Ooo, right there!"

"I'm serious, Flogg. What chance do we have against the serpent of the Sulphur Sea?"

"It has to show up first. It might have second thoughts."

"You give it too much credit. Have you seen the moons? They're all but touching."

"But they're not, are they?"

"Who's going to stop them?"

"Glass half full, Milo, glass half full."

"Have you two finished?" Zuma boomed from the bow. "Let's go!"

Milo grabbed his oar, Flogg his. Both waited to row in time with the others.

In less time than it took Milo to stop worrying, the waters darkened and, in a complicated swirl of eddying currents, the boat hit the open sea.

Met straightaway by a battery of brisk waves, the vessel dipped and bobbed, leaned in no particular direction. Zuma, his face furrowed, plucked a feather from his tunic, tossed it in the air. The feather caught the wind but swirled around as if lost. He watched it fall randomly into the choppy waters. "Stop rowing!" he ordered.

The oars were lifted. Milo held his breath; the boat was on its own. For a moment it didn't seem to know whether to creak or crack up, but then, in a dizzying moment it began to turn – started to turn to port.

Zuma's eyes shone. "We have it!" he cried. "A fair wind. It's with us!"

Chapter 47

On a hastily constructed platform in the middle of the main square, Myvan stood as straight as he could. With Circle members Revel to his right and Havoc, Rimsky and Jeeve to his left, he looked down on some two hundred Dwarfgiants who had been summoned to hear him speak. His audience, restless and talkative, was comprised of male and female fighters. Although hardened by the daily challenges of life, they did not look especially warlike. Some wore breastplates, others helmets, and there was a smattering of spears, shields and swords.

He glanced at the sky, half expecting a storm to break. He wasn't far off. The moons – sailing in tandem – were clearly visible. They'd reached the edge of the Dark Wood and would be over the ruin just after sunset. To the east, above the sea, the hapless sun hovered as if it had nowhere to go but down.

Myvan raised his arms to signal quiet. After a moment the crowd settled. He cleared his throat and began to speak.

"Fellow Dwarfgiants, tonight, when the two moons converge, the demon serpent and its devil fish will attack from the sea. If this ruin – and the settlement we are working so hard to build – is to remain our home, we must defeat this evil, make sure that it never threatens us again. It won't be easy. It will take all our fighting skills, all our courage. Now, I can't promise there'll be no setbacks, that there'll be no blood spilt, but if we stay true to our pledge of sticking together – watching out for each other, no matter what – I know we will defend what is ours. Be victorious on this night of nights."

A groundswell of cheers echoed through the ruin.

"What about Addi and Tarro," shouted a young voice from the crowd. "Will they be back from the Dark Wood in time?"

The question pained Myvan. The truth was, he'd just about lost hope that his son and stepson would return at all, let alone in time for battle. But he couldn't tell them that. Too many young Dwarfgiants looked up to them, were counting on their leadership.

"I think there's every chance of them being here," he said, as sincerely as he could. "I really do."

Doubt crossed the faces of the assembled throng.

CHAPTER 48

With the gorax left behind – the victim of a twisted, broken neck – it was good to be moving again. Jogging slowly, Addi led the way, careful not to push the others too hard – especially Sinjun, whose arm was still loose in its socket. Groff, whose heroics had led to the fall of the swivel-headed beast, had been given second spot, followed by Sinjun, Bodessa and Tarro.

Through the oval clearing – the gorax's arena of death – they entered the Dark Wood proper. Gloom was everywhere. Black thickets, deep shadows, the afternoon sky fading above the trees. In the dying light, the wood – cool and breathless – made Addi queasy. It reminded him of standing in the doorway of his room at midnight – that fearful moment before Kamistra's volcano blew.

He slowed to a walk, braced for the worst. But instead of a cataclysmic eruption, a hooting sound broke out, a pining, lonely hoot from deep in the trees. Ooo, Ooo. Whatever it was, the creature went on for some time: Ooo, Ooo – pathetic – lovelorn, almost. It made him think about Bodessa, of his own yearnings, the hope that she might think of him the same way he thought about her. He turned to catch a glimpse of her. No longer limping, she walked in Sinjun's shadow, a hand on her moonstones. Were they making some mystical connection? He began to fret. Soon he would be leaving her – his side trip to the hideaway. She still hadn't said what she thought of the plan, made no mention of wanting to go with him. He could only guess at what she was thinking, where her affections lay. What he did know was that, Jabunga leaves or no Jabunga leaves, being away from her, even for a short time, would leave his heart in a tangle.

He pushed on, lighting the way with his torch. As if stuck in the key of melancholy, the hoots persisted. Ooo, Ooo. Ooo, Ooo. In one way, at least, they brought some comfort to the woodland's brooding silence. But after a while the hoots – repeating endlessly – became distracting, annoying, even.

Ooo, Ooo. Ooo, Ooo – Agggggghh!

Addi shivered, tried not to think of what might have happened. The creature's last cry sounded as if it had been throttled. In the deep afternoon, the Dark Wood was quiet again, satisfied, it seemed, to have tallied another victim.

With little care for Sinjun's loose arm socket, Addi beat a trail – if you could call it a trail. The way forward was thick with roots and stumps, lost in crannies of shadow and shade, found only when hope sees light. Addi arrived at the fork in the trail that was to separate him from the others. Straight ahead, they would continue along the main path to the coast. Branching right, he would take the side trail to the hideaway. If he could stay out of trouble he would rejoin them before sunset, in sight of the castle ruin, armed with two bags of Jabunga leaves, ready for anything.

He sat on a log and waited. But not for long; the sound of wood snapping underfoot gave way to the approaching figure of Groff. He seemed different; his normally tottering legs were striding with confidence while his "bag of useful things" bounced on his back. What was this new boldness? All Addi could think of was the flush of glory a hero might feel after taking down a gorax. This suspicion was borne out by the look in Groff's eye – sharp as a swivel-head's tooth – and the red stain seeping through the sleeve of his tunic – a mark of pride. In the murky depths of the Dark Wood, Groff had crossed over; he'd found a new way to be – freewheeling, flying high on adventure. It was the same look Addi had seen in Tarro – a change from cautious to brazen, all in a span of just three suns.

"There's a lot to admire you for," Groff said, before Addi had time to stand up. "If we make it back, it will be b-because of you. You're a Dwarfgiant but you see things keenly, more urgently. Not only is your hair a different colour, you have a different way of looking at things, a way that goes to the core of g-getting things done. When you are selected as the next Circle member, I will be proud to stand by you."

Addi looked at him, dumbfounded. It was like being with a different person. Even Groff's voice had changed. It was him, of course – the stringy, thin-pitched tone. But now he had an edge. Now he was a conquerer! Sure-minded, his words offered no apology. And barely a stutter.

"Thanks, Groff," said Addi, even more befuddled, "but the selection of a Circle member is not up to me. As you know, there are three candidates. When we reach that point – if we reach that point – the vote will include you and Sinjun. All I know is that without your courage, the gorax would likely have had its way. We wouldn't be standing here with hope still in reach."

Groff shrugged modestly, turned his head.

The wood was suddenly noisier. Rounding the corner, Sinjun, Bodessa and Tarro came into view. They too looked lively; Bodessa, in the middle, had a jump in her step, listening to Tarro, whose voice filled the trees with some tale or other. Sinjun, though, his face strained with curiosity, looked straight ahead, eager, it seemed, to learn what Addi and Groff had been talking about.

As they arrived, Bodessa laughed: a funny ending to Tarro's story. Addi couldn't remember Tarro being so jovial, or, for that matter, Bodessa laughing so heartily. Like everything she did, her joy, like a sweet dream, rolled in waves straight to his heart. But only for a moment. Above the trees to the east, an arc of light crackled. The moons! They would be in sight of the ruin.

Tarro said, "Addi, you ready to go?"

Addi looked down the side trail. It looked bleak, full of gloom. He turned to Bodessa. She glanced at him, her shining eyes now shaded with concern. At least some feelings for him seemed to be intact.

"I'm ready," he said.

"Remember," Tarro continued, "go hard and fast. Get the Jabunga leaves – as many as you can carry – then circle back to the edge of the wood. We'll wait for you there, but not for long. Be careful, and watch out for Raslatombs."

Addi had never lacked confidence. It wasn't in his nature. But as he readied himself – checking his pouch, hitching his belt – he felt uncertain. His shoulders were heavy, his legs weak. There was, after all, a lot at stake. He was being counted on to go full tilt through the life-sapping wood, retrieve leaves that would save lives, race back and help fight a serpent. All the while he'd be living up to the expectations of a new admirer in

Groff, and proving himself endlessly to Bodessa. If it was an adventurer's dream – a mission whose success would surely seal his selection as a Circle member – why wasn't he excited? Why was he sweating? He wiped his brow, took a deep breath.

Never one for long goodbyes, he nodded to each in turn: Tarro, his oldest friend, Groff, his new friend, Sinjun, his upredictable rival. Last was Bodessa. She smiled at him – a complicated smile – her lips, not fully wide, still looked delicious. Naturally, he wanted to touch them, but he just couldn't bring himself to do it. It wasn't because he worried she might not feel the same way – it was because of her eyes. Dark and deep and fluid they slipped into his view, held his gaze, conjured a look of helpless wanting that somehow told him she was his. That was how he saw it, anyway. That was how he felt. When she blinked the spell was broken. Half dazed he turned and started down the side trail, one foot in front of the other. It was a lonely path filled with traps and snares for anything that breathed.

Chapter 49

For as long as he could, Addi kept the picture of Bodessa fixed in his mind: her lips, her eyes, the secret place where she kept her moonstones. But as the side trail bogged down – matted with wiry roots and weeds – his thoughts shifted, and her beauty began to fade from his imagination.

The trail was jumpy. Out of his flickering torchlight, vines grasped, stumps riled his senses, the smell of old vegetation watered his eyes. He and Bodessa had travelled the same trail only two nights before, but it hadn't been like this. This time there was a strange power in the air. Echoes of knife screams twisted in the trees, flights of souls, pale moons haunting. In this version, the atmosphere, sometimes restless, other times still, seemed more like the sway of life and death. Mostly death. Of things coming to an end. It was a feeling he didn't like, one he needed to dismiss before it took hold. He shook himself: a reminder of who he was, of his responsibilities. Whatever destructive forces were at large, he wasn't going to lie down and make it easy for them.

But the wooded trail had other ideas. Something slimy gripped his ankle, curled around it – a sucking vine maybe, or a lizardsnake. He tried to kick it off. No luck. He pulled his knife, but before he could use it he was yanked clean off his feet. He landed on his back, banged his head – a hard knock on a small rock. He lay still and looked up. His eyes were blurry. The tops of the trees looked separated, branches floating as if they were about to fall on him. He turned his head sideways. Nothing good there, either. He'd always liked the colour red, but not when it was his own blood. Drops were falling onto the ground beside him. He tried to lift himself but the pain in his head drove him back. Then he felt faint, and the colour changed from red to black.

He wasn't out for long. His throbbing head wouldn't let him. Neither would the slimy, snaky thing that had coiled itself around his feet, his legs, his chest, once around his neck and then to the top of his head, where it perched, licking – or was it sucking the blood from his wound like some serpentine leech? But the slimy bloodsucker had been careless. It had left Addi's right arm free, maybe because he'd had his torch in that hand. The torch was still burning, propped up against a rock from under which the slimy creature had probably come out in the first place. If Addi didn't act soon he wouldn't be around for long.

He reached for his knife, gripped the familiar knob-ended handle. A quick slice through pink scales and the slimy creature burst open, squirting red goo all over his shirt. Although lifeless, the lizardsnake still clung tight to his body. He sliced it some more, then began to pull the creature off. As he got to his feet, pieces fell to the ground. An odd specimen to be sure with its head shaped like a suction cup, its unfolded lips quivering.

He put a hand on the back of his head. Sore, messy; wet blood, dry blood, a pasty gouge in the centre. He found a cloth in his pouch, pulled it around his head, tied it under his chin. What he really needed was a Jabunga leaf. He recovered the torch, had to keep pushing, get to the hideaway while he could.

After a determined trek through stretches of knotty grass and a scratchy patch of drooping thorns, he was happy to see the trail clear. The light from what was left of the sun warmed the trees, and, as he passed a majestic stand of pines, he knew the hideaway was close.

Moments later he stood before the woodland den. The air was breathless, not a sound. He peered through the trees towards the ridge. No fires, no chanting Raslatombs, no screams from sacrificial grounds. Where was Taluhla and her horned rabble?

The hideaway was still covered with branches and leaves. He approached the entrance, didn't even have to go in. To the left, the tops of three bags poked out from a cover of leafy sticks. They were stashed full of Jabunga leaves. He took a leaf and placed it between his headscarf and his wound.

Almost at once he could feel the pain begin to ease.

The bags weren't heavy but they were awkward. Occupying both hands would leave him without the use of his torch. He tucked it into his belt on his right side, next to his knife. The bamboozie was slung on his left side. Before he set off he took a moment to take in the scene, the hideaway where he and Tarro had started this moonstruck adventure, collecting Jabunga leaves – where he'd brought Bodessa to recover from her ordeal with Taluhla and the Raslatombs. As he stood there in the cold silence he was drawn to the sound of something floating in the air, ever so faint: a distant sound, something big, something grand, like the clamour of an army on the move. It was so far away he couldn't be certain if his mind was playing tricks, wasn't sure it was real … until pine needles started to fall off the trees.

He grabbed the three bags, put one on each shoulder, the third he tied to the back of his belt. With his head aching again, he set off along the twisty path running eastward to the coast. With any luck it would take him out of the Dark Wood before the sun's glow died.

Chapter 50

Tarro was agitated. He knew from previous adventures that just when he was about to reach his destination, it always seemed to take forever to get there. He was feeling that now – a need to get through this forsaken wood, to clean up, to smell the sea again.

With Addi on his side trip, he, Sinjun, Bodessa and Groff had slogged along the Eastern Trail without threat. The only time they'd been bothered was when a strange hail of pine needles had rained down on them from out of the trees.

The problem now was Sinjun. He was back to his old ways, seeing things, things that were watching. Before, it had been trees. Trees that had eyes! Now it was flying ghosts, pale apparitions that travelled along with them, weaving among the trees, watching their every move.

"Did you see that?" Sinjun said, pointing to one side and then the other. "They're setting us up. We won't make it! We won't make it!"

"Keep moving forward," said Tarro, from his position at the back. "It's not far now."

He hoped Bodessa might settle him down, but she was absorbed with her moonstones. She had removed them from her neck and was holding them in front of her as if she was receiving some sort of magical guidance.

Groff was out in the lead. The Circle lottery candidate – suddenly acting like Addi – seemed to have a new purpose, a confidence that hadn't been seen before.

"We're walking into a trap," Sinjun said, stumbling, waving his torch in the air with his good arm. "We need to stop them, now!"

It was Sinjun who had to be stopped before his muddled brain cracked completely. He may have had a point thinking the air was simmering with a mystic presence – but not flying ghosts.

Tarro caught up with him, could smell the panic, the sweat, the aimless desperation that gripped the muscled Dwarfgiant.

"Sinjun, listen to me!"

Sinjun's eyes were glazed, otherworldly.

"Snap out of it," Tarro added. "We're almost home."

Sinjun looked at him blankly. If Tarro's words meant nothing, Bodessa did. Dropping back, she held out her hand. Like a baby, Sinjun took it.

Groff dropped back too. His words meant everything. "At the top of the r-rise," he said, full of vigour, "past the shadow of the forio tree is the end of the Dark Wood."

The end of the Dark Wood. Tarro felt a tingle in his neck. Not only was Groff's news heartening. He'd said it almost without stuttering.

Chapter 51

Addi carried a bag of Jabunga leaves on each shoulder. They gave him good balance and a feeling of well being. After all, the job of finding the healing leaves had been his and Tarro's.

"We're in desperate need," Myvan had said. "If we don't get them soon, Dwargiants will die."

That was three suns ago!

There'd been distractions, of course – a few setbacks – but here he was, at last, on the verge of bringing back the life saving leaves. He may have been fighting a headache, struggling with heartache, but as blood-black shadows pulsed around him, he knew what he had to do: get back to the ruin before it was too late.

The way ahead darkened. Without a lit torch he used the rhythm of the trail to guide him. Thin and zigzaggy, the pathway had a primeval feel to it – disorderly, out of use. His instincts, sharpened to the level of a Circle adventurer, drove him forward, first with a firm footing then, later, tramping through a maze of tendrils, offshoots and low boughs. But things got worse. He got stuck in a thicket so tangled with scrubwood and fallen branches that there seemed no way through. He couldn't be held back. Not now that he was so close.

Addi lowered the bags of leaves to the ground. He'd chop his way through. He pulled out his knife and hacked at the dense barricade. At first he got nowhere. Tough and springy, the cross-hatched web seemed inpenetrable.

In desperation, he checked for a weak spot, found a lower section to his left, looser, less packed. He went to it and, after a flurry of stabs and cuts, a parcel of deadwood collapsed. A small opening appeared. With new hope he clawed away, tunnelling through sprig and bush, his lungs pleading for breath, the blood from his head-wound running down his neck. Burrs raked his arms, shredded his headscarf and shirt. But he pushed on, found a way through.

Panting, he crawled out the other side. The terrain ahead looked clearer, the path wider. He reached back for the bags of Jabunga leaves. He'd pulled them halfway through when a noise stopped him. It sounded a long way away, but there was no mistake – a single clang, then another and another. His heart lifted. It was a sound he'd heard before: the Dwarfgiants' watch bell at the castle ruin.

CHAPTER 52

When the bell tolled, Tarro was rushing to the top of the rise. Just ahead, Sinjun was shouting, "They're on the run! They're on the run!" – which was a big improvement from, "We won't make it! We won't make it!"

Sinjun's improved state of mind was all Bodessa's doing. Still holding his hand, she pulled him along with animal fluidity, a natural grace that was a pleasure to behold. Up ahead, Groff, who had finished the climb, stood waiting in the shadow of a forio tree.

Tarro became anxious. He knew the clanging of the bells came from the castle ruin, but he wasn't sure what they meant. They could have been signalling the ending of the day, a celebration of the sun setting over the Sulphur Sea. They might also have meant danger, maybe a sighting of the serpent.

The first thing, though, was to get out of the Dark Wood. And as everyone finished their dash to the top of the rise, they finally left the miserable place behind. For a moment the adventurers stood together, inhaling the salty air, taking in a view that looked to have been waiting for them. To the right, high above the forio tree, the frosty moons hung like twins, their halos virtually touching. Ahead, down the valley trail, the castle ruin stood waiting. It looked much the same: the fragile towers and walls, the new buildings within. The entrance to the moat, though, looked to have been dammed up, posts and beams and boards keeping the sea water out – or keeping serpents from getting in. Someone had been busy.

Beyond the ruin, below the muffled cries of seabirds, waves rolled scarlet under the sinking sun.

The bell tolled on.

"It sounds urgent," Groff said. "We should hurry."

Tarro guessed it was the call to battle stations. "We need to give Addi some time to catch up." He scanned the edge of the wood. "But not long."

* * *

Addi felt dizzy. Blood was running down his neck, his back, soaking what was left of his shirt. With no way of keeping the Jabunga leaf in place, the wound made his head swim with lightness and pain. He had to sit down – before he fell. Lowering himself, he slumped against a tree, his head in his hands. He tried to recall Bodessa. But his mind was fuzzy, her memory dim. All he could remember were remnants of a battle, burning boats, her swimming away.

In the closing darkness he strained to see straight, his head pounding to the tolling of the bell.

Chapter 53

Myvan hobbled up the steps to the east battlements, reached the highest point of the castle ruin. Revel huffed and puffed behind him. Sunset warriors.

The bell had clanged long enough. Myvan leaned over the parapet and gave the sign for the bell ringer to stop. Now the air was filled with urgent voices – battle stations – the rush of the sea.

In the freshening breeze he and Revel surveyed the castle's defences. Scattered along the west, south and east walls, units of Dwarfgiants assembled, readying for the attack.

"So, Revel," Myvan said, "we have a hundred bamboozies. What about ammunition?"

"About a thousand bamboozie balls. Ten strikes each."

Myvan winced. "Ten. Let's hope it's enough. And the nets?"

"All the nets are in place, behind the dam, at the east entrance to the moat and over at the north wall."

"Good. Were we able to do anything with the north wall?"

"You know we didn't have a lot of spare workers," Revel said. "It's still a weak spot, but we managed to install makeshift barricades with firing slits."

Myvan sighed. "Barricades."

He turned his attention to the sea entrance to the moat. Working frantically at low tide, Havoc and his workers had miraculously built the dam. And though the structure prevented the tidal waters from entering the moat, it still looked puny compared to the mighty forces expected later that night.

"Our builders did a commendable job," Myvan said, "but I fear it might not be enough." The tide had turned, and for some moments he watched the swell of waves as they broke against the dam wall. "We may have been better off evacuating the ruin and taking to the Dark Wood."

Revel shook his head. "What, and wake up each morning looking into the eyes of blood-lusting predators? No thanks. If the dam holds, we'll have a chance."

Myvan put his arm around his old friend. "It's a good dam, Revel, but …" He looked to the sky. The two moons, like the eyes of a serpent, edged ever so close. "We'll soon see."

For some moments he looked out to sea, the normally soothing waves now more turbulent.

Revel broke the silence. "Myvan, whatever happens, if ... well, if things don't work out the way we hope … if the serpent has its way and we don't make it, I … I just want you to know it's been a honour to have been part of the Circle … being at your side all this time. I couldn't have wished for a better leader … or friend."

"Thank you, Revel. You and I made the best team. But it's not over yet. We can still win the night. One thing: before the battle begins, make sure Claris has mothers and their youngens go into the tunnel."

"Already done. Though I should tell you we have a strong contingent of females at the infirmary, the armoury and on the battlements ready to fight."

"Good. We'll need them all."

In silence, they watched the sun sink below the horizon. Myvan felt a tear flood his eye. Had a feeling he might be watching it for the last time.

Chapter 54

"What now?" said Sinjun, pacing around the forio tree. "Shouldn't we be going?"

Tarro was thinking the same thing. The bell had stopped clanging. The time seemed right. But he still felt guilty. They hadn't waited long. Addi might arrive at any moment laden with Jabunga leaves, eager to join them in a wild run to the ruin. A triumphant arrival.

"Well?"

Tarro didn't like Sinjun's tone – bristly, demanding. Only a short time earlier the one with the popping armsocket had been blathering on about being got at, about seeing ghosts. Tarro didn't answer.

"I think we should go," Groff said. "Myvan needs to know that most of us are safe. If the battle is about to start, he will need as many fighters as he can get."

Sounded logical. "Bodessa, what do you think?"

She looked impatient. "Addi will find his way back," she said. "If anyone can, he can."

So, everyone was keen to go. And yet Tarro was surprised at how quickly Bodessa was ready to leave her rescuer behind. Didn't she and Addi have a special bond? In the end, Tarro didn't have the energy to argue. Instead, he turned towards the valley trail, his eyes set on the ruin.

"All right, let's head out. Keep a brisk pace. Groff, you take the rear position. Keep an eye out for Addi. Bodessa, you'll be next, then Sinjun.

I'll lead."

One thing he wanted to make sure of. By the time they were in view of the battlements, he'd be the first one to be seen.

* * *

If Addi felt any better it was only because the bell had stopped clanging. The welcome silence softened the thumping in his head, gave him a chance to see straight. Well, almost. Images crossed his eyes – split and cracked and blurred. But there wasn't a lot to see. As he sat, his back against the tree, darkness crowded in – a twilight of dimming hope. If he didn't do something, he'd have no hope left. He inhaled deeply and did the only thing he knew: used his willpower to start moving again.

He remembered the Jabunga leaves. How many had there been; three bags? He reached to his right, one bag there, still tied to his belt. To his left, two more. He held a fresh leaf to his head wound until it clung to the sticky blood.

He needed to be on the trail. First, though, he'd have to get on his feet. Using the tree trunk for support, he pushed up with his legs, raising himself to a crouch. Then, with his hands flat against the bark, he straightened, wobbly, until he stood upright.

He looked down the path. It was reasonably clear. To be safe he'd need his torch, couldn't risk a fall. He also wanted his knife handy. That meant he'd have to tie all three bags behind him. He cut strands from an overhanging vine and punctured holes in the top of the bags. After looping the vines through, he knotted them to the back of his belt. It took more time than he wanted. But he'd given up on meeting with Tarro. By now, his friend, along with Sinjun, Bodessa and Groff, would have left, might already be back at the ruin. At least he could hope.

The bags were fastened. As a test, he walked forward, slowly. They trailed behind him easily enough. He paused, and using his friction stick, lit his torch. With his knife steady in the other hand, he set off, hoping to escape the Dark Wood before it ate him up.

* * *

It was hard to run, hard not to. Tarro couldn't wait to reach the ruin – to hear the cheers, the shouts of welcome, at least for making it back. Although Addi wasn't with them, Bodessa was. She would be a distraction until his friend arrived – hopefully before the battle began.

It didn't help that they'd all been injured. But the main thing was that they arrive with their heads held high, and that Groff not stumble crossing the drawbridge. He wouldn't. Adventure had changed them all – especially Groff. The timid, spindly-legged stutterer had survived the crushing arms of the dragasp, had been heroic in bringing down the gorax. His bag of useful things – his mizot repellent, his wayfinder – had all helped to find Addi and to get them back home. And now, toughened by experience, he'd turned out to be a formidable Circle candidate, his new confidence giving rivals Sinjun and Addi all they could handle.

He glanced behind. Sinjun and Bodessa were running side by side. Both looked strong. Behind them, Groff appeared to hang back, likely hoping to catch sight of Addi.

* * *

In a half-trance, Addi stumbled along the side trail. The only thing keeping him going was the smell of the sea. It couldn't be far now. Tied to his belt, the bags of Jabunga leaves scraped and bumped behind him. They weren't heavy but they were precious. And lighter. As he'd stepped over a scattering of rocks some leaves had spilled out.

He kept going, his neck crackling with dried blood. The occasional howl rode the night wind. At least it felt like night – dark wooded, cool to the bone. Keeping his torch close in front of him, licks of heat warmed his face.

The trail widened, meandered upwards. With the strength he had left, he dragged the bags to the top of the rise. Could this be it, the end of the Dark Wood? A glimpse of the sea, that was all he was asking.

He saw the moons first. They hung in perfect alignment, a double menace in the deep-red sky. His heart beat fast. A few more steps and he'd reach the spot and the view he'd longed for.

He stopped at the wood's end, allowed himself a smile. Down the sweep of the valley the castle ruin sat at the edge of the sea. Calm and restful, it looked to be in limbo – half shadow, half light. Beyond the moat, the Sulphur

Sea rolled restless under the glare of the moons.

He set off along the edge of the Dark Wood to the point where he was to meet up with Tarro and the others. But he doubted he'd find them there. And he was right. They'd gone. But not long. Down the valley trail, about halfway, four torch flames flickered. Had to be them. Had to.

Chapter 55

From the command turret atop the east battlements, Myvan gave the signal to light the torches. Throughout the ruin, along the castle walls and around the moat barricades, flames sprang up on the breeze.

"It won't be long now," he said, scanning the defences.

"Everyone's in place," said Revel. Then, with a touch of regret, "Well, not everyone."

Myvan sighed, wearily. "I wonder what happened to them, Revel. Did they lose their way? Did they come to some terrible end deep in that forsaken wood? The worst of it is, we may never know." He remembered Lucus. "I can't imagine going through the pain you went through and still do."

After a short silence, Revel said, "Whatever their fate, good or bad, it's out of our hands. All we can do now is to safeguard the ones who are here, the brave defenders of our home."

"Even so," said Myvan, "we'll leave the drawbridge down as long as we can. I'm not shutting the door on my sons and the others until we have no choice but to raise it."

He leaned over the wall, gave the signal to fire. The giant bamboozie, winched tight, was released. In the pre-battle ritual, a blazing bamboozie ball soared far out to sea.

* * *

"Did you see that?" Milo said, pulling his oar through the water.

Flogg, rowing in front of him, didn't answer.

"Well, did you?"

"I saw them."

"Them?"

"At least six. Skimming the waves."

"What are you talking about?"

"Flying jades."

Milo looked over the side. "I don't see any."

"Well, I've seen them. Cutting wings, razor sharp."

"I was talking about the fireball."

"What?"

"Way down the coast. Blazing."

"Blazing, was it? You know, Milo, we've got enough to worry about without you getting all worked up about fireballs. Let's just keep quiet, all right? Zuma won't be happy if he's disturbed."

"How long's he been down there? Isn't it our turn for a nap?"

"There's no rest for us. Not tonight."

* * *

Tarro stood, amazed. The flaming bamboozie ball had lit up the sky: glorious, defiant, warning the moons. The ritual – he knew what it meant – was the Dwarfgiants' call to arms, a pre-emptive spit in the face of evil. He'd heard rousing cries from the ruin. The defenders sounded ready. It was time to give them something more to cheer about.

The others caught up.

"Has it started?" asked Sinjun.

"Not until the moons touch," Tarro said.

"We'd better hurry, then," said Groff.

"Before the serpent comes," said Bodessa.

Tarro looked back up the trail. The Dark Wood, nothing but gloom. He worried about Addi. He'd worry about anyone alone in that place. Had he been right in sending his friend off alone? Were Jabunga leaves worth the risk? He was beginning to feel guilty when he saw something flicker. Another flicker. A torch?

"It's Addi," Bodessa said.

"How do you know?" Tarro asked. He noticed her moonstones, lying across her chest.

"I just do." She looked as dazed as twilight, but sounded convinced.

"Well, even if it is Addi, we can't wait, he's too far back. We must push on. He'll follow."

Still leading, with the other three close behind, Tarro rumbled down the last sandy stretch. The nearer they got to the ruin the more he wondered if they'd be noticed. Surely their torches would be seen. There were figures moving along the battlements, but no one, it seemed, was looking. One good sign – the drawbridge was down.

Chapter 56

Myvan had always believed in miracles. Rooted in Dwarfgiant lore, the ability of Circle members to change in size was as miraculous as the carrahock plant that spawned it. Surviving the adventures of youth and the escape from Kamistra were miracles based more on his belief in a force closer to the heavens than good luck: a kind of shiny, unbreakable thread connecting all known life to a true and wonderous power. And yet if destiny's light was indeed on his side, it would need to show up in a hurry, with bells on, here on this night of nights.

He didn't have to wait long. One level down, the bells started clanging again, faster and louder than before. Strange, he hadn't given the order. And there was more: a swell of euphoria, cries and cheers coming from the south battlements.

He was about to investigate, but Revel beat him to it, rushing to the edge of the wall to look. He waited for a report. Nothing for a moment, then Revel's legs began to twitch, and, while not quite jumping, spun around. "Yes!"

The glee in his friend's eyes was unmistakable: Miracle of miracles, they were back!

Myvan raced to Revel's side, looked down and saw the search party approach the drawbridge. There were four, all right. His son, Tarro, led the way, waving his torch above his head, side to side – the sign of friends. He looked different, his body erect, a surer step, no longer wearing a sling.

It was Sinjun who wore one now, his right arm tied to his side. And what about the one who walked beside him, someone ... he strained to see. In the bubbling torchlight he could make out a dark-haired female. Adventures conjure miracles.

The last of the four, the one with a bag slung over his shoulder, caught up. It was Groff, the lottery winner. He, too, was a surprise. No longer doddery, he fell in step with the others, and, with torch raised, crossed the drawbridge without the slightest hint of stumbling.

Myvan watched them pass through the open portcullis gate and disappear into the square. "Miracle of the heavens, Revel, this is an omen to the good. Come, let's go greet them." Ignoring the pain in his knees, he started down the steps. But half way down he felt queasy. Where was Addi?

In the square, other Circle members had gathered: Havoc, Jeeve, Rimsky, their sons. Myvan didn't stop. He hurried towards his son. "Tarro!" he said, throwing an arm around him, careful not to bump his wounded shoulder. "It's so good to see you."

"Sorry we're late. We ran into a couple of snags."

"I'm sure," said Myvan, releasing his hold. "But we'll catch up later. Right now the moons are about to converge and we'll be in the fight of our lives."

Over Tarro's shoulder Myvan could see the young female. "Who have you brought with you?" he whispered.

Tarro broke away. "Ah, forgive me, Father. This is Bodessa. She's the one we rescued from the Raslatombs."

"Bodessa. Welcome."

Overhead, thunder rumbled. Bodessa's smile was heavy with irony.

"There's evil in the air," added Myvan, turning to Bodessa. "It's best that you join some of the mothers and youngens in the tunnel."

"No, Father, she's here to help us."

Myvan shook his head. "I don't think you understand, we are about to face abomination of the worst kind."

"Maybe you don't understand –"

"Tarro, it's my job to understand."

"But she really can help us. She's the daughter of Zuma the Mystic Zenta, and a friend of Addi's."

Myvan looked at her intently. She stood clutching a pendant with stones that seemed to glow. She looked restless, a dark-eyed, smooth-skinned beauty from an ancient tribe, bloodied by adventure, the side of her leg scraped red.

"Very well," he said, as if stirring from a trance. "I'll take your word for it. Now, tell me, did you find Addi?"

Tarro couldn't quite look him in the face. "We think he's behind us. On the trail, with Jabunga leaves."

"What, on his own?"

"We arranged for him to meet us but he must have got held up."

"I can't believe you didn't wait longer."

"I know. It just seemed important that we got back before the serpent came, show we're ready to fight."

"And are you, ready to fight?"

"We've got some scrapes. Sinjun's got a loose arm, and I can't change up. But yes, we're ready."

"I see," said Myvan, trying not to sound disappointed. He turned to a nearby guard. "Take a tracker up the trail. Find Addi. Bring him home."

"Let me go with them," Groff said. "I can show the way."

Myvan was taken aback. What was this, a two-sun adventure and the spindly-legged lottery winner was jumping into the fray? He glanced at Tarro.

Tarro shrugged. "I don't see why not. He's the least injured."

Myvan frowned. He spotted the bloody bandage around Groff's arm.

"Just a puncture," Groff said.

"From a gorax tooth," Tarro added.

Myvan felt his mouth open. Good heavens. Where had they been? Suddenly, the request seemed hard to deny. "Very well," he said, "you can go. Just leave those spygoggles."

With a bow, Groff handed them over. Hooking his bag over his shoulder, he turned, and followed the guard down the tower steps.

Standing next to Tarro, Sinjun groaned.

Myvan took note of the big-muscled Circle candidate – his arm strapped to his side, his sour face. "Sinjun, are you all right?"

"Me, all right? No, no, it's wrong. Everything. It's talk. All talk." With his left hand, he pulled a knife and pointed at the sky. "I'll take the moons. Leave the moons to me."

Myvan winced, looked to Tarro for an explanation. But his son had nothing to offer, just a shake of the head, a hopeless shrug. Turning back to Sinjun, Myvan said, "Maybe you should go to the infirmary. Get your arm looked at."

As if in some other world, Sinjun jabbed at the air in front of him.

"Sinjun, stop! There's nothing there. Look, go with Rimsky. Get patched up."

Dwarfgiant cries echoed across the battlements. The bell started to clang again, this time heavily – a dark tolling that seemed to summon a terrible reckoning.

As Rimsky led Sinjun away, Myvan turned to Revel. "It's time. Let's see what we're up against."

Chapter 57

Down the trail, halfway to the ruin, Addi stopped. The sky, now black, was lit up by the moons. Watched over by shadows and with nowhere else to go, the silver circles touched. Lunar edges crunched and sparked. Flashes and flares blinded. In an act of fate and raw with fusion, the moons began to merge, seething in a brightness destined to change even the spirit of dreams. As if in tribute, rainless thunder rolled across the sky.

His head really hurt now.

Chapter 58

From the crenallated lookout, Myvan, along with his entourage, beheld the melding of the moons. At first, edges fractured, pieces broke off. But then, in the noise and chaos of flash and thunder, the points of contact began to soften.

He ordered the bells to stop ringing, and sooner than he had imagined, the lunar disruption waned. As the moons joined together they brightened, stiffened the breeze from the sea. He raised the spygoggles to his eyes, set the focus wheel.

"What do you see?" Revel asked.

As Myvan swallowed, the taste of fear washed over him. Clouds of winged rodents skimmed the waves. "They're coming," he said, passing the spygoggles to Revel.

Revel jammed them onto his head. "Flying jades. Razor wings."

With mad shrieks, the black carriers of doom stormed the moat.

Myvan raised his arm. "Battle stations!"

Bamboozies aimed, the Dwarfgiants waited.

Driven by the light of the moons, the first wave of jades assailed the dam.

"Revel, what's happening?" Myvan asked.

Revel adjusted the spygoggles. "Good news. They're smacking into the wall of the dam."

"Their eyesight's bad," Myvan said. "They'll soon adapt."

"You're right!" Revel said. "Some are flying over."

"Let me see!" Myvan took back the spygoggles. "The water's rising. We have to stop them or they'll cut us to ribbons."

CHAPTER 59

The boat rocked starboard, dashed by a freak wave.

"Ahh!" cried Milo, as a rush of sea water smacked his head. The broadside, hard and cold, sent his oar flying, swiping Flogg across the back.

"Ouch!" Flogg yelled. "What are you playing at?" He threw the oar back. "Get a grip!"

Milo gasped. He'd received the brunt of the wave, which seemed to have come from nowhere. Moments earlier the sea had been calm. Well, calm-ish. But when the moons had touched, the Sulphur Sea had begun to foam and roll.

Milo jiggled the oar back into its oar lock – not easy to do with the boat rising and falling like a churning stomach.

Behind him another wave tumbled in. Amid shouts of panic, the Zentas started to bail water. The commotion must have aroused Zuma because the cabin's deck door swung open and the Mystic Zenta appeared, looking fresh and full of purpose.

"Keep bailing!" he said, sloshing along the deck to the bow. "I'll watch for serpents."

Milo cringed. Serpents. So this was just the beginning. It would only get worse. Bad-dream worse. Quests were one thing, but missions with no chance of survival? There was something obscene about the idea of forlorn hope – arrow-fodder for the better good. Huh! How could it be better if you were dead? He had nothing against the odd adventure, a journey of discovery or rescue – as long as it had its share of running streams and blue skies, where heroes were given a fighting chance. Those he could handle. But the bad-dream variety – the ones where you're being chased by hungry beasts, your legs so heavy you can't run – well, you could forget about them.

He wiped sea water from his face, cleared his eyes. In front, Flogg rested on an oar. Considering all the activity – all the bailing of water going on around him – he sat very still. Milo was about to ask if there was something wrong when he noticed a pulsing thing, a pale yellow blob, the size of a hand and slimy enough to fall into the bad-dream category, stuck to Flogg's back. Only two parts of it moved: a sucker on its head and a spike on its tail. Milo had seen one on a fishing expedition once. It was a clingerstinger, a jelly-like parasite with sucking tentacles and a numbing sting.

"Torch!" he shouted out to anyone who would listen.

To Milo's surprise it was Zuma who turned – a questioning look on his face. With no sightings of serpents to report, the Mystic Zenta sloshed back down the deck.

"What is it?"

"Clingerstinger!" Milo said, pointing to Flogg's back. "He's already paralyzed."

Zuma winced then looked down. Another blob of yellow slime had settled above his own ankle. He shook his leg. The stinger stuck like it was on to a good thing.

"They came in on the wave," said Milo. "We have to burn them off."

"Get the torch from the cabin," said Zuma. "Hurry!"

Dodging Zentas with water buckets, Milo slithered to the deck door and descended the stairs to the cabin. Zuma had kept it neat. The smell of polish, clothes folded on a chair, a table with a map and a bowl of suli fruit. Even the bed was made. A torch burned in a stand. Milo grabbed it, and hurried back up.

On deck the flood of seawater had been mopped up. All that was left was Zuma and five Zentas plagued with clingerstingers, all needing the flame of life.

Flogg was first. In a frozen state and losing blood he sat hunched in his seat. Milo lined up the torch. It was all about aim, making sure the flame melted jelly and not Flogg's skin. With Zuma looking on, he applied the torch.

With a bitter smell of smoke and blood the clingerstinger sizzled. Once it cooled he would scrape it off. Then, with any luck, Flogg would be back to his grumpy old self.

Zuma took the torch. "This had better not hurt," he said, lining up the flame above his ankle.

"Keep your hand steady," Milo offered. "Pretend its Bardo."

Zuma smoked the creature.

The torch was passed around, and each Zenta took care of his own burn-off. Some sizzles were painless, others more clumsy. Two Zentas scorched themselves, blistering an arm and a neck. In the end, though, the cost was small – no real harm done.

It took longer than Milo had expected, but by the time the rolling thunder had stopped and the moons were finally touching, Flogg came around. His lips were limp, his eyes dozy. He tried to straighten up.

"Easy," Milo said. "Give yourself time."

Bent over, Flogg slumped back into his seat. "Milo," he grimaced. "I'm in pain. You're supposed to be watching my back."

Chapter 60

As the moons merged, getting closer to being one, they got brighter. It hurt Addi's eyes to look at them, but at least – for the sake of his head – the thunder had stopped. As he neared the castle ruin a powerful wind barrelled in from the sea; the moat's dam was lashed by white-caps. Barricades were set up at either side of the dam. Behind each one Dwarfgiants fired bamboozies. At what, he couldn't tell. Whatever was happening, it looked to be the first skirmish of a bigger battle to come.

At the bottom of the trail the land flattened, forcing him to pull the bags harder. He'd lost some Jabunga leaves, but he hoped there would be enough to help those who suffered wounds. High on the battlements he could see groups of fighters – torchlights and bamboozies ready – set to defend the ruin.

He was happy to be back. He'd been determined. But it was more than that. He believed in destiny. Whatever his fate, he knew there was at least one more part to play out. A reckoning of what had to be. And yet, at that moment, he felt strangely cut off, like an outsider. Was it because he was returning alone?

Would he be able to fight? It was more than the dent in his scalp that was leaving him dizzy. He longed to see Bodessa. Imagined she might embrace him. But he knew he couldn't count on it. She was looking for something. It didn't seem to be him.

On the fringes of quarrel and siege, in this arena of war, he stood tremulous, as uncertain as the sand under his feet. Torchlights were coming. Three of them. Turning briskly off the drawbridge they fluttered towards him.

Chapter 61

On the east battlements more than twenty Dwarfgiants cocked their bamboozies. Arm raised, Myvan held his signal.

"Be sure to aim over the dam. Ready … fire!"

With a whoosh, a battery of bamboozie balls sailed across the moat. Jades were hit. Their shrieks turned to squeals. But it wasn't enough. The waves surged, bringing with them an avalanche of slashing creatures. The defenders at the moat barricades were fighting valiantly, their bamboozies keeping the jades in check. But as each wave rolled over the dam, it carried a new threat – armoured fish, their spines lined with darts.

"Sicklebacks!" Revel cried.

Myvan stared as the hordes spilled into the moat, launching their darts, peppering the barricades. Flying jades cut and slashed. Dwarfgiants were struck down.

"Fire as they clear the dam!" Myvan roared.

A crossfire of bamboozie balls flew from behind the barricades. Another blast from the battlements.

So much for saving ammunition.

Myvan knew the fight would be hard and yet, in the midst of battle, things like nerves were often shut out. As a huge wave toppled over the dam – bringing with it legions of dragonfrogs – his spine tingled all the way up his neck.

"We've got flame-throwers!" said Tarro, reloading his bamboozie.

"They're jumping the nets."

Myvan thought about having Circle members Havoc and Jeeve change up. But at this point height wasn't needed. With so many bamboozie balls being fired, what they'd need soon was more ammunition.

"Lower the portcullis," said Myvan. "Raise the drawbridge!"

"What about Havoc and Jeeve?" said Revel.

"They'll have to stay at the barricades for now."

"And Addi?"

Myvan shook his head. Too many questions. "We'll see when he arrives. If he arrives."

With blood running from a gash over his eye, a messenger approached.

"What news?" asked Myvan.

"Not good."

"The count?"

"Eight lost."

"Wounded?"

"Fifteen. Six cuts, four burns, five stabs."

"Can we hold the barricades?"

"It's in the balance. The good news is that many jades have expired – too long out of the water. The sicklebacks are also falling. As soon as they fire their darts, they bleed."

"What about the dragonfrogs?"

The messenger shook his head. "They're burning down the barricades."

CHAPTER 62

With nowhere to hide, Addi scuffed along the trail towards the ruin. The three torches were approaching fast. He could only hope they were friendly.

Beyond the flames, the sea was as rough as Kamistra the night the volcano blew. High waves stormed the dam, flooding the moat. A battle raged. Bamboozie balls were flying.

As the torches drew near, he took a deep breath. Whoever it was, he was as ready as he could be, torch in one hand, knife in the other.

"Addi!" said one of the three. "Is that you?"

The voice was familiar.

"It's Groff. We've come to take you back."

It took a moment, but on hearing Groff's name, Addi exhaled. It felt like the best news he'd ever had.

"Groff, it's good to see you," he said, lowering his knife. "I need a hand with these."

"The Jabunga leaves, you have them?" Groff said, pointing his torch. "Brilliant! We really need … good grief, Addi, what happened to your head? Your shirt's ripped, covered in blood."

"Scrape with a lizardsnake."

"Some scrape. Here, let's help you with those bags."

Groff and the two guards took one each. Addi didn't recognize the guards, but they were dressed for battle: breastplates, swords, bamboozies. They appeared restless, anxious to get back.

"What's happening?" Addi asked. "Who are we fighting?"

"Killer sea creatures," said Groff. "Flying jades, sicklebacks, dragonfrogs."

"What about the serpent?"

"No sign yet, thankfully. Our defences are already under siege – as you've been, by the look of it. Here, give me your arm."

Addi linked arms with Groff. Feeling more stable, he tramped towards the ruin, his head filled with questions.

"Is Bodessa safe?" was his first.

"She's well enough, but absorbed with her moonstones."

"Is she with the females?"

"She's been allowed to stay up on the battlements with Myvan and Tarro."

At least that was a good sign.

CHAPTER 63

Dragonfrogs were not strangers. The Dwarfgiants had come across them soon after arriving on Helborin. More of a nuisance than a danger, the fire-belching amphibians, with their red-webbed feet and blue wings, were found in the sea pools and streams around the castle ruin. They were noisy. Some croaked all day long, a low, annoying bellow. But they were useful. The Dwarfgiants kept a few dragonfrogs in captivity, taking the poison from their skin to arm arrowheads. The creatures were also used for lighting fires at fairs and jamborees.

Lately, though, dragonfrogs had shown up in unlikely places, setting fire to the main pigpen and scorching stretches of the northern hayfields and carrahock groves. Myvan was convinced the moons were responsible for the dragonfrogs turning nasty. And now, as he looked down from the battlements, he was astounded at what he saw – a flotilla of flame-throwers lit up the moat like a thousand lanterns.

The barricades at the moat entrance were burning. Havoc and Jeeve and what was left of their forces were in retreat. As they backed up the path, Myvan could see them fighting off jades and dragonfrogs.

"We need to get Havoc and Jeeve back in," Revel said from behind the spygoggles. "Lower the drawbridge."

"No," said Myvan. "The dragonfrogs will burn it down. We'll be overrun." He turned to Tarro. "Line up your best shooters. Wait for my command."

CHAPTER 64

Edging past bulrushes at the side of the moat, Addi held Groff's arm. In sight of the castle gate, they slipped behind a low wall, took in the view. The scene looked bad. The sounds and smells of battle were everywhere – wind-blown fire, smoke, smouldering wood, whooshes and shrieks and croaks, bodies floating. In the moat, gangs of dragonfrogs huddled under the drawbridge.

The drawbridge was up!

"How do we get in?" said Groff.

Addi's thoughts were slow. "We don't. Not yet."

Chased by dragonfrogs, Dwarfgiants scurried up the path from the burnt-out barricades. Addi recognized two Circle members, Havoc and Jeeve.

"They need help," Groff said, pulling his knife.

"Wait!" said Addi. "Look!"

Up on the east turret, sharpshooters with bows and bamboozies were about to fire. An arm was raised. It was Myvan. Two familiar figures stood next to him – Tarro, who cocked a bamboozie, and Bodessa, her dress topped with the glow of moonstones. Seeing them both seemed to clear Addi's head, made him more determined to find a way in.

Myvan's arm fell. "Fire!"

The bombardment was harsh. Arrows and balls rained down. Flying jades shrieked, sicklebacks bled, and dragonfrogs, especially the ones that had cornered Havoc and Jeeve, bellowed their last fiery breath. Still, there were survivors, especially in the moat where dragonfrogs, riding the rising waters, belched flames at the underside of the raised drawbridge.

Addi watched Havoc and Jeeve and their eight remaining fighters position themselves across the moat in front of the castle entrance.

"Come on," he said to Groff and the two guards. "It's time to join the fight."

Chapter 65

More than flaming dragonfrogs, Myvan worried about the raging sea water. The moat, now besieged with waves, was rising to a level that was, at times, higher than the drawbridge, had the drawbridge been down.

From the east tower lookout he could see Havoc, Jeeve and the barricade fighters across the moat, waiting for the drawbridge to fall. From behind an outer wall, a smaller group hurried to join them. There were four of them, one bloody, his shirt in shreds.

"Revel, pass me the spygoggles." Myvan took them, turned the wheel.

"What do you see?"

"Lower the drawbridge."

"What?"

"Quickly!"

"Down!" said Revel, instructing the winch operators.

"We need to get them back in – Havoc and Jeeve, Groff and Addi. Revel, take your best shooters to cover them."

Tarro stepped forward. "Did you say Addi?"

"I believe so," Myvan said, handing Tarro the goggles, "although I've seen him look better."

While Tarro looked down, Myvan became aware of Bodessa standing next to him. She smiled but didn't speak. The wind blew her hair across her face. Her black eyes were beautiful and strange. A Zenta, Tarro had said. The moonstones hanging across her chest emitted an orange, pink glow.

For some moments she held them, stared at the colours as if awaiting some mystic message. Then, as if the news was bad, her smile disappeared and she drew a quick breath.

"What is it?" said Myvan, his own breath suddenly tight.

The answer came from a sound he'd never heard before, a kind of gushing echo that rode the sea wind, something monstrous, unstoppable. Along the ramparts the cry went out, "Tidal wave!"

Myvan looked down. The wave had not yet reached the turn of the moat. "Raise the drawbridge," he cried, "battle speed!"

"What about the boys?" Tarro asked. "We can't –"

Myvan cut him off with a stern look. On the drawbridge, Havoc, Jeeve and the barricade fighters were battling a pack of dragonfrogs. Breathing fire, the flame-throwers sent two Dwarfgiants screaming into the moat. In the thick of the fight, Addi and Groff inched forward, protecting three bags. Jabunga leaves!

Still, Myvan had no choice. The drawbridge had to be raised or it would be swept away, the ruin would be flooded, everything would be gone.

* * *

Halfway across the drawbridge Addi felt dizzy, more from a state of helplessness than from the hole in the top of his head. The way into the ruin looked bleak. A line of dragonfrogs – flames rolling – barred the entrance. All around, jades shrieked and slashed, wings flapping in the driving crosswind. When a wave crashed the bridge, it took a bag of Jabunga leaves with it, swept away like so much healing gold.

Addi crouched down, held on to the two remaining bags as tightly as he could. Another wave and he might be washed away – along with Groff, Havoc, Jeeve and the surviving guards – lost before they'd even set sight on the serpent.

"Change up!" he heard Havoc call to Jeeve.

"No, look!"

As if out of a mirage, a line of bamboozie shooters appeared under the portcullis. Without ceremony, he heard Revel give the order: "Fire!" In a whoosh, a battery of bamboozie balls flew – clipping jades, leaving dragonfrogs choking on their flames. After two reloads the onslaught was over. Except for the tumbling waves, the drawbridge was free of danger. Havoc, Jeeve and the leftover guards scrambled into the ruin.

With hope dethroning dizziness, Addi grabbed the two bags by the neck and rose to his feet. A jolt knocked him down again. Groff fell too; the two of them sprawled, face down, side by side on the bridge. It started to lift. The lurch of ropes and chains forced Addi to lie flat, but with nothing to hold on to he knew he could easily slip into the moat – into a torrent from which there would be no return. As the drawbridge angled up, their only chance – his and Groff's – was to time their slide down into the ruin just right.

With a shake and a bounce Addi turned, rolling onto his side, then his back, setting up the right moment. Then, with a judder, the drawbridge stopped. Too steep to walk, too shallow to slide, he was caught in a fix, hapless as a sea ghost, breathless and choking. But on this night of nights, in the vague, maddening course of destiny, nothing could have knotted his throat more than the sound and fury of what he saw coming towards him. Rounding the curve of the ruin, a giant wave – an indefensible monster – charged down the moat. The mountain of water, its moonlit crest foaming, was moments away.

* * *

"Get that drawbridge up!" Myvan cried. "Tarro, go help."

"It's too late. The wave's going to hit."

As it passed by, the wave forced Myvan away from the wall. If it was going to take out the drawbridge, along with Addi and Groff, it was better not to watch. Same for Bodessa; the cruel demise of a friend was not the kind of memory you wanted to be left with. He turned to warn her.

But she wasn't there.

Full of foul promise the wave swept by. More a rush than a roar, it showered spray, scattered guards, drenched Myvan to the bone. He looked to the moons. "Curse you!"

Then he waited.

He heard the slam, the thud. Nothing. No cries, no screams. There had to be screams. Trapped on the drawbridge, Addi and Groff would have taken their fate bravely, but the flood of water filling the ruin would surely have brought screams of panic.

From where he stood Myvan saw that the wave's crest had trekked around the moat, along the western wall towards the fragile north barricades. But what of the destruction it had left below? He hurried to the wall, looked down. What a sight!

Somehow the drawbridge had been raised, was still intact. But how? How could the wave not have ripped it to pieces? Then he saw Jeeve in the main square. He'd changed up, stood more than twice the size of those around him.

Taking in the scene, Myvan's heart lifted. The group included Revel, Bodessa, Groff and Addi. Then Havoc joined them. Like Jeeve, he too had changed up: the Master Builder, stretched out in his blood-red battle tunic.

It's what Dwarfgiants did when things got serious.

Chapter 66

In the square, in a daze, Addi sat on a bag of Jabunga leaves. Although there were still sounds of battle in the air, the cries and shrieks and croaks seemed more distant, less intense. He lifted his head, took in a sight that seemed unreal – a glorious one to be sure. After what he'd been through – given how he felt – this version of reality was probably an illusion, the white light that hope clings to when breathing stops. And yet his breath was steady. As for the light … well, the ruin was awash in the moons' glare, but what really warmed his heart was the glow from the torches held by a familiar group, a light as real as the smiles on their faces.

Havoc and Jeeve stood side by side, giant-sized, war-faced defenders. He remembered … the drawbridge stuck … the mighty wave … about to be swept away. Dying of hope, he'd closed his eyes, braced for the end. But then the crank of the winch – being flung? being caught? It must have been Havoc and Jeeve. No one else had the size or strength. Flying off the drawbridge he remembered. What came next had quickly faded to black. But here he was, his heartbeat steady, beginning to believe he was still alive.

In front of Havoc and Jeeve, Groff stood straight as a pole, his bag of useful things slung on his back. He looked fresh and eager. What was with him, anyway? Hadn't he also been on the drawbridge facing the wave, clinging to life?

Next was Tarro. Brandishing Groff's spygoggles and the other bag of Jabunga leaves, his friend's expression was a mixture of joy and apology.

Joy was all Addi needed. Well, maybe not all. A fond look from Bodessa would have been better. Or at least some sort of recognition. As she came towards him, he caught her eye. She was an adventurer's dream – lean and scraped and rumpled, her hair loose across her face, her smile widening as she walked. She didn't say anything, simply gave him a hug. If not as tender as he would have liked, it was warm enough. More importantly, it was for everyone to see. As he held her she whispered, "I knew you'd make it."

Myvan strode towards him. "Addi," he said. "You're here. A living miracle."

At that point he was convinced. He was alive.

Myvan spiked his sword in the ground. "The good news is that, thanks to Jeeve closing the gate, the wave has circumvented the moat and gone back out to sea. Many sea creatures have been taken with it. The moat's dam is still standing – a credit to Havoc and his builders – although the moat barricades are burnt out. We've also got flooding along the wall's northern stretch, in the carrahock fields and through the ruin's temporary barricade. Rimsky's unit is out there reinforcing it."

Rimsky. Addi had always liked the friendly Circle member – the Keeper of the Castle. His thoughts turned to another absentee. "Where's Sinjun, how is he?"

Myvan's face looked strained. "He's at the infirmary. He's gone a bit over the edge."

In the east tower the bell again began to toll. Solemn and dull, like a funeral.

"Something's afoot," Myvan said. "Must get back to the battlements. Havoc, stay here in the square. Jeeve, lend Rimsky a hand along the north wall. Tarro, give Revel the spygoggles and get these Jabunga leaves to the infirmary. Revel, Groff, Bodessa, come with me. You too, Addi, if you're up to it."

"I'm in."

CHAPTER 67

Holding Bodessa's hand, Addi followed her up the steps to the battlements. Groff was behind, Revel in front, and Myvan, wheezing on his shaky knees, led the way.

Near the top, the Dwarfgiant leader halted at the open belfry. "Stop that!" he said, waving at the bell-ringer. "I can't hear myself giving orders."

Addi was thankful. Any more clanging and his pounding head would have burst. On reaching the belfry he, too, looked in. After tying the rope, the bell-ringer pointed south, down the coast where the mudflats stretched into the distance.

Addi shivered.

The flood tide covered the flats now, but where the waves stopped their rush to shore – short of the gully that lay between the dunes and the rise to the Dark Wood – an army of torches was on the march. For some moments he watched, stunned. With the bell now silent, he began to hear it; the low drone of ugmuls, death chants drifting in on the sea wind.

"They're coming," said Addi.

"Raslatombs," said Myvan.

"Taluhla," said Bodessa.

"There's lots of them," Revel said, looking through the spygoggles. "Hundreds."

"Come on!" said Myvan, elbowing past everyone. Using his sword as a walking stick, he pushed his way up the last steps to the battlements.

From the command post, Addi watched the Raslatomb army rumble towards the ruin. At the speed they were going it wouldn't take long for the horned rabble to reach the low wall on the far side of the moat. Already he could see the lead column scuttling around the front edge of the mudflats. Armed with spears, daggers, bows and arrows, they gave escort to two sets of carriers. To the left was the bed of pointed stakes. To the right, a dark figure was being carried in a half-curtained chair. Taluhla.

Addi began to despair. With ammunition low, and outnumbered three to one, the Dwarfgiants wouldn't stand much of a chance. But wait, what was he thinking? Destiny had saved him from the giant wave. Now it was his turn. He needed to shake himself up, do his own bidding.

Spying through his goggles, Groff said, "What do they want?"

Myvan, talking with Revel, looked up. "The moons are almost one. Taluhla and the Raslatombs … they're here to welcome the return of the serpent."

Like a child, Groff said, "Why?"

"We don't know. Something about this castle ruin has got them agitated."

Groff persisted. "They've got a bed of pointed stakes."

Addi glanced at Bodessa, looked for a reaction, but she remained still, staring at the moons. Dreamily, she said, "It's for sacrificial bloodletting."

"A gift for the serpent," Myvan said, grimly.

Groff's shoulders sagged, his questions dried up.

"Revel," Myvan commanded, "spread the word. Make sure everyone has a torch. Save ammunition. Fire bamboozies only when necessary."

Revel called for messengers. He dispatched four along the battlements with the order.

A new question from Groff. "What happens if our bamboozie balls run out?"

"There's boiling water," said Myvan. "And anything else we can throw at them."

"We wouldn't run?"

Groff's suggestion irked Addi. In matters of honour, Dwarfgiants never ran. Then he realized that Groff would know little of the *Order of the Inner Circle*; the laws of conduct to which Circle members were bound by.

Myvan showed patience. "We can't lower the drawbridge, the water's too high. As for the tunnel, it's still a dead end. There was only enough time to excavate part-way under the moat. No, this is where we make our stand."

Groff's shoulders sagged even more.

"You're forgetting the strength of the Circle," Myvan went on. "Havoc and Jeeve have already changed up. When the time comes, their sons, along with Rimsky and his son, will also transform themselves. As for Revel and me – well, we'll just have to see how it goes. It's been some time since we went through a change. It's more for the younger ones. Still, we'll do what we have to do."

"But they have the serpent."

Myvan's tone was more forceful. "Groff, before we start doubting ourselves, let's see what we're up against."

Plenty, thought Addi as he watched the stream of torches draw ever closer. Past the mudflats the Raslatombs came, chanting all the way to the brink of the fast-running moat. They were now within range. His bamboozie was in his hand, a ration of six bamboozie balls at his feet. Although it gave him *some* comfort, they were hardly enough. Suddenly, he missed Tarro.

"Hold your fire!" Myvan's voice rang out.

Across the moat, the front lines of the Raslatomb army reached the low wall. Shifting right, they squeezed around the open end, massing in the area in front of the drawbridge. More and more arrived. Addi was surprised by the orderly way in which the creatures manoeuvred: the main influx formed lines – both curved and straight – until they were assembled, a putrid glut of goat-heads, grey-spiked and toothless, lit up in a sea of torchlights.

"It's like old times," Tarro said, easing in next to Addi. "I see they haven't improved their looks."

"I was just thinking of you," Addi replied, glad to see his friend. "Wondered if you'd decided to stay at the infirmary. You know, out of harm's way."

"Very funny. I wouldn't miss this. I mean, who knows how it's all going to end. But at least we get to fight together, side by side."

That was what Addi wanted to hear, the new Tarro talking tough.

Tarro went on. "I took the liberty of changing into something more battle-worthy. I've been told this doublet with extra-thick leather and metal breast studs is all but knife-resistant."

"It's enough for the two of us," Addi joked. "Maybe Bodessa, as well."

They looked her way. She stood a little to the left, near the wall. She glanced over at them.

Holding a long dark cloak, Tarro moved towards her. "I've brought this for you," he said, placing it around her shoulders. "It will keep you warm."

"Thank you, Tarro." She fastened the string at the front but left her moonstones in view.

"I also brought refreshments." He opened a small hamper laden with food and drink. "I ran into Mother in the square. She was so happy we were back she couldn't help herself. There's roast rosarri, baked bouella bread and fizzy suli juice."

Addi inhaled. It smelled like heaven. He wanted to dig in, but the timing was not so good. "Tarro, your mother's meals are the best, but given that we are about wage war, I doubt my appetite would do it justice. Better to save it for the victory celebration."

"Very well," Tarro said, filling goblets with suli juice. "Let's drink to that."

As Addi took a swig he was reminded of the victory celebration at Castle Zen the night before – the one Bardo had ruined, storming the banquet with his archers. Taking Bodessa's brother, Andros.

Would Taluhla ruin this one?

He looked down to where the mob of Raslatombs awaited their queen's command. A space had been cleared, front and centre, where Taluhla's carriers lowered her draped chair to the ground. To the discordant blare of ugmuls, a Raslatomb with double-circle horns swept the curtain aside.

Chapter 68

The last time Addi saw Taluhla she had seemed to rise out of the ground – horned and goat-headed, a half–skinned creature with a luminous face and tusks that bulged from her mouth. The figure that arose from the chair had all of this: eyes ringed blood red, a hideous grimace smeared with yellow dye. But, in just two suns, she had grown a third horn; a stubby, green node that jutted out from her forehead was already warted and festering.

As she stood, she raised a bone sceptre to the moons.

The chanting stopped.

She pointed her sceptre at the carriers of the bed of pointed stakes. The cold instrument of torture was lowered to the ground. The Raslatomb with the double-circle horns knelt before her, took the sceptre. Twisted and hunched, Taluhla seemed, oddly enough, to glide through the sea pools, coming to a stop at the edge of the moat. With the torrent running fast in front of her she raised her arms. In a hard, gravelly voice she spoke – words dark as shadows, words of some ancient dialect.

Whatever she said brought calm. The wind died, the waters settled and the sea creatures –mostly flying jades and dragonfrogs – retreated from sight.

"What is she playing at?" said Groff, refocusing his spygoggles.

"Whatever she said, it worked," Addi said.

"She's not here to make friends," Bodessa pointed out.

Taluhla spoke again. This time the language was understandable.

"I am Taluhla, Queen of the Raslatombs. This is our sacred ruin. Here we celebrate the joining of the moons. Leave now, before the serpent comes. Give up the female, Bodessa, and you will not be harmed. If not, your end will come quickly. The serpent spares no one."

In the moonlit stillness she awaited a reply.

Myvan pushed himself up onto a raised step, the highest point of the battlements. In a determined voice he responded: "I am the leader of the Dwarfgiants. We will not leave. This is our home. Find another sacred ruin. As for the serpent, if it must do your evil work, so be it."

Bodessa hurried to Myvan's side. "I will go. Save yourselves!"

Myvan shook his head. "Bodessa, all is not lost. We have Circle members with the power to change up. And the serpent … it may be a small one."

Taluhla's voice called out again. "You have sealed your fate. One way or another, she will be ours."

Tarro, bamboozie in hand, whispered to Addi, "I could finish her now. One shot. What do you say?"

"No," Addi replied, "she's not stupid. She wouldn't stand there if she thought she would be struck down. Remember, she's got a finely tuned disappearing act."

She had already moved. Now facing the sea, Taluhla looked up to the moons. Like stooges, the Raslatomb army followed her lead. Another chant – low, this time, ominous.

Taluhla raised her arms. Her voice, still hard-edged but not so gravelly, filled the air. "In the name of Phul, magic spirit of the moons, we, your servants, rejoice in your union and do summon the great serpent."

Above the Sulphur Sea, brilliant in the clear black sky, the two moons became one. A perfect circle. Now a giant eye, it glared, then flashed, lighting up the night bright as day. The flash spawned jagged moon lightning. A long, spiky arc crackled the surface of the sea, made the waters churn and bubble. With his heart beating double time, Addi watched as a whirlpool formed, foaming wider and wider until finally, out of the gurgitating depths, a monster rose like a demon unleashed. High into the moon's light the creature soared – wild and gory and twisted, its head fierce, its red eyes flaming. Even from a distance, its skin, stained sulphur gold, was clearly marked. Its scales clung to its body like heavy armour.

The foretelling had come to pass, and now it was here – the mighty devil snake, serpent of the Sulphur Sea.

The Raslatombs roared.

Addi gripped the bamboozie in his belt. It felt insignificant in the face of a creature that, by legend, took no prisoners. The serpent repeated its show of power – crashing into the water then rising again into the full glare of the moon. Addi's eyes swept back and forth over the battlements. The Dwarfgiant defenders looked on, aghast.

"It's not small," said Bodessa, excelling in understatement.

"It's higher than the c-castle t-tower," said Groff, his stutter back.

"What now?" Tarro said, meekly, his newfound toughness deserting him.

Myvan appeared dumbstruck. Revel, too, could only muster a blank face.

Addi searched for something brave to say – anything to bolster ebbing spirits. Before he could, he was distracted by an unearthly sound, a whirring emanating from deep in the tower below them. High-pitched and haunting it came – like ghosts in a wind tunnel – a rising vortex. It was broken for just a moment by the cry of the bell-ringer, blown out of the belfry into the moat below. Then the guard at the top of the stairs was thrown sideways as a green spectral stream, laced with screams, burst from the blackness of the stairwell below.

"The lost souls of the moon," said Bodessa, her lips parting in awe. "My mother?" Across her chest, the moonstones were changing colours rapidly.

Lost souls of the moon? As Addi watched them streak high into the sky, he wondered what they had to do with the ruin. He knew that fifteen summers ago Bodessa's mother and the Odanus had perished by the fury of the serpent. Had their souls been trapped ever since?

The trail of wraiths turned to the sea. Over the dam they streamed towards the serpent. The creature was thrashing its tail in the waves. Only when the stream circled its head did it calm itself, enough to open its jaws and swallow the lost souls in one gulp. Giddily the serpent zigzagged. But not for long. It began to shake its head, at times with such fury that it looked as if it might fly off. But instead, it … it grew another one.

"The serpent's got two heads!" said Groff.

Now it was Addi who felt shaky. How did it do that?

Myvan found his voice: "The Odanus scribe was right. The night of nights is upon us. Now, I realize things look one-sided – but at least we know the full extent of our enemy's strength."

Knowing your enemy was all very well, Addi thought. But what was the plan? How could they possibly defend against such a beast? One thing he knew: Myvan never panicked. It was one of the qualities the Dwarfgiant leader was revered for.

Myvan turned to Revel. "When the serpent comes we need to strike it with all we have. Position our best bamboozie shooters all along the east rampart, facing the entrance to the moat."

As Revel started off, Myvan called after him. "Oh, and have Rimsky and Jeeve come in from the north barricade. And get Rimsky to change up."

"What about us?" Tarro said. "What can we do?"

Myvan smiled, dryly. "For now, you and Addi, Groff and Bodessa stay here with me. Until we know what Taluhla and her army have in mind we need to stay vigilant. Groff, keep those spygoggles focused."

But Groff wasn't looking at Taluhla. He was looking out to sea.

"The serpent's c-coming!"

Chapter 69

With two snarling heads and at least six humps rising and falling all the way back to its tail, the serpent stormed towards the entrance of the moat. Driven by the moon and the screaming Raslatombs, the creature looked bent on finishing its task quickly, if not quietly.

This is it, Addi thought. What happened next – in the next few moments – would decide the Dwarfgiants' fate. To live or to die. He glanced at Bodessa. Her lips trembled as she watched the serpent, giant fins propelling it along the moon's reflection towards the ruin. He wanted to comfort her, tell her there was a way to survive the creature, a way out. But there was no time. All he could do was play his part in a fight to the end.

With a slow pull, he cocked his bamboozie.

Myvan raised his arm. "Don't fire until I say!"

Disobeying a command was never a good thing, but firing a large-scale weapon was especially brazen. Before Myvan could give the order, the wind-up, release and recoil of what sounded like a siege catapult reverberated from behind the ruin. Addi spun around, forgot about his head. Dizzy again, he steadied himself, then gaped as a huge rock whooshed overhead towards the dam. For a moment it looked as if it might strike the serpent, but then, in a disheartening display of failing strength, the rock fell short and crashed into the dam wall. After withstanding the force of the tidal wave, Havoc's reinforced structure finally broke; a gaping hole now let in the sea water, re-flooding the moat.

Tarro jumped onto the western lookout.

"What can you see?" said Myvan, his arm still raised.

"It's unbelieveable."

"What is?"

"Noggin!" Tarro said. "It's Noggin and the Loggerheads."

"Friend or foe?" asked Myvan.

"Friend, I think."

"Are you sure?" Revel said. "They've just destroyed the dam."

Two more rocks whizzed by. This time they cleared the dam. One flew over the serpent while the other struck the side of its original head, knocking both heads together. The second head screeched and the creature was lost from view.

"Noggin bamboozled the serpent," said Groff. "It's gone down."

"It'll be back," Myvan cautioned. "Be ready to fire."

But when another rock landed to the left of Taluhla – squashing a swath of Raslatombs – she screamed out and sent half of her forces to confront Noggin's Loggerheads.

Along the moat-side path edging the bulrushes, square formations of rock-throwers came into view. Tarro hadn't said much about the Loggerheads, only that he, Sinjun and Groff had been held at Noggin's rock quarry the previous night. Addi could see that they were stocky with square heads, armed with pails of rocks and a siege catapult. A short, lumpy-faced Loggerhead with thick arms and neck strode in front of the wood-framed weapon. Noggin.

Although outnumbered, the Loggerheads didn't flinch. Separated only by the low wall, the Raslatombs and Loggerheads began to fire at each other, one with arrows, the other with rocks. At first there were losses on both sides. Soon, though, the Loggerheads weakened. Their front lines fell back amid the screams of the injured and the groans of the fallen.

"They need help," said Tarro. "Fire a volley or two."

"Not yet," said Myvan. "Save it for the serpent."

Addi had only three bamboozie balls left.

From under the Sulphur Sea the serpent resurfaced, its two heads raging. Slithering over what was left of the dam, the beast entered the moat. Down at the low wall, Taluhla screamed orders. Ugmuls bellowed, and the Raslatombs and Loggerheads lowered their weapons, stopped to watch.

The power and speed with which the serpent romped up the moat was as frightening as it was thrilling. Its heads – jabbing and seeking – were one thing; its tail, decorated along its top edge with bony nubs, was another. One swipe might smash a castle wall.

Myvan's hand fell.

"Fire!"

Bamboozie balls rained down on the serpent. Too many bounced off its plated scales. Addi's shot was one of just two or three that found its mark; it struck the beast's second head in the spot between its eyes.

All it did was hiss.

"Hold your fire!" Myvan said.

Across the moat, the Raslatombs squealed as Taluhla, her sceptre held in salute, welcomed the serpent's arrival at the raised drawbridge.

The Queen of the Raslatombs wasted no time. "Break it down!"

Two tongues flicked, four eyes blazed and, in a move faster than Addi had ever seen, a single swing of its tail – like a cracking whip – reduced the drawbridge to splinters; chains dangled on rings.

Addi looked at Myvan – if not for answers, at least for direction.

"Revel, take the sharpshooters to cover the entrance," their leader said, his voice solemn. "Take what ammunition we have left."

Revel paled. A last stand against the serpent was no more than a forlorn hope. But everything on this night of nights was starting to look bleak. Loyal to the end, he called in the sharpshooters from the ramparts. Willingly they came, about twenty of them, scurrying into the blackness down the tower stairs.

Like the tidal wave before it, the serpent didn't stay but continued its rampage around the moat, knocking holes in the western wall, swallowing up Dwarfgiants, trashing the northern fortifications. Addi jumped alongside Tarro for a better view. Another huge rock catapulted over their heads across the ruin. It didn't strike the creature but was near enough to drive it from the moat and back to the sea.

Behind a hail of flaming arrows, the Raslatombs resumed their battle with the Loggerheads. The square-heads fought valiantly but the goat-heads pushed them back.

Dwarfgiants, too, began to struggle. Almost out of bamboozie balls, soon they would be reduced to fighting with knives, hand to hand. Addi could see Jeeve, Havoc and Rimsky in the main square. The changed-up Circle members looked big and strong standing alongside Revel and his last-stand bamboozie shooters. But they'd need more than that. Maybe a miracle. The Raslatombs were already laying planks across the moat, bridging the running water to the open entrance. Soon they would charge into the ruin.

Addi's pain was back, more from a sinking heart than his hurting head. Things looked bad on all fronts: Dwarfgiants out of ammunition; Loggerheads in trouble; the serpent circling back. And yet for all of this, his thumping head kept him alert, gave him an idea. The Loggerheads still had lots of rocks. But their arms looked to be tiring.

Addi turned to Myvan. "The Loggerheads need bamboozies."

With a pained look, Myvan squeezed his eyes. "Tarro, see to it. Give them as many as we can – from the armoury if necessary. Get Havoc and Jeeve to help. Have everyone toss their bamboozies to the rock-throwers."

"What about the serpent?" Tarro said. "It's coming back."

"Just go!"

With no time for parting words, Addi watched his friend turn, disappear down the castle steps. Now he was left standing with Bodessa and Myvan. In front, crouched by the wall, Groff was aiming his spygoggles seaward.

"The beast's driving towards the m-moat."

Addi gulped. Back to finish the job.

Next to him he heard a sniffle. Bodessa. A tear trickled down her face, hung like a pearl under her chin. Her chest began to lift and fall. The tear spun off, down to where her moonstones – struck by the moon's brilliance – pulsed to life. As if struck with the affliction of sleepwalking, Bodessa, holding her pendant, turned and passed in front of him, slowly, deliberately, towards the tower steps.

"Bodessa, wait!" said Addi. "Where are you going?"

But she was already descending the steps. He started after her – had gone only a step or two – when …

"Aaah!"

Myvan's cry stopped him dead. Addi swung around. The Dwarfgiant leader was down on his knees, his hands clutching his chest.

Chapter 70

As Myvan fought for breath, Addi helped Groff sit him up.

"You don't look well," Addi said. "We need to get you to the infirmary."

Myvan laughed, then spluttered from the effort. "No, we don't," he said calming himself. "There are more urgent things to take care of, like Taluhla and the serpent and Bodessa." Then, with a soulful look, he said, "Addi, somehow, you must find a way to save the night. You've got destiny running through your veins – a gift for dealing with the disagreeable. Use it. Groff can stay with me here. Go, now!"

"Wait!" said Groff. He opened his bag, pulled out two stones. "I've been saving these. It's not a lot, but they might help."

"Thanks, Groff," Addi said, stuffing them into his pouch. "I'll make them count." He smiled bravely, then turned and set off.

Before descending the tower steps, Addi looked over the wall, down to the entrance. On the planks that crossed the moat, clusters of Raslatombs lay lifeless, victims, no doubt, of Revel's sharpshooters. But there were no sharpshooters now, or bamboozie balls flying. Out of ammunition, they must have retreated – along with Revel and Havoc and Jeeve – onto the western battlements to hurl bamboozies to the the struggling Loggerheads. Soon the Dwarfgiants would be in a last stand of their own, with only torches and knives.

On the other side of the moat Taluhla waited to cross. Surrounded by guards, her head was raised in a regal pose, at least as much as her hunched back would allow.

"Clear the planks," she screeched.

A small Raslatomb force hurried forward. With spears, they pushed their dead into the moat.

The way into the ruin was clear. Taluhla glanced to her right, where the bed of wooden stakes stood ready to be carried in. With an air of expected victory she raised her sacrificial dagger and, with a twisted grin, waved her arm forward. A squeal of Raslatombs charged across the planks.

Addi gasped. Bodessa! Turning, he raced to the tower, descended the steps, two at a time.

* * *

Bodessa felt as though she was sleepwalking. The only difference – she knew where she was going, what she had to do. At the bottom of the tower steps she stopped. The square was awash with Raslatombs, the horned creatures howling and barking, armed with spears and knives, firing arrows up to the battlements where the Dwarfgiants were taking cover. Then, in a blare of ugmuls and protected by shields, Taluhla entered. She was followed by carriers of the bed of wooden stakes. In the middle of the square a space was cleared for the blood-spiked contraption.

Bodessa walked towards it. Her pendant lay over her cloak. A haloed light shone from the moonstones, as if showing her the way. When the Raslatombs saw her, they stood aside, gaping, unsure.

"Let her come!" Taluhla said; her dye-smudged eyes lit up with joy.

As she walked, Bodessa looked straight ahead. The queen of the Raslatombs – hunched and claw-fingered – beckoned her with the long, wavy blade.

"What a pleasure to see you," Taluhla said, her voice dripping venom, froth bubbling over her tusks. "I've waited a long time. Fifteen summers. You slipped from my grasp once before, but not this time. As the moon is my master, I promise you, you'll be with your mother – my sorry sister – very soon."

Bodessa listened with an even heartbeat.

Taluhla's dry voice went on. "I loved your father but he was taken from me. Your mother saw to that. Now she is lost, and so will you."

He never loved you. All you have left is bitterness and cruelty – emotions that never stand a chance.

Taluhla turned sideways, her shinbones sticking out of her skin. "Take her! Tie her down."

* * *

Addi didn't get far. Down just one set of steps he stopped at the belfry. It was the smell – a putrid, slimy sea smell – that drew him in. But no one was there, only the bell, cast in moonlight, steeped in stink, the stench of the demon. And what demon was that? He heard it first, above the screams of battle – a shrill, hissing sound. A head sprang up outside the open window, then another – two scaly, red-tongued heads swinging like battering rams. They began to pound the wall, knocking out stones. The serpent, the stinking demon.

He fell in behind the bell but knocked the clapper ball. The clang was so loud it clouded his ears. It was the only cover he had … unless he ran. Something, though, told him he must stay, find a way to stop the beast before it delivered the crack of doom.

He took out his bamboozie.

* * *

Bodessa felt the rough, scratchy hands of two Raslatombs grip her arms. They led her to the edge of the bed, where the wooden stakes rose in a field of sharp points. Two straps hung ready to be fastened.

"On your back," said Taluhla.

Without protest she climbed on – better to ease herself on than to be forced down. Even so, the pointed ends sank into her back like before, reopening wounds. But her mind fought it off, filled with thoughts of her mother.

"I'll take those," said Taluhla lifting the pendant from around Bodessa's neck. "What power they have will soon help only me." And with the moonstones in one hand, the sacrificial knife raised in the other, she addressed the moon. "Mighty Phul, magic spirit of the moon and bringer of the great serpent, we give you our offering, a soul for a soul, one lost, one found, forever to be, on this, the night of nights."

A moonbeam caught the knife's edge, a murderous glint. But, as though destined, the light was deflected and struck the moonstones. They shone bright blue.

Taluhla glared at them. Her eyes, set in deep-yellow sockets, widened. Her knife, poised to strike, held still, frozen as the look on her face – the look of fear.

Bodessa, sensing the time for truth had come, lifted her head to see what was turning Taluhla aghast. The face of her mother, a sublime image, emanated from the blue light: a face not unlike her own, with dark hair, and eyes keen but softened by age; a breath of illumination, of old wisdom about to be renewed.

Taluhla gurgled, began to bleed – her nose, her ears. Even for someone so wicked, the change was horrid. Eyes melted in their sockets, fingers snapped like sticks, horns and tusks crumbled to dust. Her prickled body hair began to smoke, along with the black gown and the burning image of the serpent.

As moonlight on moonstones had blinded the Queen of the Raslatombs – turned her into a lost soul – Bodessa's mother's soul had been set free.

* * *

Addi placed the first of Groff's two stones into the bamboozie. Edging around the bell, he could see the heads of the serpent about to break through the wall's gaping hole. He didn't wait. Stone number one struck the first head, a blazing shot that knocked it backwards. Addi reloaded, fired at the second head. The stone hit it in the eye. The second head shrieked. Jittery and dazed, both heads looked ready to be finished off. But Addi had no more stones. Wait, though. He rummaged in his pouch. Tucked in the corner he felt the smooth edges of the pink sapphire he had taken from Zuma's treasure vault, the gemstone he wanted to give to Bodessa if they survived the night. He had no choice. If he didn't use it he might not see the sunrise. He placed the hard pink stone in his bamboozie and aimed.

But the serpent was gone.

* * *

Bodessa watched Taluhla wither into a tortured ghost. Suspended above the bed of stakes, the one-time Raslatomb queen had changed into a writhing glob of green goo.

Raslatombs stared. All around, the horned guards began to wail, bemoaning the spectacle of their leader perishing in front of them. Bodessa felt a strange pull. It was the moment in a battle when arrows stop flying, daggers cease to draw blood; the pivotal moment when the fall of a leader transcends the will to kill. She held her breath, turned her head, hoping to see Addi.

At that moment he appeared at the bottom of the tower steps. But he looked worried.

* * *

When Addi saw Bodessa strapped to the bed of pointed stakes he almost screamed. It had been two suns since he'd first rescued her in the Dark Wood, and here she was again in the same fix. And he couldn't see Tarro anywhere. This time he'd have to save her alone. Not easy with a two-headed serpent at large. And yet she seemed in a surprising state of awareness, her head turned, looking straight at him. Something odd was happening. The Raslatomb guards had stopped fighting and were watching with alarm an anguished green spectre that hovered above Bodessa. What was it?

There was no time to guess. As the fates twisted in the shambling night, the shadows of the grim-faced moon deepened. And with a double-headed screech, the serpent raged through the open entrance and into the ruin.

Again, Addi aimed his bamboozie. But from where he stood the chances of stopping the monster – its massive body stinking of sulphur, water pouring from its scales – weren't good. In the belfry he had given it a scare, half blinding one head. But to deliver a fatal strike with just one stone left looked impossible.

The serpent – so long its tail was still outside the ruin – stopped, fixed all three eyes on the middle of the square, on the bed of stakes where Bodessa lay. Slowly it slithered towards her. Was his beautiful Zenta girl about to be lost, to suffer the most gruesome fate? He thought about intercepting it, but even had he been able to change up, the creature would still have overpowered him. And though the bamboozie might scare it briefly, the thought of confronting it was crazy.

In the end, it didn't matter.

CHAPTER 71

Moments in time – at least the ones that pertain to destiny – are rare. Sometimes they backfire. Sometimes they don't happen at all. As Addi watched the serpent – its upper body squirming, the jaws of its heads wide open – he was convinced that his own destiny path, the one that had brought him to this moment, might be turning in his favour.

The transparent green glob that writhed above Bodessa had reshaped itself. Now horizontal, the all-but-melted figure took flight and sped towards the serpent. Left behind on the ground were the smoking remnants of a black gown.

Taluhla, it had been her!

Without ceremony, the Queen of the Raslatombs disappeared into the mouth of the serpent's second head. And as if disgusted with the taste, the second head gargled then wrapped its split tongue around the neck of the first head. Eyes blazing, it pulled the first head to it and, in a snap, devoured it. Blood and bits of skin dangled. Not a pretty sight.

The serpent was back to having one head. But with only one eye, it looked unsteady. The beast struggled to drag the rest of its tail into the ruin but didn't seem to have the strength. It looked to the moon. No help there, the bright glare had started to pale. The serpent turned to face Bodessa, its giant paddlefins holding it up. But it could do no more, except to stumble and screech and then – in a sudden spiral of reptilian transfiguration – melt, like Taluhla before it, into a great glob of green goop.

The serpent – what was left of it – jetted skyward, a tracery of evil sailing towards the moon, trailing behind it what was left of the sea creatures; the sicklebacks, the jades, the dragonfrogs.

Addi stood amazed, watched the ghost stream rise above the Sulphur Sea, jumped when the stream exploded in a burst of green – dust sprinkles cascading into the silver-capped waves.

A wrenching sound from high in the sky; the moon, likely crushed by disappointment, broke in two, drifted apart, its journey of destruction ended.

Now Dwarfgiants were everywhere. The giant-sized Rimsky, Havoc and Jeeve along with Tarro charged from the battlements into the square. Taluhla's Raslatomb guards were laying down their knives and spears.

A messenger rushed in through the open entrance. "They're surrendering. The Raslatomb army has given up. The square-heads are taking prisoners."

Stuffing his bamboozie in his belt, Addi hurried to Bodessa, who was flat on her back, lying still.

"Bodessa." He loosened the strap across her chest.

Arms free, she reached for her pendant.

"Look!" she said, her white face disrupted by joyful tears. "My mother, I've found her."

Addi knelt beside her. He gazed at the moonstones. The vision of a female shone out of the pale blue light.

"I can see your beauty in her," he said.

Bodessa smiled. "When the moon struck the moonstones, my mother's image appeared, and her lost soul was recovered. Now she's at peace."

"What happened to Taluhla?"

"When she saw my mother, her own soul was lost. She melted away."

Bodessa's mother's image began to fade.

"Bodessa," said Addi, "let me help you." He undid the strap binding her feet. "You'll never have to suffer this bed of stakes again. Tomorrow, we'll destroy it." He slid his arms under her, lifted her off.

In the cacophony of victory, through crowds of jubilant Dwarfgiants, he helped her towards the infirmary. Near the entrance stood a cluster of females, chattering, excited. Claris walked towards him. She could hardly contain herself.

"Addi, it's a miracle. You came back and the battle is won." She scanned the castle walls. "Where's Myvan? Have you seen him?"

"He's on the ramparts with Groff. He just needs rest."

"Is he's all right?"

"I'm sure he is."

"What about your friend, here? She's been through a lot. Leave her with me and I'll take care of the wounds on her legs and back."

Bodessa held on to Addi's hand. Then, turning, she embraced him: a weary, yet affectionate hug that she held for some time.

Over her shoulder, he saw Reesel watching.

Chapter 72

Leaving Bodessa with Claris, Addi looked for Tarro. The square was packed, filled with the clamour and cries of victory and defeat, of Dwarfgiants rounding up Taluhla's Raslatomb guard, taking weapons, tending the injured. The bed of wooden stakes was dragged away.

Through the seething jumble, Addi pushed his way towards the entrance, where, in front of the apothecary shop, an emergency treatment station had been set up for Dwarfgiants bleeding badly, having arrows removed. But it was the leather doublet and metal breast studs that caught his eye, the battledress of a pharmacist turned warrior. Tarro was handing out Jabunga leaves straight from a bag.

"I'll take one of those!" Addi said, satisfied his side trip to the hideaway had been worthwhile.

Tarro turned. His eyes lit up. "You can have two if you like."

Before Addi could answer, he found Tarro's good arm around him, squeezing him tight. It felt good, just as Bodessa's had. In the end, though, he put the double dash of affection down to the spoils of war.

"Your head still bothering you?"

Still in Tarro's grip, Addi said, "I can't say anything's bothering me. How could it be? We're alive, aren't we?"

"And so is Myvan," said Tarro, breaking away, pointing.

Helped by Groff, Myvan emerged from the foot of the tower. At least his weak heart had got him down the steps. His lips tight with determination, he walked gingerly towards them. At the sight of their leader, the Dwarfgiants cleared a way, waving and cheering.

With an effort, Myvan hugged Tarro. "Well done, my son. The night of nights is ours. Well done to you, too, Addi," he said, with another hug. "And your friend Bodessa."

Now Groff stepped up, his arms outstretched. His bag of useful things was hanging loose in front of him, his wayfinder sticking out from his chest.

"Wait!" Addi said, holding up his hand. "Let's not rush to conclusions. The main Raslatomb army is still out there. Have they actually surrendered?"

Before Groff could answer – before he could take another step – cheering erupted from the battlements. Addi looked up, then turned to the entrance, where a curious-looking figure strode into the ruin. Noggin the Loggerhead, a torch in one hand and a bamboozie in the other, was just as Tarro had described him: short, square-headed, his face mostly broken. From his expression – sore, irritable, roguish – it was hard to tell if he came as a friend. Still, his manner was not all gristle and knots; his puffy nose and small, fidgety eyes left him looking a tad vulnerable. Following behind, Loggerhead guards, with bamboozies, herded in captured Raslatombs, the remains of an army that, only a serpent ago, had looked unbeatable.

"Come on," Tarro said. "Let's go greet him."

Addi, along with Myvan and Groff, followed Tarro through a crowd of onlookers. When Noggin saw Tarro he stopped.

"The last time I saw you," said the Loggerhead, gruffly, "you were three times as big."

Tarro laughed. "I told you we were creatures of change. And so are you, it seems. Why are you here?"

"Is there a problem?"

"No. No. Glad you came. It's just that you're a long way from home."

"We had unfinished business."

"What, you mean –"

"Headlock."

"Oh, I see. Right, well –"

"And target practice. It's not every day we get to throw at moon-worshippers and a serpent."

"Well, we thank you for your help," said Myvan.

Noggin raised his bamboozie. "It's just as well we had these. We had tired arms."

"Keep it," Myvan said, "a memento of victory."

"I might do that. But once we are finished here, you can have the rest back."

Streams of Raslatombs stumbled by, pushed and prodded towards the main pigpen.

Noggin continued. "What do you want to do with this scum? We could use them as targets."

Myvan said, "I think we'll let them go."

"What!" said Noggin, kicking up a clump of dirt.

Myvan stood his ground. "They're not going to be used for target practice."

"What about moving targets? We'll give them a running start."

"No."

"No?"

"We'll banish them."

Noggin squinted. "Banish! Where to?"

"Back to the Dark Wood."

"That's pitiful!"

"No, Noggin. They are pitiful. Look at them. They have no purpose left. No leader, no serpent. Believe me they'll never threaten us again."

"Can I just pop one?"

"No!"

There was a hulabaloo in the holding pen. The Raslatombs were packed in so tight that the pigs were turning nasty.

"Let me talk to them," Myvan said, holding his chest. "Addi, Groff, give me a hand."

The pigpen was overflowing. Changed-up Circle member Jeeve was trying to keep the gate closed, while Havoc, also towering above everyone else, bellowed, "Quiet, you rabble. Quiet!"

When Myvan approached, the prisoners hushed, their eyes filled with fear. "Listen to me," he said, his voice strained. "Your queen, the serpent and the two moons are no more. The battle is over. You who have survived, your lives will be spared. We will not keep you here. You are free to return to the Dark Wood. Go back to your village and never come here again. If you do, we won't be so merciful. Jeeve, get them out of here!"

Jeeve opened the pigpen gate and the Raslatombs scrambled out, looking both bewildered and grateful.

The pigs romped.

Out of the ruin the Raslatombs ran – every goat-head for himself. They ran until they reached the mudflats, now a bog since the tide had turned.

From the battlements, Dwarfgiants and Loggerheads watched. Out of the tunnel, females with youngens emerged, witnessed the horned creatures trudge through the sandy swamp. In the distance the torches dimmed, the lights went out, and the last remnants of Taluhla's dream disappeared.

"It's over," Myvan said. "Noggin, thank you again for your bravery, for the sacrifice made by you and your Loggerheads. If there's anything we can help you with, let us know. Meanwhile, you are welcome to stay the night as our guests."

Noggin sniffed. "Don't think so. Got target practice in the morning. Need it after wrecking your dam."

"In that case, we wish you well."

Noggin summoned the Loggerheads, commanded them to give up their bamboozies. Dwarfgiants lined up, each one getting back his weapon.

Noggin clenched his fist, began to bang himself on the side of his head. "What happened in here, to the she-devil and the serpent?"

Eyes turned to Addi. Somewhere under the burden of memory, out of the shadows of adventure, he was sure there was an answer. But could he explain it? His head started to thump again, his mind, foggy. He began, slowly.

"As much as I can piece together, it was a reckoning of sorts, about a young female, Bodessa, needing to find out why Taluhla wanted her – like her mother – out of the way. It had to do with jealousy, her father, Zuma the Mystic Zenta, a Krogul named Bardo, moonstones, moon cycles, Raslatombs, serpents, the Odanus, the secret of this old ruin, the lost souls of the moon –"

"Whoa, whoa, stop!" cried Noggin, smacking his temple hard. "What are you going on about? Just tell me how the she-devil and the serpent turned into ghosts, blew up in the sky."

Addi took a breath. "As far as I can guess, when Bodessa's moonstones were struck by the light of the moon, Bodessa was taken – as if sleepwalking – to Taluhla. As she lay on the bed of sacrifice, her moonstones released an image of her mother. When Taluhla saw this, she was the one turned into a lost soul. And when the serpent saw Taluhla's terrible transformation, it too melted away and joined the ghost stream taken by the sea."

"Did you make that up?" Noggin said, squinting.

"It's quite a story," Myvan said.

"It's not over yet," Addi said. "There's a Krogul named Bardo who –"

"Enough!" said Noggin. "That's it. We're going."

Through the ruin's open entrance, the Loggerheads departed. As Dwarfgiants cheered from the battlements, Myvan signalled to Revel.

Moments later the portcullis slammed shut.

Chapter 73

The sun rose in a blaze of triumph. Standing alone on the west wall, Addi watched the fiery orange circle float above the Dark Wood. Shining with a new brightness, it looked content to have the sky back to itself. He turned to face east, towards the sea. A soft breeze caressed his face. After a night of miracles and mayhem the scene was mostly peaceful: gently breaking waves rolling in on the morning tide, the odd moan from the infirmary.

He walked the walls, along the northern stretch: a tumbledown mess of serpent damage, piles of stones; moat water spilling into the ruin, running between houses, down alleys into the square, around the castle well, the granary and pigeon coop, through the orchard, gardens and beehives, swamping the pigpen, all the way to the farm sheds.

One of the few dry spots was the raised sleeping quarters next to the armoury. It was where Circle members slept. In the care of Claris, Bodessa would be there. Would she be awake? Would saving her mother's soul have finally given her peace, a chance to rejoice, let herself go? If so, would she be willing to be more than just a friend? It was complicated. And there was still Andros to think of. Would her brother be the subject of another quest, a journey that would take her into the sordid world of Bardo and his Kroguls? Would she give herself up to Bardo in exchange for Andros's life? The gouge in his head began to hurt again. He discarded the old Jabunga leaf, replaced it with a new one, tightened the bandage that held it on.

Addi tramped on, his mind a mix of hope and pain. Many Dwarfgiants were still asleep. For most, it had been a long night, cleaning up mess, seeing to the injured. Guards had been posted, but some of them were sleeping, dreaming, no doubt, of the sweet if unlikely victory. After the Loggerheads had gone, Myvan had addressed all the Dwarfgiants, a speech full of honour and pride. Afterwards, though, Tarro had helped his father to the infirmary. "I must visit the injured," Myvan had said, gripping his chest. But it was clear he needed to rest, take medicine for his heart.

As for Groff, he'd headed home, splashing through the streets, reuniting with his family.

What stories he'd be able to tell!

Around the walls to the eastern battlements, Addi stopped at the observation platform. Now in full view of the sea, he was drawn to the moat's entrance: the scorched barricades, the demolished dam. Noggin's siege catapult had done a job. One giant rock, and all of Havoc's work had crumbled. But it didn't matter now; a dam to keep out the serpent was no longer needed.

A squawk of birds distracted him. In the moat below, a flock of young marigores was picking at the remains of jades and dragonfrogs. Jades had cut him twice, on his arm and neck. Dragonfrogs had scorched his leg. No love lost.

He looked up, out to sea; the pull of fate. In the far-off waves, around Starbeck Point, he saw something moving. Addi stared intently until a dark shape emerged, a medium-sized vessel rounding the headland.

* * *

"Milo!" cried Flogg. "Will you stop that?"

If only he could. But his stomach, empty from a night of throwing up, wouldn't let him. All he could do was retch.

Flogg brought a bucket anyway.

Milo winced. The container had been well used, whether from the effects of the overturning sea or from outright fear. But now the waters had settled, along with whatever it was that had been blasted into green confetti.

"Phew, it stinks!" Milo said, pushing the bucket away. "I'm fine. My stomach's settling down."

He retched again.

"Nice one," said Flogg. "Look, Milo, get a grip. Zuma wants to speak to us."

Milo groaned.

"Draw long breaths and pinch your earlobe."

"What?"

"Pinch your earlobe."

"Why?"

"Just do it."

With one hand clinging to Flogg's arm, Milo doddered along the deck. He took deep breaths and nipped his ear with his other hand. When they reached the three remaining Zenta guards, they flopped into their rowing berths alongside them. Zuma stood at the prow of the boat. Haggard and washed-out, his dark eyes sleepless, his tunic almost stripped of feathers he looked nothing like a decorative figurehead. And yet, for all his bedraggled state, like all good leaders, the Mystic Zenta was able to rouse himself, find the words. With a spry lift of his head he spoke clearly.

"How we survived the night only fate knows. But here we are – on a morning fresh as sea spray – still breathing, alive under the sun." He pointed to land. "As you can see, we are in sight of our destination – the castle ruin in which I pray we will find my daughter, Bodessa, alive and well." He placed his hand over his heart. "Not so, two brave Zentas lost in the night, washed overboard at the height of the tempest. Let's honour them by completing the mission of which they were so much a part … one last push to shore and … Milo, what's the matter with you? Can't you hear me?"

Embarrassed, Milo took his hand away from his ear. His stomach turned.

Zuma continued, "If it's nausea, hold your breath."

Milo thought about it. He'd try it, but not for too long.

* * *

Addi watched the boat turn towards the castle ruin. Around Starbek Point, it would have travelled up from the Southern Extremities, contending with crosswinds at the turn and then braving the tidal mudflats before sailing headlong into the storm and the serpent. He couldn't imagine how such a modest-sized vessel could have gotten through, let alone stayed afloat. He knew that Dwarfgiants built fine boats – planks and frame construction using forio wood – but none had been out, not last night. He knew of only one other race who prided themselves on their boatbuilding – the Zentas.

He looked around; still no activity to speak of. Only he, it seemed, had noticed the oncoming vessel. In the early-morning quiet someone needed to sound the alarm. The belltower was only steps away.

One level down, Addi looked in. The bell, hanging on its crossbeam, was his for the ringing.

In the corner, in the hollows under the rafters, something moved: something restless, unafraid. Addi tucked in behind a post, reached for his bamboozie. But before he could load it a Dwarfgiant emerged, breathless and dripping wet. Although covered in weeds and mud the figure looked familiar. Walking straight to the bell, he hooked the rope, sounding the alarm.

The bell-ringer – he was back!

Chapter 74

The bell was loud enough that no one would sleep. Soon Dwarfgiants would be hurrying to the main square, confused and anxious.

From behind the post Addi turned. Two steps at a time, he ran back up the tower steps. On the observation platform he watched the boat approaching fast, riding the tide. If he'd had Groff's spygoggles he might have seen who was on board. As it was, a solitary vessel did not seem like much of a threat, even if it was filled with Kroguls. And if it was a Zenta boat, it might bring news of Zuma.

Now, it seemed, everyone was awake. Guards lined the ramparts; crowds filled the main square, sliding and skidding in the water streams.

Clang, clang, clang.

Addi looked for a familiar face. At first, no one, but then beyond the castle well he saw Tarro. His friend was coming out of the infirmary, stretching, yawning.

Addi waved. Tarro squinted, waved back, headed straight towards the observation tower. By the time he got to the lookout, he was breathless.

"Addi, what's happening?"

"A boat somehow survived the night."

"That's impressive. Who is it?"

"Not sure. But we'll soon see. How's Myvan?"

"He's resting. Revel's with him now."

"So, who's in charge?"

Tarro shrugged. "I am. I've been asked to report back."

Addi, his mind racing, saw the opportunity. "While you're at it, maybe you could ask Bodessa to report back to me."

Tarro laughed. "Your head might be damaged but your heart's still strong."

"I'm serious. I have to see her, know how she is. She's with your mother. I'm sure you could pull some strings."

"Sorry, Addi, but my authority is limited to finding out what alien boat is about to land on our beach. Bodessa will be fine. Come on!"

Tarro signalled the bell-ringer to stop. Then, along with Circle members Havoc, Rimsky and Jeeve, who were now back to normal size, he strode down to the beach, north of the moat's entrance. In the soft breeze, waves lapped to shore.

Creaking like an old sea dog, the boat moored on the beach. It was Addi who recognized Zuma, his shaved head shining in the sun. Amazing! The mystic Zenta had somehow escaped the clutches of Bardo. Bodessa would be thrilled. Clad in his feathered tunic – crossed with a studded harness belt – Zuma tramped down the boat ramp and stepped onto the wet sand with a wobble. Three Zentas followed, plus Milo and Flogg. All appeared exhausted. Milo looked sick.

Tarro said to Addi, "It's Zuma, right?"

"The Mystic Zenta."

"Bodessa's father?"

"All the way from Castle Zen, by sea."

"Father!"

Addi turned. Bodessa, dressed in a fresh green tunic, came running down the sand – not as easily as he'd seen her run before, but fast enough. She didn't hold back her smile. It was the happiest he'd ever seen her.

Zuma was running too, and without so much as a nod he charged past, slowing only to catch Bodessa in full stride swinging her around like a long-lost child. For some time they stood embracing, exchanging words that Addi couldn't quite hear.

Tarro said, "Looks like father and daughter have been reunited."

Addi didn't answer.

From behind, a familiar voice shouted, "Addi, you kept her safe!"

He turned, saw Flogg lumbering towards them. Lagging behind, Milo looked ready to throw up.

"Flogg! How did you find us? What's the matter with Milo?"

"We came to help. Milo's seasick."

"I'm not surprised if you sailed through last night's storm."

"The waves were like mountains. Lost two overboard. Somehow the vessel survived."

"We survived because destiny willed it," Zuma said, returning, his arm around Bodessa. "Bodessa tells me she found what she'd been looking for: the spirit of her mother – my dear wife, Falice – free at last, no longer imprisoned in a realm of torment, no longer a lost soul of the moon – thanks to you and the Dwarfgiants."

Addi glanced at her. Her eyes, a mix of tears and joy. He wondered if she had found more than her mother – freedom for herself, perhaps? If so, could this mean their attachment might become more permanent?

"Bodessa's being kind," Addi said. "We fought like Dwarfgiants always do, by standing together. But it's your daughter who should be thanked. It was she who was brave and determined. When the moment came, she was the one who stood up to Taluhla. The magic of her moonstones did the rest."

Zuma squeezed Bodessa's hand. "That may be so – my princess has made me proud – but Addi, more than once you've saved my daughter, protected her with your life. I can't think how to ever repay you."

You could leave her with me. I'd protect her, take care of her forever. "As I said before, I was glad to help. But it was Tarro, here, who took the arrow in the shoulder fighting off the Raslatombs. He gave me time to free Bodessa from Taluhla and her sacrificial knife."

"So you're Tarro," Zuma said. "My thanks go to you, too."

Tarro said, "I agree that destiny has played its part. Had we not been in the Dark Wood and saved Bodessa from Taluhla, we would have suffered the same fate as the Odanus. We could not have stopped the serpent on our own. As for repaying us, friendship between Zentas and Dwarfgiants is all the reward we need."

Addi felt his chance slipping away. He had to ask. "There is one thing," he said, hurriedly. "I was wondering if Bodessa might want to stay for a while, enjoy the sea air, play music on her reed, right here in the place where her mother grew up."

Zuma's expression changed. It wasn't as though his joy clouded over. It was more a look of regret. "Ah, well, Addi, as for what Bodessa does next, it becomes … well, sticky. She has now reached the age – and certainly earned the right – to decide for herself. But much as I would like to grant her that choice, I'm afraid her remaining here is impossible."

A tear ran down Bodessa's face.

"She wouldn't have to stay forever," said Addi, his world slipping away.

"It's not that. I've got a score to settle, and I can't do it without her."

"Is it Bardo?" Addi asked.

Zuma nodded slowly, his eyes filled with disgust. "I have one son, and now only two suns in which to rescue him. As soon as we refresh ourselves and restock the boat we must be off, across the Northern Strait to the Lake of Fools."

So it was true. Bardo held more than Zuma's treasure. The Krogul had Andros, and Bodessa was the bargaining chip to get her brother back. Although Addi knew the answer – the Bardo-Bodessa arrangement – he wasn't going to let his heart's desire be used as a pawn so easily. He put Zuma on the spot.

"You can't possibly agree to let Bardo have Bodessa!"

Zuma looked cornered, glanced shiftily around him. "Bardo thinks Bodessa belongs to him – a bogus claim from a long time ago."

"If it's bogus, why does she need to go?"

"I'll need to show some intent. But that's all it will be. What Bardo thinks and what he's going to get are two different things. I mean to keep both Andros and Bodessa safe. By the time I'm finished, Bardo will never threaten us again."

"I still think she –"

"Addi, it's all right," Bodessa said. "It's decided. I have to go."

"But you'll be going with only six. Five if you leave Milo. Look at him. He's hardly fit to travel."

Milo, holding his ear, looked feeble, strange.

"He'll be fine," Zuma said. "The waters are calmer now. A short rest and we'll leave on the afternoon tide."

"I could come with you!" Addi said.

Zuma held up his hand. "Addi, I admire your tenacity, your willingness to help. But I'm sure, after what you and your Dwarfgiants have just gone through, you'll be needed here to get things back to normal. Besides, this thing with Bardo is personal. I brought it on. I'll fix it."

What was Zuma thinking? How could he, with so few and in just two suns, travel to the Lake of Fools, infiltrate the Krogul stronghold and expect to come out alive? Once Bodessa was his, Bardo would rid himself of anyone who might pose a threat to him keeping her. Unless Zuma could summon his powers of prediction – concoct a favourable plan of rescue – Bodessa would become a love slave, and the Mystic Zenta a fool. A dead one.

Chapter 75

In the time it would take for the tide to turn, Addi was determined to see as much of Bodessa as possible. Now in a world that was finally theirs to enjoy, it seemed almost tragic that once her boat set sail he might never see her again.

Together they walked back up the beach, past the moat entrance to the ruin. With her hair blowing free, her dark eyes shining in the sun, Bodessa proved once again how quickly she could recover from her wounds, from the sharp points of Taluhla's bed of stakes.

"My father has a plan," she said, eagerly.

"I know. To take you away from me."

"No, Addi. It's a plan that will complete his destiny. I'm an important part of it."

"Bodessa, you're the only part I care about."

She stopped, took his hand. "Listen to me. You're a Dwarfgiant. I'm a Zenta. We met under Taluhla's spell, in the madness of flames, when the two moons ruled."

"I'd like to think it was part of our destiny. Drawn together by adventure; defying daggers; a natural attraction … even if we don't look the same."

Bodessa smiled. "We are not that different."

Addi was encouraged. "We are as different as we want to be. What matters to me is that we are together."

"I'm sorry, Addi, but I can't. Right now, all I can do is go with my father.

We have to rescue Andros. After that, maybe I could spend some time here by the sea, play that game …?"

"Chizzy?"

"That's it. The one you lose to Reesel and Kulin."

"They beat me and Tarro most of the time, but we don't lose on purpose. As I said before, they play well … you remember their names?"

"We met last night. Reesel was on her way to help defend the west battlements, carried a bamboozie. She's very striking."

"I suppose you could say that."

"She said she was pleased to meet a friend of Addi's. Gave me a hug. I liked her."

"That's good."

Silence fell.

"Hey, are you two coming?" Tarro called. Along with Zuma, Flogg and Milo, he was waiting up at the drawbridge.

Addi waved, then turned to Bodessa. "My feelings won't change. We were destined to be with each other. If I have to wait, so be it." He dug into his pouch. "Until then, I want to give you something to remember me by." In his hand shone the gemstone, the pink sapphire. "I know your mother's moonstones are precious to you. This was your father's. I took it from his treasure vault before the Kroguls did. I want your family to have it back, hope that it brings you luck."

"Thank you, Addi. Lucky Pink."

Chapter 76

During the time it took to prepare Zuma's boat – for the tide to turn – life at the castle ruin was full of joyful activity. At every corner, Dwarfgiants – males, females, young and old – worked side by side to clean up the mess: the running water, the puddles, the wreckage left by the serpent. Holes in the north wall were being patched and a makeshift castle gate put in place, cobbled together by Havoc and his workers.

Only when the bell tolled did the Dwarfgiants pause. Led by Tarro, a team of Dwarfgiants carried Taluhla's sacrificial bed of stakes into the main square and set it on a mound of fire-starters.

The bell stopped. Tarro's voice rang out across the ruin. "Let the burning of this monstrosity symbolize the end of those with evil intent. Let the flames of justice douse forever the dark shadows of Taluhla and the serpent. Our world is safe again."

From the flame of a caged dragonfrog he lit a torch. Around the square, from hand to hand, the torch was passed until it reached Addi. Bodessa stood next to him.

"Here," he said. "You must light it."

Bodessa took the torch and, following a quick glance back at him, she stepped forward. With grim satisfaction Addi watched as the wood was set ablaze, embers crackled, smoke rose in a plume.

From the direction of the infirmary Claris approached. "I've been to see Myvan. He's resting but insists on having a meeting of the Circle. Tarro,

Addi, you are summoned. Bodessa, come with me. You can select some fresh travelling clothes."

Bodessa nodded and glanced at Addi – an awkward, slightly guilty look, he thought, but that was it. Turning, she set off with Claris. For some moments he watched her, his determined, dark-eyed dream taking another step in the wrong direction.

"Come on," said Tarro. "Let's get to the Circle meeting."

Addi forced a smile. "How is Myvan, really?"

Tarro's face was stern. "Not so good, I'm told. The attack on his heart has left him deathly pale."

Chapter 77

Addi followed Tarro into Myvan's room. In the glow of candlight, hushed Circle members gathered around their leader's bed. There were seven in all: second-in-command Revel, along with Havoc, Jeeve, Rimsky and their sons. Propped up with pillows Myvan lay still, a faint smile on his lips, his eyes glazed.

"Myvan has called a meeting of the Circle," Revel began. "Given his weakened state he has asked me to speak on his behalf over matters concerning the future of the Circle and the selection of the all-important new member.

"As you will recall, three suns ago a vote was taken by the Circle as to who would replace my son Lucus. Two candidates were nominated: Addi and Sinjun. Each candidate received two votes. The deciding vote lay with Myvan. However, since Addi was missing in the Dark Wood, he put off his choice until Addi's return. A search party was formed. Led by Tarro, it included Sinjun and a surprising third candidate chosen by lottery: the carpenter's son, Groff. But with the 'night of nights' only two suns away, it was clear that the search party would have little time in which to find Addi and bring him home. And so, it was decided that if he wasn't found, a new vote would be taken to choose between the remaining candidates, Sinjun and Groff.

We are all happy, I know, that Addi survived his ordeal in the Dark Wood and, along with the others, returned safe, if not entirely sound. Tarro took an arrow in his shoulder. Addi, suffered a blood-sucking knock to his skull. Groff's arm was punctured by gorax teeth. And Sinjun has a bad case of broken courage, triggered, we believe by an encounter with an eye-plucking mizot. As we have no idea how long it will take for him to recover – if he recovers – only two candidates are now being considered: Addi and Groff. I see that Addi's here, but not Groff. So while we await his arrival, Myvan has asked me to inform you all of a decision he's made with respect to his successor."

Feet shuffled. Heads turned. This was unexpected.

"In the event that the shock to his heart leaves him unable to carry out his duties – and we all hope this is not the case – then all leadership responsibilities will be passed on to … his son, Tarro."

Addi gasped. Traditionally, the second most senior Circle member would take over as leader: Revel.

"From all accounts," Revel continued, "Tarro displayed an exemplary mix of wisdom and courage in leading the mission to find Addi. His ability to deal with the Loggerheads and keep them on our side helped us to defeat the Raslatombs. Along with his position of Master Herbalist, we are confident that he will undertake this new responsibility wisely."

The room filled with applause.

"I will, of course, be happy to give Tarro any assistance he may need."

Tarro stepped forward, knelt beside Myvan. "Father, you know I don't expect to be taking over any time soon. But when the day comes, I'd like to think that my selection was unanimous."

Myvan reached for Tarro's hand. In a whisper he said, "It was."

Addi swallowed hard, his pride forcing a tear. His best friend was to be the next Dwarfgiant leader. Amazing!

Revel clasped Tarro's hand. "Congratulations. The decision will be announced formally at a victory celebration two nights hence. At that time, the new Circle member will also be sworn in, which brings me to the further selection."

In a rush of heartbeats, Addi held his breath. Now it was his turn.

"Ah, here's Groff!" added Revel. "The timing couldn't be better."

Addi turned.

Along with his bag of "useful things," Groff strode in, carried an air of confidence.

Addi's hopes began to unravel. Could it be that Groff was a serious candidate? After only one adventure, had the spindle-legged novice impressed so much that he might be favoured? True, he had learned fast – gone from a clumsy eccentric preoccupied with peashooter stunners and stinky repellent to a fearless, even heroic adventurer. Even so, surely Tarro's assessment would have placed Groff second.

As Revel began to speak, he looked directly at Groff. "I am pleased to announce that in recognition of his skill as a navigator and his bravery in the face of a great gorm and the beast with the swivelling head, Groff has been chosen to be the new Circle Member-in-Waiting. By this I mean he will assume the postion of full Circle member as soon as he's completed three adventures, or in the event of the untimely passing of a present member. Whichever comes first."

More applause left Groff beaming.

Addi`s head began to thump. He was confused. What of the new Circle member, the one to replace Lucus? Had the naming been put off?

"Congratulations go to Groff," said Revel. "The Circle Member-in-Waiting is a new position. In future it will be open not only to the sons of Circle members but to our male population at large."

Myvan nodded his approval.

"I now turn to a final matter," Revel said, his tone giving nothing away. "We have in our midst someone who is neither the full-blooded son of a Circle member nor a youth from the general population. Myvan's late sister's son, I speak of course of Addi. He has always been popular with our young Dwarfgiants, and he has shown great vitality in everything he has been asked to do. The spirit of adventure is in his blood, even if, at times, taken a little too far. We have, however, received assurances that his disposition now includes sprinklings of prudence. And while this is a good thing, had it not been for his decisiveness, his instinct for taking risks in rescuing the Zenta female Bodessa, it is unlikely any of us would be alive today. In a world of the unknown, one in which we hope to thrive, these are the qualities we need."

Addi tingled. No headache now, his cheeks blushing warmly.

Revel led the applause. "My son Lucus was everything to me. He will be remembered fondly. I am sure that, as his successor, the new Circle member, Addi, will do all Dwarfgiants proud."

Overwhelmed to the point of dizziness, Addi felt his knees weaken. It was a wonderful moment to receive such recognition. But he needed air. He also needed to share his news with Bodessa. He was sure she would be impressed. He was about to excuse himself when a messenger entered the room.

"What is it?" Revel asked.

"Zuma, sir. He's set sail."

"Already?"

"What about Bodessa?" asked Addi.

"She's gone too. They've all gone."

With empty gaps between heartbeats, Addi ran out of the room.

CHAPTER 78

The view from the observation platform did little to ease Addi's pain. Surrounded by waving Dwarfgiants, he watched Zuma's boat head towards Starbek Point. It was said that the tide waits for no one. Couldn't the Mystic Zenta have been an exception? Couldn't Bodessa have given him a fonder farewell, more than a speck of hope? How could such a joyful day have dissolved so quickly?

He saw a figure in red moving on deck. His Bodessa? Why was she wearing red, anyway? Bardo would see her coming. Maybe it was Zuma, he liked bright, brash colours. The long stroke of oars unsettled the flat sea – Flogg and Milo – they would protect her.

Tarro eased to Addi's side. "So she's gone to finish what she started."

"More like what Zuma started."

"Destiny. It's a strange and wondrous thing. Who would have thought you and I would be standing here, in a postion of privilege, on the threshold of shaping our future?"

Addi was only half listening. He watched the vessel turn leeward, a sweep to the north. Under the meridian sun, running with the tide, it got smaller and smaller until, at last, like a Taluhla trick, it was lost from sight. As his heart sagged, he hoped for one thing: that it wouldn't be the old sea dog's last voyage.

"Addi! Tarro!" A female voice cried out from below. In the square, next to the armoury, Reesel stood holding a Chizzy stone. Beside her, Kulin waved.

Tarro laughed. "What do you think, Addi? Are you up for a game?"

"Females," Addi said, shaking his head. "I've just lost one. May as well lose to another."

The End

ACKNOWLEDGEMENTS

There's something to be said about kids at bedtime, waiting in the dark for a story to be told, especially stories that are made up, that stretch the imagination – the ones that are a bit scary. It was certainly true of my kids – Charlie, Adam and Jessica – who, before the age of ten, had developed a keen thirst for moments of desperation, close calls and blood! It's difficult to tell how well they slept afterwards (*if* they slept) but one thing I know, they were the ones who brought the idea of *Dwarfgiants* to life – a collective rooting for the little guy, who, by no fault of his own, bore the brunt of malevolence of all kinds – until, of course, he was left with no choice than to size up the situation. Today Charlie, Adam and Jessica are all grown up and still rooting for the little guy. They are three cool kids, and I'm happy to say that.

Thanks a million to the following for their encouragement, insight and constructive criticism during my time writing this novel: My wife, Jan, my parents, Harry and Sadie Jacklin, Brian Henry, d. L. shelly, Catherine Marjoribanks, Alex T. Davis, Susan Davis, Jeremy Gretton, Dyanna Prisk, Leslie Hudson, Geoffrey Knight, Yvonne Heath, Jadyn Heath, Tanner Heath, Tyler MacDonald, Jayne Drinkwater, Jodie Auckland, Bryan Dearsley, Muskoka Author's Association, Tellwell Publishing and my friends of the Vermilion Writer's Group: John Bandler, Janet Turpin Myers, Valerie Burke and Theresa Samsone.

Author Biography

Originally from Yorkshire, England, Steven Jacklin now resides in Muskoka, Ontario. *The Adventures of the Dwarfgiants – Serpent of the Sulphur Sea* follows his previously published collection of short stories, *A Slight Kink*.

Along with his love of writing, Steven enjoys theatre and has performed in stage productions in Toronto and Muskoka.

He also continues to be inspired by his three children, Charlie, Adam and Jessica. They are often in his thoughts, even as he multi-tasks at his desk – looking out the window, delighting in the winter landscape and writing a sequel: *The Dwarfgiants and the Lake of Fools.*